WATCHDOGZ

WATCHDOGZ

SHARON LEE THOMAS

TATE PUBLISHING
AND **ENTERPRISES**, LLC

Published by Tate Publishing & Enterprises, LLC
127 E. Trade Center Terrace | Mustang, Oklahoma 73064 USA
1.888.361.9473 | www.tatepublishing.com

Tate Publishing is committed to excellence in the publishing industry. The company reflects the philosophy established by the founders, based on Psalm 68:11,
"The Lord gave the word and great was the company of those who published it."

Book design copyright © 2015 by Tate Publishing, LLC. All rights reserved.
Cover design by Jim Villaflores
Interior design by James Mensidor
Author's photo by Edward Meecham

Published in the United States of America

ISBN: 978-1-63449-722-0
1. Fiction / Legal
2. Fiction / Mystery & Detective / International Mystery & Crime
15.02.04

For my late husband, Wes,
who supported my desire to engage
in a career change that fulfilled my lifetime
interests and ambitions

Acknowledgments

Despite having worked for a little more than two decades in various aspects of immigration law, I was aware that I had much more to learn and that governments all over the world continue to craft policies that impact on the migration of people. A number of persons provided me with guidance and general assistance in helping me to present an honest glimpse of extreme problems that can face Border Security and Intelligence officers around the globe, whom I wish to thank.

Andy Mavroudis has been with Border Services and its predecessor, Citizenship and Immigration, for many years. He helped me understand aspects of the department, the employees, and its operation, which I was not accustomed to dealing with. He has shared many stories with me that I have used as a basis for developing some of the situations in this story.

Dorothy Bell Reynolds and my sons, Ed and Will, were invaluable reading every chapter as the story unfolded. Each provided me with thought-provoking questions about the characters, the events, the laws. They helped in the development of the overall story.

Thanks also to Gillian Meecham for her painstaking and time-consuming initial editing and proofreading of the manuscript before it was sent to the publisher.

Prologue

The stocky, elderly man peered over the rim of his thick, dark glasses through the two-way mirror. He observed the somber face of the fellow who had recently arrived and was now seated in the workroom. He had boyish-looking features that made it difficult to determine how old he was. He figured that he was about twenty-five. He was a nice-looking youngster, perhaps a little thin.

Sometimes he could tell by studying a person's face something about his character, which was the likely reason for him being here. In this case, it was different. This fellow just had a blank look with an air of innocence about him. For just a moment, he wondered what the devil this kid had gotten himself into. He thought that he must have pissed someone off, and this was perhaps a warning.

He never asked questions about the subjects; he just followed instructions. Usually an interrogator accompanied him on these assignments, but in this case, he was alone. Regrettably, he'd been ordered that this time, the task was to be performed as humanely as possible. Importantly, he had been cautioned that future contracts were dependent on his cooperation in this particular case.

It was unfortunate that he couldn't partake in discussions with any of the subjects. He understood that it was necessary for him to refrain from talking because of his distinctive lisp. However, in this one instance, there would be no communication with anyone. No interrogation would take place. Just get him in and get it done as soon as possible. Stroking the stark white hairs on his chin, he reflected that just this once he wished he knew the whole story behind the person who had come across his path.

He always adhered to the rules regarding maintaining anonymity. This way it was safe for everyone. He slowly walked into the small washroom and carefully checked the honey-brown contact lenses and salt-and-pepper-toned hairpiece that disguised his bald head and green eyes. Satisfied with his appearance, he went back into the office and reached for his case of tools.

He glanced once more in the mirror and assured himself that his disguise was adequate. Before leaving the room, he studied the young man for several more minutes, through the larger two-way mirror, looking for signs of anxiety or agitation. There was none. Either the kid had nerves of steel or he didn't know what was about to happen. Quickly, he headed for the room.

In the hallway, he silently opened his toolbox. It was a small, nondescript little case that didn't hold much. He quickly withdrew the vial, an alcohol swab, and a fresh needle before quietly entering the soundproof room where the stranger was waiting. In seconds, he approached the man now seated in the dental chair and administered the morphine before the boy even knew he was there.

When he was quite satisfied that the young fellow was knocked out cold, he tied him securely in an upright sitting position. He followed this with some test probes on his arms and hands to ensure that there was no response. As an extra precaution, he placed a strip of duct tape over his mouth. He liked to see and hear the person's responses, but hated moaning sounds. He preferred the screams of fear instead.

This time, he was amazed that his subject hadn't even made a reactionary outburst when he first inserted the needle. The drug took some of the pleasure away from his task and made it personally less rewarding. His preference was that his subjects were awake and kicking, so to speak. During a procedure such as this one, he couldn't experience the same degree of exhilaration.

He had accepted that he would take whatever enjoyment he could derive from this experience and just follow his instructions, knowing that there would be other opportunities in the future. He sauntered over to the small cabinet over the sink, opened it, and extracted a bowl, a small pan, and some cooking oil. After placing about two inches of the oil in the shallow pan, he set it on a kerosene stove sitting on the long countertop and turned on the burner.

At the end of the counter, he opened the mini fridge and found a bag of ice in the freezer compartment, just as he had requested. After filling the bowl with the ice, he added water to it until it was half-filled. He tested the water to ensure that it was icy cold. As he rolled the small table over in front of the fellow's chair, he was salivating. His heart began pumping excitedly. This part of his task was what he enjoyed the most. Although he recognized that it wouldn't be nearly as pleasurable as usual because of the sleep-induced state of his victim, he still had a sense of titillation at the prospect of what he was about to do.

Hearing the crackling of the oil as it began to sizzle, he carefully grabbed the pan and placed it on the table. He checked one last time to make sure the young man was knocked out; then, one by one, he immersed each of the fellow's fingertips in the burning, hot oil until he was sure that they were slightly charred. After each one, he hesitated momentarily before advancing to the next digit, savoring the smell of the burnt flesh before placing it into the bowl of ice water.

With a sigh, he thought that it was most unfortunate that he didn't get to hear the screams this time. As he examined his handiwork, he grabbed a metal spoon and added some oil on the upper parts of the lad's hands and wrists, and then he scattered the hot liquid on areas of the fellow's lower arms. When he was satisfied with his work, he immersed each hand in the icy cold water. After a few seconds, he splattered more of the ice water on the remaining burns on the man's arms and wrists.

He quickly drained the oil into the container before placing it back in the cupboard. Someone would dispose of it later and replace it with a fresh container. Then he took some paper toweling and wiped the pan clean of all the remaining bits of oil. Finally, he gathered all of his tools before leaving the room, pleased with his handiwork. It wasn't his usual type of assignment, but it had given him sufficient pleasure for now.

For the next hour, he retreated to his small office in the adjoining room where he looked over the lecture notes he had prepared for tomorrow's class. He'd be presenting as a guest lecturer at the University in Frankfurt. His outward appearance was bland and unassuming. There was no doubt that few people would recognize him in the role of his alter ego. He blended in with the geriatric bunch of guest professors that travelled around Europe giving occasional lectures during their retirement and supplementing their pensions.

He had specialized in the subject of human behavioral psychology. Fear was the topic that intrigued him most because it is so primitive and powerful. He knew that all people generally exhibited the same types of biochemical responses such as increased heart palpitations and a rush of adrenaline. However, he was fascinated by the emotional reaction of each individual. No amount of research had indicated the same results from two people. They had all reacted differently.

He had never found anything in his life more satisfying than conducting research sessions like today. However, in this case, he had some degree of disappointment because he didn't have the opportunity to observe or assess the subject's fear. He wanted to witness the physical or emotional responses. This time, however, there had been a slight variation as he was advised that his subject had to be sedated, and there would be no interrogation by a third party.

As his stomach started growling, he glanced at his watch and noted that sufficient time had passed to achieve today's objective.

He had to finish up his task. Rising from the desk, he checked his disguise and then slowly gathered up his belongings before returning to his laboratory workroom.

He examined each of the man's fingers to ensure that they were adequately swollen and blistered. Then he reached for a fresh towel, razor, and tweezers to peel off and remove the blisters. He grinned, satisfied that the skin was raw and weepy. Then he placed a petrolatum layer of gauze on each area of burnt flesh.

The final layers of sterile gauze that he covered the surfaces with would absorb the moisture, which oozed from the raw surfaces beneath the original layers of gauze. He made record time in wrapping up the burns before cleaning up all the evidence of his work. Then he left the mysterious young person to continue sleeping. He went to the other office to retrieve his briefcase and stopped by the attendant's booth before exiting the premises.

He silently nodded to the attendant and tossed him the bottle of OxyContins with a typed note that advised him to follow the instructions on the bottle. The note also stated that there was enough medication to last the guy for a couple of days. It had concluded with the message, "Then get rid of him!"

1

Russ wiped the perspiration from his forehead, glancing at the new arrivals who were waiting to pass through immigration and customs inspection. So far, it had been one hell of a night! The evening crew had started their shift a couple of hours early as they were required to attend some behavioral modification training program that had been "prescribed" by the suits in Ottawa.

Presumably there had been a high incidence of complaints from visitors that the airport staff were not congenial and never smiled. Tourism was big business, so the department acted swiftly to enlist an "expert" from the local university who put a session together on friendly greetings, thanking people for coming to Canada, and learning to smile. They called it "sensitivity training."

The last part had been almost comical when he learned that some people actually didn't seem to know how to smile. It was one of those unconscious things that he hadn't seriously thought too much about. He had been aware that periodically a few people didn't seem to smile at all. Some actually scowled. However, while some barely smiled, others let loose with broad grins. Occasionally, they even did it at the most inappropriate times. So here he was at fifty-eight years of age learning how to greet people and smile on his last night on the job. The staff wasn't too thrilled with the training, and he understood why. He felt like an idiot.

In his thirty-five years employed with the department, the shenanigans that went on at the terminal had never ceased to amaze him and the reactions of various political appointees and their lackeys in addressing them. After enduring the nonsense of the mandatory training, he was relieved that this was his last shift. He was eagerly looking forward to the golden years of retirement. However, he chuckled to himself because he knew, perhaps in some sick way, that he was going to miss the staff, the visitors, migrants, and the constant commotions that went on.

As he headed toward his office, he overheard a number of the officers complaining that the management was undoubtedly out of touch with the reality of the job. Although thousands of people who were relatively ordinary folk came through the border every week, these officers were always on the lookout for the drug dealers, people smugglers, war criminals, and other criminals. Russ knew that his seasoned officers had grown increasingly more enforcement minded as they had been exposed to some of the most devious criminals in the world. For that matter, after thirty years, he was slightly jaded too.

That reminded him that he needed to contact the "boys" in customs to determine whether there had been any progress on the latest suspected drug operation. Sid, who was the customs supervisor, had called in the Royal Canadian Mounted Police. The RCMP, as they were commonly called, had alerted Russ a couple of nights before that they wanted to watch two unclaimed suitcases for a pickup. Russ had been asked to accommodate a few undercover RCMP officers by placing them in some strategic work areas for surveillance purposes.

Customs officers regularly worked with both the immigration employees and federal police officers, who they simply referred as the "Mounties," and were careful not to disclose covert operations as they fought the growing drug trade. Two days ago, Sid informed him that the dogs had picked up a scent in some luggage that had been off-loaded from an international flight that had arrived from Hong Kong. An x-ray had confirmed that there was a strong possibility that they were dealing with narcotics.

The suitcases appeared to contain some large ordinary children's dolls. However, the x-rays had revealed that their bodies were filled with finger-sized packages that contained something that was probably a narcotic substance. It looked to be a sizeable haul with a potential street value well over a million dollars.

In such cases, they had to act quickly and minimize the delay at sending the bags through for passenger pickup while allowing both the RCMP and Customs to get their operatives into place. The Mounties had indicated that they suspected that there was some inside help in this case.

Russ placed the call, and Sid answered brusquely with a slight impatience to his voice, "Yeah, what is it?" he'd asked.

"Hey, there. It's Russ. Just started my shift and thought I'd check to see if there's been any activity on the bags yet."

"Nothing yet. You've still got some guys helping out, I hope?" he said.

"Yeah, we're good. I sure as hell hope that something happens before the weekend traffic arrives though."

"You and me both. I'll let you know as soon as I hear or see something."

"Thanks, Sid. Good luck, tonight's my last. I enter the world of retirement as of the morning."

"You lucky son of a bitch! If I don't see you before you leave, best of luck, Russ."

"Thanks. To you too in catching the crooks." Russ smiled to himself as he replaced the receiver. He liked Sid. He was a good employee and had been pleasant to work with. He and his staff had made some substantial drug busts over the years.

Russ truly hoped that none of his people was involved this time. He had hired many of the officers over the years and had an almost-patriarchal relationship with most of them. Overall, the staff appeared to respect him highly and had often come to him for career and occasional personal advice, knowing that they could trust him with their confidences.

He was decisive in his direction of the personal strengths that each employee had. He not only assessed their skills in considera-

tion of the betterment of the department but also for the employee's own personal satisfaction. Best of all, if they approached him
and he couldn't help you, he usually knew where you could get the
proper assistance. He was known as the bookworm and seemed
to know every manual inside and out. In addition to that, he was
never without a paperback or magazine within easy reach.

His rugged, dark looks with a tinge of distinguishing gray in
his close-cropped military-style haircut and his large, but trim
frame gave him a commanding appearance. However, it was his
steel-edged quiet speaking tone that caused one to know instinctively that he was a force to be reckoned with. Although he was
known to be tough, he had a wicked sense of humor and was
extremely likable. Over the years, he had cultivated many strategic interdepartmental relationships that had become beneficial
to both the organization and its employees. Most importantly
he was honest and direct with everyone and always met each
challenge head-on with the force of his wits and the strength of
his personality.

This particular surveillance had been labor intensive for the
past seventy hours. Sid had his senior officers on alert, addition-
ally both Russ and the federal police force had a full complement
of staff involved. It was situations like this that had led to the
need to have staff with top-security clearance levels and prepar-
edness for the worst-case scenarios. Russ hated guns, though, and
that new requirement of border officers had been the deciding
factor that pushed him into thoughts of retiring.

Russ recalled how all of his team had felt several months
earlier when a US Customs and Immigration officer had been
gunned down with an AK-47 during a drug bust on the Mexican
border. Whether it was an admission by land, sea, or air, the cartels, terrorists, and criminal organizations had made it necessary
to arm the border officers as front line defenders. In defending
the border, every officer had become acutely aware of the dangers
they might encounter daily and empathized with their counter-

parts at other international borders. Occasionally, it had become a nasty business.

Waiting for someone to claim the suspicious bags had been getting frustrating over the past few days for the officers on every shift. As the luggage remained unclaimed, Russ wondered if someone had got their wires crossed. However, within the hour, he received the signal that something was taking place. It was like a game of cat and mouse. Clearly the dealers had been watching for an opportunity to make the pickup.

It caused a stir, though, when one lone uniformed baggage handler nonchalantly walked over and loaded the bags onto a cart. From his vantage point, Russ got a good look at the fellow, but he couldn't recall seeing this person before. That wasn't unusual, though, as a private company contracted the baggage handlers. He couldn't always keep up with their rapid staff turnaround.

Initially, the RCMP couldn't decide whether to head him off, thinking that he was going to blow the bust. They were contemplating that perhaps, he was just performing his duties and taking the unclaimed baggage to the clerk who normally handled it. Anyone in law enforcement could tell you; however, that patience was often critical. They decided to wait it out.

Russ glanced over at the sergeant and knew that he cautiously thought that perhaps this was the inside man for the drug dealers. Russ saw that as he moved away with the cart; they had put a tail on him. They watched him carefully from a distance—waiting to see if he would turn the suitcases into the unclaimed baggage clerk.

Pay dirt!

The baggage handler had headed out through a side door near the back of the terminal where he met up with two fellows and immediately loaded the bags into a waiting vehicle. No one inside made a move; they were hoping their tracking bugs placed strategically on the bags would lead them to others involved in the operation. Russ glanced at the sergeant who was engaged on his two-way radio likely giving orders to his outside operatives.

He gave a sigh of relief when the sergeant gave him the thumbs-up indicating that there were no problems, and his people had it under control. The baggage handler slid back into the terminal with the empty cart and was quickly apprehended. Everything had gone smoothly, and Russ was able to summon his officers to resume their normal duties and help out with the arrivals. Thank God! Several full plane-loads were scheduled to arrive within the hour.

Russ's bailiwick was immigration. Assisting customs guys with operations like the drug bust were an important aspect of his job, but he enjoyed the people aspect of his primary role. His staff scrutinized the people coming into the country, where customs examined and taxed the goods that they brought in. He recognized the distinctiveness of their jobs and was always amazed to see some of the things that people tried to smuggle into the country, including live animals and exotic birds.

Returning to his office, he turned on his computer and immediately noted that he had received an urgent red alert from the Intelligence Department. Since the tragic events of 9/11 in the United States, the new warning code had been developed to help identify potential risks. It was meant to assist the border officers to recognize and deal with situations that might affect overall public safety.

Opening the e-mail, he quickly scanned the contents. The briefing contained information that came from the US Department of Homeland Security, and it stated that the US State Department had received credible information that an extremist group based in Pakistan were planning acts of terrorism against the United States or its citizens. Both the location of the target and the means by which it would be carried out was unknown; however, there were indications that people were moving into the Americas in preparation for this event.

The State Department warned that, at the present time, the risk appeared to be elevated but not imminent. Their information was that operatives for the terrorist group were likely headed to Mexico, Canada, or directly to the United States. The report highlighted that the attackers could be of any nationality or ethnicity and were not necessarily from Pakistan. Russ was well aware that terrorists often used such diverse tactics as suicide operations, assassinations, kidnappings, hijackings, and bombings.

It was Russ's opinion that the vast majority of visitors to Canada were good, honest people. Some came for business or to holiday; others were seeking asylum and fleeing horrendous circumstances in their foreign countries, while others were just looking to make a new life for themselves and their families or rejoin family members who had previously migrated to Canada. He estimated that the number of people his guys had to weed out was likely less than 5 percent of the volume of travelers that they dealt with annually. Even though it was his final shift, he knew that he couldn't delay informing his staff of this latest report because one could never be sure who might be on the next flight coming into Canada.

He was confident that the experience and judgment of his senior officers furnished competent interrogations to eke out the rotten apples in the barrel. In the grand scheme of the immigration system, it was their level of expertise that was also useful to other external and internal government departments concerned with the issues involved in the overall process of keeping Canada safe. What concerned Russ the most was that the intelligence report also indicated that whatever the terrorists were up to now, there was reason to believe that the effect could be ten times greater than the events of 9/11.

2

Russ knew that it was probably going to be a long night for the RCMP and customs officers tracking the luggage until the seizure was finally made. Even though they had the baggage handler in custody, they were after the rest of the responsible group involved in the operation. He was relieved that the drug bust was out of his hair, and he'd been able to schedule all of his officers in two short meetings to inform them of the new terrorist threat.

Emerging from his meeting, Russ glanced up at the up-and-coming crowd, and he instinctively knew it would be a long night for his guys too. Two international flights had just unloaded. They were also expecting an additional two large flights to arrive before the night was through.

He headed back toward his office needing to complete the paperwork reporting the drug incident. Dammit! He had only partially completed it, when a knock at his door revealed the arrival of two federal police officers.

"Hi, Russ, sorry to barge in on you with an unexpected visit. We've come to have a talk with one of your employees, Donnie Forrester."

"What's up gentlemen?" he inquired. "The Department of Foreign Affairs received a complaint from the US State Department that one of their former congressmen was recently escorted to a backroom secondary inspection and made to remove all of his footwear. To make matters worse, after instructing the American to remove his socks and shoes, the border officer retrieved some paper and a pencil and proceeded to trace the man's feet for no apparent reason. We understand that this Donnie fellow was the culprit who performed this examination."

Hell! He was a kid, no more than twenty-three years of age, who had been with the department for a little over a year. He had a decent education, always appeared to be well mannered, never absent or tardy, and was impeccable in his appearance. He also seemed to get along well with all his coworkers. In fact, Russ had never received a complaint about his work. As he listened to the officers' concerns, he felt a knot in his gut and disappointment rise. It was a bloody shame that the youngster had tainted his otherwise-decent work record with some perverted fetish so that he had become the focus of an ongoing RCMP investigation.

Jeez! What the fuck was the kid doing? He had given the man some lame reason that they were searching for a passenger with a particular footprint pattern and needed to make a sample outline of everyone's feet who matched a specific profile. He'd proceeded to complete his artwork, pretended to check the pattern with some kind of master drawing, and then calmly told the guy he could go.

"Okay, I'll get him, and you can question him in one of the rooms," Russ replied.

Russ went along to watch the interrogation and was amazed when the kid openly admitted that he actually liked to spend time looking at and making drawings of people's feet. Russ couldn't believe his eyes when they looked inside Donnie's locker. They had shockingly discovered several large binders full of similar sketches.

It was a miracle, judging from the evidence they collected that other people hadn't stepped forward and complained about his twisted hobby. Judging by the sheer number of albums he had collected, the kid had to have been doing this for some time. Russ wondered what the tourists thought. Welcome to Canada and our own unique inspections by homegrown weirdos with foot fetishes!

Russ was exceedingly annoyed as he thought that the kid had been getting away with this for some time judging by the sheer volume he had compiled. He wondered how the hell he had gotten away with it. The airport was generally a pretty busy place, yet no one had ever complained. His fellow officers had to have covered a hell of a lot of downtime for him. He mentally made a note to recommend in his report that the installation of cameras in the interrogation rooms could prevent future similar instances.

Hell, what was the world coming to? He thought most people were pretty much aware of their human rights. Clearly, Donnie's collection indicated that at least a couple hundred people or more had either seen nothing wrong with this kid's activities or were too embarrassed to have complained.

It was likely that Donnie would be lucky, though. It appeared that he hadn't done anything other than make drawings of people's feet. He was only grateful that at least there hadn't been any complaints about him trying to lick or suck someone's toes! That could have been construed as an assault with criminal charges being laid. The kid wasn't off the hook yet, but Russ knew that the government wasn't likely to air its dirty linen in public and expose itself to a bunch of potential lawsuits by the victims.

The whole affair would be swept under the table like so many other things that he had seen over the years. In this case, the American politician was predictably as embarrassed as hell. He probably didn't want it plastered all over the papers, especially if he wanted to make a political comeback. Oh yes, then there was the bleeding-heart union who would claim that the guy needed psychological help, not punishment.

He had no doubt that the powers that be would make up some damn story to satisfy the US government. They'd probably claim that it was actually a part of some ongoing weird investigation. He could hear it now that the kid had mistakenly thought their fellow fit some profile that they were working on.

With all the crazy things going on in the world, the Americans were likely willing to buy any flimsy story that Foreign Affairs would concoct to save face. Apologies would be made. The situation would be discreetly defused with and kept under wraps. He thought that he had seen it all, but this one seriously took the cake!

Russ knew that the media wouldn't get a hold of this report. It would be prevented at all costs, not only for fear of opening floodgates to lawsuits, but the government would also be prudent to assess the harm of such a potentially humiliating international scandal. He figured that an executive decision would be made to move the kid somewhere else in the organization away from the public eye, likely pushing a pencil; send him for some counseling and no one would be any the wiser.

Hell, what had the kid been thinking? He would have been better off taking a job as a shoe salesman or in one of those sports gyms. He had missed his calling. If he'd invested in a little education, he would have been in his comfort zone as a chiropodist or podiatrist. Who else gets hung up on people's feet?

Russ was relieved when they finally gathered all of the evidence and escorted Donnie out of the terminal. He wanted to contain any damage from the incident so that it didn't appear in the morning newspaper. Shit, he thought, now he was down a man for the shift, and he also had additional paperwork to complete that he didn't welcome. He headed back to his office.

3

Damn! Russ thought as he read his e-mails and was reminded that one of his officers, Mike, had called in sick tonight. With both Mike and Donnie out, he was now going to be down two guys for the night. He would have to do some urgent juggling of the staff lunch and coffee breaks to keep the lines moving. While he hoped that no other surprises were in store for him, he decided to give Corby a quick call and see if he could come in a few hours early and help out.

Russ noted that his watch showed that there was still almost four hours to go for this shift. Corby never seemed to mind helping out whenever they were in a tight jam. Of course, it helped that he was a single guy and lived close to the airport.

The terminal schedule indicated that there was going to be a hefty number of arrivals, and true to form, Corby quickly agreed to come in. Russ didn't mind getting in himself and helping out; however, tonight he was also encumbered with the two evening incident reports.

He was glad that this week had been relatively quiet except for the alert on the drug bust, but he had hoped that his last night on the job would be peaceful too. He had purposely chosen not to work Friday night in deciding his retirement date because the weekends usually brought most of the problems. Nowadays, the airlines offered cheaper fares during off-peak flying hours, so assignment of work had become more difficult to predict. Today, they had an emergency landing just before the end of the afternoon shift that had already increased the workload for the guys on both shifts.

Russ sat back thinking about what to write in the report on Donnie, but his mind drifted. He was looking forward to spending this spring somewhere hot and sunny. He was in the mood for a little fishing and lots of relaxation. Perhaps, he'd play a little euchre or maybe even some bridge. He had enjoyed playing cards at some of the local clubs for more than twenty-five years, but after his wife, Sally, died he hadn't done much socializing.

He now felt out of place in the mixed couples clubs they had frequented. However, up near their cabin there was a local Legion Hall where the old guys gathered one afternoon a week and hung out for companionship and cards. It was perfect. No single women, a few beers, and he expected to hear some good war stories that would add some light entertainment to his life.

He had drifted from the friendships that Sally and he had made over the years, mainly because he hated the sympathy and all the reminders of the memories he liked to keep reserved and cherish with their only child, Katy. He also resented the fact that everyone seemed to believe he was single and available. They were always calling him to make up a fourth for bridge and hook him up with some recent divorcee or widow.

No, thanks, he wasn't up to cultivating a long-term relationship. It wasn't that he didn't enjoy being with people. The truth was that his work had provided him with an adequate social life since Sally's death. He'd had a strong marriage and was satisfied with that aspect of his life. Perhaps sometime in the future he might want some companionship with sexual benefits, but another marriage wasn't in his cards. He figured that he still had to watch over Katy and that he would find out in due time whatever other purpose God had in store for him.

He had a neat little nest egg, set aside from all the overtime he had done in the past four and half years. The work had not only helped him to bury his grief, but it also provided the means for any adventuresome inclination he might develop. He was also entitled to a fairly half-decent pension, so he was content that he had enough money to maintain his own humble lifestyle.

He contemplated that he might want to travel a little, but he certainly didn't need a companion to complicate matters. As a matter of fact, women were naturally drawn to him, and one-night stands away from home was tempting. He finally had accepted the fact that Sally had died and felt that he was prepared to handle that void. He had needs the same as most men, and for that purpose he was ready to move on. He had met many fascinating people from all over the world in his work and had developed some curiosity about the countries that they had come from. He thought that he might also like to visit some of the intriguing sights he had only had the opportunity to read about.

A lot of his friends had cautioned him that he'd be bored with retirement. Once he announced his retirement, the staff had jokingly teased him that he was certainly getting old at fifty-eight and just couldn't keep pace with the job anymore. They knew it wasn't true, but they liked to rile him. The staff he worked with were actually disappointed to see him go. He had been a pleasant taskmaster, always honest, fair, and he didn't micromanage his team. Although a few of the older women had shown an interest in striking up a more intimate relationship with him, he maintained a professional distance with most of the other employees. His one exception was his reliable employee and fishing buddy, Corby Dunn.

Russ was aware that he still had a lot of living to do but liked the idea of choosing how he did it. He figured the time had come for a change. He was enthusiastic about the prospect of not having to report to anyone anymore and the opportunity to sleep in if he felt like it. He needed to move on to another stage in his life. Change didn't frighten him; it was part of life and inevitable. He had enjoyed his career and grown with the job. It had provided security for his family and for his own future.

One thing he had hated over the years was the politics. Now more than ever, he didn't like the new political signs that were emerging throughout the government. There would be massive changes in the near future, and how those changes were managed by bureaucrats was often distasteful. In particular, he felt that the government was one of the largest perpetrators of abuse toward older workers.

Age discrimination was becoming a challenge to a lot of the older people. He had heard biased comments against senior staff regarding their capability to keep pace with the job. These were all arguments that pitted the younger workers against older ones. Some of the supervisors and managers were openly abusive or discouraging of their older workers. They pushed young people ahead before they were ready and failed to recognize the inherent strengths of the mature staff.

He agreed that it was time for the next generation to step up to the plate and deal with the issues that were now confronting governments with modern technology, equipment, and new laws. However, he knew that most were ill-prepared, having a general lack of experience and naivety. He speculated that responsible government meant altering the pathways of customary practices by changing the playing field, but whenever laws were changed it also provided an immense learning curve for the staff, and modern thinking was that all jobs could be handled by a template. What a crock of hogwash!

Guidelines were good, suggestions were helpful, but no two situations were the same, and templates were often used restrictively without thought. Flexibility was essential to performing any job well and kept the staff on their toes. Interviews couldn't be done in a vacuum, with the belief that everything would fit nicely into some predetermined pattern of behavior.

He'd given it some thought and concluded that while he was still quite fit, of sound mind, and financially able, he'd recapture some of the fantasies of his youth and protect himself from ageism. He hadn't done much travelling throughout his life partly because he couldn't afford to while paying for a home, private school and university for his daughter, and the cabin property up near Kelso. He had made a lifelong commitment to public safety and now wanted to sit back and enjoy the rest of his life.

When Sally and he had bought the property, they had decided that holiday money would be better invested in something that would provide long-term equity and years of entertainment for the family. They had hoped for several children, but they were only blessed with one. He didn't get the same use of it in recent years, but he hoped one day to have enjoyment there with his grandchildren. He enjoyed the camaraderie of some of the locals, which had softened the hard realities of his career.

Once the properties were mortgage free his family had begun to take a few small trips and see some of the places that had captured their interest, but then again, it wasn't ever about his personal fantasies. Their travels were always something afford-able and inclusive for the family such as trips to Disneyland, the Calgary Stampede, and once to the nation's capital to see the parliament buildings. Over the years, he had also attended a few conferences in Toronto and Montreal, courtesy of his employer, but that was about the extent of his travels.

Now he hoped to see some of the finest golf courses, do some deep-sea fishing—heck, maybe even visit the space center. He had plans to go to Australia the following week, but who knows, he also thought of visiting places like the Galapagos, the Arctic, and the tombs of Egypt. What could be boring about that? Someone else could worry about the crooks, the contraband, and guys who liked to play "twinkle toes." He had been working for as long as he could remember. He figured that he'd earned the right to do something different while he was still physically able.

While completing his reports, his thoughts were interrupted by a large commotion that was taking place in the terminal. Following a brief knock on his door, a junior officer barged in. "Russ," he breathlessly said, "we need a medic and you at the entry lines. We've got an emergency."

4

When the plane hit the tarmac, Hassan had felt the muscles in his face grow tense. He had known that the next few hours would probably determine the course of the rest of his life and the success of his mission. He had been over this a hundred times in his thoughts as he had crossed the Pacific. His gut feeling had been that this was undoubtedly going to be a different experience, unlike any he had ever encountered before.

His previous travels had all been done in the name of the cause, never with the intention of setting down roots in any particular place for a prolonged period of time. It wasn't that he didn't have an ulterior purpose in coming to Canada. It was that this country just didn't figure into that part of the plan. This would be his base of operations, not his target.

He liked the idea of staying here and the prospect of carrying on his business in proximity to his ultimate objective. He intended to stay here and establish himself. Strategically, Canada was better for all his future plans with regard to his activities on behalf of the organization. A Canadian passport was a free ticket to almost any country in the world. Importantly, it provided him with the best access to the United States. That was his target!

As the plane emptied, he had slowly gathered up his jacket and small carry-on bag, and he carefully made his way toward the crowd who were waiting for inspection by the Canadian customs and immigration officers. He went to the back of the longest line, hoping that most of the passengers would be cleared by the time he was interviewed. He didn't want to become a public spectacle, but he still wanted to get it over and done with quickly.

After what seemed to be at least an hour, he glanced at the wall clock and mentally confirmed that he had actually been waiting more than an hour. His medications were starting to wear off. It was almost two thirty in the morning. He anticipated that, by all accounts, he would be up for a couple more hours. He knew it was necessary for him to remain alert and work through the throbbing pain.

Thinking that a night flight would be less crowded, he had intentionally chosen a late flight. The travel agent had reported that this was a slow travel time. He wondered how long it would take during peak travel hours. The airport was pretty busy despite the hour. He was beginning to get agitated by the long wait, the stench of sweaty people, and the noise of crying kids. What parents would bring their kids on a flight this late? he pondered.

These people were undisciplined, he inwardly scoffed. Children should be in their beds. Of course, why wouldn't Canada be just like its neighbors, the permissive society of the Americans where discipline, morals, and structure in daily living were absent? No wonder people complained that kids didn't respect their parents these days. It was a two-way street. Parents needed to respect their children, guide them, teach them, and understand their basic needs like being in bed at a sensible hour.

As he looked around at others waiting to clear Immigration, he noted that many of the women were brazen, underdressed, and had, in his opinion, no business having children in the first place. He was annoyed with looking at their vulgarity and listening to their uncouth language. His patience was wearing thin. He had heard many stories of the way North Americans lived, but nothing could fully describe the extent of human degradation that he was now witnessing firsthand.

It never crossed his mind that these were people seeking to come into Canada. His assumptions with regard to their nationalities were unfounded and flippant. Had he given it any real thought, he would have realized that the people in the lines were likely not Canadians. Most of them were seeking entry into Canada like himself; therefore, they were from other countries.

He wished he had had another pill to pop before getting off the plane. The medication was no longer very effective, and he could feel the searing pain. He hoped like hell that they would get him some medical assistance quickly. He was a firm believer in the adage "No pain, no gain"; however, his tolerance was reaching a new low.

Moving closer to the booth, he glanced at the young officer at the counter wondering what would be her initial reaction to him. She spoke to each person with an impassive monologue, detached from the person with whom she spoke as if going through the customary routine from some ridiculous template. She stifled a yawn revealing either boredom or tiredness.

He'd give her some excitement and awaken her curiosity, he thought as he fumbled in his jacket pocket for the crumpled piece of paper containing one word, which hopefully would help him achieve his objective. He could speak some of the English language, but he wasn't going to reveal that. At long last, he approached her cubicle in response to the light indicating she was available for the next person.

"Passport, sir?" she requested.

He slowly shoved the paper toward her. Her eyes flew open as she simultaneously hit the small button to her right when she read the word written in bold and full capitals: "**REFUGEE.**"

"Do you speak any English, sir?" she inquired, resuming her composure.

He gave her a blank, impassive stare, shrugged his shoulders, and raised his hands, crossing them back and forth, to show that he didn't understand her. The strains of the night were beginning to show on his face. She could see that the man appeared to be in a lot of pain as she glanced at the bandages that covered both of his hands.

"Do you have a passport or any other documents?"

He inwardly smiled at how easily rattled she had become by his impassive stare and the sight of his bandaged hands. It was obvious that she was out of her comfort zone as he stonewalled her with a lack of response. He guessed that she hadn't been expecting anything out of the ordinary tonight, and she was a little hesitant on how to proceed.

Even then, her reaction was a little surprising considering that Canada was reported to have between twenty and thirty thousand refugee claimants a year. He would have thought that Vancouver must be one of Canada's larger airports, and they probably got a few claims every day. Someone had told him that more than fifteen million people came through this port of entry, annually.

She must be fairly new at the job, he thought. She didn't have the haughtiness you found with some customs and immigration officers in countries all over the world. However, he had to hand it to her; she regained her composure pretty quickly and reacted with an appropriate air of authority as two other officers approached.

"Just go with these gentlemen, sir, and they'll assist you," she commanded, pointing to two uniformed men who had abruptly joined them.

Then he collapsed to the floor.

5

Hassan's eyes fluttered open in confusion as he found himself lying on the floor with people crowded all around him. He had actually been unconscious for less than a minute, but he was slightly disoriented. His light-headedness persisted as he tried to bring himself to a sitting position and regain his composure.

He had been about to request a drink, when he recalled that he was at the Canadian customs and immigration checkpoint as he spotted an officer in full uniform. His mouth felt incredibly dry, and he desperately needed some water; however, he knew that he couldn't blow his cover by speaking the language. Moments later, he was startled by the arrival of an intimidating guy, who was at least six feet tall and weighed close to two hundred pounds.

"All right, everyone, let's clear the area a little and give the man some air. He's fainted, but he appears to be okay, and we've got a medic on the way." Russ spoke as he arrived on the scene. Hassan was thankful that someone had arrived with some common sense and the voice of authority.

Quickly, Russ noted that both the man's hands were all bandaged and wondered what the hell had happened to him. Using his first aid training, Russ felt the man's pulse and was concerned with his rate of rapid palpitations. He knew that this was often associated with dehydration and called for someone to bring some water and a wheelchair. His attempts to communicate with the arrival were met with a weak response in a foreign language.

"Let's get him into the infirmary where he can lie down until the doctor gets here," Russ ordered.

The wheelchair arrived a few minutes later, and Hassan was helped to his feet, but he felt exceptionally weak and thought that he might collapse again. Two officers assisted him into the wheelchair and offered him some water while he heard the man who seemed to be in charge inquire on what documents he'd entered with.

The male officers seemed much more accustomed to this type of situation than the girl had been. They informed the man that he hadn't shown a passport and had only produced a piece of paper with the single word, "refugee," written on it before he fainted.

"Roger, contact the airline, see if they can identify him. We need to get an interpreter here, so we've got to figure out what language he speaks. Can somebody see if Corby's come in yet? Tell him to come to the infirmary as soon as he comes in." Russ looked at the man's hands and immediately speculated that they would play some role in his story for refugee status.

Several of the officers tried their hand at communicating with the arrival all to no avail. After a few minutes had elapsed, Hassan winced as he reached toward his right pant pocket, and he attempted to retrieve the British passport with another crumpled note that had been written on with the foreign words: "هە انگلیسی ی." [note to layout: foreign words] It was written in his native tongue and intended to convey to them that he spoke no English. He waved his injured hands horizontally crossing each other back and forth as he shook his head slightly from side to side, then pointed to the pocket.

Russ stepped forward and placed his hand in the pocket, extracting the document that the man had indicated he needed help in retrieving. Just then another officer walked in. He was tall, with a pockmarked face, soggy and unkempt hair, and a small gold ring on his left eyebrow. He glanced at the man lying on the cot and asked Russ if he could help.

"I'm glad you're here, Corby. You're just the man I need. You look like hell, though. Did I catch you in the shower?"

"It's pissing down hard out there." Corby laughed.

"Take a look at this note and see if you can make out what language it's in, will you? I think it might be written in Arabic."

"Yes, I agree. It could be Arabic. Let me see the passport."

After leafing through the passport, Corby continued, "The passport shows he was in Dubai. There's a lot of Iranian people there. You know, it might be Farsi. He looks Iranian to me, and they usually speak Farsi."

He took the British passport and checked it under a magnifying glass with a peculiar light. He glanced at the senior man and continued, "I'm pretty sure that this is a photo sub. I don't think we'll get much help from it. I doubt that this is his real identity. What happened? How come he's in here?"

"It's hard to tell with some of these languages, but I think you're probably right. Do you want to see if you can get a Farsi translator? We had to bring him to the infirmary because he fainted, and we've got a call in for Doc Ryan. Somebody needs to look at what's under those bandages," Russ responded.

"Okay, I'll be back in a few minutes. Do you want me to grab Roger? We can take it from here."

"Yeah, that sounds good, but I think I'll stick around for a few minutes until the doc takes a look at his hands. I don't like the looks of this one. There's an urgent intelligence report with respect to a suspected terrorist operation. This guy conveniently has not one, but both of his hands all bandaged."

As Corby left the room, Hassan studied the man they had called Russ. It was likely that he wouldn't have talked so freely if he'd known that Hassan could speak perfect English and understood every word he uttered. He wondered if the man really had some information from a so-called intelligence report or had he just thrown the statement out there to impress his underling.

Hassan's scrutiny was interrupted by the sound of a rap at the door, which was abruptly opened by a scrawny, bespectacled young guy carrying a black bag. His appearance was slightly disheveled as if he'd been aroused from his bed.

"Good evening, Mr. Norman, I heard you have a patient for me?" The man stated in a cheerful tone, despite his earnest attempts to stifle a yawn.

"Dr. Ryan, I'm sure glad to see you. Sorry to call you out at this ungodly hour. Yep, we've had a little medical emergency here. Doesn't seem too serious, but he collapsed at one of our booths. Came around pretty quick, though. The man doesn't speak English, and Corby Dunn's gone to get an interpreter, which shouldn't be too long.

"No problem. Perhaps, you can fill me in on anything you know?"

"There's not much to tell until we can communicate with him. Like I said, he fainted waiting in the lines. Seems thirsty and still wobbly on his feet. Heart palpitations were elevated quite a bit. What has me fascinated is that both of his hands are completely bandaged, as you can see."

Hassan made a mental note that now he had the names of the men he was dealing with: Russ Norman, Corby Dunn, and Dr. Ryan. The latter two didn't really concern him too much; however, Russ Norman appeared to be a smart man with attention to details, and Hassan thought that he might pose a possible threat to his entry. He'd be very careful in his presence and hoped that he wouldn't be conducting the interrogation, which Hassan knew would happen sooner or later. He had never underestimated an adversary, and he wasn't about to start now. Despite his weakened physical condition, he was mentally alert and on guard.

6

Bashir—an unshaven, bushy-haired, fifty-five-year-old Pakistani-Kuwaiti—silently drove the van around the airport to the passenger pickup area. His two passengers quickly opened the suitcases, which each contained four-dozen toy dolls. The men began slitting open the bodies of the dolls that were found inside to extract the packets of white powder, the proceeds of which would be used to finance their mission. Despite the annoyance of the thin surgical gloves, it took the men less than ten minutes to transfer the contents into their two backpacks. When they had finished there still had been no phone call.

"Shahid, is your cell turned on?" the driver asked.

"Yes, it doesn't look good. They must have grabbed Tarik."

"Khurram, I don't see a tail yet. I'll slow down near the taxi stand, and you'll need to get out fast. Make sure your backpacks are secure. Don't hesitate, just go. If we make it, we'll meet you at the studio."

Khurram looked into the rear-view mirror into the steely eyes of the older man and gave a slight nod. Bashir had been a trained reconnaissance expert back in Pakistan, and Khurram knew that he had planned every detail of this task. It was now up to the thirty-year-old, agile younger man to complete the job and make the delivery. This shipment was vital to pumping money into the hands of the operatives in both Canada and the United States who were working to bring about the greatest mission the world had ever known.

Glancing out the window, at the heavy downpour, he felt confidence in the assurance that Allah would protect him. As the car swept around to the departures area, Khurram thought that they were equally lucky that the area had a fair amount of traffic. On second thought, luck had little to do with it. Bashir had likely checked the scheduled plane arrivals and had known the weather forecast. The taxi stand came into view, and Khurram reached for the door handle, uttered the traditional blessing *"Rahimahullah"* to the other two men, and without a look back, he jumped out as the car approached the front of the taxi lineup.

Shahid secured the door the minute Khurram had safely exited, and the car began travelling quickly onto Grant McConachie Way heading toward the Arthur Laing Bridge. His job would be to ditch the suitcases into the Fraser River, just in case the customs people had placed tracking devices on them.

"Any visuals?" Shahid asked.

"I can barely see out of my window, so I think they'll have a hard time seeing us. I'm sure Khurram made it. Are you ready? We're getting close to the bridge," Bashir responded.

Despite the fact that he was in excellent physical form and had trained for this operation, Shahid could feel the old injury from a previous mission was aggravated by the evening downpour.

"The suitcases are a little heavier than I thought. You'll have to get as close to the side as you can."

Bashir edged the car closer to the right side of the roadway as Shahid slipped the side door of the van open. With all his strength, he heaved the first bag over the rail and breathed a sigh of relief as it cleared and fell below to the waiting river. As he grabbed the second bag, the lid swung open, and the contents spilled out all over the inside of the vehicle; the catch hadn't been secure. He didn't hesitate, though, and pitched the bag anyway. However, the open bag had caught on the rail and fallen back onto the roadway.

Bashir didn't blink; he just kept moving the van toward SW Marine Drive heading for Granville Street. The area was known to have an active night life that he hoped might buy them the opportunity to get away if someone had followed them. Once they left the vehicle, he had figured that both he and his accomplice would be difficult to spot in a crowd as they were completely attired in black. With the night particularly dark from the pouring rain, he did not immediately notice the unmarked black Dodge Charger that picked up his trail as he exited the bridge.

Shahid opened the glove compartment and drew out a small box as Bashir moved the car farther into the heart of the downtown. On W. Sixth Avenue, he turned left and then made a right on Burrard Street heading for the vehicle and boat storage facility. The plan had been to dump the van there and switch to a Toyota parked nearby; however, Bashir became a little suspicious when he caught a glimpse of the Charger that seemed to be following his route.

As they pulled up in front of the storage gates, Bashir sucked in his breath and commanded with a militarized tone, "Don't move, I think we might have company!"

The two men sat in the parked vehicle for another few minutes while they waited to see if the other car continued on past them. It didn't. Shahid peered at the dolls that had spilled into the back of the van, cursing the evidence that linked them clearly to the operation.

"If that's the case, there's no way to get rid of all those dolls. Without them, they can't link us. Are you sure someone's following?" Shahid asked.

"I'm pretty sure. He's made the last three turns with us. I don't know where he picked us up. You take the Toyota. We'll do the backup plan and drive around the area for a bit; then I'll meet you at that pub on Granville in fifteen minutes. I don't know how long this guy has been with us, and I'm not sure if he's alone. I didn't see any other car that might be tailing us, and I'm fairly certain that he didn't pick me up inside the airport."

"He must have gotten us off the bridge. I think our mission has been successful. If they saw us drop Khurram, they wouldn't have to keep following us. I think that they'd just surround us. They're trying to get us to lead them to Iqbal," Shahid replied.

"Yes, I agree. We have done our part. Bahrami will be pleased."

They synchronized their watches, and Shahid exited the van to walk over to the other waiting car as Bashir pulled back into the road and slowly began an unsure game of cat and mouse. No one appeared to follow him, but that didn't mean that he was safe yet. He weaved in and out of the short blocks, and in less than ten minutes, he heard a resounding explosion. He had been right. He hoped that Shahid had taken the infidels with him. He would be rewarded for his work in paradise.

He reached into the box that Shahid had left on the seat and placed the second detonator close by his leg; then he pulled into an all-night service station. He got close to the attendant booth and got out, holding the device securely in his palm. This time he didn't miss the second black Charger as it slid into a parking spot close by. He asked the attendant for directions to the airport, thanked him, then drove out heading in the direction of the surveillance car.

Stroking his scraggly beard, Bashir grinned with a surging pride that Bahrami had chosen him for this mission. As he approached the Charger, he looked directly into the face of the driver, shouted "*Allah Akbar*," and then he pushed the button on the detonator and veered directly into the parked vehicle.

7

Corby returned to the interrogation room, and after a brief conversation with his superior, he turned to the refugee claimant. Pointing at his own chest, he asked, "Mr. Dunn...and you?" Then he pointed at the newcomer.

The man nodded slightly and responded, "Hassan."

Corby noted that the claimant had a boyish appearance, hair cropped extremely close to the head, almost as if it had recently been shaven and just started growing back, but overall his face was bland and expressionless. His eyes were like shards of steel, hard and cold. There was not even a hint of warmth anywhere in his face, and his overall demeanor was aloof.

Corby had once heard that a person's eyes were the window to his soul. If that were the case, he thought, this man was totally devoid of any human sensibility. He lay quietly, passive and unreadable. Corby checked his watch, then took some papers from the desk drawer, and began to write while glancing periodically at the man lying on the cot.

After several moments, Corby decided to try a different tactic. By smiling at the man, he tested him to see if he could elicit any type of reaction. However, Hassan maintained a poker face and displayed no emotional response or acknowledgment of the gesture. After Russ had perused the passport a little more thoroughly, he tossed it to Corby and suggested that he busy himself by making a copy until the interpreter arrived.

While Corby photocopied all the pages, stamped, and then initialed the copies before sealing the original in a plastic bag that he labeled, the other two men stepped out of the room.

The time dragged silently on as Corby engaged in reviewing the records he had written for the file, examining the passport and the notes that the man had presented. It appeared to be another fifteen minutes before the door was suddenly opened by another shorter, heavier, uniformed officer who was accompanied by someone whom Hassan instinctively knew was one of his fellow compatriots.

"Good evening, Mr. Dunn. I hope you weren't waiting too long for me. I came as fast as I could get here," he gushed apologetically.

Hassan was a little taken aback as he felt waves of disgust rise within himself while he observed the newcomer's subservient responses to the beck and call of the two border officers. He hated to see people kowtow to others, regardless of their position. It was one thing to do the job and follow instructions, but it was quite another to allow others to exercise control over you.

He wanted to lecture the man about human dignity and remind him that the Qur'an speaks of human equality and submission only to the will of Allah. Why would he apologize? It was the middle of the night, and he was doing them a favor. He probably only received some menial remuneration. His thoughts were quickly interrupted as he tried to catch the words Dunn spoke to the newcomer as the doctor and the boss man also joined them.

"No, I'm sorry for calling you at this time of night, Mr. Azizi," Dunn replied. "He doesn't seem to speak any English, and he appears to have a few injuries as you can see. We want Dr. Ryan to take a look at him first. He had a little mishap when he entered. I think he might be Iranian."

"Okay, I'll ask him some questions and see if we can communicate all right," Azizi responded, showing some concern.

"Did Roger show you the note?"

"Yes, it is written in Farsi. It just says he doesn't speak English."

"Well, note or no note, we figured that one out. Go ahead and see if he understands you. I think his name is Hassan," Corby said with sarcasm.

Hassan was addressed in Farsi as Mr. Azizi identified himself. He explained that he was an interpreter who was present to provide translation for all of the parties and then queried whether Hassan understood him. After acknowledging that he did, and a brief conversation, Azizi told the two officers that the man's name was actually Hassan Zadeh and clarified the spelling of both names.

"Would you just start by introducing us and tell him we're Border Security officers who need to ask him a few questions after the doctor has examined him. I don't know if you know my colleague, his name is Roger Wayne, and this is Dr. Ryan. You have met my boss before, Mr. Norman, of course."

After a few minutes of interpretation, Azizi advised, "Mr. Zadeh acknowledges that he understands."

"Could you ask him what happened to his hands and why they're all bandaged like that?" Corby continued.

After a few moments of discussion, Azizi informed them that Mr. Zadeh had been in a fire and had suffered severe burns to both hands, arms, and even his hair had been somewhat burned. He went on to say that the man indicated that he was in considerable pain and wanted to know if he could get something to alleviate it.

Dunn instructed Azizi to inform Hassan that the doctor would need to remove his bandages so he could examine his injuries. All the while, Russ Norman stood silently observing and had the uneasy feeling that the entire scene was being carefully orchestrated exactly how the stranger wanted it to be. The doctor spoke to Hassan through the interpreter and began unwrapping Hassan's bandages. Russ and Corby stood close by filled with curiosity at what they would see.

"We need to take his fingerprints," Corby informed the doctor.

"Whoa! Not so fast, Mr. Dunn. What have we here? There's no chance of getting fingerprints right now. This fellow's got some very serious burns, and there's a real threat of infection setting in," the doctor replied. "Perhaps a couple of these burns aren't too bad. They might only be second degree. My God, there appears to be third-degree burns on all of his fingers."

"Just the fingertips," Russ commented, making a quick observation.

"How can you tell? What's the difference?" Roger asked.

"You see where the color is red and white? The redness indicates second-degree burns, and they're the ones causing him the pain. Notice how they appear moist. There's evidence that he has had some blisters that broke, too! Where the skin is white and dry or leathery, that's a sign of a third-degree burn. He's going to require removal of that skin—and the sooner, the better!"

"He fainted when he arrived. Can that be attributed to the burns?" Russ inquired, moving closer for a look at the extent of the man's injuries.

"Yeah, it's a sign of dehydration caused typically by a severe burn. He needs electrolyte-enriched water immediately and lots of protein. I've got one bottle with me. He won't feel pain from the worst burns because of the nerve damage, but they pose the greatest danger to him. When the nerves are damaged, people don't feel the pain if an infection sets in. I'll dress the wounds for now and give him a few painkillers, but he needs to get to the hospital for further treatment. Where's he going tonight?"

"We're sending him to the detention center," Corby responded without giving it a second thought.

"I recommend a hospital, but it's your call," the doctor quickly stated, looking at Russ.

"Corby's right. We'll have to detain him tonight. I can't free anyone up right now for guard duty. Can we get more of that special water at the all-night pharmacy?" Russ asked.

"No, they only stock it for children in emergencies. I'll call the Richmond Hospital and see if I can get you enough to last for twenty-four hours if someone can slip over and pick it up. You know, Russ, he'll probably hold up until tomorrow."

"We'll go over to my office in a minute, and you can make arrangements with the hospital. I'll get someone to go over and pick it up or go myself if I have to. We need to get him to a hearing tomorrow, legal procedures and all. Do you think he can weather it?"

"In that case, I'll give him some antibiotics and painkillers, which should get him through until later tomorrow. I'll check in on him in the morning around eight, before the hearing. Then I think you should get him to the hospital. You'll need to let them know that he requires hospital treatment in the burn center," the doctor responded.

Before the doctor left the room, he had rebandaged both hands and had given Zadeh a couple of pills to swallow immediately. Then he handed Corby two small bottles with a few pills in each, instructing him to convey to the staff at the detention center when they were to be taken. Turning to Azizi, he told him to inform Zadeh that he required hospital care, and he would see him the next day to make arrangements.

"Can I ask him a few questions, now?" Corby asked as he walked with Russ and Doc Ryan into the hall.

"Yeah, go ahead. If he's up to it. He seems pretty stable for now. I'd suggest that you just let him lay on the cot and go easy."

"Thanks for coming, Dr. Ryan. We can head over to my office and take care of getting some of the special water that you mentioned. I promise you, we'll get him through as fast as we can in the morning. Corby, get what information you can, and when you're through, I'll escort him over to detention," Russ said.

8

Corby returned to the room holding Hassan Zadeh and asked Azizi to inform the man that he would like to ask him a few questions if he felt up to it. Zadeh had been waiting for this day for some time. He was eager to get on with the interview, and there was no point in delaying things any longer than was necessary, but his face remained impassive as he took his time to respond.

After several minutes, he asked Azizi if they would permit him to stay lying on the cot as he thought that the prone position might be helpful in preserving his strength. Once they had agreed and assured him that they would stop at any time he needed a break, the officer named Dunn began with the obvious question with regard to how he burned his hands. Zadeh closed his eyes for several moments, causing everyone present some concern whether he was able to proceed with the questioning.

Then he suddenly opened them in a hooded fashion and slowly answered the question. After a few moments of discussion, Azizi informed the two border officers that Mr. Zadeh had been in a fire and had suffered severe burns to both hands, arms, and even his hair had been somewhat burned.

"How did he get the bandages? Who attended to his burns?" Corby asked.

After questioning Zadeh, Azizi replied, "He explained that his friend's father is a doctor. The doctor treated his wounds and took him to Dubai where someone had arranged that another doctor came to the hotel for further help."

The next few questions posed to him were routine and basic fact-finding. Dunn asked him where he came from, his parents' names, his date of birth, all the addresses he had lived at during the previous ten years, where he went to school, and where he worked. It was all straightforward and didn't provide any surprises for him.

Dunn turned to the photocopies of the passport and asked Azizi to find out whether the document was his. Hassan thought that the question seemed ridiculous because the passport was obviously in another name. However, he didn't comment on that subject and just played along with their games.

After a brief conversation with Zadeh, Azizi translated, "No, he denies owning the passport. He bought it from a smuggler so that he could get to Canada for help. He also said that he is aware that someone else's name is in it and reminded me that his name was Hassan Zadeh."

"Where did he get it?" Corby continued.

"He said that he got it in Dubai," repeated Azizi, after conferring with Zadeh.

"When did he leave Iran?" Corby asked.

"As soon as he could travel, several days ago."

"How did he leave?"

"His friend got him on a plane to Dubai," Azizi repeated Zadeh's response.

"Did he use his own passport for that plane?"

"No, he used his friend's."

"Where is that passport?" Corby probed, wanting explicit details.

"He gave the passport back to his friend's father."

"Is that the same person who treated his hands, the doctor? Is that the person he gave the passport back to?"

"Yes."

"What are the full names of his friend and his father?"

"Ali Shirazi and Dr. Shirazi, he doesn't know the doctor's first name," Azizi repeated.

Corby was taken a little aback by the response that Zadeh had provided. He contemplated that it was rather strange that anyone would behave so trustingly with a man whom he didn't even know his full name. He decided to delve into the relationship a little closer. Carefully watching Zadeh, he queried, "Did this doctor give him any special instructions about his hands?"

"Yes."

Azizi took several minutes to clarify Hassan's response before he continued, "The doctor told him that although he might not feel pain from some of the burns, it was because they were bad and that he needed immediate medical help because he could suffer shock or get an infection. He also suggested that he needed specialized hospital care. Mr. Zadeh said that he couldn't go to a hospital in Iran, and regardless, his hands were too injured to travel immediately. That was part of the reason Mr. Zadeh didn't travel right away. The doctor said that as soon as he was safely out of the country, he should go to the hospital for special care."

His response was consistent with Doc Ryan's assessment, and without medical training, Corby was at a loss on how to continue with this line of questions. His approach had veered off course. He really wanted to know if Zadeh had been attended by a professional physician, so he moved on.

"Did he get any more treatment for his hands before he came to Canada?"

"Yes, he saw a doctor in Hong Kong."

"How did he find this doctor in Hong Kong?" Corby asked.

"A smuggler in Dubai provided him with the photo-subbed passport, and he had arranged for someone to meet him at the airport in Hong Kong. That person took him to see the other doctor, but he doesn't know the doctor's name."

"What were the names of the smuggler and the person who met him in Hong Kong?"

"The smuggler indicated his name was Haydar, and the person in Hong Kong was Farid, but they didn't provide him any other information. He doesn't know their last names."

"How long was he in Hong Kong?"

Hassan closed his eyes again, took a deep breath, and murmured a response, following Azizi's translation. "About three days. He stayed because his burns needed treatment. When the doctor permitted him to travel, he came to Canada," Azizi repeated in English.

"How's he doing? Perhaps he needs a break or something?" Corby sensed that the man was tiring, and he himself wanted to confer with Roger. He wasn't picking up anything and was beginning to feel that this part of the interview had been pointless.

Azizi spoke to him sympathetically and asked if he felt okay to continue. Hassan was tired but determined to get through the interview. After several minutes, he nodded his head and informed Azizi that he wished to complete the questions. Corby looked down to his notes and then picked up his questions where he had left off.

"Where did he stay in Hong Kong?"

"He doesn't know the address. He was taken to an apartment somewhere but doesn't remember much about it because they gave him medicine to put him to sleep."

"How much did he pay the smuggler?"

"He doesn't know what was paid. His friend, no, he said it was probably his friend's father who took care of all the arrangements. Mr. Zadeh says that he didn't have any money except for a bit that Dr. Shirazi provided to him for his journey."

"Did the doctor pay for the passport in Hong Kong?"

"No, the money for the passport was paid to the smuggler in Dubai, and he thinks that it was the smuggler who paid the person Farid for the passport," Azizi conveyed.

Over the next hour, Hassan watched passively as the second officer wrote down everything Azizi translated while Dunn did all the questioning. Inwardly, Hassan was satisfied that little did these guys realize, but he was well prepared for this interview. He was perfectly aware that those notes would be a part of the record in subsequent hearings if he wanted to stay in Canada.

Some of his friends had been through the whole nine yards before him. He could have almost anticipated every question, and he was cognizant of the importance of providing minimal facts that couldn't later be used against him. He had been warned that details of the interview were often used to confuse claimants and impugn their testimony at a later date in an actual formal hearing for asylum.

To the unwary these seemingly unimportant questions gave the immigration officers the ammunition to make inferences about a claimant's credibility. They could even cost a person a positive ruling at the eventual hearing for asylum. He had carefully crafted his story to be tight and as close to truthful events that he was familiar with so there would be less of a chance of tripping him up later. He had spent countless hours researching indisputable facts that he could throw at them. These would make his story plausible if some of the circumstances were objectively verified.

This is all nonsense, he thought with an air of intellectual superiority. Anyone who prepared themselves with knowledge of actual events could tell them anything to tie themselves to the event. At the end of the day, the interrogators had to prove he was lying. Whoever trained these guys were idiots.

He had seen transcripts of many similar interviews, and they were all the same. Their questions were all predictable and followed a routine pattern. Governments seemed to be unable to hire people who could think for themselves. He'd heard that the Canadian government had created employee templates for all these matters. Now these same tools could be used by people such as himself in preparation to circumvent the system that was in place. If they ever actually caught someone in this process, it was either pure luck or just stupidity on the part of the claimant.

Once everything was standardized, almost everyone knew how to deal with it. The lawyers and the people who did their homework had easily obtained access to the templates. The whole process utterly amused him. He could have asked all of the questions that were being put to him. He began to relax, letting down his guard.

Then suddenly, they had caught him! All the coaching he had received and his carefully crafted responses still did not prevent him from a slight falter when Azizi asked him if he had ever been out of Iran before. He wasn't sure how to answer this and had to think about his answer. His hesitation caused the two officers to glance at him and then at each other. Damn! He didn't miss their silent communication that perhaps they had stumbled on something that he didn't want to share.

There it was. His own stupidity. He knew that the question was standard, but somehow he hadn't prepared a spontaneous reply. It was so simple, and yet his hesitation could arouse some suspicion. He took a deep breath and allowed his cool-headedness to prevail.

He cleared his throat and told the interpreter that he needed to stop for a bit, he wished for some more water. Personally, he hoped that this would explain his hesitation with the question. Dunn appeared a little annoyed at the interruption before remarking that the doctor had instructed that he had to be kept well hydrated and indicated that they'd get something for him. Roger agreed to check to see if Russ had managed to get the special water from the hospital and promptly left the room.

9

Russ sat in his office and listened to Sid in stunned disbelief to how the drug bust had gone awry and ended up with two suicide bombers taking out four RCMP federal police officers and apparently destroying all the evidence that was connected to the drug bust earlier in the evening. There had never been an event like it on Canadian soil. Hell, he didn't recall an incident anywhere in the world like what had transpired right here in Vancouver on this night. Drug dealers becoming suicide bombers was a new one!

He suggested to Sid that even though they had the baggage handler, they didn't have much in the way of hard evidence to hold him on a charge of conspiracy to engage in drug trafficking. Russ suggested that they needed to look at Transport Canada's Air Cargo Security Program and see if they could keep the guy on a breach of security. Disappointedly, Sid informed him that it was not designed for this type of situation, and technically speaking, each airline is responsible for its own unclaimed baggage.

The RCMP had interviewed the baggage handler, and he had given them a simple explanation that a guy offered him a sizable tip to bring the luggage to a rear door where he had his car parked. Although, he acknowledged, it was unusual to use that particular door, he just figured that the person was someone who worked at the airport and needed a helping hand due to his incapacity.

"Christ, even with the seized contraband, some judge would likely buy his story," Russ commented.

"Yeah, we want you to run him through the immigration records and see what status he has in Canada. If we're unable to keep him on criminal hold, we might be able to transfer him to an immigration hold. Here's his name and date of birth," Sid replied, shoving a piece of paper towards Russ.

Glancing at the paper, Russ signed into his computer on the Federal Immigration operating site and quickly entered the man's name. Nothing came up.

"Any idea where he might be from?"

"Hate to tell you this, Russ, he says he's born in Canada, but his parents are Egyptian. Not sure if I believe him, though."

"This is about as serious as it gets. I'll get a hold of my director and get him to bring the contractor in. The employee file might help identify this guy. You didn't get any other information?"

"No, I'll tell the Mounties we need more, and I'll check back with you in about an hour." Sid could barely mask his disappointment as he prepared to leave.

When Sid opened the door, he almost walked right into one of Russ's officers. Roger had arrived. Russ pointed to the bottles of water that had arrived just before Sid had come in. "Sorry, I suppose you're looking for that. I hadn't had a chance to run it over to you before I catalogued it in. I'll just be a minute with the paperwork. How's it going? Are you finished with the Iranian?"

"Hah! That's wishful thinking. You know, Corby, when he gets going, he'll keep at him as long as he can. I'll give the guy credit, though. He seems to want to cooperate."

"All right. Get back to me as soon as you're finished. We've got some pretty serious stuff going on tonight. We've lost four RCMP officers in the drug bust."

"Do you mean killed?"

"I'm afraid so, Roger. Worse than that, it was the act of suicide bombers right here in downtown Vancouver."

"What! Oh my God!"

"It's hard to believe, I know. I'm a little concerned about this Iranian guy too! I wonder if the two incidences are somehow interconnected. I want you fellows to be as thorough as possible. I think it's going to be a long night."

10

Roger delivered the enriched beverages to the interrogation room and offered to get Azizi and Dunn a coffee before the interview resumed. Several minutes later, he returned with the hot beverages, and they all settled back down. Corby knew that he'd lost his momentum from the first round. He began to see a pattern with this fellow. Every time Zadeh had been led outside his comfort zone, the man came up with something to distract everyone.

After the refreshments, Dunn glanced back at his notes and reiterated the question he had asked before the interruption. This time there was no hesitation.

Hassan simply stated that he had travelled a little with his family on holidays when he was younger. Dunn was persistent. He wanted the name of every country where he had been, when, and why he had gone there. Hassan had to admire the focus of the man, and he instinctively knew he was dealing with a slightly more worthy adversary than he had initially thought, even if he wore that ridiculous jewelry above his eye.

He responded that his family had taken some vacations to Turkey and Dubai, but he couldn't remember the dates; he had been a kid. It was so long ago, and he had never had the opportunity to travel anywhere else. After a moment, he breathed a silent sigh of relief that his answer seemed to satisfy the officers.

Dunn picked up the photocopies of the passport and began checking the entry and exit stamps shown on the pages within it. He went over the trip to Dubai, again. Zadeh repeated that he travelled with his friend's father to Dubai where he was put in contact with the agent who helped him get a flight to Hong

Kong. That agent arranged for him to get the British passport, which he used for his entire trip from Dubai to Hong Kong and then to Canada.

Then he added that the agent told him it was easiest to fly to Hong Kong and then to Canada. As Dunn continued leafing through the pages of the passport, Hassan was confident that it bore entry and exit stamps from Hong Kong that would match his story. He had been careful to make sure that anything that could be used as physical evidence supported his claim.

Dunn repeated a few questions about whom his friend and his father were. How long had they known one another? Why would they risk helping him? Hassan knew that these questions were well beyond the scope of any template, and it had been his misfortune to get this particular officer. The man was pretty thorough in looking for loopholes in his story, and he suspected that his boss, the one called Russ Norman, had known he would be.

He decided it was time for another diversion to slow Dunn down and asked Azizi to assist him with more of the liquid. Then he lay back and closed his eyes again, mumbling that he needed a few moments. Corby had had enough and decided it was time to get down to the real purpose of this interview. He gave him a few more minutes. Then he questioned Zadeh about why he was claiming refugee status. Hassan opened his eyes and relaxed a little more because he knew this story well. He had researched facts and rehearsed it several times. He was confident that it was solid.

Hassan related that his family were members of the Baháʼí faith. These members, as a group, were recently targeted by the Iranian government as apostates from Islam. Because their religion varied from the traditional Islamic teachings, many of their people were condemned by revolutionary leaders. Their deaths had been not only condoned but also ordered by the new regime. Some of their leaders had been held for almost a year in Gohardasht Prison on the western outskirts of Tehran.

It was not uncommon for the Iranian government to confiscate or destroy the property of members of his faith. His parents had been falsely accused of spying for Israel and promulgating propaganda against the Islamic republic. Corby had read that similar accusations had been made against many of the leaders of the Bahá'í. He was also aware that there were numerous articles verifying that even the religious followers of the faith were dealt with by false imprisonments, torture, and even death.

As Hassan continued and informed Azizi of the recent history of Gohardasht Prison—where people were beaten, tortured, imprisoned for life, or executed—it confirmed what Corby already knew. Azizi too showed instant recognition of all that Zadeh related to him, and as he translated this to the immigration officers, one could detect a glimmer of sympathy toward the man in his eyes.

Hassan was pleased with the passion that Azizi used concerning every horrific detail that he described regarding the burning of his family home and his personal attempt to locate members of his family amid the fire. He had duly conveyed the story of his escape and his overwhelming fear that his entire family had been annihilated. He had further described that his hair had been on fire, and his hands and arms badly burned in his desperate attempt to find family members. Azizi was a good envoy of the message he wanted to convey.

Hassan concluded his story with a strong summary statement that he wasn't sure if any of his family members had survived. He suggested that perhaps if they had, they too had been taken to the prison. He couldn't find either of his parents or his younger siblings, a brother and sister. He knew that the government would look relentlessly for him too.

The officers appeared to mellow a little and took a slightly less aggressive approach in the questions that followed. It was generally thought by Hassan's people that Canadians were both exceedingly gullible and compassionate by nature, and he wasn't disappointed. He had almost stumbled, but he was thankful they hadn't seemed to take too much notice.

After that there were just a few more elementary questions about his identity and whether he had some identification that would confirm who he actually was. Wincing as he attempted to get something from his pants, he motioned to a pocket and asked Azizi if he could help retrieve his wallet, explaining that he had his Iranian National Identity Card.

He was slightly startled when Dunn seized the wallet from the interpreter and began rifling through it. There was very little inside, besides his identification and some cash. However, there was a folded sheet of paper in one of the pockets, with what appeared to be two names and a couple of Canadian phone numbers. He didn't want them to take the paper, but it was too late.

Dunn placed the identity document, boarding pass, and the folded paper in a clear envelope. Then he sealed it and returned his wallet. Hassan calmly told Azizi that he needed the information that was on the paper as it had the phone number of one of his relatives on it. It was where he was planning to stay while in Canada.

As Azizi explained this, Dunn unsealed the envelope, photocopied the paper, and handed the copy to Hassan. He then placed all the original documents back in a new envelope, resealed it, and initialed over the seal. However, at the mention of a relative in Canada, another barrage of questions ensued. Dunn wanted to know whom he knew in Canada and how he knew them.

Knowing that there are fifty thousand of his fellow countrymen in Canada, Hassan smugly informed them that the phone number was for a man named Noe. He was a relative from his mother's family who had come to Canada more than ten years earlier. Azizi spent several minutes trying to determine more details about how this person was a relative and told Dunn that Canadians would call him his cousin, and that was the reason he had chosen to come to Canada rather than to seek asylum in Europe.

Hassan had been alerted that people could name just about anyone as a maternal relative without the Canadians being able to prove otherwise. It was more difficult to trace family connections through that lineage and virtually unverifiable by any foreign government. In his case, though, it was probably one of the few truths he had spoken.

His organization had several people who were experienced in the Canadian immigration process. They were lawyers and consultants who attended hearings regularly. They never represented any members that could be tied to the organization, keeping a distance in case anyone was identified. However, they had been instrumental in providing training materials to operatives wishing to base themselves in Canada before they came to the country.

Lawyers and consultants were able to obtain transcripts of the admissibility hearings for the people they represented and passed them onto their clients. They even obtained tapes of actual asylum hearings from a number of countries. The continuing practice of Western societies to have their employees use templates and common research materials had led to the ability for organizations such as his to learn how to circumvent the procedures for many countries, not just Canada.

Their education systems were so atrocious that government workers had to use a group of standardized questions in these hearings to narrow the focus of their inquiries. People generally were incapable of thinking for themselves and didn't know how to follow up what was being told to them. The real investigative work could be initiated in this interview, but he had been told it seldom was and was, in fact, discouraged by their management teams.

Hassan had received extensive coaching in preparation for the hearing processes in Canada. He had also been assured that the Canadian courts required the government to show that a refugee claimant was lying; otherwise, the judge had to accept whatever he was told by an applicant for asylum. Dunn was a lot more thorough than the majority of his colleagues according to what Hassan had seen in some of the sample officers' notes that were passed around. This guy and his boss showed little compassion. Heck, he had probably been trained by that Norman guy; he was razor-sharp even though he looked a little ridiculous, he concluded.

Quite frankly, there was plenty of evidence about the persecution of members of the Bahá'í faith and about conditions in Gohardasht Prison produced by all kinds of human rights organizations. He certainly didn't have to prove anything. It would be up to the Canadians to disprove his family's fate, which was nearly impossible for them to do.

However, he knew that some people became too confident and got tripped up on their stories, failing to recognize that the initial interview was important for what was to follow in the months ahead. No doubt about it, these guys were primarily on a fact-finding mission, and they were making meticulous notes of every word. The responses he had given appeared to have served his purpose. Fortunately the system averted any deeper questioning, at least for now.

He wasn't happy, though, that they had kept a copy of the paper from his wallet. There were two numbers on it; he didn't want the immigration people or anyone else to have one of them. He'd have to alert Nazreh as soon as possible to ditch the cell phone.

11

The door opened again, and Hassan observed that another officer had brought in his single checked suitcase. This latest recruit turned to Dunn, indicating that all hell had broken loose, and Russ was wondering if he'd be much longer.

"What's going on?" Dunn asked.

The officer blurted out that four Mounties had been killed during the course of two terrorist attacks downtown. He informed his colleague that they had also lost most of the evidence from the events earlier in the evening, and they were trying to identify either one of the attackers. None of the officers who were present during this outburst appeared to have noted the instant satisfaction in Hassan's eyes as he carefully listened to the conversation and swiftly recovered his masklike expression.

"Tell him we need about ten more minutes. That should do it."

As the officer left, Dunn pointed to Hassan's carry-on and the piece of luggage that had just been brought in and asked if it belonged to him. When Hassan confirmed that it did, Dunn informed him that they were just going to take a look at what he had brought with him. Hassan shrugged; he knew that all they'd find was his toiletries and a few changes of clothing. He had travelled light, and there was definitely nothing incriminating.

He watched the second officer, Roger, explore every nook and cranny, check each item, and even run his hands in all the pockets and seams of both of the suitcase and its contents. Hassan thought that they'd probably had them x-rayed too. Satisfied that there was nothing of interest, Dunn spoke some more to the translator.

Azizi informed him that they needed him to stand for a body search, empty all his pockets on the table, spread his feet, and raise his hands clasped above his head. He quickly reminded him that it was difficult to either clasp his hands or empty his pockets due to the condition of his hands but had no problem if they wanted to conduct a search. After some discussion, they agreed to let him just raise his hands, and they would check his pockets.

The shorter guy, whom they called Roger, frisked him quickly before he finally permitted Hassan to return to the cot. Dunn instructed Azizi to read him everything that they had recorded on the sheets and then have Hassan sign the forms to the best of his ability. As he did, Azizi assured him that there would be just a few formalities at a place where he would spend the rest of the night called a "holding center." In the morning, he would appear before an immigration judge for an admissibility hearing because he didn't come to Canada on a visa. Hassan nodded.

He had been alerted to all of these procedures, and though he was tired, he was aware that it was just one more necessary step in the process. They didn't have to tell him that he'd probably be issued a removal order at the morning hearing. It was something else he knew that didn't truly matter.

The judge's order would mean nothing unless he lost his refugee claim, months down the road, maybe even years as he had been told that some of these hearings took. It was just another mere formality. More of a nuisance than anything, and they couldn't even attempt to remove him for a long time if he lost his refugee hearing. He knew that there were lots of other things he could do to prevent them from kicking him out if they ever tried.

He had learned that there were several avenues to appeal to higher courts and then, another branch of the department could even give him permanent resident status on humanitarian grounds or if he married someone in Canada. In the meantime, he would have some of his basic needs met. He knew that he'd be given money and free health care until his asylum claim could be heard. It would happen in another location, maybe in a year or two.

He glanced at his watch and discovered that it was just past 3:00 a.m. No wonder he was tired, he thought. He'd been on the go for about twenty-two hours. He asked Azizi where they were sending him and if he could make a phone call to his relative who had been expecting him when the plane landed. Without answering the first question, Dunn asked Azizi for the number, dialed it, and then passed Hassan the phone.

He was given no privacy, although they feigned disinterest. Hassan didn't trust that the phone call wasn't being taped anyway, so he planned to be particularly cautious. The phone was picked up immediately on the first ring. He heard Noe's deep voice ask, "What's up?"

"Noe, I've arrived," he muttered in Farsi.

"How was your flight?"

"The food was terrible. The agent was supposed to order me a vegetarian dinner, but I'm sure it was mixed with some pork. It smelled bad, too. I couldn't eat anything and had to sit in the washroom until they cleared the plates. It was making me nauseous. I need some real food. I'm also in need of a few hours' sleep. My hands are throbbing. I saw a doctor, and I might be going to a hospital tomorrow, but I'm done here, and they're taking me to something called a holding center for a hearing tomorrow before a judge," he replied.

"I think I know the place. Ask if it's called Wolmer Center," Noe requested.

He glanced at Azizi, and with an open display of struggling with the language, he inquired, "Wolmer Center?" Upon receipt of an affirmative nod, he then confirmed his destination with Noe.

"It's not far from the airport. I'll be there bright and early, around eight. The hearings usually start about eight thirty or a little later, and we should be able to get you out by noon, or shortly after. I don't know about going to the hospital, though. It might be a good idea," Noe responded.

He promised that his wife, Maryam, would have a sizable plate of *khoresht* and basmati ready for his arrival, voicing his shared contempt for English foods. He closed with, "Sleep well, my friend, you're almost here. You should be free and clear by noon."

After hanging up, Azizi advised him that Mr. Norman would accompany Hassan to the holding center until he was settled in, and the next day another person would assist him with the language at the hearing. Feeling relieved that the initial interrogation was over, Hassan stood to stretch his slight five-foot-eight-inch frame. His relief was short-lived as the man they had called Russ sauntered into the room. He reached for Hassan's hands and then stopped. He was dangling a pair of handcuffs, but hesitated when he again saw the bandages.

Dunn told the burly guy, "Russ, it's your call, but I don't think that the cuffs are necessary."

"Yeah, I think you're right. Is any of the water left? Who's got the meds?"

"He's got them. Perhaps you should take them over and hand them back to him there. For that matter, Mr. Azizi, could you carry these three extra bottles of water to take with him too?"

Russ asked Azizi to get the pills, grab the carry-on, and bring the bottles of water as he took the small suitcase in his free hand and gently pushed Hassan toward the door.

"Hey, Russ, thanks for helping out. I'll see you when you get back. I want to discuss something with you. I think I'll require your signature for a referral to Judd," Corby stated.

Russ nodded as he led Hassan out of the interrogation room through the back passage to the vehicle transport area. "Thanks for coming so late, Mr. Azizi," Corby mumbled as everyone dispersed.

12

After turning the detainee over to the detention center, Russ returned to hunt down Corby Dunn. He ran into Sid and a couple of Mounties who asked if they could meet with him for a bit. He noted that he would have had just a little more than a half hour before he would have been finished for the night and with his career if providence hadn't intervened.

"Okay, gentleman, but I should inform you that I'm scheduled to commence my retirement very shortly. I'll be back in a minute and go grab Corby Dunn so there's some continuity with communication around here in the weeks ahead. " Russ knew that this would entail a lengthy investigation and took the bull by the horns to assure the men of a reliable collaborator.

He liked working with Corby, and he felt that he had the smarts to move on up in the department. He picked up on little things. He was thorough in his examinations, and the officers who did the hearings welcomed his reports. One realized that he was a person who looked at the whole picture. Some people found his appearance a little disturbing, suggesting that a facial piercing was inappropriate for a man working border security.

The issue had recently raised its head when the Health and Safety Committee had objected to the departmental dress code demanding some revisions. Management had seized upon the opportunity to object to the wearing of jewelry that could be used to injure an officer during a confrontation. Russ was glad he wouldn't be around for the new policy. Russ also knew that Corby wouldn't be a happy camper when it came out because he prided himself on his "barbells" and had confided to Russ that they gave him sex appeal. Russ had merely nodded his head while thinking everybody had their quirks.

Otherwise, you had to respect the guy. His hunches had periodically led to fruitful intelligence investigations that caught up with some of the worst criminals to land on Canadian soil. It wasn't that he was overly aggressive. He was just thorough and paid careful attention to the details.

He recalled how Corby had instantly suspected that an Indian passport was one of a series that the intelligence boys had alerted the immigration officers to, about seven months earlier. They had advised the officers of a report from the Indian government that a block of passports had been stolen, and they provided the sequence of numbers. A passenger from India presented a passport at the port of entry one night, and Corby had recalled the number sequences of the missing ones. Bingo! His memory had served him well when he checked the document out.

Some thought it was impossible to remember such minute details, but Corby proved time and again that he had either a remarkable knack for it or incredible luck. He had confided to Russ that it was the man's demeanor that had led to his suspicions, but even so, he had kept the list handy and checked it out. He had all his tips organized in a big binder prepared to handle such matters in minutes.

Indeed, Corby caught a lot of people off guard. Aside from being acutely observant, he was adept at questioning. Russ liked to use him in training sessions for the new border officers because he was straightforward and to the point. He was also forthcoming in sharing his knowledge as a member of the team.

Corby was soon going to be forty, seemingly a confirmed bachelor, and he dutifully looked after the needs of his elderly mom. Overall, he was married to his work. He didn't treat people differently either. He believed that everyone was, above all else, a human being. He had always had a penchant for treating each person to come across his path with dignity and respect—even when he sensed that something wasn't quite right.

His manner was relaxed and thoughtful. Moreover, he had become Russ's close friend. After Sally's death, they had enjoyed summer weekend fishing trips up at Russ's secluded cabin where they shared a quiet camaraderie that had helped Russ through those difficult days. If he wanted to talk, Corby was a good listener and could be trusted with his confidences.

When Russ approached the interview room, he found Corby completing some paperwork and Roger busying himself at the copier. Corby seemed to be putting another requisition together for further investigation, Russ noted as he caught sight of the familiar forms. As the immigration supervisor on duty, Russ was required to sign off on all investigative referrals. He smiled to himself as he wondered what had caught Corby's eye this time; unfortunately, it would have to wait. He needed Corby's help in trying to identify the baggage handler.

"Hey, Russ, thanks for getting back to me. Sorry to make you come back. I need your concurrence and official John Hancock one last time. Did you have any thoughts on the guy you just escorted?"

"Knowing you, perhaps I should ask the question. We'll have to get back to this guy later. Grab your file, the RCMP and Sid are waiting in my office, and I think we could do with your help. Roger, can you take charge of things on the lines and brief Sheena when she arrives," Russ asked.

Roger nodded and went off to see that everything else ran smoothly until the morning shift showed up, while Russ briefly filled Corby in on the events of the evening, explaining that they didn't have much to go on. They had the baggage handler and an x-ray film of the contents of the bags, but that gave them little proof that the dolls had contained narcotics. One of the bags had been retrieved on the bridge. It had nothing inside of it, and the only fingerprint belonged to the worker. There wasn't anything to identify it other than one of the active tracking bugs was still intact.

Corby stated that he'd learned that four RCMP officers had been taken down, which Russ grimly confirmed. Russ informed him that they assumed that the second bag had also been tossed, probably cleared the bridge and had fallen into the Fraser River. He commented that no doubt a search would be on for it at daybreak. At some point, one of the drug dealers had transferred to a second vehicle close to the downtown hub, and both vehicles had subsequently been intentionally detonated.

The traffickers, the federal officers tailing them, and any evidence, including the vehicles, had been blown to smithereens in two separate, apparent suicide bombings. At one of the two locations, they had recovered some pieces of the dolls that had been used to transport the drugs into the country, but not much else. There was no sign of the drugs.

"Suicide bombers make it sound as if it could it be linked to the terrorists," Corby commented.

"There's been some word that drug money is becoming the primary source of financing terrorist activities. I've called Judd in from Intelligence based on their recent report involving a terrorist lookout. There could be a tie-in. What we're left with right now is the baggage handler and not much evidence to hold him on."

"Who is he?"

"That, my friend, is why I need you. We're trying to find out who the hell he is, and we're coming up empty."

Several minutes later, they arrived at Russ's office, where they were met by his boss, Dan Newbury, the director of operations; Sid; and two federal police officers. Russ and Corby were hastily brought up to date on the attempts that had been made to identify the fellow in custody. He claimed to be of Egyptian ethnicity and a Canadian citizen. However, the RCMP officers explained that they were highly suspicious that he was a possible illegal.

They had interviewed other employees working for the contractor who knew little about their colleague. Dan apprized everyone that he hadn't been able to reach the contractor yet to see if he could provide any other information about his employee. The RCMP had found both a social insurance card in his wallet and health card in the name of Tarik El Safty, which corresponded to the information he'd given them. Someone had mistakenly thought his surname was spelled "El Safety" and had recorded the incorrect spelling in his officer's notes; however, the matter was quickly rectified. There was nothing else, save for some cash.

They'd also run the worker's fingerprints, but, again, they hadn't gotten a hit anywhere. El Safty claimed that he was born in Montreal, had no family, and that of course he was innocent of all knowledge in the drug operation. His story had been simple. He stated that a man wearing a sling had approached him and offered him twenty dollars to retrieve his bags from the carousel and bring them to his vehicle parked at the side door.

During the discussions, the RCMP informed the other men that there was a major problem in verifying the worker's birth in Canada. Before 1994, the churches maintained the register of births in Quebec, although they sent a second copy to the local courthouse called the protonotary. After that date, the records post-1899 were transferred to government registries maintained in Quebec City and Montreal, but there were occasional errors by the local clergy in recording of the information.

El Safty had also informed them that while he had been born in Canada, his family had never actually lived here. His parents had temporarily been visiting in Canada when medical complications had forced them to stay until after his birth. He had spent most of his life in Egypt but had the right to Canadian citizenship by virtue of his birth.

Corby noted that the Egyptian's social insurance card was a fairly recent issue from British Colombia or the Yukon as denoted by the number 7 starting digit. He also applied the Luhn algorithm test, which was often used to verify the authenticity of a social insurance number. Once the number passed the test, Russ suggested that they could contact the Department of Social Insurance in Bathurst, New Brunswick, and get a copy of the application record to find what identity documents he had used.

Within an hour, they had contacted the New Brunswick department's director and received faxed copies of the man's birth record, verifying that he was indeed born in Canada and that his surname was actually spelled "El Safty." The formation of the letters on the birth records also left open the possibility that his first name could have been either Tarik or Tarek. One of the RCMP officers had also received word that they had obtained a search warrant for his home at a rooming house, but there had been little found at the location other than a few personal belongings. They had nothing.

13

As Russ's visitors exited the office, Dan turned to Russ, acknowledging that he recognized that it was Russ's final day on the job, but he asked if he would prepare a comprehensive report before he left.

It had been one hell of a night! It was the worst that Russ could recall since the Air India disaster, a flight that had killed over three hundred people in 1985. He turned his attention to the file that Corby was fingering and suggested, "Well, I guess we better attend to the Zadeh file now."

Before Corby could respond, Roger entered the office carrying the men coffees and to tell them that Sheena, the night shift supervisor, would be late. She had asked if Corby could manage until she got in and said it had something to do with a flat tire.

"Yeah, tell her I'm good," Corby replied and rolled his eyes at Russ.

"Actually, Roger, I need Corby here for a bit. Can you stay on until she gets in or Corby can relieve you?" Russ asked.

"Sure, I'll stick around. I'll need you to authorize the overtime, though. She gives everyone such a hard time."

"Don't worry, Dan's in, and I'll speak to him myself. Could you also see if Judd's in yet and tell him I need to speak to him if he wouldn't mind dropping by?"

As Russ sipped his coffee, Corby began leafing through the Zadeh file gathering his thoughts. Judd popped his head through the door and joined the two officers. Both Corby and Russ could agree he was the best intelligence officer in the government. He always reminded Russ of the American actor Laurence Fishburne and his screen portrayals of a forceful authoritarian.

Russ brought Judd speedily up to date on the events of the evening, and then Corby got right down to business with respect to the Iranian following his arrival. He summarized the results of his interview with Zadeh and expressed concern about the man's identity.

Judd thought for several minutes before asking, "Russ, did you have any initial impressions about him?"

"Well, when I first saw him, he had fainted and was a little disoriented. He appeared to catch his bearings pretty quickly and was quiet and reasonably cooperative. He didn't present any difficulty or resistance. He just seemed to have a blank, icy stare on his face the whole time that I was in his company. He's the type of man that is difficult to read as he doesn't display any outward emotions."

"Yeah, I wasn't sure what to make of his lack of expression. I thought that maybe he was just trying to deal with the pain in his hands." Corby was nodding his head, indicating his agreement with Russ's observation.

"You know, I had a funny feeling that he was trying to appear to be detached from everything that was going on, but he knew exactly what to expect when I took him over to Wolmer. Did you get the same feeling?"

"Yes. Exactly! As a matter of fact, I didn't notice it in the beginning, but as we got deeper into the interview, he just seemed to come across too pat. Also, I had the distinct impression that he was bored during much of Azizi's translations. I couldn't quite put my finger on it. It could be that he already knew what I had asked."

Judd reckoned that a lot of Iranians spoke fluent English and asked, "Did you ask him if he understood English?"

An embarrassed Corby replied, "No, I didn't think to because he had a note that said he didn't. You know, he was quite a cold character too. He didn't even display any emotions while telling what amounted to a horrific story concerning the loss of his family. The only time I saw any reaction from him was when he attempted to retrieve a passport from his pocket and let a whimper escape that I attributed to the pain in his hands."

"That sounds like a reasonable assumption." Judd smiled at Corby. "Anything else?"

"I got the distinct feeling that he came totally prepared for our interview. Like he had rehearsed most of his answers. He just wanted to spit out his response almost as if he had known the questions before we asked them," Corby replied.

"How old is he anyway? This picture makes him look like a teenager, but I can see that his eyes have a hollowed, wizened appearance that I find a little disturbing. I'm sure he's older than he looks," Judd queried.

"He says he's thirty-two, but he looks a little younger. Perhaps it's because of the brush cut."

Russ shared that his main concern was their inability to get a set of fingerprints at this time. He knew that there had to be a story behind the burns and was anxious to learn it.

"His claim is that his family home got torched by the Iranian government because of their faith, and he burned his hands trying to get inside to rescue his relatives. He maintains that he wasn't successful and doesn't know what happened to them."

Judd became increasingly interested when he found out that they couldn't get any fingerprints. Russ informed them that he had spoken with Doc Ryan after he saw the burns and felt that something was amiss just looking at the location of them. He had noticed extensive burns that were confined only to his fingertips. There were very few burns on the rest of his fingers, remaining parts of his hands, and lower arms. No markings of his trauma anywhere on his face or elsewhere, either.

Corby added that he had asked Zadeh about that very issue, and he provided the explanation that the flames were so bad that he had to turn back. "He had also added that a lot of his hair had been burnt too, and that's why he had it cropped off after he left

Iran, but I didn't see any evidence of burns to his scalp, back of his neck, or even his forehead."

"If you were trying to save someone's life, how the hell would you have conveniently just scorched your fingertips and not the rest of your hands? I see what you mean. He certainly seemed to have all his answers down to what he thought would satisfy your investigation," Judd commented.

"Well, it struck me as peculiar too, so like I was saying, I spoke a little to Doc Ryan, in the hallway after he had administered to his burns," Russ remarked. "The good doctor felt skeptical, too. His opinion was that although it was possible, it wasn't probable that those severe burns would be confined to just his fingertips with a few other isolated smaller patches on the top of both hands and lower arms."

Russ continued that the doctor had said other than the burns to Zadeh's fingertips, the remaining burns appeared to be first or second degree. Interestingly, though, every last one of his fingertips was definitely scorched with third-degree burns. Turning to Judd, he revealed that there had been some light at the end of the tunnel. Doc Ryan thought one of his thumbs wasn't quite as bad as the rest of the fingers, and they might be able to get a partial print in a few weeks after giving it some healing time.

"I'll put a heads-up on my calendar and track the bastard. We might not get prints now, but we can be patient. I don't like the sound of this guy either," Judd agreed as he began to gather his notes, but Corby suddenly remembered something else.

"You know, guys, there's something else about Zadeh that made me even more uncomfortable. I think the guy is hiding something. He almost stumbled once, and he appeared to need a little time to recover. He's not dim-witted, though. He answered everything I threw at him, but I got the impression that he was toying with us. There were times when he carefully orchestrated a break in our questions, by asking for some water or medication.

It was as if he was trying to buy some time to decide upon an appropriate response."

Both Judd and Russ looked at each other and then asked Corby what had caused a crack in Zadeh's composure. Corby explained that it was a seemingly simple question about his foreign travels, and that when he had posed the question later, it appeared that the man had no trouble giving a suitable response. They all agreed that another country must have information about Zadeh that he's trying to hide if Corby's hunch is correct. However, they'd have to be patient and try and figure out which countries to run his prints with, if and when they could get one or more fingerprints.

"We can likely rule out Hong Kong, the UAE, or Turkey, or he wouldn't have given us those countries," Judd thoughtfully surmised.

"It sounds to me like he's definitely hiding something, and I don't think we'll know until we can verify his identity. That should hold him in detention for a while," Russ commented.

"Oh, he arrived on a British passport that he said he got from an agent. Maybe it's genuine, but, Judd, you might want to look at it. He's also got an Iranian National Identity Card, complete with a picture that's five years old. Of course, we can't verify it, but it does look pretty authentic. I don't think they'll be able to hold him in detention for lack of identity because the card's good for seven years. He also states that he has a cousin who lives here and was going to meet him at the airport. He's coming to the detention hearing in the morning," Corby replied.

Russ threw up his arms in disgust as he turned to Judd, making the comment, "Isn't that just great? He looks all set. He's got a place to stay, adequate ID, and a story to qualify for his refugee claim. It's almost a sure thing that he'll get released at the admissibility hearing."

"There's another thing I want to mention," Corby hesitated. "You know, he had a handwritten note that was in English indicating that he was a refugee. He didn't say a word, He just presented that at the wicket. However, in the examination room, he presented another note to say he didn't understand English, and it was written in Persian. I wondered why they weren't both written in the same language. Come and take a look at the two notes."

"I can see some similarities in the writing. The notes are set out pretty much the same style, but I don't know the Persian language," Russ commented after examining the papers.

"I'd put money on it that both of those notes were written by the same person. However, I also examined the signature on his Iranian identity card, and I think it might match the writing on the note written in English, meaning that it was likely that he was the author of the English note. Here, take a look at the identity card!"

"Judd, you can take a look at all the documents and see what you think. You're the expert document examiner. That's about all we've got for now, except one thing I wanted to raise. Perhaps it's coincidental, but that drug shipment came from Hong Kong, and so did Zadeh." Russ threw out a possibility that didn't seem too far-fetched according to the experiences of the three men.

"Damn, I almost forgot," Corby excitedly chimed in. "I thought the asshole slightly smirked when Roger said there had been bombings downtown. I shook it off because it was over in a split second, and I didn't think he understood what was being said. I thought I was mistaken."

"That's a very interesting observation. I'll keep it in mind as I work both of these cases, guys. Thanks for filling me in, and, Russ, good luck on your retirement. We're sure as hell going to miss you," Judd remarked.

14

Roger dropped by to let Russ and Corby know that Sheena wouldn't be making it in that morning and had sent an e-mail to the staff advising them to report to Corby. Russ assured him that Corby would relieve him shortly, and he reminded him to bring by his overtime sheets before he left.

"You know, I swear that one of these days that woman is going to land herself in some hot water. This is the third time this month that she's called in and asked me to cover for her."

"Be patient with her, Corby. She's good at her job, and she's going through some personal shit right now."

"To tell you the truth, that possibility had crossed my mind. I've always found her pretty much reliable before now. Now what were we talking about? Oh yeah, do you really think that Zadeh could be connected to the drugs?"

Russ sat back in his chair and thought about it for a few minutes before answering. "Think about it, Corby. Terrorists are relying more and more on the drug trade for financing. We got that drug shipment from Hong Kong three days ago. We lost it, thanks to suicide bombers. That's not something that drug cartels normally do. It smacks of terrorist involvement. I keep asking myself why they didn't pick up the luggage for three days, and I think the timing was critical."

"How so?"

"Perhaps, they wanted to create a diversion when one of their own was about to arrive, also coming in from Hong Kong. It's just a hunch. I can't put my finger on any direct connection. Let's just say I find it very suspicious."

"You know, Russ, it's an interesting theory. Did you observe anything else out of the ordinary when you were with him?"

"Yeah, as a matter of fact, at the detention center, we were all seated in the intake room, and I had done the paperwork, explained the medications, and said that I'd be on my way when Zadeh got up as if to make for the inner door. However, one of the guards had distracted me and delayed my departure with congratulations on my retirement. No one else in the room had moved a muscle to indicate that the meeting had been concluded. Suddenly, I think, Zadeh seemed to realize what had happened. He pretended to be looking around the room and then told Azizi that he wanted a drink. His drink supply was on the desk in front of me. He couldn't miss it."

"Incredible! It sounds like he knew what was being said?"

"I hope not, it could have been just a coincidence, but I certainly was surprised."

"Usually when they arrive they are a little reluctant to give too many details about their claims for refugee status. Not this guy, though. He put me a little off guard as he provided such explicit detail of the salient aspects of his claim as if to ensure that he crossed all his t's and dotted all the i's. I had the impression that he carefully selected and had prepared information that he knew we could never hope to verify or dispute, and he was trying to ensure our sympathies and solidify his claim. He tied it all together with other easily verifiable information about Iran's persecution of people of his faith," Corby added.

"You know, that's a little unusual. Most claimants don't give too much detail about the objective third-party evidence until they talk to a lawyer. Then again, playing the devil's advocate, a smuggler might have given him a tip off."

"Russ, I don't buy that. I'm sure he was playing us. I have the distinct feeling that he knew exactly what he was doing. It also sounded to me that he was pretty much aware of what goes on at the actual hearing for asylum, too. He was pushing all the right buttons in preparation for his eventual hearing. Sometimes, he offered up a little too much information for what we were asking. Furthermore, I also thought that he understands English because he barely gave Azizi time to translate the full question, occasionally blurting out an answer he had ready. Hell, there's a lot of people who speak who more than one language. I'm curious to why he'd try to hide it."

"It's possible that he was afraid that the discovery might open up other questions that he'd need to explain it, or he thought it would buy him some extra time to think through his responses to our questions."

"It doesn't make sense. He could have said that he had studied it in school or even privately. There are places that teach English in Iran. My guess is that his English is more American rather than the British dialect taught there."

"You may have a point there. He could be concerned that his particular dialect of English might give something away. He might speak in more of an Australasian dialect. I doubt that he has any American connection, so I think if he's hiding any connection to another country, your best bet would be to focus on Southeast Asia," Russ commented.

"Jesus, you're so damn logical. God, I'm going to miss you. We always seem to work through some off the beaten track issues when we discuss the disturbing details of some of these claims."

"Corby, guys like him always appear to be well prepared, and it's our job to find the little loopholes. You're good at it. I wish more officers would open their minds to trying to discover the reasons why or how a particular story does or doesn't fit together. That's why I love reading mysteries—the whodunits. They help keep a person on their toes and teach you the little innuendos and tricks to watch out for."

"I don't know what happened to his hands, but I'm pretty sure that they weren't burned in the way he presented his little tale. If you were battling a fire, surely the burns would be widespread and not be confined to his fingertips. Assessing his personal background information alone, there was little real history or detail of overt acts of persecution toward his family as opposed to other members of his religion with the exception of the night of the so-called events."

"By the time he gets to his hearing, he'll probably have other tales to tell that embellish all kinds of direct acts against his family. Any decent legal representative will have him well prepared before he files his written claim. As for his fingertips, I've seen guys come in with them sliced off to try and prevent us from identifying them. Did you ask Azizi what's written on the papers you got from his wallet?"

"As a matter of fact, I did," Corby replied as he pulled a copy out of the file. "Azizi said it was Zadeh's cousin's phone numbers, but I think I'll get a translation and do a check of those numbers as well."

"This one might be a cell number."

"Yeah, I know. I don't know what the second number beside it is. I think that they belong to the same person. Take a close look at it. It appears to be a seven-digit phone number without the area code."

"It looks like it. The additional wording might go with it, too. Did you ask about it?" Russ inquired.

"Azizi indicated that the word was a reference to the Dasht-e Naz Airport in Iran. He said that it had just been abbreviated to "Naz," and apparently the general population refer to it that way. He also said it was his cousin's cell phone. As a matter of fact, I tried to see if I could track the numbers, but I'll have to get some help to see if we can trace them. I also toyed with a Farsi translation service on the Internet for the word 'Naz' too, but I came up empty, and I was able to confirm that there is an airport by that name."

"It's written in a strange place as if the second number is possibly connected with the word. I'd bet money that even though it's missing the telephone exchange, it could be another Canadian number," Russ observed. "I'll say one thing you're absolutely right about—he sure does have answers for everything. Did anyone search the plane he came in on?"

"Roger sent a couple of guys over to it when he went to get Azizi. They didn't find anything, but that's no surprise. You know he could have just visited the washroom and fed the Pacific with more debris."

"One look at the passport makes you wonder how the airline let the guy on," Russ replied. "They've sure got liability here. First thing I noticed was that the guy's bio data page should have alerted the airline that something was wrong. His height is shown as the same as mine, and this guy is definitely much shorter than I am. Somebody didn't do their job. Don't forget to send them notification of liability, too!"

"Will do. You'd think the airlines would get smart and try and reduce their costs. They need to take a closer look at their undertakings with governments. They could establish some preventative tools to avoid those hefty fines. I hear it can cost them anywhere between three to six thousand dollars for each inadequately or undocumented passenger they bring in. Makes you wonder when they might learn to scan the bio data page, complete with the picture, of every passport into a computerized system, whether they suspect that they were fraudulent or not. I'd probably make them provide a thumb print as well."

"That's a good one, but in this case, it wouldn't have helped."

"The way I see it, most of the time, they'd at least have some mechanism in place justifying why a passenger was allowed to board. Being a little more proactive would reduce airfares for everybody else overall. Most of the other countries are also charging them, and it's got to be factored into the average cost of a plane ticket for everyone."

"It's the old story. Everyone else suffers because of a relatively few abusers. Well, I've got to do up a report for Dan and get myself out of here. Here's an overtime requisition, just fill out the details, and I'll sign off on your overtime."

Moments later, as Russ scrawled his signature, he added, "There's another thing that crossed my mind. His name kind of bothered me because of an article I just read last week. The Brits have developed a guide for examining names from around the world because of the way people are playing with their names when they go asylum shopping. If I recall correctly, Zadeh may actually be a suffix to his surname. His full last name might be 'Hassanzadeh'—spelled all as one word, two separate words, or perhaps contain a hyphen."

"You could have a point there. He told me his name was Hassan, then Azizi spoke to him, and he stated it was Hassan Zadeh. Perhaps, we made an error. I just assumed that we now had his full name. I'll make a note on file for the hearings officer to ask Mr. Mehregan to go over it with him. I checked, and he's the scheduled Farsi translator for the admissibility hearing tomorrow."

"This is a fascinating case. I'm pretty sure that there's fire behind all the smoke he's blowing at us. I'd be interested in knowing how the investigation pans out. I'm going away for several weeks, but I'll be back by the long weekend. You can come up to the cabin in August if you'd like. If anything comes of your sleuthing, you can let me know." Russ grinned.

"I'm always interested in fishing, in more ways than one." Corby laughed. "And I'll definitely take you up on your invitation. I look forward to seeing you then. I'm sure as hell going to miss you around here. You always have backed me up. We make a great pair of gumshoes the place just won't be the same without you. Take care of yourself, Russ, and happy retirement."

"You just remember, there's a difference: up at Kelso you get to catch and release. Here, hopefully, you can catch him, detain him, and deport him." Russ chuckled. "By the way, congratulations, I hear you're getting a promotion. Don't spread it around yet, but

I've been told you're the lucky guy that's getting my job. Good luck and I'll see you in a few months."

He knew that he'd be seeing Corby a lot sooner but didn't want to spoil the surprise party some of the guys were planning for his big fortieth-birthday bash. It was rumored that Muscles, as the guys referred to him, had never had an intimate relationship with a woman. The guys had planned to take him to a strip club to get a look at what they referred as some good eye candy. Russ wondered if Corby actually had ever envisioned the dirty fantasies that those places seemed to evoke with dancers who knew how to use the pole like a vibrator before venturing into the sea of men for some lap dancing. It should be an interesting night.

As soon as Corby had left, Russ completed his report, spoke briefly to Roger, and signed off his overtime. He headed out of the airport to take a short drive over to the main office to turn in his badge, his piece, his computerized pass, and to say a final farewell to the gang over there.

Russ had a sense of satisfaction and was glad to know that there were gatekeepers like Corby safeguarding the Canadian borders. No officer would pick up on every bad guy that came into the country; however, most of these guys were pretty quick to pick up on little nuances so the hearings officers could take it to the next level. Corby was one of the best front men in the business.

15

Meanwhile, across the Pacific Ocean, on the small Island Republic of Temesekia, twenty-six-year-old Jaslyn Koh was eating lunch with her coworker Sherlyn Jung and fantasizing about travelling the world. She attempted to convince her friend that they both needed a vacation beyond the confines of their small nation's borders. Her latest fantasies were about North America, somewhere that Sherlyn had no interest in visiting.

Jas had that signature Asian look with flawless tan-colored skin; long, silky black hair; mysterious, dark, and sparkling almond eyes; a slight frame; and average height. No doubt about it, she was a real classic beauty! She carried herself in such a graceful manner that one sensed that she also had an inward beauty that matched her outward appearance. The moment she became engaged in conversation, Jas exhibited acuity, humor, and the strength of character that brought respect along with the physical admiration of the listener. Women were in awe of her! Men found that Jas was just downright awesome! She had everything going for her. In a nutshell, she had class!

Sherlyn was her best friend and knew better than anyone that Jas felt stifled living on the island. World travel was becoming an obsession with Jas as if she sensed that the course of her life was meant to take her in a different direction away from the security of her comfortable but unsatisfying life. Sherlyn had the uneasy feeling that her friend's discontent was pulling her somewhere else to meet her destiny. As smart as Jas was, Sherlyn knew that she was also naive about the ways of people throughout the world.

"Jas, I know how much you would like to travel, but I'm not the adventurer you are. Frankly, I've told you before, I'm saving my money to further my education. This is one time you're not going to change my mind."

"You're hopeless. Think about Canada. It's another place I'd like to visit. I've heard that many Asians live on their west coastline."

"My cousin's friend was a foreign student there, Jas. He said that country is a disaster waiting to happen. Do you know that people go there from all over the world with false documents and establish a totally new identity usually without getting caught? They can even buy fake degrees and credentials that are accepted in other countries as if they were real."

"That sounds ridiculous! Surely, they can't do that."

"Stephen's friend knew another exchange student who worked in the administration offices of a major university that employed people who issued phony degrees to anyone willing to pay the price. These were forged on thick watermarked paper and stamped with the actual seal of the university. He even had access to official signatures, copies of real transcripts, and obtained official envelopes that could be sealed and provided to unsuspecting employers all over the world."

A wide-eyed Jas peered at her friend almost in disbelief before finally asking, "Did he get caught?"

"Eventually, but who knows how many people had benefitted from the enterprise before they deported him? Do you know some people actually received professional accreditations?"

"If what you say is true, then you can't say the fault lies with Canada, but rather it's the nefarious people who go there and take advantage of the privileges that they get to work in the university," Jas protested.

"Yes, that's probably true, but a lot of those people stay in Canada. Would you believe that they also give asylum to people claiming persecution from one group and then allow people from the other group also to claim asylum against people from the original group?"

"I don't think I follow you. What do you mean?"

"Well, for instance, there's a lot of Sunni Muslim people that say they are persecuted by Shiite Muslims. That's how they get asylum in Canada. Then a few months later, Shiite Muslims go to Canada and claim they are being oppressed by the Sunni Muslims, and they get asylum, too. They flee persecution from one another but are now both living in Canada, side by side. How come they can get along in Canada and not in their own countries? It doesn't make sense to me. I think all countries should foster tolerance. If you ask me, Canada is building their country with all the conflicts of the world being brought together."

"It sounds dangerous, but I suppose that they think that future generations won't have the same ridiculous prejudices and that teaching tolerance to the next generation would eradicate the problem in the future, don't you think?" Jas was familiar with the saying that the United States was an "immigrant melting pot," and she assumed that the same attitude prevailed in Canada.

"I don't know, and I don't want to find out. I still think that one bad apple can destroy the whole barrel, so to speak. Anyway, I wouldn't want to live there. You of all people should know that I've been saving forever to go back to school."

"I'm not talking about going to live there, silly. I'm just interested in visiting the country. I couldn't imagine leaving the island forever. Everything I hold dear in life is here." Jas laughed.

"You never know what might happen! You should go and work with your brothers in the family business. They'll look out for you. You've got the best brothers in the world. Before you know it, you'll meet some nice young man who'll sweep you off your feet and get married. When you're settled, you can travel with someone who'll be glad to show you the world," Sherlyn wittily responded.

Jas pressed further. "I've read a little about the province of British Columbia in western Canada, and I think that it sounds very intriguing. It has historical native villages, artwork, and carved totem poles from the aboriginal peoples. They lived there long before the Europeans settled there. I think I'd like to try skiing in the mountains and visit some of their dinner theaters, parks, and maybe even a winery. Think of the education you'd get there."

"To tell you the truth, fun or no fun, I simply can't afford a vacation. You need to get it through that thick skull of yours I've always wanted to teach, and I'm almost twenty-five years old, so if I'm going to do it, I'll have to get on board soon."

Looking slightly despondent, Jas half-heartedly conceded, "I feel that I'm in a rut, Sherlyn. It's getting worse so that I hate going to work every day."

"I know what you mean. I need a change too. One way or another I'd like to fill my life with little ones. Oh, oh, speaking of work, we better get back. I think our little dream fest is over, and reality is beckoning us back to the grind." Sherlyn giggled as the room began to fill with the late-lunch crowd.

As the girls hurried back to their work areas, Jas scrambled to reach the ringing phone at her desk.

"Jaslyn Koh," came the voice on the receiver.

"Speaking," she replied.

"Yes, Ms. Koh, this is Ms. Sung calling from Mr. Tan's office. You're required to attend an emergency meeting at two thirty this afternoon in the company auditorium."

"Am I supposed to attend?" Jas inquired as she was caught by surprise. "I'm in the clerical pool."

"Yes, it's for all employees, and we'll expect you there."

"Fine, I'll be there and thank you for advising me."

Jas was filled with curiosity and hoped that there might be some sort of promotional opportunity in it for her. She couldn't recall ever being summoned to the auditorium for a general staff meeting. However, an hour later she entered the small but regal-looking hall of the auditorium and was greeted by senior partner Melvin Tan. He was smiling generously, like the proverbial cat who had swallowed the canary, acknowledging each staff member as they arrived. It looked as if everybody in the firm was present.

She could see that others were just as puzzled as she. Everyone around her was talking in hushed whispers, asking if anyone knew why there had been the sudden summoning to the "great" hall. Whatever the reason for this sudden occurrence, it had been a well-kept secret.

She scoured the room hoping to find an empty spot on one of the fifty to sixty theater-style red-cushioned chairs. She hoped that she could get a clear view of the slightly elevated platform at the front. Great! She spotted Sherlyn frantically waving to her and motioning to an empty seat that she had managed to secure. Jas gratefully made her way over to it.

The company partners, who were all seated on the stage, looked just as pleased as Mr. Tan. She had no recollection of ever seeing a gathering of all twelve partners of the legal firm assembled together in one meeting as they were that day. It was so unusual that one could feel that there was unquestionably excitement in the air.

"What do you think is up?" Sherlyn asked.

"I've no idea. I guess we'll soon find out," Jas replied.

"Maybe they've got some major new case, and they want volunteers to work on it."

"I wouldn't bet on it. That wouldn't require everyone in the firm to be here. No, something else is up. Shhh, Mr. Tan is heading toward the stage now."

The meeting commenced quickly, and it didn't take long before the bombshell was dropped! The corporation had merged with another large, well-known legal firm. They had been awarded an exclusive in-house contract to provide legal services for the largest business conglomerate on the entire Island Republic, the Sang Corporation, and they had needed to expand. In a less optimistic and slightly condescending tone, Mr. Tan stated, as a result of this amalgamation, there would be some restructuring and reorganization.

"I told you," whispered Sherlyn.

"Shhh," came hushing sounds from the people around them.

Mr. Tan went on to say that this restructuring was required to meet with their new business lines and could result in some layoffs to the sound of several low groans around them. He was quick to assure everyone that there would be new opportunities and challenges for many of the staff. However, the changes would result in the transference of some of their current business lines to other smaller firms.

Mr. Tan thanked everyone for their dedication and years of service before promptly turning the meeting over to the human resources director, Mrs. Wong. Her presentation was direct and to the point beginning with notice that the changes would be taking effect almost immediately with appropriate compensation for those who would not be retained. She reminded the employees that transfers and retrenchment clauses contained in their contracts would be applicable.

Mrs. Wong indicated that the small companies who had taken over some of their clients were willing to offer work to some of the employees affected by the layoffs. Others would receive letters of reference by request to their immediate manager. Finally, she instructed everyone that persons who received letters of retrenchment would be entitled to a retraining allowance, and they could book an appointment with the Human Resources Department to discuss these options over the next two weeks.

At the end of the meeting, each of the employee's names was called up to the front of the auditorium to receive a preaddressed letter outlining the impact the restructuring would have on them personally. As the company directors shook their hands, they thanked the employees for their service.

Walking numbly to the front, Jas knew that she inwardly felt all of the emotions of shock, anger, and uncertainty that she saw in the faces of her coworkers. It was one thing to choose to leave your job at a given time but quite another to find that your life had been thrown into a sudden limbo. She had wanted change but on her own terms. Whether she liked it or not, her life was about to drastically change.

16

Later that day, Jas sat quietly rereading the letter she had received at the staff meeting. It simply thanked her for six years of service, gave her two weeks notice of termination, and stated that due to a change in business operations, her job was eliminated.

She was informed that she was entitled to two weeks of pay for each full year of employment service, and she could opt to accept an education allowance for approved course of up to twelve months in duration as a surplus employee. On the face of it, she felt that it was little compensation for turning a person's life upside down; however, she knew deep down that it was fairly generous.

"Did you get a heave-ho letter?" Sherlyn approached her desk and interrupted her thoughts.

"Yes, unfortunately, I did," she hastily replied.

"Oh, Jas, I did too. But you know what, maybe this is really a blessing in disguise."

"I'm not so sure about that," Jas remarked.

"I know that this is the right time for me, and I'm going to take advantage of the retrenchment pay and this educational allowance to get my teaching certification—now."

"It's just the right opportunity for you. I just don't know what to think right now. It was all so unexpected, and I think I'm in a bit of shock at the moment."

"I think that there's lots of opportunities out there, and you're also in a position to take advantage of it now, Jas. Think of this as a new door opening to your future. For people like us, Jas, this educational package would likely be the most beneficial."

"You know, you're going to be such a fabulous teacher." Jas smiled at her friend as she inwardly admired her quick acceptance of the situation. "There's no doubt in my mind that this is probably the best thing that could have happened for you."

Sherlyn was such a confident, patient, and compassionate person. It was Jas's opinion that she even had the look of a teacher with her shoulder-length black hair always placed atop her head in a neat bun. Jas instinctively knew that the career path she wanted to take would be the right thing for her to do. Sherlyn would provide an incredible depth of understanding and support to her students. As she reflected on her own life, she couldn't help but agree that she wasn't meant to work behind a desk typing out endless contracts and hiding the strengths of their abilities and character.

Sherlyn was bursting with enthusiasm as she explained to Jas that the teacher's program would take two years to complete, and it appeared that the company would fund the first year of tuition and books. Half of her costs would be paid! Sherlyn lived at home, and she had been saving up for a number of years hoping to put herself through school. Now, she was sure that combined with her savings, she had enough money to achieve her goals. Jas felt a twinge of envy that Sherlyn was focused and knew exactly how to get where she wanted to go. Yet she was happy for her friend as she looked at the enthusiasm shining in her sparkling black eyes.

"What about you, Jas?" Sherlyn eagerly asked.

"I'm not sure what to do yet. I just wasn't expecting something like this. I want a change too, but I wanted it at the time of my choosing and not to be tossed out the door like my years of work weren't valued in any way. I need to think about it."

"Jas, I think the company is acting fairly about it. You have to look at it from their perspective, too. I don't think that they are tossing anyone out the door. They're just seizing upon an incredible business opportunity. They don't have to give us these generous compensation packages. What about your dreams? You've been toying with ideas about that line of software for over a year now."

"Thanks for reminding me, Sherlyn. I just needed a bit of time to digest the events of today, but come to think of it, I may have a few ideas of my own. I'm going to Colin's place for dinner tonight. I'll break the news, and perhaps my wise brother will provide me some guidance."

"You know it's a thought, but you might consider going back to school and focusing on a more meaningful career, too. I think you're right to think about this as an opportunity, but not just for me, for both of us. It's something to look into."

"I wonder whether there are any conditions attached to the education allowance."

"First thing I did when I went back to my desk was set up an appointment for next week with HR. I fully expect that whatever is the outcome, it won't matter too much. It's my understanding that they'll pay the first-year costs of any acceptable education program. Since I began helping with the children's music program at the center, I've known that teaching is what's right for me. This is just going to help me achieve what I want a little bit sooner."

Checking her watch, she continued, "Listen, it's getting late, and I've got to gather up some things. Jas, I mean it, don't look for another job like this. You've got too much going for you, so don't sell yourself short. Whatever you do, don't let Colin talk you out of something you really want. I've got to run now. I've got such a busy weekend ahead preparing for the kids' music festival. We'll talk next week about all of this."

When Sherlyn departed, Jas decided to make a quick call to HR to set up an appointment for herself for the following week, too. She was slightly envious of her friend's sense of direction. Jas was no stranger to sudden change, and she was confident that she, too, would land on her feet. Her brain was already buzzing with thoughts of what the future might have in store for her.

She glanced again at the education training package provisions that were in the letter and with a slight smile thought maybe she could accomplish several different things at the same time. Travel, education, and launch her software—in that order! After making her call, she snatched up her purse, and with a skip in her step, she exited out the main door. She welcomed the refreshing, cool island breeze as it caressed her skin as she briskly walked to the family home for the regular Friday-night dinner with her brothers Patrick and Colin and her sister-in-law, Faith.

17

Colin was the oldest of the siblings, and due to the untimely death of their parents, he had assumed a parenting role to Jas. There was a four-year age gap between Jas and Patrick, who was five years younger than Colin. Her elder brother had already been active in the family business, which provided medical supplies to many of the doctors and medical offices on the island, at the time of their parents' sudden deaths in a car accident.

Colin was proficient at management, and while he provided the business skills to keep the company profitable, it was Patrick who possessed the people skills. Patrick was good-natured and usually kept the customers and suppliers happy. His best attribute, in Jas's opinion, was his willingness to listen to what others had to say.

The company wasn't large, but it provided a decent income for the owners largely because of their complementary contributions. Colin was the boss. In their society, a leader was given a degree of deference. In the business, he never gave orders directly to any of the employees, and he was always addressed formally. He was a strict taskmaster, but all communication was done through Patrick. He often reminded Jas of her father. He was not only tall and slim, but he exuded the same austerity. He even wore the same rounded wire-rimmed glasses.

In such a small office, Patrick had a reputation as a peacemaker. He was also Colin's closest friend, but as the younger brother he still conceded a degree of hierarchical authority to him. They worked well together and provided some level of cooperation and harmony as a team. Jas knew that her father would have been proud of both of them.

Jas relied upon Colin's wisdom. He was dependable, and she had faith in his ability to make the crucial decisions for the good of the family. Jas didn't experience the same type of overt attachment to him as she did with Patrick; however, she greatly respected him and felt comfortable in seeking his advice, and she was assured of his love.

On the other hand, she viewed Patrick as her ally. His jovial personality and smiling face always made a person feel comfortable. Usually, she could count on him for support when disagreements arose within the small family. He provided her with an opportunity to vent her frustrations and talk things out. Colin always watched Jas with the protective eye of an overseer, much like her father had done. Colin was her teacher, but Patrick had been her confidant.

Friday nights, Faith always prepared a scrumptious dinner for the three siblings as a stable and focal meeting ground. This was the time of the week that the family members set aside to bring one another up to date on their personal achievements, discuss problems, and examine events in the political and social aspects of their lives. Jas thought that it was probably the only time that Patrick ate a proper meal as was evidenced by his slightly plump frame. Of course, he probably didn't weigh anymore than Colin did, but he was a half a foot shorter, barely taller than Jas herself.

Tonight, during the course of their dinner conversation Jas divulged to the family that she was joining the ranks of the unemployed. Colin voiced his immediate concern that the economy had recently been lagging and that it was not a good time to be looking for a job. Faith knew by the look in Colin's eyes that they were in for an extended discussion and interrupted the conversation to suggest that they take their beverages outside to the patio.

Jas seated herself comfortably as she observed the metaphorical wheels as they worked in Colin's mind. She waited for the onslaught. A few minutes later, the always-practical Colin suggested that Jas should bring her résumé up to date immediately and start looking for a job. He reminded her that the unemployment rate was at an all-time high on the island.

Talk about mental telepathy! Good old Patrick jumped in and suggested that he didn't think she should hurry off and just take any old job. He felt it was an excellent opportunity to take stock of her life, rethink her career goals, and rediscover what she thought would truly make her happy. When Jas described Sherlyn's plans, Patrick enthusiastically clapped his hands together and said, "That's what I'm talking about. Make a plan!"

Jas sensed that Patrick had provided her with the opportunity to discuss what she had been coming around to all evening. She confessed that, like Sherlyn, it honestly didn't appeal to her to move from one job to another that didn't offer her a chance for upward mobility within the firm, either. Hesitantly, she broached the subject that Sherlyn's aspirations had awakened the seeds of a plan that was now forming in her own mind. Perhaps she too would go back to school.

"What really interests you, Jas?" Faith had asked.

"I have a business idea that I've been thinking about for some time, months, as a matter of fact. Sherlyn and I have discussed it at great length, and she agrees that it has real potential."

"Jaslyn, this is not a good time to start up a business. A lot of new, small businesses are not able to make it beyond the first year. Right now there are a lot of problems with disruptions in supplies from our trading partners, and because the economic situation worldwide is tumultuous, there is a weak external demand for our products. I can't stress how difficult it would be for you to try and establish some new venture," Colin counseled.

"Come now, Colin. Our own father began a medical supply business that few people encouraged, and even today, in this economic recession, we are surviving quite well. What's your idea about, Jas?" Patrick asked.

"In a nutshell, I want to create software for the small business community to help lower their costs and provide more efficiency in doing some of the simpler tasks. For instance, a computerized reminder system. In the legal community, it's called a tickler system, and it helps you to keep your responsibilities organized," Jas proudly explained. "I've spent six years of my life typing out contracts in many areas of law. I understand some fundamental things that would be useful to smaller landlords, for instance. I know I could design software packages for residential and business leases. I can set up templates that would enable small business operators the opportunity to purchase some self-help tools that can cut their operating expenses. Technology is the way of the future."

"You have to be careful with that kind of thing, Jaslyn. You're not a lawyer and shouldn't be giving legal advice. You might be sued," Colin responded.

"I understand that. I'm not talking about giving legal advice, rather providing tools to help a law office or small business to run more efficiently. Besides, I'm pretty sure that you can protect yourself with a disclaimer clause."

"Jaslyn, the country is in the middle of a recession. There's not many people that are going to risk starting up new businesses right now. I just don't see a big-enough market for you, at this time."

"Colin, I know that you have some valid concerns; however, I've thought about that too. I know that there's a large English-speaking marketplace for my products in North America. I'm particularly thinking of Canada," she reluctantly replied.

"Canada? Jaslyn, you can't be serious. You know nothing about their legal systems. Furthermore, you don't have the programming skills. Use your common sense, this is not a viable option," Colin quietly countered.

"Think about it, Colin" Jas sheepishly began, "there's a newly emerging small business and personal use technology business market overseas. Their legal systems are based on the same British common law that we use. I've been studying computer programming in my leisure time, and with some additional training in computer software development and technology, I hope that I can acquire the necessary skills to make this happen. It might take some additional research, but I think I could bring this idea into fruition relatively easily."

"You're better off focusing on a career. If you want to go back to school, why not go to law school?"

"Does anyone want to play a board game?" Patrick asked to try and lighten the conversation. He knew that Colin would take some time to really think about what Jas was hoping to do. He'd investigate the possibilities, and once satisfied, he'd stand behind her. There was no use getting into a heated argument now.

"Not tonight, Patrick. I've had an exhausting day today. I'd really like to go home. I'm planning a nice, hot bath, and I'd like to retire early," Jas replied.

Although Jas could see the disappointment in everyone's faces, she felt the need to be alone. Shortly thereafter, Patrick let her off the hook and offered her a ride home. She gratefully accepted it, knowing that he wouldn't press her further on the whole topic of the earlier discussion.

Later that night as she lay wide awake in her bed, Jas found she couldn't sleep. She got back up and slowly paced up and down the hallway in her small apartment. She wanted more in her life, and she longed to see the world. She had been curious and wanted to explore how other societies were structured. Meet people from far-off lands. See how they lived. Travel!

She envied Sherlyn's focus on what she had always wanted to do. Perhaps, she thought, with the education allowance, her trust fund, and savings, she might be able to fulfill some of her own dreams too! She wondered if the education allowance could be applied to an overseas program for foreign students. Turning to her computer, she began an extensive investigation into the business programs that were offered in Canada. She had made up her mind; she felt a burning compulsion that this was the place of her destiny.

18

It had been an interesting three weeks that Russ had spent in Australia, although he'd soon discovered that he wasn't really cut out for travelling by himself. Perhaps, he'd been wrong when he opted not to take a tour. However, he thought that it would be restrictive, and he had chosen Cathay Pacific Airways because it provided him a three-day stopover in Hong Kong. He didn't expect that he'd ever get back to this part of the world again and preferred to set up his own itinerary.

He'd visited the Canadian visa offices in both Hong Kong and Sydney and had been treated to some idle banter and a couple of good meals. In Sydney, he was advised that he'd be smart to buy a multiday transportation pass, which would give him unlimited bus, train, and ferry travel around the town. On his first day, he went to see the Wild Life Sydney Zoo to satisfy his fascination with the unique animals that live in that part of the world. He got to see and filmed some great pictures of a koala bear, a wallaby, the kookaburra bird, a cassowary, and even a Tasmanian devil.

The following day he visited the Sea Life Sydney Aquarium and explored its themed habitat zones. He was really pleased that he'd brought his camcorder along on the trip. He got phenomenal close-up shots of the crustaceans, rays, penguins, seahorses, octopuses, and dugongs among other aquatic life. Hopefully, he thought, Katy would provide him with a grandchild one day that would enjoy seeing the wonders of this part of the world. On his last day, he purchased some local aboriginal art at one of the galleries on the Rocks to go with his North American aboriginal art collection.

He was pleasantly surprised in Hong Kong, when he had a day to kill and contacted the Canadian embassy. He found that the newly appointed mission integrity officer, or MIO as they were usually called, was an old colleague by the name of Keith Curran. Keith got off work at three thirty and arranged to meet Russ for something to eat and show him around town. More than that he showed him around the city on what was called the "hop-on hop-off" tour bus, and they managed to visit a temple, before travelling to Aberdeen for the best seafood Russ had ever tasted in a floating restaurant that was designed like a Chinese imperial palace.

The next morning, Russ had arrived early at the Hong Kong International Airport and decided to visit the Duty Free shop to pick up a gift for Katy. Once that was accomplished he headed toward his boarding gate but stopped halfway there when he observed two men. He immediately recognized that one of them was the baggage handler El Safty who had been involved with the big drug bust that had occurred on his last night working at the airport in Vancouver.

As their eyes locked, there was no doubt that the other man instantly recognized him too! Suddenly, El Safty and his companion quickly turned and ducked down a nearby corridor. Russ hustled toward them and tried to catch up to them without thinking about what he might do if he caught up to them. It seemed to have slipped his mind that he was in a strange country and had no authority to question either man. However, they had disappeared, and then reality struck Russ that there was little he could say to the men anyways. He went back to his boarding gate and wondered who the second man was. Checking the time, Russ decided to put in a call to Keith and ask him to contact Judd, explaining to him what had happened both in Canada and just moments before.

Tarik had been sure that the Canadian border officer that he'd seen many times at the Vancouver airport had somehow followed him and Khurram to Hong Kong. He wondered which one of them the Canadians had picked up on. The two men were distressed that one or both of them had been a weak link to the organization. They decided to alert Bahrami and let him know that they had been tailed by a Canadian border officer that Tarik thought was named Norman, although Tarik couldn't recall his full name.

Tarik or Khurram were not too concerned about being found in Hong Kong; however, they were disturbed that they had been spotted together. Canadian officials had taken Tarik's fingerprints, and now this Norman character probably had a description of Khurram. They soon decided that they would have to ditch their identities, and they wouldn't be able to play any role in the future Canadian operation.

After the plane had settled into the return flight to Canada, Russ made some notes about the encounter he had experienced. He was particularly interested in El Safty's travelling companion who appeared to be Pakistani, East Indian, or Bangladeshi. Russ couldn't be certain which. He wondered where they had been coming from and going to. Was it possible that they were both part of that drug shipment that had come from Hong Kong?

He thought that the second person was less likely to be East Indian or Bangladeshi as his complexion was fairly light, and his nose appeared to be longer than countrymen of those nations. Russ had training on facial recognition, and he was fairly sure that the man had the facial characteristics that were more prominent with the Pakistani people. Pakistani people tend to have a fairer skin coloring than most Bangladeshi or East Indian males. The faces differ from East Indian men in that they are generally longer, with deep eye sockets, and a sharp nose. However, Russ noted that he had learned that the men in Bangladesh were often a little taller. His gut instinct was that it wasn't credible to generalize about the characteristics of the entire population of peoples and probably not too helpful, but it was the best he could do and perhaps it would be helpful in trying to identify the mysterious man.

19

During Hassan's first eleven months in Canada, he had remained much to himself. At first, he had experienced somewhat of a cultural shock and was very apprehensive on what he had let himself in for. He was astounded by the behavioral quirks of a few of the individuals that he had witnessed while in the holding center.

There had been one little scrawny person who had caused quite a ruckus refusing to eat his breakfast until someone else volunteered to taste everything on his tray first. Hassan had lost his appetite as he watched the other person dissect each slice of toast and examine it microscopically before eating it. The guy was crazy. In fact, he was paranoid.

He had approached Hassan first thing in the morning to warn him to be very careful that the guards were putting mind-altering drugs into all the foods to prepare him for further interrogations. He insisted that the food contained chemical poisons that the Canadians were testing for American warfare activity. Hassan didn't know if the guy had lost his mind, or there was some truth in what he claimed. He was thankful to Allah that Noe had faithfully arrived fairly early the next morning with a lawyer by the name of Jordan Connors, who had taken charge at the admissibility hearing and secured his release.

The hearing had been initially delayed for a while as they had to wait for an interpreter to arrive, but then it progressed fairly speedily. Someone from the government had begun the proceeding by arguing that Hassan should be kept in detention as his identity was unknown. He had reasoned that because Hassan had travelled on a forged passport, he was not a Canadian citizen or permanent resident, and since he hadn't had a visa to come to Canada, they needed to be sure of his identity before he should be released.

His lawyer, Connors, had persuasively pleaded that his client had escaped with his life from an unbelievable situation, was severely burned requiring extensive medical treatment, and that indeed he had a genuine Iranian identity card, which contained both his photo and his thumb print. The judge looked carefully at the card before glancing at Noe, Hassan's cousin, and asking him to step forward. After several questions, the judge commented that Hassan had a family member, who was a Canadian citizen who had confirmed his identity. Hassan felt immense relief when the judge decided that he was satisfied that he was whom he said he was and gave him an unenforceable departure order as he ruled he was to be released from custody.

Later, he had asked Noe to find out from Connors what the departure order meant. He had thought he was going to be issued something called a removal order. Connors explained that Canada used three different types of removal orders for different circumstances and that the departure order didn't mean too much at this point because he had made a verbal claim for asylum.

Hassan learned that he would have another interview in a few days to determine his eligibility to claim asylum; then he would attend Connor's office to make the actual application for refugee protection. His lawyer assured him that it would put an automatic hold on any removal process once all these formal processes were concluded. His first hurdle was to be found eligible. Anyone found eligible couldn't be forced to leave the country until after a hearing before an immigration judge. If the judge ruled in his favor, the order would never be enforced.

Noe posted a personal thousand-dollar bond for his release from the holding center. The judge imposed terms and conditions on Hassan's freedom, which required him to report to the Immigration Office regularly, notify the government if he moved, and to be of good behavior. Noe had come prepared with his bank statements and some pay stubs from his work in case he needed someone to act as a bonds person. There had been a bit of a kerfuffle when the judge had stated that one of the terms would require him to remain living with Noe.

Noe explained to the court that his apartment only had one bedroom that he shared with his expectant wife. The judge accepted the reason and removed that stipulation but told Hassan that he had to keep the Immigration Department informed of his address. The whole process had been finished in just over an hour. He went back to get his belongings and was surprised to see that the doctor was waiting to see him. He reexamined his hands and prescribed a couple more days of medication before giving him a referral to a local hospital burn center.

It had been a bit of a setback in his plans; however, after Connors and Noe conferred with the doctor, he had been admitted to the hospital and remained there for three weeks due to the severity of his burns. He subsequently enrolled in a local community college and started attending regular language classes while using a local library to do his own research on the things that were most important to him in his spare time. He had received money from a government office for food and shelter and even had his own little room, thanks to all the help Noe had given him.

Naz assured him that Khurram had made a successful delivery, had safely returned to the camp in Pakistan with Tarik, and the finances for the operation were secure. He was slightly disturbed about the incident in Hong Kong and wondered if the man Tarik referred as "Norman" was the same man he'd encountered on his own arrival were one and the same person. With that one exception, everything was going according to plan!

20

Hassan's hands were healing nicely, and he had received continued medical treatment at the hospital after he had been discharged. Hassan was genuinely grateful for Noe's assistance in finding a room, and he was relieved to be able to live alone. His cousin wasn't aware of some of his activities, and he needed the privacy. Most importantly, his room was located close to the public library where he could access the Internet and within easy walking distance of the Douglas College where he was attending.

The location had been absolutely vital. It was cheap and had easy access to reach his contacts and do preliminary research for the next phase of the planning stages of the operation. It was amazing the things one could get on the Internet if you knew how to search. He was also ecstatic with his proximity to the research libraries at a local university. Everything he would need in the months ahead was pretty much at his disposal.

The openness and trust expressed by many of the Canadians he had met certainly had continuously astonished him. He had heard that the generosity of the average person was almost laughable, and his informants had suggested that Canadians were gullible and naive. On the other hand, Hassan suspected that because of Canada's declining population, its undeveloped land, the largely Christian values of its population, and its leaders' political will to maintain a reasonably high standard of living, they adopted immigration policies that were invitational to just about anyone who wanted to migrate.

In both the holding center and at the school, he became aware that the Canadian government was not only allowing a peaceable takeover of the country that allowed almost anyone to migrate, but they were also actually complicit in encouraging it. It was ironic that they sought to change the very reasons why many people chose to come to Canada in the first place once they settled into their new communities. Canadian society, in protecting everyone's freedom, lost its moral values. He could see all around him that Canada was fast becoming an undesirable destination to raise a family.

Hassan surmised that his next big hurdle would be getting through the refugee hearing, which would determine if he would be allowed to stay in Canada, but he had no cause to worry about that for at least several months. At the college, he had heard the boastful claims that many people had been granted refugee status using a false identity. They had boasted that purchases of supporting documents were readily available at the nearby university campus from some young enterprising person engaged in making forgeries.

Some bragged about the stories they'd invented for their hearings and laughed that they had stood up to the test. He had been surprised by the openness of the students in sharing their experiences trying to impress one another with their inventiveness. If they could do it, he figured that it wouldn't be all that difficult for him! However, he only listened to the stories that circulated and refrained from revealing his own situation.

Canada's immigration policies catered to the big businessmen who wanted to see a broader population base to feed their insatiable greed for wealth. Throughout the world, Canada had developed a reputation as a nation with a high rate of acceptance and a soft spot for asylum seekers. The political climate also appealed to the numerous Christian groups who believed that they were fulfilling the commandments of their God in opening their doors to the world's underprivileged and persecuted, regardless of faith, presenting them with opportunities for a better life.

At the end of the process, he had no desire to stay here permanently. It would be nice to have a country he could return to whenever he wanted, but if he ever married again, it wasn't the type of country he'd want to raise his children in. A Canadian passport would provide ease of movement throughout the world. However, he felt confident that the lengthy delay in hearing his claim would take a least a couple of years, long enough to complete his mission and get out.

In the meantime, he would be patient and do what he had to do to enable him to accomplish his personal goals. Canadian immigration status was only a means to an end. A lot of people he had met over the years used it for their own nefarious purposes and freely travelled wherever they wanted. Many even went back to where they had come from as soon as they got status, and the Canadian government rarely bothered to do anything. While others had so many identities and passports from all over the world, they just blended in and out of one country after another.

Connors spoke to Noe, instructing that Hassan should mix into the local community, take some language courses, and get himself reasonably established. If he didn't want to go to school, he suggested that he get a job as it would be at least a year before his hearing, and either way, it would create a favorable impression at his hearing.

He also boasted that the legal processes provided refugee claimants all kinds of opportunities to stay, receive financial support, and roam the country freely over a period of several years. He had chuckled as he assured Hassan that money would be provided courtesy of the public purse for appeals if their journey took a turn for the worse. Hassan had concluded that the system was basically a sham and provided a false sense of security that the government was actually vigilant in protecting its borders.

Hassan had enrolled in the English-language classes almost immediately. He had carefully not revealed the extent of his own knowledge of the language in case the immigration folks did any checking on him as he knew that this could spark questions about the validity of his entire claim. He had carefully crafted the picture he intended to create for his hearing and divert any additional attention that might arouse anyone's curiosity of the basic facts of his claim.

His seemingly limited knowledge of the English language gave him an advantage in that it allowed him to consider any questions put to him under the guise of waiting for the translation. Overall, the English classes had progressed pretty rapidly, though, and they only took up twenty-five hours a week. While this gave him ample opportunity to do the other personal tasks that he had undertaken, he found that attending the school relieved some of the loneliness of his existence.

Douglas College also ideally suited him as it catered to international students and persons like himself who were either somewhere in the immigration stream within Canada or had been. He was an excellent listener and learned a lot about their stories while revealing nothing about himself. He had intentionally scuttled the language proficiency tests, allowing him to start at the beginner level of the program; however, he moved up quickly and was now in the ninth and final level. He was ready to move on to the next phase of his plans and hoped that he would be able to connect up with some of the other members of his terrorist cell, soon.

After completing the language classes, he applied for admission to the computer technology program for the fall. He had some background with computer training before coming to Canada. He had Noe contact his father to get his transcripts of grades from his two years at the Amirkabir University of Technology in Tehran and submitted them as soon as they arrived. He was now anxiously awaiting to hear whether he had been accepted.

21

Hassan picked up his cell phone and made his biweekly call to Jordan Connors's office, checking to see if his asylum hearing had been scheduled. It had become somewhat of a ritual that allowed the lawyer an excuse to bill for a few hours of time just to tell him that the case hadn't been scheduled yet. He wondered how many other clients were in a similar situation.

Every single call, Connors reiterated the same series of general questions and failed to provide any new information to Hassan regarding the status of his hearing. Sometimes, he felt that Connors was using a checklist of questions that allowed him to get the maximum full hour of billing time that the legal aid system would pay him fortnightly. It looked like he was running a pretty good scam, billing for the same repetitious questions that he used with all of his clients. All of his office overhead was likely covered by just twenty clients doing their check-in calls.

Hassan figured it gave the lawyer a fairly dependable income of several grand a month coming in, apart from any other billings he made. It just went to show how recklessly the government handled the public purse. Hassan thought that it would be a lot cheaper if the government had a pool of salaried lawyers for claimants similar to the duty counsels in the criminal courts so that they could stop funding half of these idiots in their gold-digging private practices.

Over the course of a few months, he began to detest Connors. He found him to be an arrogant jerk who justified his existence by continuously boasting about all of the people he had helped to a better life here in Canada. However, Hassan wasn't fooled; he knew that all those people that Connors had supposedly helped had only given him the opportunity to acquire his extravagant lifestyle.

He sported loud Hermes ties, with matching colored socks; wore sharp, expensive suits by Hugo Boss or Giorgio Armani; and had flashy rings with giant stones on the fingers of each hand. Continuing in this pretentious manner, he even drove a leased one-year-old BMW. He thought that his flashy lifestyle gave him some added class; however, it was Hassan's opinion that he needed to go back to the classroom.

What annoyed Hassan the most, however, was that he perceived that Connors had the filthiest and most annoying habit of belching and ejecting streams of phlegm across his desk at anyone who had the misfortune of sitting across from him. Hassan had learned to move the chair in front of his desk to the side to avoid the direct pathway of this foul habit. He had to attend at Connors's office several times in the beginning, but now, he made regular phone calls, avoiding his presence, whenever possible. Once, he had mentioned to his cousin his dislike of the lawyer, but Noe had laughed and informed him that he was worth the time and money because he rarely lost a case.

"Jordan Connors's office, may I help you," came the melodious voice of his office assistant, Jeanine.

Hassan loved the sound of her voice, but he couldn't figure out how someone so professional and pleasant could work for that oaf. Occasionally, he thought that he preferred to call the office just to hear her voice. She was slightly older than him and wasn't at all physically attractive, but her voice always stirred his testosterone levels and gave him a surge of wishing there were something more to his life.

Eerily, the sound of her voice reminded him of a past he thought he had forgotten. It was a lifetime that he had briefly found rewarding and satisfying, but it had left him hardened and bitter. He felt the memories were better buried away. As time went on, waiting for his hearing, he had revealed his newly acquired English-language skills in these brief conversations and tried to ignore the beckoning sound of her musical tones.

Quickly recovering from his daydreams, he identified himself and asked to speak to Jordan Connors. Much to his surprise, she advised him that she had been waiting for his call because Mr. Connors needed to see him right away, although he wasn't in the office at the moment. Jeanine informed him that the government wanted to schedule his hearing in September or early October.

After a few more exchanges, they agreed that he would come into the office the following week. As he ended the call, he was glad that the ESL classes were finished because he didn't want any distractions in preparing himself for the hearing. He pondered whether he should amend his application for the tech course and request admission for January, instead of September.

As numerous thoughts raced through his mind, he finally decided to delay his studies. He headed to the library computers to send the amendment request through to the admissions office and then sent a brief but telling message to his contact, Nazreh, just to let him know that he was now "moving to stage 2." After Hassan had sent the messages, he went over to the geographic mapping section of the library and scanned several maps of Los Angeles and the surrounding area, before deciding on the specific ones he wanted to copy. He was deep in thought and busy at the photocopier when he was quietly approached from behind.

"Planning a holiday, Hassan?" came a low query in accented English.

With a quick backward glance, he recognized the tall man who sported a chin beard in the style of a committed North African fundamentalist to be a fellow student from the college. He had the face of an intelligent and confident man. Hassan recalled that one of his classmates had mentioned that the man was called Hamid and that he had recently been granted his permanent resident status. The other student had pointed him out to Hassan as the guy had been successfully found to be a convention refugee awhile ago. He was a little surprised at the intrusion and made a mental note that he might have to change his research place.

"Not yet, but hopefully I will get to visit some of my relatives who live nearby. Just checking the maps to find the best way to get there. I'm sorry, you seem to have me at a disadvantage. I don't recall your name," he smoothly responded.

"Oh, I apologize, my name's Hamid, and I attend the college, too," the stranger said.

"Yes, I remember now, someone told me that you had recently obtained permanent resident status, and I should talk to you about the process. Congratulations, I'm a long way from that step, I'm afraid. I've just heard that my immigration hearing for asylum is going to be in the fall."

"That's great that you've got a hearing date," replied Hamid. "We both have good news and should go out for dinner and celebrate—my treat," he added.

In the many months that he had been coming here, he had never run into anyone that he knew. For that matter, he hadn't been formally introduced to this person, either, and Hassan was a little surprised that he knew his name. He wasn't happy about this encounter and thought that it should have been avoided. He wanted to keep his business private, and he couldn't risk screwing up.

The problem was that this particular library had the best resources in the city and was likely the only place he could get some of the information he need. In fact, Naz had advised him that everything he would need could be found here. It would be difficult to find an alternative location with the specific resources he required. Damn! He had thought it wasn't too close to the school, and it was unlikely that he would run into anyone who knew him.

Hassan thought further about the unexpected invitation. Why not? He had nothing else planned, and it was a Friday night, which often proved very boring. Except for Noe, his lawyer, and school, he had little contact with anyone and felt that he was long overdue for some companionable relaxation. Hamid was probably harmless and would likely provide good company for a few hours.

His only concern about this meeting was that Hamid had witnessed him photocopying the maps, but he felt confident that his response had diverted any curiosity that the student might have and equally sure that he didn't know specifically what he had been copying.

"Sure, but don't expect me to know where to get a half-decent meal. I haven't found one good eating establishment in the whole time I've been here," Hassan said with a slight smirk.

"Trust me, I know a great little place. It's called Karimi's. It's just a short ride from here on the sky train, and it always has good home-style *ghormeh sabzi* on the menu and occasionally some duck or chicken *fesenjan*. It's right on the main subway line."

"Mmm, now you are making me hungry. It sounds good."

"I'm meeting a couple of friends there in about an hour if you can wait. They won't mind if I bring a guest."

At the mention of friends, Hassan was slightly taken aback and quickly reconsidered his acceptance. He had a personal policy in which he avoided group activities. He wasn't the type of person who needed to socialize with "the guys." He valued control over his privacy above all else and didn't want to relinquish it in any way. The fewer people he interacted with, the better it would be in the long run for everyone. He sensed that Hamid meant well, but he decided to back out of the engagement, tactfully.

"Oh, wait, I just realized that tonight isn't really the best time. You kind of caught me off guard. I was surprised to see someone who knew my name here. I just remembered that I have another commitment that I almost forgot about. Perhaps another night," he replied.

"I'd think you might like to come tonight. I'm actually going to a meeting and dinner that has been prearranged by a mutual friend of ours. I think you might know him. His name is Nazreh," Hamid mumbled in a barely audible tone.

22

Hassan was relieved that he had finally met his contact. This operation had already been in the planning stages for more than four years. It had begun with Naz's sponsorship to Canada. Gradually they had been able to get other operatives into strategic positions in both Canada and the United States. Hassan knew of all the players but had never personally met any of them, and he was unaware of the names that they were going by.

"Come to think of it, I may be able to rearrange my evening. I just need to make a quick stop at my rooming house, first."

"Good, I'll walk over with you," replied Hamid. "Then we can catch the sky train."

This was the third major operation that Hamid had been asked to perform by Bahrami, and he felt honored to have been chosen for the mission. It had surprised him that this man, Hassan, was Bahrami's lieutenant in charge of this operation. This meant that the young man could directly communicate with the mastermind. Hamid had seen Hassan around the campus a few times, but he was still in the ESL classes, and they had never spoken.

As the two men walked to Hassan's room, they engaged in little meaningful conversation. Hamid revealed that he had been at the school for a few years now and had taken English-language classes, too. He told Hassan that the men they were going to meet were called Giv and Sammi. He had met the men himself at a local mosque a few times before; however, all such meetings were arranged by Naz.

Giv was from an Iranian family that had fled to the United States during the Iranian Revolution, and he had a US green card, which allowed him to live and work in the United States, but he had never bothered to apply for naturalization as a US citizen. For the most part, he travelled freely back and forth between Canada and the United States for short trips with little difficulty. Sammi, on the other hand, was from Kuwait, and he had no legal status in Canada or the United States. He worked illegally as a cleaner at the airport.

Hassan knew more about the two men than Hamid did but didn't say anything as he listened to Hamid's background information. Sammi had managed to get a job at the airport in Vancouver, and working in tandem with Tarik, they had facilitated the receipt of some shipments of supplies for the organization. He also kept a finger on the pulse of the activities and the gossip at the airport. His friendly manner had enabled him to get inside information from one of the customs officers who seemed to know everything that was going on at the terminal. It was through him that they learned that the Canadians thought that the entire drug shipment had been lost in the carnage of the bombings. Sammi also had found out that they suspected that Tarik was involved, but they had no way of holding him.

Hassan himself, personally, had chosen both Giv and Sammi when he had been discussing the operatives that would be needed for this mission. Giv was an able helicopter pilot and had recently been employed as an instructor at a flight training school in Los Angeles. He was getting aerial shots of various potential target cities throughout the western US states.

Giv had been assigned to take the photos of the aqueduct, water treatment, and reservoir systems feeding midsized cities in several states. These photos would be matched with Hassan's research and mapping to assess potential targets with a high degree of vulnerability to the chemical attack that they were planning. After dinner, they would go where they could hold these serious discussions without fear of intrusions.

As much of the city of Vancouver was at or below the sea level, travelers used a light rail rapid transit system that was known as the SkyTrain to transport about the city. Hassan didn't particularly care for buses, and this form of transportation suited him fine in contrast to underground subway systems that made him feel claustrophobic. Hamid informed him that the place where he was meeting his friends was only a few stops, so once under way, they arrived at the diner within half an hour.

"Hi, Giv, where's Sammi?" Hamid asked as he approached the table at the far end of an outdoor patio attached to the restaurant.

The man shifted his eyes back and forth between the two men who had joined him while hesitating to answer. Sensing his discomfort and the unasked question in his eyes, "Oh, by the way, this is Hassan. Hassan, Giv," Hamid continued by furnishing an introduction.

"Hello, Hassan. Naz told me that you would be in touch soon," Giv spoke with the sound of relief in his voice. "Sorry Sammi couldn't make it. I'll tell you about that after dinner. Let's eat."

The men each picked up a menu and took their cue from Giv that they would continue that part of the discussion later. Over the next hour, they filled their empty stomachs and made small talk about their lives in Canada. During the course of the conversation, Giv confirmed that he lived and worked in the United States. He complained that most of the women he met were either Hispanic or Russian illegals.

"They all hope that they can latch onto the brass ring either by marriage or as the next big movie star discovery." He jokingly asked the men whether there were any girls at the campus worth looking at.

"I've only seen one that strikes my interest," responded Hamid.

"Do tell." Giv laughed. "Does she have a friend?"

"She's in the same program as I am, and she's Lebanese. I'm not really that interested if you know what I mean. However, she's nice, not the normal trash, and I've gone with her a couple of times for a meal. Nothing more. I don't mix business and pleasure as a general rule."

"Would I know her?" Hassan asked.

"I don't think so. She's on some committee that helps new foreign students coming from overseas, but she doesn't do anything with the refugee claimants. Her name's Dana. Does that ring a bell?"

"Never met her. I keep pretty much to myself at the campus. It's my ticket into some of the library systems and bolsters my public image for staying here. Well, gentlemen, I think we should hightail it out of here. Has anyone a suggestion where we might go?" Hassan inquired, getting impatient to get down to the purpose of this meeting.

"There's a mosque a few blocks up the road. It's about a fifteen-minute walk. It's good and has lots of privacy," Giv responded as he rose to his feet.

Giv was approximately the same height as Hassan with a similar slim build, while Hamid stood slightly taller than the other two men. Hassan had seen pictures before of Giv, but he had always been garbed in a long white flowing robe, which was his traditional dishdasha, and he had worn a head covering and headband. Here in North America, he had apparently adapted to the casual dress of the western world, wearing jeans and a checkered shirt. He had a good, trim, full beard that stretched from one ear to his other one, but it was only about an inch in length.

The three men walked companionably to the mosque in the warm summer evening as the sun slowly sank down on the horizon. Upon reaching the mosque they removed their shoes, performed the ritual washing or *wudu*, and repeated their prayers before finding a quiet room where they could get down to business. Both Hamid and Hassan were anxious to know what had become of Giv, but Hassan was also concerned whether they had been able to get the pictures that he had been waiting for. As soon as the door closed, he inquired whether their mission had been accomplished successfully.

"I've got the pictures that we've taken to date, at least the undeveloped rolls. I usually stay at Sammi's place, but when I arrived, I saw some strange people entering his apartment. They had vests on and were carrying guns, which they were trying hard to conceal. I figured they were cops, and I didn't know what to do," Giv stated.

"Shit, I wondered what's happened with Sammi. Where are you staying?" Hamid asked.

"Nowhere. I got to Sammi's place about two hours ago, and when I saw what was happening, I tried to contact Naz but couldn't reach him. So, I decided to keep our little dinner rendezvous by myself because I have all the film."

"We've got a photographer who'll print the pictures. I'll give him a call and see if he can put you up for a few days while you work on the photos with him," Hassan said as he reached for his cell phone. "Excuse me a few moments, gentlemen."

Hassan went down the hall and made a call to Iqbal, a Pakistani national who owned a photography studio near Noe's work. He had been recommended by Naz and did quality work often supplying the photos for the forged identification documents, which Naz produced. Hassan had dealt with him on a couple of previous occasions to arrange documents for operatives before he came to Canada and considered that he was thoroughly trustworthy.

Iqbal quickly agreed to put up Giv and work at developing the films for the organization. He told Hassan to have Giv meet him at the shop where he had a small room in the back with a cot that the fellow could use for a couple of days. However, he warned that once Giv was in the shop, an automatic alarm system would kick in when he closed the shop around 9:00 p.m., thus preventing him from leaving the building until Iqbal arrived in the morning.

As Hassan hung up, his phone rang immediately. He glanced at the number, and after recognizing that the call was from his cousin, he answered it. Noe informed him that Sammi and a few of the cleaning staff at the airport had been picked up for working illegally in some random sweep. They were holding a hearing the next morning to deport him. Hassan thought for a moment and told Noe to give Jordan Connors a call and see if anything could be done for him. As an afterthought, he asked him to discreetly try and find out if a man named Russ Norman had been involved in the arrest.

He didn't like coincidences, and he felt that they were beginning to add up with this Norman guy at the airport. First, he had his own experience with him, then he heard Norman was involved in the drug investigation, and most recently he'd been spotted in Hong Kong by Tarik. He wasn't sure if the man was speculating or if he was actually on to some weakness in the operation, but if Russ Norman didn't stop turning up, he might have to get rid of him.

Hassan returned to the room where Giv and Hamid waited and advised of the arrangements that he had made. He suggested that it was the best that could be done on such short notice, and it was going to be a long and boring night. He gave Giv directions to Iqbal's shop, which was about a ten-minute drive away, and suggested that he should pick up any necessities he might have need of for a boring night. He did not divulge anything about Sammi.

"How is Mohammad faring in Los Angeles?" Hassan asked Giv.

"He thinks he's being watched. He says that he's noticed some guys hanging around his work, his home, and even when he's been out shopping. He wants to lie low for a little while and suggests that one of the other guys who are working on the inside of the system might be able to get more useful information for the operation, for now."

"Okay, tell him not to use any computers, everyone should only be using disposable cell phones, and I want to make sure that everybody touches base with Naz every week, advising what the status is on the suspected surveillance. I don't think the mail systems are safe to use either. I heard that one of the students at the college got caught by a mail seizure of documents that had been sent to him. We can't take any unnecessary risks at this point," Hassan instructed.

"Did Mohammad get anything for me?" inquired Hamid.

"I don't know. Like I said, he's skeptical about the situation right now. He thinks he's being watched, so he's staying away from the other guys." Giv hesitated. "We've got inside employees in five other locations. Decent-sized cities that include Tacoma, Washington; Boise, Idaho; Portland, Oregon; Peoria Nevada; and Orem, Utah."

Although Hamid had watched Hassan on several occasions, he hadn't observed any emotional response in his face until now. Hamid was sure that he detected a hint of worry in both his response and his eyes. "Naz sent me an encrypted message from Mohammad. As soon as I unravel it, I'll pass on anything that might be relevant to your end, Hamid. If he's being watched, we may have problems brewing in California."

"You should let Bahrami know. He may have to send some more operatives in," Giv said.

"I'll discuss it with him," Hassan said authoritatively as he got up. "Now I think we should head out. Thanks for the good work, Giv, and it's been a pleasure meeting you."

23

When Russ Norman returned from his extended vacation, he met the boys from the airport at the newly opened Oasis Men's Club to celebrate Corby's birthday. Russ had to admit that the girls were attractive and certainly physically fit exotic dancers. They were rather friendly with outgoing personalities, some had some light tats and piercings, and they ranged in age between twenty and thirty-five. The guys all chipped in to buy Corby a couple of lap dances, embarrassing the shit out of him. It was a fun night, though, and Russ was sure that it had opened a whole new world to his friend.

After his vacation and the night out with the guys, Russ had learned a valuable lesson. Although, he hated to admit it, everyone had been right about one thing: He hated retirement. He wasn't cut out to be a man of leisure he sheepishly confided to Katy one night when she invited him to join her and her fiancé, Kendrick, for a barbecue.

She had acknowledged that it was a common mistake that many people made. In her experience as a social worker at a small women's shelter in the city's west end, she had seen the gung-ho attitude about long-awaited retirement with some of the older women in the community. Without fail, they all eventually suffered in what she termed as the "retirement shock syndrome."

Katy reminded her dad that he had been getting up out of bed every day for the past thirty years at the same time and completing the same daily tasks that were always associated with his work. Then—*poof*—overnight, the routine ended. In fact, he hadn't socialized much since her mom had passed away, and his work had overpowered his life entirely. She expressed genuine concern that her father really needed something significant and substantive to occupy at least some of his time with.

Katy knew that her father had taken a lot of pride in his work and had received several departmental recognition awards because of his dedication and enthusiasm. However, after her mom died, her dad had just worked and worked to the exclusion of anything else. When he announced that he was going to retire, she had been taken aback.

Although he denied it, his job had provided the central purpose in his life that allowed him to cope with her mother's death. It also had kept him going on a day-to-day basis. She had tried to warn him that perhaps he should look at the preretirement program that the government offered its employees. It was transitional to help prepare people for retirement and allowed them to work just three days a week for a two-year period after which they fully retired.

The transitional program also allowed them to continue contributing to their pension at the full-time salary rate. It was ideal for people like her dad, but he had stubbornly insisted she was talking poppycock and that there would be plenty of things for him to do and enjoy once that door on his life was closed. She was so relieved when he finally made the admission that he was bored. Then it struck her! Perhaps now she could bring the two men in her life together in a more meaningful way.

As if on cue, Kendrick arrived, arms laden with a bottle of wine and some fresh blue-eyed African daisies that he must have cut from his mother's extensive gardens. It was her favorite because it was one of the few that she didn't seem to have an allergic reaction to. That he took the time to pick them himself always made her feel the strength of Kendrick's love. The pure-white florets with the blue centers filled her with calming tranquility, reminding her of a heavenly sky.

Kendrick gave her a peck on the cheek as he handed off his bounty and proceeded outdoors to help her dad get the barbecue going. She was glad that the two men got along well and were perfectly at ease in each other's company. They were both good men, and she counted herself lucky to have them.

"Hi, Russ, good to see you back. Did you catch any of those trophy-size black basses down in Florida?"

"You bet I did. I actually caught several good ones over the last couple of months, and I've got some pictures to prove it. It was a good trip, but to tell you the truth, I am glad to be back as I've not quite adjusted to becoming a layabout. How are you doing with the Watchdogz? I caught something on the news that the PI agencies are a little disgruntled these days. What's up?"

"Geez. You wouldn't believe it. I've got my hands full. They just passed a new provincial law that is becoming my worst nightmare. All security guards, even bouncers in the bars if you can believe it, and private investigators have to comply with a mandatory basic training and testing program before they can get licensed to work in the field."

"Ouch! I wonder what they'll come up with next," Russ commented. "You say they've been even requiring the bouncers in all the bars to get a license? That doesn't sound like a smart move, I'm sorry to say. Back in the day, that was a good way for a young fellow to put himself through university."

"They say it's to professionalize the industry, too many hotheads out there and no training on how to handle difficult situations. It's probably long overdue, but I wonder how efficient it will be. It certainly will close the door to students working in the industry because they can't afford the courses on top of their other student fees."

"Do you think it's just to keep some people working in the teaching end of it? Sort of job creation?"

"I don't know, I think it could be a good thing, but you know how it goes, just because someone's got a piece of paper doesn't mean they know how to do the work. Then again, how many people will want to make a career out of it? Some people are a whiz in the classroom, but can't apply the teachings to a given situation. On the other hand, other good employees can't pass the written test. It's a real headache."

"Does it affect people already doing the job or only new hires?"

"Everybody. A few of my employees didn't have to do it this year, provided that they already have a valid license that expired up until the date it was passed. They received an automatic renewal for a year. But I've got thirty-two employees who have to do the training now if they want to stay in the field."

"How about business owners, like yourself? How does it affect you?"

"It's mandatory. I just completed the private investigator course and passed the test. Shit, it took a total of fifty in-class hours and tons of reading over the past three months and cost me almost four grand."

"Christ, what were they teaching?"

"Actually, there is some pretty good stuff. They give a fairly intensive overview on civil and criminal laws and a lot of federal and provincial statutes that we deal with in our work or that affect us. I really learned a few things that hadn't even crossed my mind. They also taught communication and investigative techniques, which I think is helpful for the new guys, in particular. I didn't have any trouble with the content, and at the end of the day, it helps me to know what they've covered in their training. The courses are tax write-offs, too."

"Well, at least that's finished. Did you have to write an exam?"

"The exam was a bunch of multiple-choice questions. It wasn't too difficult. However, because I'm an owner and I have security guards in my employment, I have to do that program too."

"God, they have you coming and going. Is that another four grand?"

"I got lucky. I found another agency offering the security guard course that was also accredited. Incredible as it is, it was another eleven hundred bucks and forty intense hours of in-house training. It takes an additional week, but shit, a few guys found that the reading is just as many hours as the in class course hours."

"Do they issue the licenses, or do you still have to apply and pay for them separately?" Russ asked.

"Oh yeah, there were fees for both writing the test and for the damn licenses. The courses are all once-in-a-lifetime requirements, at least for now, for anyone holding a license. But of course, the license has to be renewed every two years. Hell, a lot of the guys are going to say fuck this, I can't afford either the time or the costs of training."

"Have you lost any employees so far?"

"Three so far. A lot of the guys haven't had to do it yet. I'm worried like shit that I'm not going to have enough qualified staff for the contracts I've got. I'm so short on staff already and busy with the summer students. We have to do employment contract background checks for them, and it's going to start soon. I can't keep up with the demand. Security is becoming big business, and a lot of the top investigative workers are looking at starting their own companies up."

As if on cue, Katy interjected, "Say, Dad, why don't you take the course and help Kendrick out. You'd be good at the investigative work. Corby always jokes that you are the best detective he ever met. I think deep down he's telling you the truth. You've always enjoyed that part of your job."

"That's a great idea, Russ. You know I could really use your kind of knowledge, international contacts, and investigative skills at my back. You could pick and choose your own hours too. Even work part-time if you want," Kendrick jumped in.

"Sure, I can just see it now: Russ Norman, Private Eye," Russ retorted.

"The investigator's course and license would be all you need, and you could do it full-time much quicker than I did. The security positions are easier to fill; however, the investigative work is interesting but so sensitive that I only have a couple of guys that I can put on those cases," Kendrick pushed.

Before the day was through, he didn't know how they'd done it, but amid the barbecued steaks and steaming corn on the cob, Russ felt that he had been snookered into a new career. Inwardly he felt satisfied; in fact, he even felt a little eager to begin. The prospect of doing something meaningful on his own terms that allowed him the freedom to do other things was ideal.

He had dreamed about retirement almost since he had begun working, but it wasn't all that it was cracked up to be. He'd figured he'd be rid of punching a clock and battling traffic. It had surprised him that lazy days of travelling about, fishing, or playing golf without a companion were actually boring and dissatisfying. He missed the social interaction, but more importantly he needed to feel that he was making a worthwhile contribution to society in general.

The prospect of working part-time had a certain appeal in improving his quality of life. Katy was right even though she appeared somewhat overly optimistic about his ability to pass the necessary course; she had recognized that both his mind and body needed something more. Perhaps one might say she was even a little pushy, because before the evening was through, she had pulled out her laptop, acquired all the necessary information, and got him to register online for a program that was beginning in just over a week.

24

Jas wondered where all the time had gone. She had spent the last two months researching so many computer and business programs that were offered all over the world. Patrick and her sister-in-law, Faith, enthusiastically encouraged her as she explained her software ideas and the educational benefits of studying away from the island.

Patrick often did the overseas travelling for Koh industries, and he was willing to approach his contacts once she had developed her product. Even though the family worked in the medical field, all of the businesses he worked with had legal departments. He suggested that one or more of them might be able to open doors for her to meet her goals.

When speaking with Colin on the topic, she used calculated persuasion. She emphasized how she had been informed by her company's Human Resources Department that a portion of the actual tuition cost and books would be covered with the training allowance provided by her former employer. It might have been an oversight in the company policy, but there were apparently no restrictions limiting training to an accredited program on the island.

Both of her brothers had told her that they were certain that programs could be found in Temesekia, which would enable her to acquire the technical training she needed. They were even willing to have their own computer specialists work with her within their business, at their own expense. She argued that she wanted an opportunity to examine other legal systems and see how their business practices worked. She explained that it was the best solution, in her opinion, if she were able to access information about international business practices firsthand.

It had taken several lengthy discussions to convince Colin that this was right for her; however, he eventually relented and pledged his support. Jas didn't need her brother's consent, but she valued both of their opinions and wanted their approval. It was so reassuring. She had dared to dream of something far reaching and at the same time to quench her beckoning thirst for travel. Now she felt completely confident enjoying the luxury of knowing that they would have her back if she needed them.

Jas was elated when she found a computer programming course at a place called Douglas College. The program was operational year-round and enabled her to enroll either in the fall, winter, or spring terms in Vancouver, Canada. The city was advertised as very multicultural and attracted people from all over the world. The city of Vancouver had always been her first choice as a Canadian tourist.

It was a two-year program in computer sciences that included some business courses well within her budget. She had played with the numbers and concluded that even after taking money from her trust fund, in addition to the education allowance she was eligible for, she would still have enough money left in her savings account and her trust fund to develop and market her product after graduation.

She wasted no time in putting the wheels in motion. She completed her applications for both the education allowance and to the overseas college within the ninety-day period stipulated by her employer. Then, with some guidance from the college's website, she applied for a visa as a foreign student as soon as she had received her acceptance three weeks later. It had been amazing how quickly she had been accepted into the start of the winter program, now just a month away.

The college had also provided her with a lot of pre-arrival information, assistance in finding suitable housing close to the campus, and they were going to send someone to pick her up at the airport. Patrick had accompanied her to the Canadian embassy when she made her visa application, and he was impressed with Canada's new foreign student program, which allowed an international student to work on the campus of the school they attended.

As Jaslyn packed, she was eager to begin her adventure. Everything seemed to be falling into place, she thought while waiting for Sherlyn to pick her up. This would be their last get-together before they each embarked on the road to their chosen career paths. It was getting close to Christmas, and they had decided to do a bit of shopping, see all the festive lights, and attend the business community annual concert of carolers.

Sherlyn was the perfect shopping companion, for they both knew that this year they would have to be exceptionally frugal. Sherlyn had been accepted into the local teachers' college and would also begin her studies at the start of the New Year. Despite her parents' willingness to assist in her educational expenses, Sherlyn didn't want to place too heavy a burden on them knowing that her parents were living on a fixed income since their retirement.

As Sherlyn's green Nissan pulled up to the curb, Jas recalled how proud her friend had been when she first got her car. It hadn't been new, but it was serviceable. It certainly had provided them with a means to visit the galleries, the theme parks, and the bazaars over the past few years. They had become good friends, almost like sisters, and Jas wondered how their separate paths would affect their future friendship.

She sincerely hoped that today would not be the final chapter in their close friendship, but an unsettling feeling came over her as if sensing that their destinies might drive them apart. She sincerely hoped not because, in her opinion, Sherlyn was a keeper. Although Jas had been quite close to her father growing up, her mother had been her best friend until fate had snatched her parents from her. Sherlyn had helped her to deal with the void their deaths had caused.

Her mother had displayed incredible tolerance and patience, always eager to make her feel secure and happy but had never been overly indulgent. She was a petite and beautiful woman who quietly demonstrated the strength of steel, and yet one always felt the softness of a gentle breeze in her presence. She recalled how her mother sharply displayed a razor wit but did so as calmly as still water to get her point across. She was masterful at dealing with the men in their household even though they clearly lived in a man's world.

Jas's mother had been the nucleus of their family. Her father had been the provider. The sudden loss of both her parents had left her with intense grief and longing as she had no opportunity to prepare for their deaths, to say good-bye, or to thank her parents for all they had meant to her. In her grief, Jas had felt such total despair and hopelessness; her sense of order had been shattered and forever changed. Two years later, she had met Sherlyn, and she began to heal.

When Sherlyn had stepped into her life, she had recognized and embraced Jas's needs for female companionship. She had displayed incredible understanding and compassion for her new friend, providing a shoulder to cry on while encouraging her to begin to live again. Sherlyn had also quenched her thirst for a trustworthy confidant that only another woman could provide.

From the very first day they had met, Sherlyn had reached her inner soul and not only made her smile, but she had also eased her pain. Eventually, as their friendship grew, Jas found her laughter and her spirit somewhat restored. Sherlyn was so sincere and such fun to be with that as time went by, Jas found herself sharing and exchanging the trials, tribulations, and the pleasantries of her daily life. Each young woman offered the other the support that only best friends can do.

"Hi, Jas. Sorry if I'm a bit late. I went to pick up my book list at the college. I wanted to check out prices if I saw anything that I might need while we're browsing around," came the interruption to her thoughts.

"Great idea, Sherlyn. We could stop off at the University Book Exchange and see if there are any deals. Also if the car park is full, other parking is less expensive near there."

"A neighbor told me that the Exchange is the best place to buy the math texts, or at least it was when she went a few years ago."

"You have to do math?"

"Ha! Ha! You caught me on that one. Because I'm going into the primary stream, it's really basic arithmetic." Sherlyn laughed.

They had come early enough and were lucky to find there were still a few good parking spots available in the bookstore parking lot as they maneuvered into a well-shaded space near the back. The side trip had not been in vain. Sherlyn was ecstatic that she had managed to find two of the texts listed for the next semester at almost half the regular price.

After making purchases and placing the books in the car, they decided to visit some of the shops in the immediate vicinity while they could still take advantage of the free parking. They made some small talk and agreed to stop at one of the local hawker stalls at lunchtime for some spicy "Muslim food," which was the name all the islanders gave to the delicious fried bread with curry sauce called *roti prata*. Neither one of the girls could resist the treat whenever they were in the shopping district.

Bearing in mind that the real purpose of their excursion was to obtain a few Christmas gifts, Jas informed her friend that Colin and Faith were expecting their first child. She had decided to purchase a nice family photo album for them so that they could capture their first memories of the newborn to share with her. She laughed at how Patrick was so much more difficult to buy for because he was so particular and such a snappy dresser. Finally, after visiting numerous stores, she settled on a gold tie pin with a crystal embedded into its center, which both women agreed would suit him perfectly.

Sherlyn liked the tie pin so much she found something similar, but conservative, for her father. To finish their shopping, Sherlyn settled on a beauty wash set for her mother that even included foot scrubs. Heading back to the car, they reflected how it had been a busy but fun-filled morning.

In the afternoon, after getting some of the *roti prata*, they visited another hawker stall for some fruit before continuing to the central shopping district. They found an outdoor bench to watch the rich, multifaceted display of dance, music, drama, and fine art by world-class performers, various ethnic groups, and people from the local churches taking place in the square. The air was filled with the sounds, sights, and aromas of the holiday season, and one readily became consumed by the atmosphere of revelry.

After an hour, they took a stroll around the entire area. They looked at the bargains in Chinatown, in the Arab center, and in the Indian village while carefully restraining themselves from buying anything further. Parents and children alike delighted in the window displays, decorations indoors and out, and the excitement that permeated the air.

As evening approached they jokingly treated each other with a holiday gift of dinner at the International Cafe famed for its assortment of rich cuisines from all over the world, before finding a spot to watch the evening float procession. At the end of the day, they both were exhausted, but there seemed to be some reluctance to end the camaraderie that they had shared. They lingered a little longer as if sensing that this day might also be the end of the free-spirited times of their friendship and uncertainty about where each of their lives would take them.

When Sherlyn dropped Jas back at her flat, she remarked, "Jas, you come back after you've finished this course. Don't you be going and finding some handsome guy over in Canada and forgetting about those of us back home."

"I don't think you have much fear of anything like that happening. My brothers would never forgive me if I didn't give them an opportunity to check out a potential future husband and give their stamp of approval. I'm not going there for a relationship. I'm going to enter the world of business." She smiled.

"Ah, but love works in mysterious ways, and sometimes it interferes with the best plans we've all made." Sherlyn laughed. "But seriously, I'm going to miss you terribly and want you to promise to write as often as you can. All I can say for now is best of luck, Jas—to both of us."

25

Hassan reflected on his growing distaste for Jordan Connors as he read the notice of decision that had found him to be a convention refugee and a person in need of protection. Although he was pleased with the result, he was quite annoyed that Connors had delayed his original hearing date as he recalled the man's actions the night before his first scheduled hearing.

At the last minute, Jeanine had called claiming that her boss was too sick to attend and that Hassan would have to stop by the office early the next morning for a letter to present at the hearing. Hassan fretted and worried as he imagined all sorts of possibilities for this delay. He surmised that Connors might be in cahoots with someone, perhaps that Russ Norman guy, in the government, trying to delay the hearing.

Despite Noe's assurances that delays happened for numerous reasons, he had worried continually until the hearing was over. During this time, he avoided contact with any of the other members of his cell for fear that if the Canadians had discovered something about him, they might bring down the whole operation. He even kept his distance from Hamid at the school campus, alerting him to the possibility that there could be a problem.

The weeks of waiting kept him mostly in isolation, but he welcomed the opportunity to fine-tune some of the intricate details of the operation. Occasionally, he felt a little starved for some companionship and made contact with Noe for a meal. Thinking about Noe's newborn son, Hassan realized that he had come to enjoy these visits. His cousin had done well. Hassan's Islamic faith led him to believe that a son represented security of his father's lineage.

He further believed that a child is an extension of his father throughout his life, and when he dies the child will continue to represent his father's prior existence and give him immortality. In Islam, it was common knowledge that a son inherited all of his mental qualities and traits from his father. Thinking back to a time several years before, Hassan recalled how he too had hopes for the immortality of a son, but it had not happened. He accepted that it had been the wisdom of Allah and that he had a different calling.

Hassan spent hours at the library researching the targeted areas that the organization was concentrating their efforts on. He had been amazed and thankful at the amount of information that was publicly available. Giv had taken some excellent shots around the Hoover Dam, and he examined them carefully for potential vulnerabilities but decided that it was too risky.

At the end of Hajj, Hassan celebrated Eid al-Adha by attending prayers at the mosque with Noe's family. They watched the Eid al-Adha parade arranged by the Muslim community and attending a lecture and buffet dinner at a fund-raiser. The events had raised his spirits during his lonely existence. Hassan believed that Allah had condoned his behavior when a few days after Eid al-Adha ended, Connors divulged that Hassan had been deemed eligible for a simplified refugee hearing process.

Apparently, this meant that some claimants were selected for priority processing of their claims in an expedited manner. Noe explained that nationals from selected parts of the world were from countries that the Canadian government viewed as posing a humanitarian concern. Iran, his homeland, was one of those countries on the current list that had been identified as being high risk for their own people.

When Hassan pressed Noe about what "high risk" meant, he shrugged and sought an explanation from Connors. Noe translated that the government developed policies directing their employees to go easier on refugee claimants from certain parts of the world. He repeated that it was often because foreign governments felt that a particular country's police or judicial system appeared to be nonfunctional, undemocratic or ineffective. Connors had assured Noe and Hassan that this was good news. Iran was such a country.

He really disliked the lawyer despite what Noe or anyone else thought of him. Initially, Noe told Connors that Hassan was upset because he was concerned by the change in the hearing procedure. However, Connors reassured him that Canada was getting too many claims for asylum and trying to find a way to manage it. They were fast-tracking cases from particular countries that the judges had given high rates of acceptance.

Instead of a formal hearing, he was scheduled for a half-hour interview with an employee who would complete a report and make a recommendation to the judge. Neither party would necessarily have any formal legal training. If the officer thought he was credible, he wouldn't have to appear before the actual decision-maker. Hassan felt that Connors was a poor advocate and that his fate depended on the story that he himself had authored. As long as Connors didn't change or try to embellish anything, he figured his story provided little opportunity for anyone to question his credibility.

Hamid had suggested that the less information that he provided to both the Canadian government and Connors, the less likely they could disprove any part of his claim and trap him. It was simply just a game, Hassan later thought as he listened to Connors make one reference to the contents of the documents provided by the officer about conditions in Iran for members of his faith during the course of the interview.

Connors acted surprised by how quickly his hearing had been scheduled. He stated that he thought that he had been given a security clearance rather quickly. The security issue was rather interesting to Hassan. No one had interviewed him, apparently no input was required from him, and it appeared that it was solely based on the minimal information he had provided them on the forms and during the interview when making his claim for asylum.

Who gave these so-called security clearances? He asked. He was told that it was an organization that was called CSIS, the Canadian Security and Intelligence Service. How their information was gathered seemed to be a mystery to everyone. Astonishingly, the entire session had taken less than an hour. The interview itself was restricted to a discussion of the information he had provided on his arrival, and fortunately there had been no surprises.

After making an affirmation to tell the truth, Hassan had been asked a total of about a dozen questions. The female officer simply canvassed some basic information and had examined his identity documents. In the end, he seemed satisfied that his story was truthful, and he was whom he claimed to be. An interpreter had done pretty much all of the talking for Hassan and appeared to be sympathetic to his claim, sometimes adding stronger words to his translation.

The officer asked why he was claiming status, and he told them that his family were members of the Bahá'í faith whom the government thinks spy for Israel. He emphasized that the political authorities in Iran think that religious gatherings of their members spread hatred and lies against the leadership of the country. He was quick to add that it wasn't true.

Hassan passionately told that the government had tortured many people of his faith, imprisoned them in horrible conditions, and executed some of their leaders. He concluded by telling them that his parents' home was burned down, and they had been missing for many, many months because his father was considered to be one of the leaders in their community.

"Did you go to any police authority or complaint bureau in your country?" the officer had asked.

He thought that the question was incredibly stupid and grudgingly said, "How could I? The people who do those things are all part of the government. They would have likely taken me for immediate execution had I done so."

"Can't you go anywhere else in your own country and be safe?" she replied.

Hassan knew that the question was meant to address her concerns that he might have an "internal flight alternative" somewhere that was safe for him in Iran that the government wouldn't bother him. All part of their standard questions.

"My family, if any of them are alive, are all marked. I would be hunted down. I couldn't work or go to anyone for food or money as they would be tracking everyone who knew me. The government runs the country. There is nowhere I could go safely, and if I stayed, it would bring great danger to those around me."

Finally, Connors opened his mouth to say that the documents concerning "country conditions" indicated that there was a great deal of persecution of the members of the Bahá'í faith.

"What do followers of your religion believe in that has caused the government to want to destroy your religion?" she continued.

"Our people follow the teachings of Bahá'u'lláh. He taught us that all of humanity are like branches of a tree, and we are one. Peace on earth will come with a new world order under one leadership and a common language to all of humanity. The new order will provide balance and harmony to furnish the needs of all people. No one will hunger and be overburdened with responsibility."

"I see. Is there anything else?" the woman had stated, but Hassan knew that she didn't understand at all. He didn't even understand the religion, but he aptly continued to confuse her.

"All persons shall be equally entitled to education, including both men and women. No one should dictate religion, but rather all of humanity should look for a common understanding of religious values grounded by scientific verification. My government feels that we threaten their power, but mankind is beginning to recognize this need throughout the world and is also working in this direction through the organization that is called the United Nations," Hassan responded passionately.

The woman had asked a few silly questions about his documents, and he was thanked for coming to the hearing. As they were about to leave, Connors advised him that he would have the result in about six weeks and then quickly went his own way for the day. Hassan felt relieved. In retrospect, he had put his school plans on hold and fretted needlessly while Jordan Connors had walked away with a quick and easy five grand.

It made absolutely no sense to him why the government didn't just let people come and go as they pleased. Tear down the borders. It would save a lot of money that could be better used in providing food, shelter, and clothing to the needy. There were so many people who were left impoverished and uneducated, while the politicians protected their imaginary borders—borders that had perpetuated wars and caused men to fight over these imaginary man-made obstacles.

He believed that propagandists really bullied and mislead the average person. People were fed crap to mask the greed and egos of a relatively small group of men throughout the world. Long ago, he had decided that one country wasn't really any different from any other except one might appear to be democratic while another might be seen as a dictatorship. This greed for wealth and power was the real cause of so much bloodshed.

When Hassan arrived home, he carefully folded the document and placed it in his lockbox with all his important papers and glanced at his watch. It was just after two o'clock. If he left now, he probably could get a message off to Nazreh from the library computer and catch Hamid at the end of his classes, assuring both of the men of his successful hearing.

Hamid had recently begun a three-year program in chemical engineering technology, and Hassan was eager to know how it was going. As Hassan headed out the door, he wondered whether Hamid's function in conjunction with the overall operation would be enhanced or hurt by his field of study. He hoped that now they could move forward with the real work that he had come to Canada to accomplish, but he was cautious about tipping off anybody that might begin to put two and two together.

Most of their discussions to date had been cautious, and no one, including himself, had shared details about the operation known to them. He had figured that when the time was right, he would eventually have to share more of the intricate details of the overall plan, but everyone had been content to play along, knowing that they were following Bahrami's instructions.

26

After retrieving her luggage, Jas scanned the arrivals lounge, eagerly looking for a sign with the words "Douglas College," which a "welcomer" from the college would be holding. She was exhausted from her long journey with the four-hour layover in Hawaii; however, she was excited about the opportunity to meet someone from Canada. Suddenly she saw a placard bearing the name of the college, and her eyes travelled upwards meeting the eyes of a young Middle Eastern woman, probably about her age.

Noticing the jeans that the woman wore, she felt slightly overdressed in her customary casual business pants with its smartly tailored jacket. She had boldly complemented it with a bright satin red blouse that was obviously not the attire of a student in this country. However, she had never been one to wear jeans. The woman was petite with a rounded face, light complexion, honey-brown eyes that were accented by her bushy brows. The soft waves of her shoulder-length hair provided some life to its mousy brown color. She didn't appear to wear any make-up, and her lips were naturally an envious luscious red.

"Dana?" she asked.

"Yes, you must be Jaslyn. Welcome to Canada. This is another student, Hamid, who kindly agreed to accompany me today to help with your luggage. Do you have much?" the young woman cheerily remarked.

Jas shyly looked at the other student, and she could sense his discomfort. She was curious how he had been coerced into lending a hand. She noted that, despite his moustache and uneven chin beard, they made for a striking looking couple. He was handsome, tall, and thin, with piercing dark chocolate-brown eyes that were almost black. Jas thought that perhaps they *were* a couple, and that was what had induced him to come. Whatever the reason she was grateful that they both came, and she heaved a sigh of relief that there were some fresh hands to deal with her belongings.

"Well, thank you both for coming. Please call me Jas," she replied demurely. "I am sure you will be relieved to know that I don't have much luggage, but I am a little tired from my long journey and sincerely appreciate your assistance."

"Hamid isn't an official member of the greeting committee, but I found him working at the college and enlisted his help when no one else from our group was able to make it in today. We have encountered a rather bad storm outside, so I am also indebted to him," Dana revealed.

"No problem, glad I can be useful." Hamid shrugged.

The trio headed toward the parking garage, and the icy cold reality of a Canadian winter hit Jas. The wind was howling, and the snow was coming down so hard that it stung her cheeks as small beads of ice hit her face. She was glad that her brothers had the foresight to give her some warm clothing for Christmas, anticipating her inexperience with this type of weather. Temesekia was located close to the equator, and it had a tropical climate.

She discovered by reading the weather forecasts that the west coast of Canada enjoyed uniform temperatures year-round, though it was normally very wet. One of the magazines on the plane predicted a lot of rainfall, yet it carefully noted that Vancouver also occasionally had heavy snowfalls. It was just her luck that she had arrived on one of those days.

With the horrendous weather conditions, the traffic was backed up, and it took the students almost two hours to reach their destination, an all-girls rooming house, inhabited by college students similarly situated to Jas. The rooming house was reasonably priced, and the operator provided breakfast for the students during the school week for an extra fifty dollars a month.

On the weekends, she would be on her own, but Jas thought that it still made good economic sense and would help her stick within her budget as she had purchased a meal plan from the school as well. Dana had come over on Friday and picked up the main-door key and another one to room number 5, which would be her home for the duration of her stay. Dana also handed her a set of instructions titled *Rules of Tenancy*, which the landlord had given her.

The house was silent when they entered except for the soft sound of music playing somewhere down a long and narrow hall. She noted a large bulletin board in the dingy hallway just after entering the building. It had a bright-red "No Smoking" sign posted on it and directly underneath a black-and-yellow sign that read "No Male Visitors Beyond This Point," emphasizing that this was the biggest "sin" that one might commit in the house.

Glancing at the sign, Hassan assured the women, "I guess this is the end of the road for me. I'll just leave you to settle in. I can make my own way home. Nice meeting you, Jas. Perhaps we'll see each other around the college."

Jas smiled and then hastily appealed to his familiarity with the neighborhood and the probability that he was knowledgeable about the local restaurants.

"Since it's Sunday and they don't have meals here, Hamid, do you know a good eating place nearby? I'm not sure I could handle North American food, but I often eat Muslim cuisine."

"We all need to get some sustenance. Why don't we all go," Dana quickly responded, "I'm sure Hamid's not in any rush in this weather, and I know of a quaint Lebanese café that's not too far away. At their prices, there's nothing too fancy, mind you, but I'm sure we'll find something palatable on the menu, and it's only about a block away."

They agreed that it was a good idea to share a meal, and Hamid went out to the small front porch to wait for the girls. Peering through the falling snow, he happened to notice Hassan crossing the road and heading his way.

"Where are you heading off to on a day like today?" Hamid called out.

"What else? Looking for something to eat. What are you doing over this way?" countered Hassan.

"One of my chemistry lab classmates is on the hospitality committee, and she needed some help in picking up a new foreign student at the airport. Everyone else in the welcoming committee didn't get in today because of the storm. We bumped into each other, and she talked me into lending a hand. But, my friend, you're in luck. If you'd like some company, we're all going out for a bite to eat at a spot that's nearby. Why don't you join us? It would do you some good to come out for a change."

At that precise moment, both of their eyes riveted toward the sounds coming from the door as Dana stepped onto the porch. She was immediately followed by the most beautiful young woman that Hassan had ever seen. She was petite and exceptionally proportioned with dark, black bewitching eyes. She had long, silky, healthy-looking black hair, and velvet brown leather-toned skin. Hassan felt as if someone had thrown him a sucker punch. He couldn't take his eyes off her.

Jas looked into the steel-blue eyes of the newcomer and also immediately felt a physical attraction like nothing she had ever known. When he flashed a smile at her, it reached the corners of his eyes emphasizing a glint that ignited sparks of interest into the mysteries of the man. He exhibited straight white teeth, closely cropped hair, and a small dimple on his cheek that gave him a contrasting boyish charm. She could have sworn that her heart had stopped beating as she experienced a tingling sensation throughout her entire body. For the first time in her life, she felt an emotional response to a member of the opposite sex that was so powerful that she was unsure of how to control it. It was as if she had met her soul mate. Jas had almost forgotten that they were not the only persons present.

Hamid quickly introduced Hassan as a fellow student at the college to both of the girls. Jas gave a slight smile in a demure manner, and with a musical lilt in her voice that he loved so much, she said, "Oh, just call me Jas."

"Hassan was just heading out for something to eat, and I suggested he join us," murmured Hamid.

"Oh yes, please do, I know a nice Lebanese café nearby that's not too expensive if you'd care to join us," remarked Dana.

Without taking his eyes from Jas, Hassan replied, "Great. Sounds good."

During the course of the next couple of hours, Hassan learned that Jas had come to Canada to study at the Douglas College in the computer technology program, which was starting in a few days. He felt overjoyed that they probably would be seeing a lot more of each other as that was also his field of study. Suddenly, he felt a growing enthusiasm for the classes to begin. This was a chance meeting that he hoped to take to another level.

Hold on, he thought, could it be because he had been without a woman for so long? No. She was not only a vision to behold, but she was also refreshing yet very modest the way a woman should be. In fact, she was breathtaking, and her smile was intoxicating. She was definitely not the type of woman that you'd use just to satisfy your passions. He relished the idea of getting to know her better over the next few months. He'd bide his time, but he knew she was a person of special interest.

As Jas sat and enjoyed her dinner, she was well aware of the man sitting opposite her. Although he wasn't much taller than herself and quite thin, she noted that he took care of his body. His close fitting black turtleneck revealed the contours of his broad shoulders and well-developed upper body that narrowed to his trim waist. Throughout the evening, she felt his quiet presence stirring newfound emotions. The little conversation they had engaged in had been interesting. It was particularly fueled by his shared interest in computer technology and that he too was enrolled in many of the same courses she would be taking at the college. She felt her nipples harden every time she looked into those compelling cold, hard eyes that continued to overpower her senses and inner thoughts.

They were just getting acquainted really, but she observed that he had become slightly startled when she revealed that she came from the island of Temesekia. She wondered if it had any significance to him, but she was careful not to intrude on his privacy. All in good time, she hoped he might reveal more of himself, but she noted he was quite withdrawn about himself, and he seemed just to want to know everything that he could learn about her.

Later that night, each reflected on their meeting with each other. Their instantaneous attraction had been both mutual and overwhelming. Jas had never felt anything like it before. She lay in her bed, drifting into a euphoric mesmerizing trance where she envisioned that this man was exactly whom she been waiting for all her life. At the same time, Hassan similarly couldn't stop thinking about the extraordinary woman he had the good fortune to encounter as he too fought to sleep amid the continuous images of Jas floating in his dreams.

27

Russ honked the horn as he settled in Corby's driveway. He looked forward to spending the weekend up at his cabin and hearing the latest gossip from the airport. It had been nothing but record snowfalls this past winter, but even then Kootenay Lake was always ice free with superb fishing year-round. It was a still a little chilly from the colder winter, but he always enjoyed these little excursions with Corby, and it wouldn't take long to get the fire burning.

"Hey, how's it going, old man?" Corby greeted him as he hauled his gear into the back of the car.

"Who are you talking to? I'm a long way off being an old man yet," countered Russ with a chuckle.

"Oh yeah, that's right, I keep forgetting that you just started a new career. How's it going anyway? Have you learned anything new?"

"It's good. I've learned some new things such as surveillance and stakeout techniques. The work involves nasty little matters like child custody, false insurance claims, and employee theft. I stay away from the lovers' triangles, though. Those situations can get downright dirty."

"Sounds as if it could be interesting, though."

"We're just gearing up for employment background checks for companies hiring students for the summer, and there's an assortment of people looking for missing persons who generally don't want to be found. The employment checks can be time-consuming. It's all good, though. Makes life intriguing and the company have been doing such a brisk business that Katy and Kendrick have finally decided to tie the knot."

"That's great, Russ. Give them my congratulations. Anytime soon?"

"Matter of fact, they've planned it for the end of the month. Just a simple ceremony at city hall with a very short honeymoon. They're both so busy these days, it's about all they can manage. Hopefully, with my help in the business, this time next year I'll finally have a grandchild to brag about."

"Sounds as if you've got your hands full; I hope you're not overdoing it, though. It's time that you enjoy yourself a little. A grandchild sounds like a good idea to help slow you down, at least for a couple of years."

"Funny enough, the job keeps me busy, but I truly am enjoying myself. The stakeouts can be really tricky. First one, I did I really screwed up. I'd been sitting in my car watching this house trying to see if I could check out the legitimacy of a WorkSafeBC compensation claim. I'd actually been there for a few days. I didn't think about the kid's schoolyard a few doors down the street, and it seems someone thought I was a pervert looking for an opportunity to grab some kid. Before I knew what hit me, I was surrounded by cops who were even more suspicious when they saw my camera equipment."

"Oh, shit! You must have just about pissed yourself," Corby managed to say between his gales of laughter.

"Yeah, well, it took some explaining, but eventually I think they were actually a little sympathetic when I told them it was the first time that I'd done a surveillance job. One of the cops suggested to me that it sometimes helps to keep the little old ladies out walking their dogs happy if you just sit in the passenger side of the car as though you're waiting for someone. Then another wise guy piped up and said women were generally considered less of a threat, and I might try to dress like one the next time."

"Christ, I guess you don't want to do those jobs anymore?" Corby smirked.

"Actually, I really enjoy the insurance claim investigations to get a break from some of the office routine stuff. Had no idea there was so much insurance fraud going on. Gets me out and about. Did enough paperwork before, and the employment checks involve hours of it. How about you? Anything new at the airport?"

"Well, there was an interesting development in that big drug bust that involved the baggage handler that happened on your last week. After Judd had received word from you about running into him in Hong Kong, they reexamined the video surveillance at the rear door that he'd used to transfer the goods to the dealers. They now think that the guy you saw with the employee might be the guy the caught on the video."

"No shit? I thought that they had found the tape was useless because of the weather conditions."

"It's pretty blurry, and it isn't good enough to make a positive ID. You've got to remember, they don't know how many people were inside that van. The only thing they got was a hazy view of a man at the side door while he loaded the goods. When those two guys blew themselves up, everyone thought the criminals were all accounted for."

"I wonder if it is him." Russ dragged his hands through his hair. "Then the question is, how the hell he got away?"

"Your information took a few people by surprise, Russ. The guys in Hong Kong took the photo we had of El Safty along with your description of the second guy and got some assistance from the authorities over there. They checked outgoing flights the afternoon you spotted them, and an employee at Qatar Airlines thought they might have boarded a plane to Dubai. They found a match on the passenger list names for El Safty."

"Interesting, what about his companion?" Russ muttered.

"They came up with another name of a passenger seated beside him that matched your description."

"Christ, don't keep me in suspense. Who the hell is he?"

"According to his passport, he's a Pakistani national named Khurram Noorani, but Pakistan has confirmed that the passport was fraudulent."

"Son of a bitch!"

"We checked the federal operating system and found a foreign student by that name. He got a visa in Islamabad, and he recently dropped out of the college. Nothing else of any use," Corby continued. "Speaking of college students, I have a scoop about the guy you escorted over to detention on your last shift. Do you recall the Iranian fellow that we dealt with that same night?"

"Oh yeah, I remember. Zadeh was the name. Hassan Zadeh." He couldn't seem to get away from the guy.

"Yeah, that's him. Judd lifted a fingerprint off his Iranian identity card, and on a hunch, he sent it over to Homeland Security in the US. Seems that the owner of the fingerprint is on some kind of watch list there. Some guy in the States requested a whack of information on him from the boys in Intel. The name doesn't match, though, and we can't match our guy to the print that was lifted."

"Have they got pictures of their guy?"

"Judd sent pictures from Zadeh's file down, and it turns out they're waiting for photos from another country where the guy is on their radar. Judd says this may be really big stuff."

"Ah, still no fingerprints on Zadeh?"

"Not yet. The asshole got refugee status, but they caught him off guard, and they've called him in for an interview regarding his permanent resident application. They're going to surprise him and try to get prints."

Russ let out a low whistle. "Finally. I can't see how he can refuse under those circumstances."

"I hope we've got a chance to at least pin him down on his ID, if nothing else. But you also know that if he's using a phony identity, then chances are there's more to this guy than meets the eye."

"It's interesting you'll have to let me know if they get anything else on him. Anyway, that's enough shop talk for now! Let's just enjoy the weekend. I plan to catch me a couple of nice rainbows. Did you remember to get your fishing license renewed?"

"Of course, I did. I got it three weeks ago, you're not the only one who needs some relaxation, and for sure I'm law-abiding." Corby laughed. "Oh, but there's one more thing I wanted to tell you. Transport Canada has a big fiasco going on right now."

"How so?"

"The US got a tip at one of their airports that the cleaning contractor they were using had more than a hundred illegal immigrants employed who were cleaning both the terminals and the planes. Apparently they were using forged papers to get their jobs. The illegals got security passes from the company, and they could pretty much get in anywhere."

"This contracting out can be dangerous. The unions here have been fighting with the government about this for a while now, but the damn politicians are so frigging naive, and our management just keeps trying to please them with condescending approval of their cost-cutting measures."

"Well, the Americans tipped our guys off, and we ended up conducting a similar investigation at all the major airports in Canada. We've found a few in our terminals, and so did Montreal, Halifax, and Toronto. Just goes to show you, you don't know whom the guy standing next to you might be."

"Did we have any immigration files on any of them?"

"Nope. Don't ask me how they got in the country. They're all here illegally. Some guys were from Southeast Asia, and they've now put in refugee claims. There was another one from Kuwait who decided to leave and return home because he said the problems over there have settled down. I was over at the detention center the day they were arranging his departure, and you won't believe who brought his passport in?"

"Don't tell me. Was it Zadeh?" Russ exclaimed.

"Nope, but you're close. It was the guy that acted as a surety for Zadeh. I think he was Zadeh's cousin."

Russ let out another low whistle. "Now how did the cleaner explain his relationship to him?"

"Apparently the cousin works near the guy's home, and he claims to have met him at the mosque a few times. He added he didn't know many people and anyone else whom he could call."

"Sounds as if you guys have been busy with this bunch. I don't trust anyone connected to Zadeh. That's what happens with privatization. Most of these contract employers are small-time operators and don't have connections to do too much in the way of screening the guys they employ. Did you get any of their names?"

"Yeah, I think the employer was pretty shocked because each one of these guys had provided phony immigration or identity papers and had somehow managed to get legitimate social insurance numbers. So their contractor can't be held responsible. They managed to produce passports, which we sent over to Intelligence to authenticate. Three of them have already been removed from the country, including Sammi, uh...the Kuwaiti."

"How have you been doing otherwise, my friend? How's your mom these days?" Russ asked.

"To tell you the truth, I'm not sure if she's gone senile, or she's just lonely. She's got herself a boyfriend."

"You don't say. Well, good for her. Where'd she meet him?"

"At church. Other than the grocery store, it's the only place she ever goes."

"Be happy for her, Corby. It's time you found yourself a partner, too."

"I know, I've been thinking about it. Say, Russ, can I ask you something confidentially?"

"Sure, Corby, you know my lips are sealed."

"You won't laugh at me?"

"Nah, what kind of foolish talk is that? Fire away."

"You know that club the guys took me to for my birthday," Corby said hesitantly, "are what those girls do legal?"

Russ almost burst out laughing but caught himself just in time before he solemnly answered, "Of course, it's legal. Those establishments are all licensed. Why do you ask?

"No particular reason. I was just curious, that's all."

Russ decided not to push the matter. What did you know, it looked like a sleeping dog had been roused. Obviously, it was a hard topic for Corby to discuss, but if he felt like it, Russ would be a good listener. For now, he changed the subject to talk of the fishing weekend ahead.

28

Over the next four months, Jas, Dana, Hamid, and Hassan became close friends. They each had found a study mate in their respective field of studies and some comfortable companionship. But for Jas and Hassan, there was an extra little spark that seemed to draw them close to each other. Occasionally, they went for long walks exploring the city. Even when they were separated, they sent e-mails back and forth, mostly sharing little humorous experiences, short poems, and their hopes for the future. Most importantly, Hassan conveyed his belief in Jas and offered her encouragement and support to achieve her ambitions. Hamid and Dana didn't pursue a deeper relationship beyond their friendship, but Dana and Jas had also formed a bond as had Hamid and Hassan.

Early in the new year, Dana and Hamid began looking for summer employment. They sorely needed to make some money to help get them through the next year of schooling. Hassan and Jas had both decided to accelerate their study programs when the college offered some of the computer courses over an eight-week spring semester, after which Jas planned a trip home, and Hassan hoped that he would find some work.

It seemed like no time before the semester was over. While Dana had found a half-decent job, Hamid had no such luck. Although he was disappointed, toward the middle of May, a frustrated Hamid informed Hassan that he was going to visit a friend in Victoria who knew of some work on Vancouver Island he could get with another friend. He said that he'd see everyone at the end of August. Jas and Hassan continued at the college until the end of June, becoming inseparable as their relationship flourished. It was obvious to any observer that the two were falling in love.

Jas reluctantly left for home at the end of July. She felt compelled to visit her brothers for a few weeks before classes resumed for the fall semester. She was also eager to tell her family and Sherlyn about the man who had won her heart. She had known that she was going to miss Hassan dreadfully and promised to contact him once a week until she got back.

She was unaware that two days after she left, Hassan had made plans of his own and joined Hamid in Victoria. Jas knew nothing about his desire to go out of town and tried to contact him repeatedly as she had promised while on vacation. She became increasingly anxious that something had happened to him as she hadn't been able to connect with him once since leaving Canada.

Nearing the end of her vacation, she was almost desperate to return, just so she could reassure herself that he was safe. Inwardly, she was confident that everything was okay, and they were just failing to hook up. She talked about him incessantly to her brothers, sister-in-law, and Sherlyn. She neglected to see their growing apprehension about the stranger who had captured her heart.

Two days before she left the island, she finally connected with Hassan, who pretended that he had been doing odd jobs to make some money. He scoffed at the imaginary menial tasks and long hours that he had endured and apologized for missing her calls. The sparkle returned to Jas's eyes after her brief conversation. Her brothers recognized that Jas was hopelessly in love and inwardly worried that she might permanently leave the island.

Colin's and Patrick's concerns were an eerie premonition of the events that were about to unfold. Shortly after they were reunited in the fall, Hassan asked Jas to marry him. He had applied for permanent resident status, and he explained that as his wife, he would be permitted to add her to his application.

They could become permanent residents of Canada at the same time. He reasoned that they would be graduating soon, and they agreed that they wanted to stay together. In the meantime, Hassan had rationalized they could pool their expenses, minimizing them to prepare for a better future together.

It all made so much sense, and a deeply in love Jas couldn't imagine refusing. She decided that it was better not to include her brothers in her wedding plans for fear of their disapproval. They arranged a quiet ceremony with Dana, Hamid, Noe, and Maryam present. After it was over, they all gathered for a small lunch at the new sparsely furnished flat Jas and Hassan had rented and had already begun moving their belongings into.

Jas decided to wait until her next visit with her family to tell them about her marriage in person. Hassan informed her that he didn't have any relatives other than Noe to invite. Hassan had also revealed that he thought all of his immediate family might have all perished at the hands of the Iranian government, and she sympathetically accepted everything he told her.

Jas had been shocked when a few days before her marriage, Hassan confided in her that he had once lived, worked, and married in Temesekia. He complained that his wife's family had interfered in the marriage from the beginning, and it had been a bitter experience. He revealed that his former wife's brothers began to make false accusations against him to alienate his wife, and they constantly were encouraging the Temesekian authorities to investigate him for no reason. He assured her that after they were divorced, he had no further problems. It was all in the past, and now he wanted to forget that part of his life and live for her to accept who he was now.

In the following weeks, Hassan further disclosed that he would never go back to either Iran or Temesekia again. Jas, reluctantly, accepted his statements without explanations and realized that discussions about his past were taboo.

She hoped that time would heal his wounds and that eventually he would come with her to Temesekia to meet her family. Their lives fell into a routine pattern with their shared studies, visits to the mosque, and occasional outings with Dana and Hamid or Noe and Maryam. Jas continued focusing on her career objectives, and Hassan occasionally offered her some excellent suggestions for improving her software.

He understood her need for her own space and obliged her by going off to do his own thing with Hamid. They never argued, and he was always accommodating in every way. He made her feel like a princess, and every day he told her how much he loved her. It was a blissful and dreamlike existence, and she thought her whole life couldn't have turned out better. She was sure that it was destiny that had brought them together, and he was her soul mate.

When the winter break came during the Christmas season, she made excuses to her brothers that this year, she would be staying in Canada because of her study load. Being a newlywed, she truly just wanted to be with her husband, and she hadn't yet told her brothers about her marriage because she wanted to break the news in person. She promised that she would see them at the spring break and told them not to worry.

Jas had been working in the school administrative offices, but she was paid hourly, and the college was closed half the month of December. It was a welcome surprise when family sent her a generous gift of money during the Christian holidays, to the tune of almost five thousand dollars. The money was certainly going to come in extremely handy in the months ahead and make things a little more comfortable for them.

The forecasts predicted that it was going to be a bad winter, much worse than the previous year. They were more than grateful to have the money to buy the few articles of warmer clothing that each of them greatly needed. Neither one of them had yet adjusted to the cruel harshness of winter weather that came to this part of the world.

During the holidays, they also splurged a little to offer their small circle of family and friends a dinner that both Dana and

Maryam helped Jas plan. As Hassan and their friends did not celebrate the Christmas holiday, Jas had felt a twinge of remorse for the loss of a custom that had always been typically filled with family and happiness. However, she adjusted to the Muslim celebrations and enjoyed their traditions as she regularly attended the mosque now.

The winter semester at the college was grueling. For several weeks, they spent hours locked away in their separate study quarters completing assignments and preparing for exams. Time flew by, and before she knew it, Jas was eagerly looking forward to the trip home to Temesekia for her planned spring visit.

She genuinely wanted Hassan to join her, but even though she knew that they couldn't afford it, she sheepishly raised the question. He fielded it easily by explaining that he didn't have a valid passport. Although he'd had an interview for permanent resident status in Canada, he would have to get a special travel document if he wanted to leave the country before he became a Canadian citizen and was eligible for a passport.

She'd be so happy when the day came that he had his Canadian citizenship, and they could travel together. On the positive side, she was close to completing her courses, and she was confident that they had a bright future ahead of them. Hamid and Dana were madly scrambling to get in job applications again for the summer, hoping to land a job in their fields of study. Little did she suspect that this was actually the calm before the storm!

29

When the plane finally touched down in Temesekia, Jas was exhausted. This time she was glad that she had the six-hour layover in Hawaii. She had pampered herself and rented a day restroom for a few hours. She didn't want to worry her brothers that she was in anything but the best of health.

Jas hated hurrying to change planes and worrying about her luggage with little opportunity to sleep. She found it both uncomfortable and tiring. It felt good to be home, she thought as she headed off the plane and down the ramp. However, two uniformed officers suddenly approached her and peremptorily inquired, "Ms. Koh? Jaslyn Koh?"

"Yes?" she hesitantly replied.

"Come this way, please," commanded one of the officers as he took her arm.

She was led down a corridor to a room where several persons were gathered awaiting her arrival. Her government was exceedingly strict about what you brought into the country, and Jas could think of nothing in her luggage that might have prompted this reception, so she became a little worried that they were bearing bad news about her family.

She nervously looked about the room and obeyed when she was invited to take a seat but declined the glass of water she was offered. The person seated at the center of the round table began with some alarming introductions of the four people in the room who were from the Ministry of Internal Affairs. He began by introducing himself as the assistant director of the Home Front Security Division, Mr. Kwan.

Having worked in the legal profession, Jas knew from the introductions that these were some of the highest-echelon bureaucrats in the country. One would expect that they would only be involved in extremely serious matters of concern to the government with respect to issues of national security. She was flabbergasted that they had summoned her to a meeting.

"Ms. Koh, we'd like to ask you a few informal questions about your recent trip to Canada. Specifically why were you in Canada?" the questioning began.

"I went to attend school and further my education."

"Why not attend school here? You have a degree from the National University, do you not?"

"Yes, but I hope to obtain further qualifications. My future plans involve work with foreign markets. Nothing illegal but extending my training to be able to develop a product for those markets in English-speaking countries."

"There are many other English-speaking countries like Australia, New Zealand, or the United Kingdom. What attracted you to Canada?"

"Canada has the lowest tuition fees for international students, and there's a good-sized population from Asian countries. I was very nervous about going to the United States by myself, and Canada has a lot of foreign students from all over the world. I thought that the products I'd like to design would reach the large North American market from a Canadian base. Why do you ask?"

Mr. Kwan had been toying with a folder in front of him, and he slowly pulled out some photographs that he pushed toward her. They were utterly beautiful shots of Hassan.

"Do you know this man?" he queried.

"Yes, he is my husband."

"What is his name?"

"Hassan Zadeh."

"When did you meet him?"

"I met him on my first day in Canada. Why?"

"How did you meet him?"

"Two students picked me up at the airport from the college's hospitality committee. He was a friend of one of them. We bumped into him as we were going to find a place to eat, and he joined us for dinner."

"Do you know that he is married to another woman?"

"I know that he was married to another woman. They are divorced." Jas calmly shifted in her chair and didn't bat an eye.

"No, Ms. Koh, our records indicate that he is not divorced. As a matter of fact, his wife lives here on the island. He used to live here also. Did you meet him here?"

"I told you that I met him in Canada. He told me that he was married before. He also told me that they were divorced a long time ago. I believe him. You are mistaken."

"Did your brothers know him when he lived here?"

"No, I don't believe so. I don't think my brothers know anything about him yet. I only told them just after I met Hassan that I was seeing someone. I am planning to tell my brothers about him on this trip."

"Does your husband know any of your friends or your former employer here on the island?"

"I don't think so. He's never indicated that he did. Over four million people live on the island, and he said that he lived in the northeast, while I have always lived in the southwest area. Also, he is six years older than I am, so we wouldn't have been likely to be involved with the same people. Why are you asking these questions?"

"What else do you know about this man?" The men ignored her questions and continued with their own.

"I know that he is good and kind. He shares my interests in computer technology and is very interested in helping me to achieve success in my business plan. He loves me, and I love him. He has told me that he is from Iran. He went to Canada to seek protection from the Iranian government. Canada has given it to him. We're planning a new life together."

"Do you know Mahmoud Bahrami?"

"Who? I have never heard this name. Who is this person? The name means nothing to me."

"He lived here in Temesekia."

"My husband has never spoken of him, and I have never met him."

"Your husband is a very dangerous man, Ms. Koh. You shouldn't return to Canada. You need to leave this man—now," Mr. Kwan stated emphatically.

"That is not possible. I don't think he is a dangerous man. With all due respect, I wouldn't leave him on what you are saying, we are expecting a child, and I know that I am in no danger from him. We are happy, and he is very good to me. I think you are mistaken about him. I need to talk with him."

"Listen, my child, you cannot have a family with this man. You are in grave danger. We can help you to make arrangements for an abortion. You should not go back to Canada. You need to forget this man."

Jas was both shocked and totally distraught. She had never heard of the government stepping into the private matters between a husband and his wife, never mind suggesting that someone should abort a baby. She had come home to share the good news of her marriage and the impending birth of her child. She had been so overjoyed with her life and eager to tell her family and friends. Jas found it unbelievable that her government would interfere in her personal life.

Now, her government was telling her that Hassan was a threat to her and that she should destroy the child growing inside her. She was devastatingly appalled at their accusations. She concluded that they were wrong and that they were overstepping their authority. Temesekian authorities had Hassan confused with someone else. She needed to get out of there—now!

"I will think about what you have said. My brother is waiting for me in the terminal. Are we finished?" she boldly demanded.

"Your brothers are outside, Ms. Koh. We would like you to think carefully about what we have told you today. If you require my assistance, this is my card. Our job is to protect the citizens of this country, and we believe that you are in grave danger from this man. We need to stress the importance that you must place on this matter. We are here to help you if you change your mind. That will be all, at least for now."

Jas was shaken. She had never had any personal dealings with the police or the government before. It was strange that such prominent people thought that it was necessary to speak with her today and to suggest the extreme measures that they felt she needed to take to avoid personal danger. She was also embarrassed that they apparently had informed her brothers of their concerns.

She was led out the door where she found both of them anxiously waiting for her. There was a puzzled look in their eyes, and she sensed their unspoken questions. She felt comforted by their presence as if encompassed by a protective embrace. However, she felt disappointed that her joyous news had been snatched from her, and she had no answers why.

30

When Russ got back from his short holiday, he found that Kendrick was swamped with contracts for employee background checks for the upcoming seasonal job market. According to Kendrick, owing to the growing numbers of international students coming to Canada, the demand for employee screening services was increasing at a phenomenal rate.

The college and university students were highly competitive, eager to work, and it appeared that all were looking for summer employment. Most employers sought only very basic information, and the searches were easy to conduct. He checked their identities, civil suits, criminal records, driver's extracts, school, and prior employment records. However, some were not so straightforward, and obtaining information about foreign students was often hit and miss.

His biggest concern was for the jobs that entailed possible exposure to highly sensitive or confidential materials. Some positions required comprehensive security investigations into the prospective employees' backgrounds. Kendrick had thought Russ would be not only interested in doing this work but that he also had a background that gave him a kind of sixth sense of wariness.

As these postings could involve highly sensitive undertakings, he needed someone with both skill and thoroughness. The municipality had been bombarded with applications this year and had contracted Kendrick's firm to do their security screening. This was an important new contract, and he wanted his father-in-law to do the job. He wasn't disappointed when Russ agreed to take on the task.

After several weeks, Russ found himself learning about interesting jobs that he'd actually taken for granted and never thought about before. He was particularly fascinated in a contract for the city that involved two positions for one of the city's water treatment plants. It was one of those places that you knew somewhere in the recesses of your mind existed to ensure the safety of the public water supply, but you usually didn't give it a lot of thought.

He vaguely remembered that he had read about some trouble back in Ontario, a few years ago, where a number of people had gotten very sick, and a couple had died because an E. coli contaminant had leached into a town's well water supply. Generally people just accepted that the Canadian drinking water supply was safe, and they didn't seriously think about the whys and how. In reviewing his screening criteria, it became obvious that the city was pretty cautious about whom they hired and wanted a thorough background check on more than just academic credentials.

There were only about six applicants for two positions. All of them had taken the Douglas College drinking water operator course. The majority of applicants were near completion of the first three levels of the water treatment technology certification, but one applicant, Hamid Al Zain, had been taking some additional online courses from the United States on wastewater treatment.

This guy had excellent grades. However, his background information was insufficient. He'd been born in Kuwait and entered Canada about three years ago. He was found to be a refugee and had been attending the college almost since his arrival. He studied English before getting into his current field of study and had clearly mastered the language to achieve the grades that he had in his certificate program.

His primary reference was a company in Kuwait whose line of business involved sewage treatment. However, there was a note attached to the application indicating that many people had been killed, and he was unaware whether anyone who knew him was still with the company. Russ knew that during the invasion by Iraq, many business records had been destroyed, and many people were killed.

It was an interesting but plausible read, and Russ was unsure what to make of it or whether he should try and contact the company and see what he came up with. According to the application, Hamid didn't have any living relatives, didn't possess a driver's license or credit card, and his only phone appeared to be a pay-as-you-go cell phone because he was living in a student residence.

He had listed a Canadian college professor and a fellow student as his references, but they had only known him since coming to Canada. Russ felt a little frustrated because it was well known that it was difficult to obtain accurate and complete school records from Kuwait. It was also just as likely that he'd obtain limited information from his former employer, so his task was going to be challenging, to say the least. He decided to start by contacting the Canadian references. The student was named Dana Jahel. He was unsure of her relationship with Hamid, but Russ wanted to see what relevant information she might have about the fellow.

It took a few days to make his contacts, and the instructor had provided a superb reference. He then contacted Ms. Jahel, introduced himself, and asked a few basic questions; however, he'd been taken aback when he asked her if Mr. Al Zain had any other friends at the school that might have more information to offer. She stated that because of their student workload, most students didn't have much time for socializing. Then she added that Hamid usually spent his free time with a student by the name of Hassan Zadeh and his wife, Jaslyn, other students whom he had met at the college.

He and Hassan had some friends they met when they were taking English classes that they sometimes got together with, but she didn't know their names as they were no longer attending the school when she had met him. Just as casually, she mentioned that her friend and Mr. Zadeh were currently visiting someone;

she thought his name was Naz and that he lived in Victoria, but she didn't know their host personally. She wasn't very sure of his name or how long they'd known him. Russ thanked her for her time and asked that she keep the reference check confidential. Hanging up the phone, he felt a surge of alarm bells going off in his brain.

It was a small world, he thought as he contemplated the chance meeting that he had previously had with the Iranian guy. Later that night, as he dialed Corby's home number, he thought about the Iranian and what this job applicant, Hamid, might know about him. By the fourth ring, the call hadn't been picked up, so Russ decided to try Corby at work.

"Corby here," roared into his ear.

"Ouch! You must be having a bad day. It's Russ. Sorry to call you at work, but I just stumbled on something of interest that we've shared a few conversations about. You know how I hate coincidences, wondered if you might be up to dropping by for breakfast after your shift, in the morning."

Corby lowered his voice a notch or two. "Sorry about that. You know what a racket there can be around here. Sometimes you have to assert yourself to get heard. Which conversations?"

"Would you believe, our favorite Iranian?"

"Oh, okay, sounds interesting. There's no problem. Should be there before eight o'clock. I'll have scrambled eggs, bacon, toast, and coffee if you're taking orders."

"Sounds good, I think I can manage that. I'll see you then."

After he'd hung up, Russ thought that it might not amount to much, but he didn't like coincidences. The more he thought about it, the more he didn't like the fact that everything came to a dead end on this fellow Zain. He knew darn well he was going to nix the application and validate his decision by reporting that he couldn't obtain enough information from a security standpoint.

It was a legitimate excuse because verification of documents was almost impossible in Kuwait. The Iraqis had destroyed records and obliterated an essential paper trail for many. During the invasion, they had also killed people who could have provided valuable references. Russ would have been very cautious with any applicant under these circumstances; however, he had a gut feeling that, in this particular case, there might be a lot more to this man than met the eye. He was a true man of mystery, and he had lousy taste in his choice of friends.

31

Dana weaved in and out of the heavy traffic in one of the borrowed school vehicles and headed to the airport to pick up her friend. She was anxious to see Jas as both Hamid and Hassan had gone away for the spring break, and she had been quite lonely over the holiday. She was bursting at the seams curious to find out how Jas's family had taken the news of her wedding. Catching sight of Jas, she pulled into the passenger pickup at the arrivals ramp and lowered the window as she called out to get her attention.

"Hi there, how did the trip go?"

"Very tiresome. Even though I love my family, I'm just glad to be back. I thought Hassan might hitch a ride with you to pick me up. I've truly missed him."

"Oh, he went with Hamid to Victoria, and they aren't back yet. They suddenly decided it was too boring without you and up and left the day after you did for a visit to Hamid's former employer. Hassan thought he'd like to see the island. I think I overheard Hamid say that they could stay with a man named Naz or something like that. I'm the only one that didn't have any place to go for a break," Dana responded with a playful pout.

"Victoria? Are you sure? Hassan never mentioned that he went there. I talked to him a few days ago, and he was at home."

"I think they just decided to go on the spur of the moment. They were restless, and boys being boys they just decided to go. I guess they didn't stay long. I hadn't realized that they'd returned. So how did your brothers take the news of your nuptials?"

"They were a little shocked and somewhat disappointed that they didn't get to meet Hassan first. Overall, the trip was okay, but to tell you the truth I'm exhausted."

Jas inwardly thought that was an understatement. She didn't want to divulge details of what had been a harrowing vacation. She had learned that her brothers had also been interrogated, shown pictures of Hassan, and had their business investigated by the Ministry of Internal Affairs. Apparently, the ministry had interviewed Sherlyn and her former employer, too. It was scandalous! In fact, it was more than that. It was an *outrage*, and her head was still reeling from the whole trip.

"That's too bad, Jas. They'll get over it as soon as they see you two together. Everyone can see that you're made for each other. Look, I've got to return the car to the school, so I can't stop for a visit right now. Moreover, you look exhausted. Get some rest, and let's do something tomorrow. It's the start of the new Muslim festival, and it's going to have art, music, and film in my culture that I would really like to share with you."

"Sounds like fun, but I'll have to let you know how I feel tomorrow. You're right, I'm terribly tired from the trip, and I haven't told you the news yet, Dana, but I'm expecting a baby."

"Oh, Jas, that is fantastic. I'm so happy for you. When?"

"Around the end of August. I didn't want to tell you before. I told my family that was the main reason I went home now as I won't be able to travel come the summer. So I had to tell my brothers not only that I was married, but they are also going to be uncles. They were stunned, to say the least. Of course, it didn't take them long to figure out that I would be moving to Canada permanently."

As they turned the corner to her street, Jas spotted Hassan entering the flat. Dana offered to help with the luggage, but Jas waved her off and told her that she had noticed that Hassan was home, and he'd give her a hand. As if on cue, when they pulled up to the curb, he opened the door and stepped out to greet her.

Dana made a hasty exit, letting them have some time together but again suggested that perhaps they could all go to the festival the next day.

Jas glanced at her husband with the shy smile of a woman hopelessly in love; however, she felt her heart beating a mile a minute as she scanned his features for some reassurance that he would make sense of all that had happened. Could he explain these accusations? Had he deceived her, or was her government wrong? She had done nothing but think about this night for the past two weeks, and now that it was here, she was extremely nervous about the responses she would receive.

After settling in the flat, Hassan inquired if she were hungry, but she quickly told him no, she had eaten on the plane. The truth was she needed to talk to him now. It couldn't wait. Until they had this discussion, she knew that she couldn't eat or sleep.

"Did you have a good trip, Jas?" Hassan inquired, sensing that something was amiss.

Jas didn't quite know where to begin. She had so many questions. This latest revelation that he had gone to Victoria without bothering to tell her disturbed her as well. Hadn't he told her just a few days again that he'd been working?

"My trip wasn't good at all. Something very troubling has happened, and we need to talk." Jas didn't believe in mincing words. "I haven't been able to eat or sleep for the whole trip." Then Jas quietly and calmly told him all that had happened and waited for his response. She witnessed the initial shock in his eyes but quickly saw a cold mask and stone-like stare that came over his countenance. It was a look that she had never seen before. She found it disturbing, and it made her shiver.

"Jas, of course, I am divorced. Regardless of what the Temesekian authorities may say, in the eyes of my God, I divorced her long ago. There were witnesses to the divorce ceremony as is customary. I can contact them to clear this mess up if it creates a problem. I don't know why the government of

Temesekia would think this. Perhaps her family is just trying to make trouble for me again. This is preposterous! I'll get to the bottom of it."

Jas believed him. She trusted her husband and accepted all that he said. To her, there was no question of the depth of this man's love for her nor hers for him. He was the love of her life and the father of her unborn child. She was satisfied that this incident had been caused by his former wife's family, and there was no validity to it.

She knew that some people could never let go, and when relationships soured, retaliation by one of the parties often resulted. She had seen many divorce contracts and listened to the lawyers talk about the spiteful actions by one or both parties who weren't ready to move on with their lives. She would not allow this woman or her family to come between her and Hassan nor the love that they shared.

She'd almost forgotten, but she was still curious about his trip to Victoria. "Oh, Dana thought you went to Victoria with Hamid. Did you go away?"

"Yeah, Hamid talked me into it. I'd never been there before, and we just took a boat over for a couple of days and stayed with a friend of his. It was nice. We'll have to go there sometime together. They've got lots of places to go shopping." He laughed. "It's more European style than Vancouver, and it's the capital city of the Province."

"I thought you said you were working," Jas said.

"Yeah, well, we did some work for his friend over in Victoria. He has a print shop, and we helped him out a bit and earned a few dollars. Gosh, it's so hot in his shop I couldn't do that for a living."

Hassan reached for her and gently kissed her until the intensity of their passion exploded, destroying in its wake all uncertainty about the strength of their relationship. After they had made love, they talked about their plans for a new life, in Canada, and the bright future that they would share as a family in this country. She soon forgot about the warnings from the government of Temesekia as if the incident at the airport had never happened. She was also happy that he had got the opportunity for a little vacation too.

32

When classes resumed, Dana approached Hamid to let him know that someone named Mr. Norman from a company called Watchdogz had called her regarding a security check for the water treatment job he had applied for. She advised him that she couldn't provide much information and that she had suggested he might like to call Hassan. Hamid didn't think too much about her revelation until he mentioned to Hassan about the possible reference check.

Hassan was flabbergasted. He wasn't absolutely sure it was the same man, but this Mr. Norman character kept cropping up into his business, and he didn't like it. Every time he heard the man's name, he cringed. The guy had been intruding in his life for more than two years now, and he wouldn't quit. "You can forget about that job." Hassan assumed.

"Why do you say that? My grades are excellent, and my history is unavailable to anyone trying to obtain information. Do you know something that I don't?"

"This guy, his name is Norman, has been tailing everyone in our operation since I arrived in Canada. I don't think he's figured out my connections or what is going on, but I guarantee you, he keeps digging and won't let up. I had the unfortunate opportunity of meeting him when I arrived, and he ordered an investigation on me. He followed Tarik and Khurram in Hong Kong, and I'm sure he was behind Sammi's deportation. If it's the same guy, now that he's got a connection between you and me, he'll be on your case too."

"Damn! I was hoping to learn about the mechanics of their fluoridation program. I think that when the fluoride is put into the water supply, it might provide us with easy access to put in our own additive. Hell, I hope this guy's not as smart as what you seem to think he is. He might start putting two and two together and figure out what our general target is."

"He's smart, all right. No question about it. We're going to have to take him out. I'll contact Iqbal to help with arrangements. We need to get a positive identification, though. If it's the same guy, Norman's days are numbered. I don't want to do it at the airport, though. What I can't figure out is how he got to screen a job application for the city unless he moonlights for this company? Watchdogz did you say?"

"Maybe it's not the same guy. I have a letter that says that this Watchdogz is a private firm who was screening all the applications and references for the summer jobs. Doesn't sound as if it could be connected to your guy if he works at the airport," Hamid hypothesized.

"I'd be willing to bet it's the same guy. Get me a copy of your letter with the name and address of the company that did the screening. I'll get Naz to do some sleuthing."

"Do you think he can find out?"

"He'll call them about hiring some students for the summer and inquire about doing some background screening. Perhaps, he can get the full name of this Mr. Norman. I know the guy at the airport was called Russ. If we get a match, Iqbal can try and get us a picture of the man. I happen to remember what he looks like. I don't ever forget a face."

"Yeah, maybe you're right. He might be connected somehow with this other company. Come on over to my place now, and I'll get you the correspondence I got."

An hour later Hassan spoke with Naz and reiterated the events involving Russ Norman. He supplied him with the company name of the Watchdogz agency and their address as he asked him to do some research of his own about the company and its employees. Within a week, Naz hadn't disappointed him.

He had obtained a mother lode of information and learned that Russ Norman did indeed work for the company. He had retired from his former job and was now working for his son-in-law, Kendrick Freeman. The offices were located in a low-rise complex, in a small plaza centrally located, in Vancouver. He didn't know how Naz had got so much information, but he had been pretty thorough.

Without hesitation, Hassan called Iqbal and ordered him to get some pictures of the employees at Watchdogz. He had a plan on how to arrange for the demise of Norman.

33

Hassan and Jas resumed some degree of normality in their life except that Jas began to have severe bouts of morning sickness, and she struggled to complete the school semester. Neither one mentioned anything further about what had transpired in Temesekia. Instead, they became engrossed in making plans for the baby.

Hamid had held out hope that Hassan had been wrong about his prediction that he wouldn't get the job at the water treatment plant until he received a letter telling him that his security checks could not be completed. Meanwhile, Hassan anxiously awaited word from Iqbal on his efforts to identify Russ Norman from the description that Hassan had provided him with. The sooner they had taken care of the man, Hassan felt the sooner that everyone could get on with the real purpose of their operation in Canada.

Iqbal had taken several photos of older men both entering and exiting the building where Watchdogz were located, but a disappointed Hassan revealed that none of the pictures had been the elusive Mr. Norman. Discussing the problem with Hamid, one afternoon, they had wandered over to the general vicinity of the Watchdogz company when suddenly Hassan caught a glimpse of the elusive Mr. Norman.

"I knew it!" he'd exclaimed as he ducked behind some shrubs. "It is that bastard, and I've devised an ingenious plan to take care of him once and for all."

"How's that?" Hamid inquired.

"You know, I've been thinking Naz could provide us with a facsimile of the letter that you received from the city's HR

Department that could help us get directly to this Mr. Norman," Hassan pondered.

"Go on." Hamid became suddenly interested.

"We could send him a note from them with a little thank-you gift for his recent assistance."

Hamid thought about his failed attempt with the mails in Britain. Government postal workers were on the lookout for suspicious packages. He had sent a small package to the American ambassador in London that contained a small charge that he had designed to explode a vial of nerve gas when it was opened, but somehow it had never reached its target.

"It would be hit and miss for us to get anything through the mails."

"I know, I remember London," Hassan agreed. "There are other ways. We could find someone on the street willing to make a personal delivery for a few bucks, I'm sure."

"I follow you. Do you want me to rig something?"

"We'll get the letter to Naz first. Can you go over and see him? This is urgent, and if I go, Jas will want to come with me."

"I'll leave first thing in the morning."

"You said that a lot of chemicals hydrolyze in water. Is there a lethal one that we could get into a bottle of wine?"

"Absolutely. That would be simple. Tabun would be a good nerve agent. It's clear and tasteless. Wine would mask its faint fruity smell. I have a small quantity that I smuggled in that I got from Iraq, enough to do the trick, I'm sure."

"You never cease to amaze me. Let's get it done, then," Hassan enthused.

Hassan decided that he would go job hunting and try to earn some extra cash during the summer. The Guidance Department at the college advised that they had some potential summer placements, and he began the search immediately while he eagerly awaited Hamid's return from Victoria. Each morning, he would get up at his usual time and head to the college early to check the job postings, while Jas was able to catch a little extra sleep.

On the fourth day of Hassan's new routine, Hamid caught up with him at the campus. He cheerfully advised Hassan that his "undertaking" had been completed. He'd even arranged for delivery to their nemesis, sometime on that afternoon. Satisfied that the problem was taken care of, the two men looked over the job board and placed all fears of Russ Norman to rest.

The other students were encouraged when Dana had successfully landed a summer job. Hassan optimistically would meet up with Hamid early each morning to spend the day job hunting together until late each afternoon. Hamid had conveyed to Jas and Dana that he had been hugely disappointed that the city job with the water treatment plant hadn't worked out because they couldn't complete his background checks in Kuwait. Both girls assured the men that something would turn up. However, the following week, Jas received a call about nine thirty in the morning from Hamid asking where Hassan was as he hadn't shown up at their meeting place that morning.

During the next several hours, both Jas and Hamid fretted and checked with Noe, but Hassan was nowhere to be found. As the day slipped into evening, no one had heard from him, and the three of them became increasingly concerned. They called the hospitals and the police. Eventually, Noe had become so worried that he visited the local mosque to see if he had been there while Hamid checked the libraries.

Jas felt exasperated when the police advised her that she couldn't complete a missing persons report for twenty-four hours. She was certain that something had happened; it just wasn't like Hassan to disappear. However, Jas began to panic when he didn't arrive home that night and she'd heard no word on his whereabouts by morning. Hamid put in a worried call to Naz, who had no information to offer either. Hassan had apparently vanished!

34

Hamid was far more concerned than he wanted to admit to Jas. He had stayed late with her the night before, and there had still been no word by 2:00 a.m. He called her first thing in the morning; even if she'd managed a couple of hours sleep, he knew she'd be up. She sounded crushed, and he could hear the pain in her voice as she relayed that she had still not heard from Hassan.

She had said that she was going to try to call the hospitals again and figured that perhaps the police might take a report now. He told her that he'd keep looking for him and get back to her.

"You keep your chin up, Jas. Everything will be all right," he'd told her. He felt decidedly uneasy as he hung up and then noticed he had a call waiting message on his phone.

When he checked the message, and in an unusually low voice, which was almost inaudible, he heard Hassan's voice, "Retreat." It was followed by a quick click. Hamid listened again to make sure that he had made no mistake about the message, quickly erased it, then he called Dana on her cell and told her that Jas seriously could use some support as Hassan had gone missing. He suggested that she went to stay with her friend after work, and he would check around a few places to see if he could locate him.

He also informed her that he had just received a call about a personal family emergency and that he needed to go out of town for a while. He would check the school, the library, and a few other places, and if he didn't find him, he would need to leave Vancouver by midafternoon. He promised to be in touch as soon as he returned. A half an hour after hanging up, he called Jas back and apologetically also spun her a story that he had a family emergency and needed to go out of town, but he still hadn't been able to locate Hassan either.

"I wouldn't leave, Jas, but I think they may have found my brother alive," he remarked.

"I'll be okay. Dana called, and she's coming over. I'm sure Hassan's got a silly explanation of where he's been," Jas replied, trying to appear optimistic.

"Yes, I called Dana, and she said that she'll be over to your place after work."

"Thanks and good luck, Hamid. I really hope it is your brother. You'll let us know, won't you?"

"Sure thing. I'll call you and see how you both are. You'll hear from Hassan soon. Bye, Jas."

After hanging up, Hamid took the phone apart and hurriedly packed his few belongings. He didn't want to leave a trace of anything in the room. Checking every nook and cranny, he burned any documents that he didn't need, dropped the keys on top of the dresser, and headed for the door. Carefully scouring the outside to see if he could see anyone out of the ordinary hanging about, he made his way to the bus stop. He changed buses several times before arriving at the terminal for the Sea Bus, an island ferry service, which would take him to Vancouver Island. With any luck, he'd make it to Victoria by two o'clock.

He spotted a sewer grid after assuring himself that he wasn't being observed; he discarded the sim card from the cell phone down it. Then he proceeded into the restroom where he changed his clothing, shaved his beard, and covered his head with a ball cap; in case anyone had followed him, he would be more difficult to recognize. As he approached the ferry dock, he made a detour to the storage lockers and took out a small key from his wallet. Opening the storage unit, he retrieved the envelope that contained some emergency cash, a small suitcase with clothing and personal items, and replaced them with some documents. Eyeing a nearby pay phone, he put in a quick call to Naz.

"Hamid here, I don't know what's happened, but it sounds pretty serious. Hassan is missing, but he sent me a message to retreat. I'm taking the ferry immediately."

"Okay, I'll be there," came the response after a slight hesitation.

"It's urgent. I'll head to Dubai. Can you call Iqbal and tell him I've left my records in the ferry dock locker? He has a duplicate key."

"I'll check for flights, probably Cathay Pacific is the best flight out to Dubai, wait in the washrooms near their sign. Do you know if anything has happened to anyone else?"

"Noe heard from Sammi. He got caught working illegally and was deported a couple of days ago. You probably know that Giv said he thought there was trouble with Mohammad. I think we're too late for Hassan. Don't know what's happened, but I think you might contact Bahrami and tell him the operation may need to be regrouped."

"Shit! Are you and Iqbal his only other connections in Vancouver?"

"I think so. You'll need to get hold of Noe and see if he knows what's happening. Hassan said that he's not involved with our plans, though, and I've noticed he doesn't discuss anything when he's around. Tell him I've gone to see if they found my brother. That's what I told Jas."

"Will do. Do Hassan's or Noe's wife know anything?"

"No. I don't think either of them has a clue. Hassan said to keep them out of everything."

"All right, I'll see you soon. I'll find out what time the ferry comes in and give you one hour to get to the airport. Hopefully, you'll be waiting in the men's room nearest to the Cathay Pacific airline sign. I'll walk in and leave the package at the sink. I won't stop to talk just in case you've been tailed. You enter after I leave. In the meantime, I'll call Iqbal to empty the locker."

"Sounds good. Thanks, Naz."

Hamid felt bad for Dana and Jas. They wouldn't understand any of what was happening, but he was confident Naz would speak to Noe, and Hassan's cousin would support the girls through whatever broke. Damn, he had spent three years preparing for this operation and was disappointed that their plans might not come to fruition. This had been one of the most critical missions he had been assigned by Bahrami. The world had never seen anything like what they had planned.

He had been training for such a long time, and now, regrettably, someone else would have to begin the work again. Hamid hoped that Iqbal would be able to pass on his research to someone competent. He'd found that most of the organophosphorus compounds weren't suitable for the majority of the facilities they'd identified for contamination of the water. Still he knew that there were other possibilities, and he'd isolated potassium cyanide as their best bet.

He heard the boarding call and made his way to the Sea Bus. He felt an adrenalin rush. He wasn't going to relax until he was safely out of the country. He wondered where they'd send him next. He'd liked it in Vancouver, and he liked the few friends he'd made. His biggest disappointment was leaving Dana. They'd gotten remarkably close without crossing the line.

He'd managed to keep their relationship uncomplicated as he hadn't been prepared to put her through what he knew Jas was going to face in the next few months. He wondered if Jas had been the weak link. Did she know anything? Hassan shouldn't have gotten involved with anyone. What was he thinking? He'd married her and fathered a child, knowing that he couldn't provide them with a secure future.

He speculated about how the hell the Canadian authorities had found Hassan out. He hoped that they didn't know his real identity, whatever it was. For that matter, did Jas? He had so many questions racing through his head, but right now, he just had to cover his own ass and get the hell out. He figured they might come looking for him too if they asked Jas or even the school if Hassan had any known associates. The perspiration was pouring off his forehead as the ferry began its short crossing of the Burrard Inlet. Partway across the waterway he dropped the rest of the cell phone and some other shredded documents into the water.

After reaching the airport and glancing about nervously, he located the Cathay Pacific airline desk. Then he grabbed a coffee and a newspaper, which he pretended to read. Within ten minutes, he felt a small wave of relief as he spotted Naz, who made a slight motion toward a nearby men's room. As soon as Naz left, he entered the washroom, washed his hands, and picked up the small satchel that Naz had placed on the counter. He then headed into one of the cubicles to extract its contents.

35

Fortunately, Naz had an older picture of Hamid when he had been clean shaven, and as planned, he'd used this in the new passport. Hamid almost didn't recognize himself as he moved his hand to stroke his barren chin. He carefully studied the bio data page in the name of Yusuf Alhammad born in Kuwait now a citizen of the UK.

As he glanced through the pages, he found earlier entry and exit stamps from Dubai, and a stamp into Canada three weeks ago. The passport indicated that it had been issued just shortly before the Dubai trip, and there was nothing else that he actually needed to know as the birth date remained the same as what he had been using for a few years now. He checked the other document. It was a birth certificate written in Arabic and identified his parents as Fahid and Munirah. Naz had also gotten him an e-ticket to return to Vancouver with a connecting flight leaving for Dubai several hours later.

He wasn't too thrilled about returning to Vancouver and hanging around the airport, but he knew that it was the only way he could get to Dubai from the west coast of Canada. Otherwise, he was satisfied that everything looked in order. He put everything back in the satchel. Naz had left, grabbed his suitcase, and headed to the Air Canada counter to check in for the flight back to the city often referred to as "Hollywood North."

It would be a short flight back to the other airport, and he had about an hour before boarding, so he decided to grab a quick bite to eat and some reading materials for the longer flight ahead of him. He reflected on his past four years in Canada, and in some respects he knew that he was going to miss it. He'd enjoyed the school and the companions he had gotten to know.

Apart from that, he found that he could satisfy his personal needs unobtrusively. He had easily blended in with the bar scene where girls were a dime a dozen, and morals were generally out the window. He'd had some pretty decent one-night stands to quench his insatiable sexual appetite with no strings attached. The city was large enough that his occasional excursions into the bar crowds were isolated from his life as a student and removed from his tight circle of friends.

The flight to Vancouver had taken less than half an hour leaving Hamid almost six hours to kill until he could board his flight to Dubai. He decided to purchase a couple of bottles of water, a few snacks, and to rent one of the new sleep pods that were positioned around the airport. He'd watch some television, perhaps get a couple of hours' rest, and more importantly, keep out of sight.

The sleep pod was fairly expensive, about fifty bucks an hour, and from previous experience, he knew that it would be extremely confining, but it would give him some down time to reflect on the events of the past twenty-four hours. He'd barely settled in before he fell fast asleep for the next three hours—unaware that someone had taken up watch nearby.

Hamid was slightly disoriented when he woke up and thought he might have been dreaming the whole experience of the past twenty-four hours. Reality set in with the sounds of the airport drifting in through the thin walls of the pod. He was saddened that this phase of his life was over, but now he had to concentrate on getting out and moving on to another assignment.

The organization generally frowned on failure, but he was assured that he wouldn't be faulted. It looked like Hassan had messed up big time, and hopefully both he and Jas would get through it without too much trouble. He'd enjoyed their friendship; however, he sincerely had liked the woman that Hassan had married and felt sorry for the situation she was now facing.

He flicked on the TV and checked the channel guide when he noticed the time and realized that he had less than ninety minutes to go. He decided to make use of the facilities and freshen up before checking in for his flight. Reluctantly, he left the safety of his hideout. Within half an hour, he was checking in his baggage for the flight when he happened to recognize a student from the college working behind one of the counters. Shit! Just his luck. He hoped the guy didn't know him without his beard, he thought as he put the ball cap on and turned in the opposite direction.

"Hey, Hamid," he heard as he walked quickly away from the voice.

He went into the men's room and decided to wait it out until the boarding call. He honestly didn't believe that the other student had actually had a close look at him but didn't want to take any more chances. Hell, it was just his luck! He checked his watch and decided to give it about forty-five minutes before he ventured back out to the boarding line.

In the meantime, the student had walked over to the other airline employee check-in clerk and inquired whether the person who had just checked his baggage was someone by the name of Hamid. The clerk glanced at the baggage still on the ramp and said that he thought his name was something like that.

"I thought it was somebody I know. I could have been mistaken because he was clean shaven, and the guy I know has a beard," the second clerk responded as he went over to the luggage and flipped the name tag, "Oh, it was my mistake. This guy's name is Yusuf Alhammad, not Hamid."

Two men strolled up to the counter and pulled out their identity badges while identifying themselves as immigration intelligence officers and asked to speak to both of the employees, somewhere discreet. After speaking briefly to their supervisor, the men were taken aside and questioned by the officers. In particular, they were eager to learn more about the passenger that they had overheard the student remark about. When the employee indicated that he had thought that he recognized him as a fellow student at the college he attended, but he had been mistaken, they persisted and asked what name the student knew him by.

The second officer checked the name shown on the computer terminal and baggage tags with the other employee. Noting the details for the boarding time, the officers calculated that they might get a half hour to make some quick checks. They decided to speak to the airline authorities and ask them to be prepared to delay the plane, if necessary. A third officer kept up her surveillance of the subject to the best of her ability, while waiting near the outside of the men's room.

The officers had followed the print shop owner Arz to the airport in Victoria, hoping to catch him in the act of handling of fraudulent documents. They'd had the printer under surveillance for a few weeks, but they hadn't been able to catch him in the act. Even today, they didn't observe an actual delivery of documents to anyone, although they had found it particularly intriguing that the printer had apparently driven to the airport just to use the washroom.

They had a telephoto shot of the printer entering the washroom carrying a satchel and one of him leaving without it. They also managed to get a photo of a second man exiting the men's room moments later carrying a bag that appeared to match the one that the printer had been carrying. Glancing at one another, the officers had exchanged knowing looks that indicated that they believed an illegal transaction had occurred. It was just circumstantial, the two men didn't acknowledge each other, and they didn't have any proof of an actual handover, but they thought something might break in their favor!

They called the Border Services Immigration office at the terminal, and after identifying themselves, they checked the name that the student had thought belonged to the passenger. This is where things had got a little more interesting. Surprisingly, they were informed that Corby Dunn had placed a flag on the guy's name and that the computer carried the message that all queries should be referred to either him or Judd in the intelligence unit.

Moments later, Corby picked up on the second ring; however, he had been reluctant to talk to them and insisted on referring them to Judd. Quickly they placed a call to the intelligence officer.

"You say the guy's here in the Vancouver terminal?" Judd asked after he listened to the nature of the call.

"Yeah, we've got him under surveillance. He's hidden himself away in the can."

"Okay, pick him up and take him over to the AFIS machine. We've got his prints on file. You may get to hold him on passport fraud. I'm very interested in this fellow. We think he could be involved in a terrorist plot. I might be interested in the printer, too! You say his name is Nazreh Arz. You better pick him up. Do you think you've got enough on him to justify getting a warrant for his place, perhaps on the grounds of suspected people smuggling? We need to move fast before he empties out his office. This could be a long night and the very break that we've been looking for."

36

Russ was in New York for a five-day conference at a private investigators' convention where he had attended a seminar about some of the growing areas of fraud investigations. It had proved rather fascinating, and he looked forward to sharing a summary recap of the newest trends in the business with Kendrick's team, who worked extensively in this area. Of course, there were problems the United States that were not really a big threat in Canada—such as the con artists who were selling bogus health insurance plans to consumers. The market for the product would be substantially limited by public health care in Canada. But it certainly didn't hurt to be aware of the latest schemes that were afoot south of the border.

The devastation in the US economy had bred some new unscrupulous operators that Russ felt were worth knowing about. He was certain that when Kendrick met the insurance companies to market the services of Watchdogz, the information that Russ gathered during the conference would be helpful in promoting services that Kendrick's company could provide them. Some of the fraud trends and insurance scams were universal. One of the interesting ones that Russ learned about had been labeled "Vehicle Give-Ups."

Recently, the Americans had found large numbers of torched vehicles that had been sunk in rivers and lakes after owners had reported them missing or stolen. In some cases, the owners had even sold them to the chop shops or the gangs selling vehicles overseas before submitting fraudulent insurance claims. These incidences seemed to coincide with job losses, rising gas prices, or even when the depreciated value of the vehicles exceeded the balance on their car loans.

Russ stopped at Timmy's and picked up a fresh assortment of doughnuts for the meeting. It had become customary that whoever arrived first in the morning always put on a fresh pot of coffee, and he knew that the staff would appreciate the morning snack. He was in a good mood and looked forward to the day ahead and the beginning of a new week. It seemed though that the day was only going to get better as Donna, the company receptionist, handed him a nice gift-wrapped present that she said had arrived for him while he was out of town.

"What's this? Hey, Donna, I'm the boss, not him," Kendrick joked as he entered the office and witnessed the exchange of something that looked like a bottle of alcohol.

"It's not from me, Kendrick. I guess Russ has got a secret admirer." Donna laughed.

Russ opened the envelope and frowned as he saw that it was from the HR person at the water treatment plant. He'd worked in the federal government for a long time where it was a policy that you didn't accept gifts from other people or agencies. It was surprising that a municipal government agency employed such a practice. He asked Kendrick if Watchdogz had a company policy that prohibited employees from accepting gifts as he advised that he didn't feel at all comfortable about it.

"Never had it happened before. Usually they just pay the bill, and I hope they'll come back to us again for their next assignment. I can't see any harm in it. You probably deserve it, just say thanks, and be done with it."

"Looks as if it's a bottle," Russ deduced as he undid the wrapping.

"Oh, oh, it's wine. Sorry, old man, we didn't tell them that you're allergic to the stuff. I guess you'll have to give it to your boss." Kendrick laughed as the contents were revealed.

"Not so fast, buddy. You did say it was my gift to keep or do whatever I want with it. Seeing that Donna took such good care of it, I think she should have it just for babysitting." Russ handed the bottle to the beaming receptionist, who shyly took it from him.

"Fair enough," Kendrick replied. "We couldn't function without her around here. Enjoy it Donna, with my blessing."

"Thank you both so much. I've got guests coming on the weekend for dinner. It'll be a nice touch."

"I guess I'll send our benefactor an e-mail and thank her for her thoughtfulness. Now I've got some interesting data to share with the team, so I better get to the boardroom," Russ added as he gathered up the wrapping paper and the letter and dumped them into the garbage.

Having been away for several days, Russ found himself busy with the morning meeting and spent the rest of the day catching up on some of his files. He completely forgot about the gift he had received until he had gone to Katy's for dinner and Kendrick had teased him about it. He reminded himself that he'd have to send off the thank-you the next morning.

Three days later, Russ sat staring at the reply from the client on his computer, which politely denied having sent the gift. Russ couldn't figure out what to make of this new development. The source of the gift was now a puzzle. After speaking with Kendrick, they called Donna into the boss's office to see if she could recall who had delivered the package, whether the garbage from Monday had been removed, and how the parcel had been addressed.

A cleaning lady came in during the day and emptied all the trash cans, so they were gone. Donna only could remember that the delivery man was actually just a teenage boy who was rather nondescript. She recalled that it had been addressed to Russ Norman, in large black letters in care of Watchdogz. It struck Russ that they were in a dangerous business, and there were a lot of mentally challenged people around. As the trio exchanged worried glances, Kendrick asked Donna to bring the bottle back to the office for precautionary measures.

On Friday morning, Kendrick gave Donna a fresh bottle of wine in exchange for the one that had been delivered, despite her protests. Russ tried to recall the details of the letter that had accompanied the wine, indicating that it was from the water treatment plant. He was pretty sure that it had looked official, and that led him to the recent work that he had done for them. The only name he kept coming back to was Hamid Al Zain.

Kendrick and Russ carefully examined the bottle, looking for possible tampering. Fingerprints that they might have been able to obtain had probably been compromised, but there might be an off chance of getting something. With the use of a magnifying glass, the men agreed that it appeared that there was a tiny hole in the center of the cork that was no bigger than something made by a pin. Russ picked up the phone and called his friend Judd at the Border Security's Intelligence office.

37

Dana arrived at Jas's flat and found her to be worried but amazingly under control. She couldn't help but admire the strength of this woman. How could Hassan just disappear?

"I haven't seen Hassan since yesterday. It's as if he's gone from the face of the earth. Oh, Dana, I feel so powerless right now. I don't know where to begin looking for him. I called Noe, but Maryam said he wasn't home, and she'd have him call as soon as he came in. I also tried calling the police station and every hospital in the city, several times, but all to no avail. I just have no idea where he could be or where else to look."

"Jas, there's sure to be a simple explanation. Are you sure that he didn't say something before he left? Maybe you were half-asleep and just don't remember. Perhaps he went over to that place in Victoria, where he went before. Let's get some food in you and have a cup of tea while we think this through." Dana struggled to calm her friend's fears.

"I couldn't eat anything, but tea sounds good," Jas replied as Dana headed to the kitchen.

Dana was in the process of making the tea when a knock came on the door. Hoping that it was not bad news for Jas, she quietly stepped into the hall as Jas answered the door.

"Is Jaslyn Zadeh here?" boomed an irritatingly loud voice.

"Yes, I'm Mrs. Zadeh. How may I help you?"

"May we come in?"

"Certainly, Officers! Do you have some news about my husband?"

As Dana watched Jas usher in two uniformed police officers, she heard them advise Jas that Hassan had been arrested and that he was being held in the local jail on an immigration matter. Jas was no wilting flower and never resorted to fits of hysteria or emotional outbursts at this news; she seemed to take it calmly in stride. At least outwardly, she appeared strong but cautious and seemed able to brace herself for whatever news they had brought.

"We'd like to ask you some questions," one of the officers said.

"How long has my husband been in custody? Where are you holding him?" Jas inquired.

"We've had him about twenty-four hours, ma'am, at the central jail."

"I've been concerned, and I've called the police many times. Why didn't they tell me when I called the police station?" Jas gallingly responded.

"It probably wasn't in the computer system when you called. However, we're here now to let you know."

The phone rang, and Dana called out that she would get it. It was Noe, Hassan's cousin, and Dana quickly advised him that the police were present and that Jas had just been advised that they were holding Hassan. She explained that they had just arrived and the girls had little knowledge of anything yet, although the police had mentioned that it was an immigration matter. Noe told her not to worry, and he asked her to stay with Jas until the officers left and then call him back.

"Wild horses wouldn't drag me away," Dana responded. "I'll be in touch as soon as I can. Noe, there is something else you might want to know. I don't want to upset Jas any more, but I am worried about Hamid, too. He was here last night, and then he called this morning to tell me that he had to leave town for a family emergency. Seems Jas and I are on our own, and I don't know what's going on around here."

Noe told her that he had also heard from Hamid. They had found his brother during a raid in Iraq. Apparently, he was barely alive. Fortunately, one of the rescuers knew Hamid was in Canada, and he contacted him. Noe assured her that there was nothing to worry about. As far as Hamid was concerned, it was really good news. Again, he asked her to call him back as soon as the officers left, and then he hung up.

Dana hurried back into the small sitting room full of curiosity but equally concerned for her friends. When the officers turned toward her, one of them asked her name. Before she could get out a word, Jas brazenly beat her to the punch.

"Excuse me, Officer, you are not here to question my guests. I'd like to know exactly where my husband is. Where is this central jail, and why you are holding him there?"

"Well, Mrs. Zadeh, this matter is confidential, and in the interests of protecting your husband's rights, we are required to be cautious about whom we give personal information to."

"This is my friend Dana Jahcl. She's a student at the college we both attend. I met her as a member of the school's hospitality committee when I arrived in Canada, and she met me at the airport. We have become friends, and I have no one else in Canada other than my husband. She is staying with me at present, and you can speak in her presence."

"Okay, Mrs. Zadeh, your husband is currently on an immigration hold. We don't know all the details. We just responded to your missing persons report and located him. He's at the downtown police station and is being held about some misrepresentations he made to immigration authorities. He'll have a bail hearing tomorrow morning. You may want to get him a lawyer."

"I see, this is all some silly mistake that will easily be resolved." Jas recollected her experience with the Ministry of Internal Affairs in Temesekia. "This must be because my government has alerted the Canadian authorities that they believe that my husband is still married to his former wife. However, I can assure you that Hassan has witnesses to his divorce, and we are able to obtain affidavits from them to attest to this."

"I'm just the messenger. We don't know any details. What makes you think that this is about the validity of your marriage?" the officer asked.

"When I visited my homeland recently, my government interviewed me and warned me of this matter. I have discussed this with my husband, and I believe him. He is divorced from his previous wife. He has told me that the witnesses are available."

"Did your government tell you anything else?"

"My government is very strict. They felt that I should leave my husband and not return to Canada to finish my studies. They were wrong. My husband is an honest man. I believe him that he is divorced."

"Does the name Mahmoud Bahrami mean anything to you?"

"No, should it? I have never met this person." Jas felt prickles in the back of her neck as she recognized the name of the person that her government had also asked about. She had forgotten that point and meant to ask Hassan if he knew this person. However, she was completely flabbergasted with one of the officer's response.

"We understand that your husband is also known by that name."

Dana could not conceal a slight gasp, and an officer turned to her and asked, "Does that name mean something to you, Ms. Jahel?"

"No, I only know him as Hassan. I was just surprised that you say he has another name."

Jas grew impatient. This was all utter nonsense. She thought back to her conversation with the authorities in Temesekia and recalled that they had also mentioned that name but that it hadn't seemed to have been their primary concern at the time.

"I think you are making a mistake. My government told me no such thing. My husband doesn't know this person. If my husband used another name and my government wanted to convince me not to return to Canada, why did they not tell me this? They didn't mention anything other than the fact that they believed he was never divorced from his former wife. They certainly didn't say he was known by a different name to them."

"We don't know, Mrs. Zadeh. You'll have to ask them. As I said, we don't know too much about it at the moment. Right now it's an immigration matter. Does anyone else live here other than you and your husband?"

"No, just my husband and I."

"We'd like to take a look around here if you don't mind?" The loud officer had pushed. He had done all of the talking, and Jas was now thoroughly annoyed by him.

"Oh, but I do mind, Officers. I am not naive. I have worked in the legal profession for a number of years in my country, and I do know that both my husband and I have rights. Do you have a warrant? You said this is an immigration matter, not a police matter, didn't you?"

"Do you have something to hide, Mrs. Zadeh?"

"Of course not. I just don't want to answer any more of your questions. I need to see my husband. I'll have you know that you cannot intimidate me. What would I have to hide? I would like you to leave until I can speak with a lawyer."

"That's fine, Mrs. Zadeh. We wanted to let you know that your husband has been located. If you have any questions, you or your lawyer can call me at this number," he said as he handed her his business card.

As soon as the police had left, Jas turned to her friend and apologized for not telling her about the small problem she had on her holiday. Dana gave her a quick hug and advised her that Noe had called and wanted her to call him back as soon as the officers had left. She reasoned that Noe was more familiar with Canadian laws, and hopefully he would know what could be done to get Hassan's release. Jas wasn't sure if Hassan had confided to Noe about the divorce problem; however, she saw no harm in letting him know and immediately placed the return call.

As Noe listened to Jas, he felt a twist in his gut knowing that the situation was probably far more serious than had been revealed to her at this point. If indeed the police were questioning Hassan's marital status and they also knew that Hassan had lived in Temesekia under a different identity, it was a sure thing that his cover had been blown.

He had no doubt when, seconds later, Jas confirmed his fears as she conveyed the problems she had in Temesekia and that they too had mentioned the name Mahmoud Bahrami. He immediately denied any knowledge that Hassan had used an alias and advised Jas that he thought Hassan needed a lawyer. He suggested that since it was an immigration matter, he would call Jordan Connors and get back to her.

As he hung up the phone, Noe felt that he too might be in jeopardy as authorities knew that he was Hassan's cousin. He wondered why Hassan hadn't told anyone that Jas had been questioned over a month ago on her trip home. Why didn't Hassan alert the other members of his organization that this happened? If they now knew that Hassan was also known as Mahmoud Bahrami, he was not surprised that Hamid had suddenly found some reason to leave. Noe didn't believe that his brother had been found; he thought it was more likely that Hamid was in the process of aborting their mission and simply left Canada.

He thought that if he himself were questioned, he could claim convincingly that he didn't even know that Hassan had been married before. He would explain that they were actually only second cousins and hadn't seen each other for a long time. The plan had been that if anyone got pinched, he would state that they kind of lost touch after secondary school.

Noe would stick as close to the truth as possible and state that while he went to university, Hassan had gone to technical college, and they'd known little about each other's lives after that. The story would be that his dad contacted him and told him that Hassan was coming to Canada and needed some help in getting established. He'd feign ignorance about Hassan's other identity and the years since he had attended the university; these were the agreed facts that he had worked out with Hassan, long ago, should either of them ever find themselves in this position.

38

Russ had been badly shaken when Judd had enlisted the RCMP to examine the "gift" that he had received and learned that it contained a nerve gas that was intended for him. He shuddered as he recalled how he had innocently given the present to Donna, who was a middle-aged single mother of two teenage children. Even though there was an ongoing investigation, there was no evidence on where the package had came from as they had discarded the letter and the wrappings that it came in.

With little evidence to go on, he doubted that the feds would be able to link anyone to the act. This meant that he was the target of somebody who had access to a weapon of mass destruction, who was likely involved in terrorism. The only real link he had was that the letterhead had certainly connected someone that knew he had done the security job for the treatment plant. Although two of the applicants for work had failed on their reference checks, it was only Al Zain who hadn't passed the security clearance.

As if he didn't have enough on his plate, the hairs on the back of his neck had stood on end when Corporal Jeff Coulson, from the Kelso RCMP detachment, had alerted him a few days later that there had been reports of some vandalism near his cabin property. Jeff assured him that he had personally gone over to check his property and hadn't seen anything out of the ordinary there, but he had figured that Russ might want to check on it as soon as possible. It wasn't that he had much up there to take; it was just the thought of someone intruding on his private domain and the lengths someone had already gone to bring him harm that had Russ worried beyond anything he had ever felt before.

The next morning, he told Kendrick that he was going to take a bit of a break and go up to the cabin for a few days if he didn't mind. Russ didn't reveal anything about the call from the local police detachment to prevent causing his family any more unnecessary worry. He surmised that the two events were a mere coincidence and probably unrelated. Few people knew about the whereabouts of his cabin, and it had been his little hideaway for so many years. It also wasn't unusual to have some vandalism in some of the nearby larger cottages, and his little shack had never been a target. However, as a precaution following his receipt of the tainted wine, Russ decided to take his old .30-30 Winchester hunting rifle that he hadn't used for years with him on this trip.

He felt uneasy during the entire drive to the cabin and made the decision to stop off at the detachment office and tell Jeff Coulson about his concerns. The two men had been friends for more than twenty years, and when Jeff had learned about the attempt on Russ's life, he insisted on going to the cabin with him. He agreed with Russ that it was unlikely the break-ins were connected, but he had learned long ago that caution was the best course of action.

When they arrived at the cabin, though, they had found an entirely different kind of intruder: mice. It seemed that all manner of vermin had been looking for shelter from the unusually harsh winter they had experienced. Needless to say, he had a lot of work to make the place habitable again. Clothing, furniture, books, and many other household items had been contaminated by their droppings and urine or damaged by their gnawing.

They had somehow managed to get into the cupboards too, probably in search of food. Most troubling of all, they had gnawed their way through some of the electrical wiring that could have caused a fire. Jeff hurriedly made the decision to get back to town because it was going to take his friend a lot of time to clean up the mess his unwanted visitors had left.

Russ called Kendrick and told him he was going to take a little more time to clean up the mess he'd found and make sure the place didn't burn down from the damage to the wiring. In the coming days, he worked hard sealing every nook and cranny, clearing the foliage and tall grasses close to the cabin, and cleaning the cabin from top to bottom in the hunt for any nesting grounds. Some of the furniture and wiring even had to be replaced as the damage had been fairly extensive. Most notably his favorite chair would never be useful again.

When he was finally satisfied that the place had been sufficiently restored to some semblance of order, he decided to give Corby a call and invite him up for the long weekend. He was missing some companionship, and Corby was always willing to oblige to get in some fishing. He was delighted when Corby asked to come and stay for the entire week. Hell yes, he'd answered and thought that maybe he'd talk him into contributing some muscle to his fence repairs too.

A few days later, Corby had arrived stocked with food, beer, and fishing gear. He was in a particularly good frame of mind and seemed as pleased as punch with himself. Russ sensed that he had some news he wanted to share and waited until Corby had settled in before asking him how things were going.

"I've got some interesting news that I think you'll be glad to hear. I helped snag a really dangerous dude while you're off just sunning and fishing," Corby teased.

"Sunning and fishing? In my dreams! My cabin practically got destroyed this past winter by mice and what a mess! It's been nothing but hard work since I arrived. However, I noticed that you've packed on a few pounds. There's no need to worry, though. I've saved some outdoor work for you so you can earn your keep while you're here," Russ chuckled. "All kidding aside, what did you do now?"

"Well, Russ, old boy, actually you helped me out with this one. You remember that Iranian fellow?"

"Now let me see, you said Iranian? I wonder which one of the thousands I've met over the past thirty years you mean."

"Yeah, you're right. Do you recall the guy by the name of Zadeh, who had his fingertips burnt off, and you escorted him to the detention center on your last night?"

"Christ, that guy keeps popping up like a bad penny. What's he up to now?"

"Some big wheels are in motion now. He said his name was Zadeh, but now no one's sure who the hell he is. The US have discovered another identity for him from the one single good fingerprint we got off his permanent resident application. They say he's an RBG. He's been sitting in the clink for a few weeks now. He got refugee standing with one of these expedited hearings that they're doing these days. They don't even wait for the security clearances anymore. It's all about pushing the numbers through."

"An RBG—gee, I haven't heard that expression since I left the department. What makes them suddenly agree that he is likely a 'really bad guy'?" Russ laughed.

"Not sure what all they have, but it's enough that they're talking about taking away his refugee status with a security certificate."

"A security certificate's a difficult way to go. He can tie us up for years with all his appeal rights now that he's been found to be a refugee. What do they suspect? Do they think he has violated human rights, is a member of organized crime, or is he perceived to be a threat to national security?"

"National security—they think he might be a terrorist!"

"It's a shame, I had a feeling that he was somehow connected to the terrorist group they were on the lookout for, just by looking at the burns on his fingertips. His story never rang true with me. He's been here for more than two years now. I wonder how long it'll take to get him through the system."

"That's not the only problem. If they can prove the case they have against him, there's a little question about where we can remove him to. Our hands are tied with the moratorium on removals going to Iran. It's on the list of respite countries."

"Do we even know who he is and whether he's really from Iran?" Russ glumly asked.

"Who knows if they'll ever establish his real identity?" Corby replied.

"You know that's what scares me the most about our immigration system. So many people have all kinds of documents giving them several individual identities from different countries all over the world. Some of them have three or four identities and several citizenships so they can move in and out whenever they want. I heard that in some countries, they just buy phony attestations of birth and obtain legitimate passports to travel around."

"The other problem, of course, is that nobody wants them back in their country."

"It's still going to be tough for our guys to get a security certificate on him. Some of these guys have been in this country years, and we're still trying to get rid of them."

"I don't understand the process required to take refugee status away. If you don't know who a person is, that should be a no-brainer. In my book, that's logically described as a straightforward misrepresentation, supposedly the primary ground to lose their status," Corby said.

"Sometimes, Border Services are fighting our own Immigration Department, who also give them genuine identity documents based on their phony information. I recall a terrorist whom we successfully removed but gave his entire family, including six teenage children status, even though the father acknowledged that he had bought phony identity documents for them."

"What morons."

"Yep, I would argue that our own government is complicit in helping them to establish secondary identities that they can move about the world with. Might not be a problem when they're sixteen, but ten years later it can come back to bite you that John Doe and George Smith are one and the same person."

"I hear you. There has to be political will to deal with these problems and a willingness to stand behind the public servants who try to deal with the situations that arise. The politicians and a lot of the bureaucracy dealing with these matters have no idea what we deal with. Even if a person is found to be inadmissible to Canada, there's no guarantee that they'll ever be removed."

"That being said, they must have something pretty serious on Zadeh, though. What do they think they know about him?"

"Personally, I don't know a lot right now. I've been told that they think he might be the mastermind behind a very active terrorist cell. He's been busy since he arrived here. He married a foreign student from Temesekia while he's been here. What she sees in him, I can't figure out. It's too early to tell what's going to shake loose on him, but I'll tell you, there's a lot of interest in him. He never did sit right with me."

"Yeah, when I did an employment check on his friend, I was told that he had a wife. Wow, he's done all right for himself. Got his refugee status and a wife in what, just over a year? Is there any information about the girl and how he met her?" Russ said.

"They've been checking her out with the Temesekian authorities. She might not have a clue whom she's married and what he's into. I think they met at the college where they both attend."

"There was something about the guy I didn't trust from the minute I laid eyes on him, too. Gives me great comfort knowing that someone's on to him and he's locked up."

"Oh yeah, I've heard that it's pretty heavy stuff that they've got on him, but it's all hushed up right now. Supposedly he's considered by some as the mastermind behind a number of terrorist actions that have taken place in various countries over the last ten years."

"Has Zadeh got legal representation?" asked Russ.

"Oh yeah, of course, and he's lawyered up. The US and Interpol are pretty interested in him. I don't think that they have real hard evidence against him though, just a lot of circumstantial stuff that may meet the test of serious reasons to consider."

"Did he include the wife in his immigration application?" Russ inquired.

"Yep, when they were checking her out, her government got extremely interested in the case, too. They claim to have quite a dossier on him. He's a real man of mystery! No one is sure what his true identity is. Everything comes up that he is Iranian so that presents the removal problem that prevents us from sending people back to Iran. I've heard he's a real shrewd dude who's been involved in some pretty nasty stuff, but it's all classified."

"How about associates or the wife? Do you know if anyone else is involved? I'm particularly interested in his friend Hamid Al Zain."

39

"Oh yeah, there's plenty of news on Al Zain. I forgot about your little episode that you suspected him of." Corby's face lit up as he recalled the tampered wine that Russ had received. "I don't know if you remember the piece of paper I copied that Zadeh had on him when he entered Canada. He said it just had his cousin's phone number on it, but it also had the word *Naz* written on it."

"I vaguely recall it. What does that have to do with Al Zain?"

"The Mounties had some fellow by the name of Nazreh Arz under surveillance for about five months."

"What for?"

"People smuggling. They suspect that he operates a little side-line business providing all manner of forged documents for identity purposes. They haven't been able to nail him yet, but they've been monitoring him rather closely."

"So what were you saying is Al Zain's connection to him? Unless he was planning a name switch."

"Gets even better." Corby grinned. "You won't believe how Al Zain entered the picture. As I said, the feds have been tailing the printer for a while trying to determine the extent of his operations. Recently, Arz went to the airport in Victoria carrying a package and paid the men's room a momentary stop. The tail went into the washroom right after he left, and there was only one person in it. He came out carrying the same package that Arz had seemingly left behind. They got photos of the incidents. It looked pretty suspicious, so they decided to keep an eye on the second guy in the washroom, too. Arz didn't appear to talk to anyone else. He left so fast it took them by surprise."

"Christ, I wonder what that was all about," said Russ.

"Hold your horses. The surveillance team split up and called for backup. One man followed Arz back to his shop, and the guy in the washroom grabbed a flight to Vancouver within half an hour. Then the son of a bitch rented one of those sleep places and parked himself in it for a few hours while the Mounties just had to wait him out."

"Boy, I bet they were they pissed," Russ commented.

"Yep, don't know what the bastard was doing in there, but he sure took his time. It wasn't long after he reemerged that they found out he was trying to take a flight out to Dubai. It was his misfortune that someone working for the airline recognized him in a name other than the one on the photo sub passport he was using."

"Do tell me, it was Al Zain." Russ figured they could have gotten lucky.

"Yes, sir. A fingerprint scan identified him. He was your student."

"Holy shit! I knew it. I knew there was a good reason to be a little suspicious of what that one was up to. It confirms my opinion that he's involved with Zadeh in some nasty business."

"Off the record, the RCMP has been working closely with Judd on the whole case. Apparently, the printer guy wasn't initially aware of the pinch as they picked him up soon after the whole thing went down. They were also able to get a warrant for his shop based on what they got tying him to Al Zain. They've also found some information that he's involved with a photographer here in Vancouver who does all his photos for what looks like phony documents and got a warrant to search his premises too."

"Interesting. Seems this started a roller coaster, and it's getting scarier by the minute. Sounds like a bad bunch to me. Now that I come to think about it, I may have some notes in my file on Al Zain that can make another connection to the printer. I seem to remember that the girl I interviewed for his reference check said that Al Zain was with Zadeh visiting someone in Victoria.

That might be the printer guy. I'll check out my notes and let Judd know."

Corby wasn't finished and continued, "They also managed to grab a cell phone from the printer. It hadn't been in use long, but they were able to trace some interesting numbers that belonged to a couple of guys in the States. They've contacted the FBI and Homeland Security. It might help to focus this investigation even more. They both work in water reservoirs."

"Christ almighty! That's a similar angle to the job application for Al Zain. He was applying to work at the water treatment plant," Russ exclaimed. "It sounds as if this could be the terrorist ring that we were warned about. Biological weapons and the drinking water serving some US cities. I don't know why the hell they'd go after me, though. How did you find out about it?"

"They scanned Al Zain's fingerprints at the airport and came up with his identity, and then they called me looking to see what information we had because I posted a watch on the national computer base. He had a one-way ticket to Dubai and another whole new identity, in a British passport, when they nabbed him. They suspected there was an identity switch from what they've learned about Arz and some of the comments by one of the airline employees. The airline clerk had been a student at the same college and thought he recognized him. He knew him under a different name. When they called, I had them talk to Judd."

"Wow, that was a stroke of luck!"

"Yeah. Judd said that they called his bluff on the passport, but he was real smooth and said he'd found it a few days earlier and had made the photo exchange himself. They questioned him extensively then charged him for uttering a forged passport. Fortunately, they were able to later lift a fingerprint belonging to Arz off the package. They're both in custody. Al Zain's over at the Wilkie."

"After Zadeh had been picked up, it sounds as if Al Zain was in a hurry to get out of town. Has he made any contacts for bail?"

"Well, he won't be going anywhere in a hurry now, he's been denied bail as a flight risk because they're also holding him on suspicion of murder, they found his cellmate dead when they went to pick him up for his bail hearing after his first night."

"Whoa! Murder? How does he connect with the cellmate? How did the guy die?"

"Everybody's waiting for the autopsy results and trying to find out the connection. Last I heard, he didn't even have a lawyer. He was using a duty counsel. Seems to be reluctant to contact anyone and I don't think that Arz knows that he's in custody. Everything is very much under wraps. Top security."

"It seems rather strange that he'd kill the cellmate."

"They haven't got a clue what that's all about yet. Personally, I'm not surprised that they went after you. They found a passport photo of the baggage handler that was involved in the drug bust on your last shift at the photographer's studio. He's connected to this group somehow. They must have realized that they kept running into you, even in Hong Kong. They probably think you're on to them, Mr. Super Sleuth."

"It's not by choice, I assure you. This murder thing is a whole other matter, though, I can't see how it fits. Why would he murder someone if he just had the passport issue at the end of the day?"

"Like I said, they're trying to find a connection, but they haven't come up with anything yet."

"I'd be interested in seeing how it unfolds."

"All I can say is that I hope somebody finds out what these guys are up to." Corby was exhausted from talking about the whole situation. "Let's forget these fellows for now and enjoy the fishing. Sounds as if the big fish are all locked up."

"Are you sure about the wife or the cousin?" Russ asked again. "How do you know that they're not involved?"

"They say the wife appears to be pretty naive, has a few bucks, gorgeous as hell, and she's expecting a kid soon. She apparently met him here and likely doesn't know much about him unless he's confided in her. Her government vouches for her and her family. Apparently she checks out, and she may be in for a rough ride before this is all over what with the baby and all. Right now she's backing Zadeh to the hilt and thinks we've got him all wrong. She's even paying for the lawyer—no legal aid here. As for the cousin, Judd's checking him out with the help of our friends south of the border."

"You said the wife's from Temesekia. It's my guess she's likely a babe in the woods and doesn't have a clue what she's got herself into. As for the cousin, I'm just not sure," Russ commented.

40

The day following Hassan's arrest, Jas woke late and was concerned that she might not be able to get into see Hassan. Checking the schedule in the pamphlet that Jordan Connors had given her, she noted that she had to book an appointment. Wednesday, today, was the only day of the week a visitation was allowed. She called the prison and was disappointed when she was advised that all visits had to be scheduled at least twenty-four hours in advance.

She was also informed that, at the present time, her husband was not permitted visitors at all as he was being held in temporary detention, and no risk assessments had been completed. Dana had called just as she hung up, and Jas relayed to her the gist of her conversation with the prison officer. She also told her that she needed to keep busy and was going to the school that afternoon to see if they had courses open for enrollment for the fall semester. That would let her keep her medical coverage and occupy her time before the baby arrived in October.

After checking on Jas, Dana caught the bus and headed over to the courthouse in New Westminster. She tried to slip quietly into the building to ask where she might find the duty counsel office. She was shocked that she had to adhere to some customary procedures before she was instructed to go to the far end of the large hallway. The room that was not much bigger than a closet was situated next to a long counter with a window.

Dana was quite surprised at the large numbers of people milling about the courthouse. She sincerely hoped that she didn't run into anyone from the school as she bowed her head low and promptly proceeded to her destination. It was a congested area, and the crowd of people appeared to be lined up at the counter to see the same person she needed to.

It took close to half an hour before Dana made it to the front of the line and asked to speak to Mr. Dean, the lawyer who had called her that morning on what he said was an urgent matter regarding Hamid. He had refused to discuss the matter further over the phone, and she had agreed to come to see him today.

Dana had felt intimidated when she first arrived. She had been made to empty her pockets and open her purse for inspection by the court guard. After she had been directed to a counter at the end of another hallway, the person there asked her the purpose of her visit and made her show her identification. It had taken almost another hour before a short, balding, and bespectacled man opened the door of the small room and called her name.

As she identified herself, she was invited into the little room next door to the reception office. The attorney quickly decided that she was a shy and nervous young woman of Arab background who likely had little exposure to what he was about to divulge and decided to handle her as tactfully as possible. He wondered what type of relationship she had with Mr. Al Zain.

"Thank you for coming, Ms. Jahel," Mr. Dean said. "Are you a close friend of Mr. Al Zain?"

"We attend classes together at the Douglas College and occasionally join other students for a meal away from the campus. I don't think he knows many people in Vancouver. How can I help you, Mr. Dean? Is there something wrong?"

Mr. Dean informed her that Hamid had asked him to contact her because he was being held in the Pacific Institution with an extremely serious charge of uttering a forged passport and needed a lawyer.

"I'm the duty counsel here and represent people when they don't have a lawyer or until they get one. Mr. Al Zain said that he has no family in Canada and doesn't know very many people but thought you might be able to help him get in touch with some-one who knows a lawyer that would be willing to represent him."

"Oh dear," replied Dana, "I'm not sure what I can do. How long has he been there?"

"Well, they arrested him a couple of days ago, but I'm afraid he won't be leaving anytime soon. He's also being investigated for, hmm, murder," he said hesitatingly in a low voice.

"Murder did you say?" Dana gasped and appeared to be physi-cally frightened.

"The morning after he was arrested, the prison guards found his cellmate dead. The circumstances seem rather suspicious, and they're being investigated. I've spoken to your friend, and he says he had nothing to do with the fellow's death. As a matter of fact, he was adamant that he didn't even talk to him as he was already sleeping when Mr. Al Zain arrived." He cleared his throat before continuing.

"There's going to be an autopsy, but it takes time for that to be completed. There are some very serious things going on here. For now, the main thing is to get him representation for the pass-port charge."

Taking several minutes to regain her composure, Dana explained that they were both students who had first met each other at the Douglas College; neither of them had any relatives in Canada. She had only recently developed a friendship with him and a few other students. Although she considered him to be a friend, she confided that she didn't know anything about his family or life before he came to the school.

"He keeps pretty much to himself as I told you, though a few of us occasionally go out for a meal, together. You know he is such an excellent student. Sometimes he helps me with my studies. I don't know what to say. I can't believe that he has committed any crimes and certainly not murder."

She recalled that he had told her that he had to leave the coun-try for a short time as he had a family emergency, but she had no idea how she could be of any help with his current situation.

"Can you hire a lawyer for him?" Mr. Dean asked.

"I'm sorry, but I don't have any money. As I said, we're students. I'll check around with some of the other students at the college, though, and see if we can raise some money. Do you know how much it would cost? Many of the students have had lawyers who represent them on immigration matters. Perhaps, I can see if I can find someone to help him," Dana cautiously replied.

"Well, I'll continue to represent him for now, but you might contact the legal aid office and see if they'll help him out. As I said, he's been taken over to the Pacific Institution, a regional assessment center, and he said he would like you to pay him a visit. Maybe he's got something in mind," he stated gloomily as he handed her his business card.

"Where is this place, and when can I go there?"

He quickly gave her directions and said that she'd have to check with the institution about public visiting hours; then he thanked her for coming and ushered her to the door. He hadn't even given her more than ten minutes of his time. The place was like a factory line shuffling people in and out in short intervals.

Mr. Dean reminded her of an automaton. She felt that he was close to being useless. He was a lawyer, yet he didn't seem to want to help Hamid. How could that be? she wondered. Don't lawyers take an oath that they have to assist people they are trained to help? To tell the truth, she was surprised that Hamid had asked for her help.

Feeling overcome by the whole situation with both Hassan and Hamid, Dana was on the verge of tears and struggled to get home without breaking down. She had never found herself confronted with such a situation before and wondered how on earth she could help with the situation. She had just reached the door to her room as her cell phone began ringing and was never so glad to hear someone's voice.

It was Hassan's cousin, Noe, calling. He inquired whether Jas was with her as he had tried to reach her at home, and there was no answer. She recollected that Jas had gone to the college before she burst into tears. Taking deep breaths, Dana apprised Noe of the situation with Hassan.

"Damn, what else is going to happen? You say he's been charged with murder?"

"No, they haven't charged him with that. According to the lawyer at the courthouse they need to perform an autopsy. He said they were going to hold him on suspicion of murder. The only charge he's facing right now is for uttering a forged passport."

"Who is he supposed to have murdered?" Noe asked.

"I don't know. Apparently, they arrested him for using a phony passport when he tried to board a plane with it. Then someone in his jail cell died, and they think Hamid might have killed him."

"Okay, Dana, this doesn't sound good. I think you had better stay out of it. I'll get hold of Jordan Connors. He practices both criminal and immigration law, and I'm sure he'll take care of matters. Do you have the phone number and name of the lawyer who contacted you?"

Dana pulled out the business card and repeated all of the information on it. Feeling relieved that the entire matter was no longer in her hands, she thanked Noe for his support while suggesting that they shouldn't discuss it with Jas; it just might be too much for her.

"I couldn't agree more, Dana. If you need anything, please feel free to call me. I'm sure that there is an explanation for all of this. I don't know too much about Hamid, but I doubt that he'd kill some guy just out of the blue. Connors will get to the bottom of it, he's good at what he does, and I think for charges like this, Hamid would likely get some sort of legal aid. Try not to worry about Hamid. I suspect Jas needs your support more than anyone else right now. I'd actually appreciate it if you'd just concentrate on helping her."

"This lawyer said that Hamid wants me to come to the prison and visit him. I don't know what to do."

"Dana, if you want to go, it's up to you. You don't have to, though. I'll contact the lawyer there, and I'll let you know what he says. Then you can make up your mind."

"Thanks, Noe. I've never been around all these kinds of problems before, and I'm finding it all a bit overwhelming. You're right, though, Jas and the baby are the most important people, and don't worry, I'll be there for her. As a matter of fact, I don't think we should mention anything about Hamid to Jas. She's just so worried about Hassan. I think it's not wise to burden her with more."

"You're absolutely right. My lips are sealed. You're a good friend to have, Dana."

41

Jordan Connors had become extremely frustrated while waiting for the information that he hoped would allow for Hassan Zadeh's release. He had other clients who had used fictitious names, and they hadn't been detained indefinitely. Personally, he felt that the government was overreacting and for some reason had taken a very hard line in this case.

Sitting in his office, he felt that this might be his lucky day! His physician had finally been able to determine the cause of his gastrointestinal problems. He hadn't known anyone in his family to have lactose intolerance before, but apparently that was the culprit. It had not only caused him a lot of discomfort, but it had also been a source of embarrassment to him for some time.

His thoughts were briefly interrupted as Jeanine stepped into the office. She handed him the envelope that had arrived from the prosecutor's office regarding the man from Kuwait that Noe had asked him to look after. As he glanced through the disclosure notes, he found that the autopsy report on the cellmate who had died was finally available.

"Ah, thank God, Jeanine, it appears that the luck of the Irish has stayed with us today!" he exclaimed. "It seems that the inmate who died out in the Pacific Institution had swallowed several packets of narcotics, and one burst open in his stomach. That's what caused his death. He died from an overdose of cocaine. This is indeed excellent news for our client."

"What a horrible way to die. I recently learned that some guy in Brazil did something similar. He had swallowed a whole bunch of capsules filled with cocaine, but the authorities were on to him, and they pumped his stomach. He lived, but then they charged him with smuggling drugs."

"Well, this guy wasn't so lucky and certainly caused our client some serious anxiety issues. Can you see if you can reach Noe Akbari on the phone?"

"Okay, I'm sure he's going to be relieved too," she said and returned to her office to make the call. A few minutes later she buzzed her boss and told him that Mr. Akbari was on the phone.

"Hi, Noe, how are you today?" Connors cheerily said.

"Pretty good, have you some news for me?"

"I won't keep you too long. I just called to let you know that the murder investigation against your friend has been dropped. Now that we're only dealing with the passport charge, he'll need to have a surety so we can get him released at the bail hearing scheduled next week. By the way, the cellmate died of a self-inflicted drug overdose."

"This is good news, at least for Hamid. How do I do this surety thing?"

"I'll put Jeanine back on in a minute, and she'll fill you in on what you need to do. However, I'm going to have to put some information together about your friend and thought you might be able to help me."

"I don't know too much about him. He is really Hassan's friend and apparently doesn't know many people in Canada. They met at the school. What kind of information?"

"Oh, the usual, would you know if he had any other friends or relatives in Canada?"

"Like I said, Hassan met him at the college. He said that he didn't have any family except that they recently found his missing brother overseas. I think in Iraq. Of course, he was also a friend to Hassan's wife and her friend, that girl named Dana, at the Douglas College. Hassan said that Hamid didn't know anyone else in Canada, and so they brought him over to our house for dinner a couple of times. A few times, the six of us, including

Dana, went to activities at the mosque. Hamid had told us that his family had all been killed by the Iraqis when they invaded Kuwait. Then he recently heard that his brother had been found alive. We haven't told Jas anything about what is happening with Hamid. We think she has enough on her plate."

"Ah yes, that is the reason he was in a hurry to leave Canada. I agree, there's no reason to involve Mrs. Zadeh in this nasty business with Mr. Al Zain."

"Yes, you're right, he was on his way to see him. That's the last I heard and really all I know."

"Did he know that other fellow that you referred to me from Kuwait? You know the illegal worker from the airport."

"You mean Sammi?"

"Yes."

"No, no. I hardly knew Sammi myself. I met him when he came to the carpet shop where I work. I don't think Hamid knew any of my patrons or even my friends for that matter. As for Sammi, he was new in town too. I don't even know if he knew many of the local shopkeepers near my job. I'd see him sometimes when I went for coffee at the doughnut shop, and he also went to the mosque where my wife and I usually attend."

"Isn't that the same mosque that Hassan goes to?"

"No. Hassan and Jas attend the mosque near their school. Occasionally, they attend our mosque, or we go with them to theirs for a special occasion. I think Dana and Hamid attend that mosque by the school, too."

"Yes, well, it does sound like you barely knew him. Why did this Sammi call you?"

"Although I'd given him a copy of my business card for sales referrals, I was pretty surprised to hear from him. When he got arrested, I guess he didn't know anyone else to call and used his one call that he was allowed to call me. I knew that he didn't know many people in Canada, so I took the responsibility to call you. Why do you ask about him? I thought he was deported."

"Yes, yes, he was deported. I guess I'm just trying to grasp for anything that might help out your friend. Your connection to the two guys from Kuwait suddenly struck me as a strange coincidence. I thought they might be part of a larger Kuwaiti community here in Canada that could provide some support to Hamid, and you might know of it."

"Lots of newcomers to Canada don't have family here and don't know many people. We meet in the mosque or at work, and often we become friends. I don't know if there's a Kuwaiti organization, though, where they may have connected."

"I guess that's understandable. It's no big deal. If you think of anything that might be useful to this chap Hamid Al Zain, please give me a call and give my regards to Mrs. Zadeh. I'll put you over to Jeanine now." And with that Connors abruptly ended the conversation.

Connors sat back and reflected on what he knew about Al Zain. He had no priors, he was going to plead guilty to the passport charges, and his explanation for committing the crime would hopefully elicit some sympathy from the judge. He claimed that he received word from someone in Dubai that his brother had been found by the British in an Iraqi prison. All of his relatives had been killed during the invasion, and his brother had been presumed dead for more than four years.

He'd also argue that Mr. Al Zain had no passport, and as he wasn't a Canadian citizen; he wasn't eligible for one at this time. As a former refugee, he couldn't approach the Embassy of the State of Kuwait. He hadn't been aware that he could ask the Canadian government to issue him a travel document. Foolishly he'd taken another approach to try and get to his brother as quickly as possible.

Connors was confident that he had a reasonable chance of just getting a basic slap on the wrist for the passport charge. The only significant problem that he saw was that Hamid had provided a rather sketchy story about the person who had supplied him with the passport. The Mounties were trying to get him to rat out on some guy in Victoria, but he swore he didn't know him.

He had insisted that he had panicked when he learned that his brother was alive. He asked around the college how to get a passport to leave the country, and someone told him to go to the men's room located nearest the Cathay Pacific airline counter at the Victoria airport at the time he did. He didn't know the person who advised him. He was Asian and might have been from China.

He said that the man snapped his picture, and Al Zain gave him five hundred dollars. When he got to the meeting place, he'd found the package beside the sink containing the passport with his photo in it. He said he didn't have any contact with any-one else and didn't know who had left the package. Although his story was suspicious to the authorities, it was plausible to Connors, and he was satisfied that he could offer a reasonable defense to his client.

Connors planned to spend the rest of the day catching up on some of his paperwork, including the preparation of sentencing arguments for his Kuwaiti client, which he would base on the mitigating circumstances. He felt somewhat confident that the man would get a decent break. Now, he also had to get to the outstanding written submissions to make on another complex case for an unaccompanied minor, and he had to prepare for an extradition hearing that was taking place in the morning. He was glad to have a little time to get back on top of his work.

His reprieve was short-lived. Opening a courier package that was handed him soon after lunch, he felt a disturbing sense of unease as he read that he was being served with notice that the solicitor general of Canada had signed a copy of a security cer-tificate put forward by the immigration minister from a security intelligence report that involved Hassan Zadeh. The government was applying for a danger opinion against him.

Connors hadn't handled a security certificate before. A danger opinion allowed the government to deport anyone who was not a

Canadian citizen, on the supposition that they are a danger to the Canadian public or to Canada's security. As both the ministers of immigration and public safety have to sign off on a security certificate if they want to remove someone, he figured that there had to be some very serious grounds that the government would be arguing to make Hassan inadmissible.

The annoying point was that some of the information would be protected from disclosure by law. A judge at the Federal Court would examine the security intelligence reports in the absence of both Connors and Zadeh before giving them a summary of it that would eliminate any information that might be considered a risk to any other person or national security in general.

There weren't many prior cases that had been before the courts in Canada. He was astounded by this new allegation and was curious to know what the young Iranian had gotten himself into. He had heard that such cases usually involved a deadly combination of political and religious fanaticism that resulted in accusations of terrorism.

Connors recalled that during his own youth everyone had an interest in the politics of the day. He and his friends had chosen their legal career paths according to their political leanings from those early days at the university. Some had been drawn to corporate governance, while others fought for human rights. There often appeared to be competing interests, and he had found that the corporate mentality usually prevailed.

He had laughed at the words of the great Winston Churchill, "Any man who is under 30, and is not a liberal, has not heart; and any man who is over 30, and is not a conservative, has no brains." Yet to this day, he still considered himself to be a centrist liberal. He was a devout believer in policies promoting civil liberties and human rights, as well as economic and social liberalism. His father had been active in the labor movement and had done his fair share of work on political campaigns for candidates who advocated progressive taxation, collective bargaining, and social welfare provisions.

His Irish roots had also made him wary of mixing religion and politics. The human costs were too onerous. It seemed senseless to him that so many wars had stemmed from religious differences. He had never understood how two Christian religious factions could condone the use of violence in Ireland, for example. The Catholics and Protestants had been doing this for centuries. Then again, the Christians had fought Islam as long ago as the Crusades, yet there were a lot of similarities between the two religions.

He had seen a number of cases in the courts where young men and women had been indoctrinated into a fanatical religious frenzy and advocated violence as a duty to preserve their religious beliefs. He had heard from his father how his own dear grandfather had carried a shotgun on his property and forbade any protestant to set foot on his land. He sincerely hoped that his young client was not involved in such extreme notions.

He set his written submissions aside and concentrated on the hearing that he was scheduled to attend in the morning. It was going to be a tough case, and he wasn't very confident that he'd be successful. Connors was going to go out on a limb and try to obtain a stay of removal to the United States. He was going to argue that Canada Border Services had abused their powers by cooperating with the Americans in what amounted to disguised extradition contrary to the objectives of the Immigration Act. It wasn't often that cases of this nature were successful, but it was the only argument he had left.

42

Jas arrived at the prison for her scheduled two o'clock visit but still had to endure a lengthy wait before she was allowed to enter the barren room. It was equipped with just four chairs placed before a windowed counter that was compartmentalized with four phones. Now eleven weeks since Hassan had first been brought here, this was only her fourth visit to the jail.

Jas still felt uncomfortable in these surroundings as she quietly waited for Hassan to appear garbed like all the other prisoners in orange. He moved to the stall opposite her, sat down, and picked up the phone in front of him. She did likewise as they couldn't hear through the glass. It was annoying and didn't provide them any real privacy.

"Is there any way we can talk privately?" she asked.

He shook his head from side to side; then he thanked her for coming. He seemed to be in good spirits, considering his situation. It was difficult to read the thoughts that were in his mind; his expressions and mannerisms reminded her of the reactions he displayed on the night she had returned from Temesekia. He showed little emotion as he inquired about her well-being to which she simply advised him that she was doing okay.

"Jas, they still haven't been able to get the documents in time for the next hearing," he warned. "Mr. Connors paid me a visit yesterday and said that even if we can get them, another matter has occurred, and he's not very hopeful that the judge is going to let me out of here anytime soon. Maybe Dana could move in with you so you won't be alone?"

"You make it sound as if you expect to be here for quite a while longer?" Jas asked. "I'm doing fine, and I really don't know Dana all that well. I'd prefer not to involve her in our personal affairs. Don't get me wrong, she has been a good friend in the time I've known her, but it is quite another matter to have her live with me. I have faith that you will be home soon, and Mr. Connors thinks that he might be able to get them to accept your identity card. In any event, Dana has her own life to live and is busy preparing to graduate and get a job."

"Jas, things are not easy. This government may make things very difficult. I don't know why, but they believe that I'm a danger to this country or some kind of security risk." Hassan warily continued to advise her, "Connors is waiting for further information to see what we're up against."

"Danger? Security risk? This sounds crazy. It sounds as if somebody has quite an imagination. Have you done anything that would make them think you're dangerous?"

"Jas, right now I don't know where these accusations are coming from or what they're about. I'm a simple man and just want to be with my wife and make a new life together. You know that."

It became apparent that Hassan's conversation was cautious, and Jas sensed that he was unwilling to say too much under the circumstances.

"Do you think that Iran is causing this problem? Perhaps when Noe's father tried to get your birth certificate, it tipped them off that you're alive and well, living in Canada. Surely, knowing what happened to your parents, Canadian authorities won't listen to them?"

"Hmm! That could be the problem. We'll have to wait and see."

"How long do you think this is going to take? What does Mr. Connors think?"

"Like I said, Jas, I don't know anything more right now. Has anyone come to the house at all?" he asked nonchalantly.

"Only the two officers who previously came to tell me that you were on some sort of an immigration hold, in the beginning. They asked to look around the apartment, but I didn't let them. I understand that they can't without a search warrant. I don't feel comfortable with strangers going through my house."

A worried look spread across Hassan's face. He signaled for her to remain silent, motioning with his finger, and then he changed the course of their conversation to ask how she was feeling. "If they keep me in here for much longer, I've heard that they have a program that allows for private family visiting where you can come and stay for a few days."

"What do you mean? Stay in the prison cell with you?"

"No, Jas, they have small units. Each unit is a small private cottage that has a kitchen, bedroom, and living room located somewhere on the grounds. You would have to place an order with the prison canteen for groceries for the duration of your visit, and they have to be paid for in advance of your visit. Some guys have their kids, parents, or grandparents come and stay."

"I hope it doesn't come to that," Jas replied. "The time is getting close for the baby, and I really want you home."

"Did Mr. Connors tell you to give my laptop to Hamid? He's got some things on it."

"I haven't heard from Hamid since the day following your arrest. He had a family emergency. He thinks that his brother was found alive. He said that someone overseas contacted him, and I think he went to Iraq."

"Really, that sounds like good news for him. Hope things work out well for him. He's a good guy. How's school going?"

"I'm taking an interesting course on product marketing. I attend each of my courses for three hours, two days a week. I'm finding it's helping me to focus on developing a business plan for my software. However, I love the graphic design program. The good thing about it is that it applies to both print and web-based products. I had to take three courses to qualify as a full-time student and maintain my medical insurance, so I also took a related course on graphic and package design."

"I don't know how long you're going to be able to keep going to school. The baby should be here in less than two months."

"Don't worry. I spoke to a counselor at the college, and they're going to try and let me complete the course work from home if it comes to that. I've more than halfway completed the term now. In any event, the baby will be a Canadian citizen, so he'll be entitled to free medical coverage. After the baby's born, I'll spend some time at home working on the software, and I think these courses will be helpful."

"Jordan Connors said that you're paying him. I have to warn you that he can get very expensive. Will you ask Noe to remind him that he was going to see if I could get legal aid?"

"I don't know about these things, but Noe mentioned that he thought you could apply for legal aid here in the jail. If this doesn't get resolved soon, you might have to do that, but I'm okay for money right now. Mr. Connors only asked for eight hundred dollars as a retainer. He's charged me three hundred dollars for his preparation time; then he said it would be five hundred for each hearing he attends. I was hoping it won't cost more than that, will it?"

"It'll just depend on how long they keep me in here, and he'll definitely slap me with a bill for his trips here, in addition to his travel time. I should warn you that every time you phone his office, he bills his time. He charges by the minute at a rate of three hundred dollars per hour. With these new allegations, it might get really expensive. I'll see if I can get the paperwork in here and make the legal aid application, just in case he decides he wants more money."

Suddenly, the guard stepped into the room and informed them that their time was up. They quickly said their good-byes. Jas assured Hassan that she would drop by the office before she left and find out how to deposit some money in a prison account for him.

"Let me know if you need money in your prison bank account. I'll see you next week at the bail hearing. Remember, I love you," Jas remarked as she prepared to leave.

Back in his cell, later that night, Hassan thought about the contents on his computer and how he could get it somewhere safe without arousing the suspicions of his wife. He lay restless while he recalled the sheer agony of the days following the burning of his hands. He'd barely caught a glimpse of the elderly man before he jabbed Hassan in the arm with a needle, and he'd been put out cold. Several hours later, he awoke with an intense pain in his fingers and patches of his lower arms and upper hands.

He had had an insatiable thirst and desperately wanted a glass of water. At first, he wondered why there was an intravenous tube in his arm before he realized where he was. He was alone in the most sterile surroundings he had ever seen. The walls were starkly white. In fact, everything was white, including a bar-size fridge and a double cupboard topped by a small counter. The chair he'd sat in was gone, but he was sure that it was the same room that he briefly remembered being ushered into. The only difference was that when he had awakened he had found himself lying on a cot that had been brought into the room, and a nightstand with a small lamp atop had been placed beside it.

When he woke his heart had been pounding, and his mouth was dry. A strong animalistic instinct came over him with a driving need to be free. He had been disoriented and had barely felt anything beyond the throbbing pain of the burns when he ripped out the intravenous tube. Shakily he'd risen from the cot and edged his way toward the door.

His vision had become distorted, and his body began to shake with tremors that became almost violent. He was sure that he was going to collapse before he made the short crossing to the other side of the room. Just as he had reached for the handle of the door it had suddenly opened. The fellow he recalled from the front reception entered and caught him as he began to stumble.

Distantly, he remembered hearing him ask, "Whoa! Where are you going, buddy?" Then he had half-carried him back to the cot where, to the best of his recollection, he subsided into a near-comatose state. He had slept for what he thought was a few more hours, and when he woke his eyes had adjusted easily to the darkened room. The small light had been turned on, and he saw that the intravenous tubing had been restored.

He had sat up slowly and gratefully noticed the pitcher of ice water on a small table located beside the bed with a couple of wrapped sandwiches lying beside it. He wondered what day it was. How long had he been here? His hands were throbbing, and he wasn't sure that he could pour the water into the paper cup that sat beside it. He had felt like hell!

He'd actually been quite relieved when suddenly the guy from the front desk had reappeared and asked him how he was doing. He acknowledged that he had seen better days, but was sure he would survive. He asked him to help get a glass of water and unwrap a sandwich; then he watched as the guy undid the bandages. His fingers looked brutal. He had to turn his head away as the fellow checked each of the burns before putting on some salve and rewrapping them as he explained how he was to take care of them in the days ahead. Again, he asked the attendant to pour him some more water. He had an unquenchable thirst. He was certain he couldn't use his hands for even the simplest of actions and wondered how long he would be there.

He took some more medication for the pain, and when the man explained that some preparations had to be made, he had taken his picture for a passport. He would have just one more day before he needed to get moving on his journey. Hassan hadn't asked any questions; he just accepted whatever he was instructed to do. Then he'd slept soundly again until the next day.

As he lay in his cell now, more than a year after his arrival in Canada, he looked down at his hands and could still see the pink scars that served as a reminder of the pain he had suffered. It had

taken months for his hands to heal. In fact, they were still healing. He gritted his teeth and hoped that he had not endured that
pain in vain.

When they first brought him to this jail, they had taken his
fingerprints, but Hassan had felt pretty confident that his prints
couldn't be matched. He believed that all possibility of identifying him had been destroyed. Now he was a little worried, though,
because the government lawyer had said that they had matched a
fingerprint on his Permanent Resident application to Mahmoud
Bahrami. He wondered how could that be.

At the time that he had arranged to have his fingerprints
burned off, he'd been assured that it would be a permanent solution. He examined his fingertips more closely now. Then he realized that one of his thumbs showed some of the familiar swirls
of an identifiable fingerprint. Son of a bitch! That old man had
been sloppy. He was disappointed with the sick old bastard. The
organization had been using his services for years for interrogation purposes, and though the professor pretended that he did
the work for research, Hassan knew exactly who and what he was
and that he was sexually stimulated by his torture tactics. Men
like him disgusted Hassan, but he supposed they were a necessary evil.

43

The screaming wouldn't stop! The noises were replaying over and over again as if emanating from a broken record. Then she felt gentle hands wiping her brow and a distant voice telling her that she was safe. Jas knew then that the initial sounds had been her own as she slipped back into a coma.

She reawoke a little later and could hear people around her. She could feel that everyone was staring at her, but she was powerless to open her heavy eyelids. She tried to lift her hand, and she heard someone say, "Look! She moved her finger!"

A hand grasped her own, and its owner started rubbing the back side of her thumb, talking to her in a soothing voice. Jas had many thoughts and emotions but didn't have the power over her body to express them. So she lay there very aware of people around but unable to communicate as she struggled to focus on their conversation. Then she drifted off to sleep, again.

This pattern continued for several days as Jas struggled to catch the sounds and focused on the smells around her as she tried desperately to open her eyes to no avail.

"I think she's coming round," a voice interjected amid her thoughts. And again she tried to force her eyes to open, but instead she saw the vehicle heading straight at her and heard the shouting of people all around.

"How's the baby doing?" another person asked.

The baby! Oh god, the baby, thought Jas as she inched her arms toward her stomach. She couldn't feel the baby! Panic set in, and then she softly began to cry. "The baby was gone! No," she whispered.

Almost immediately, she felt someone pat her hand and offer some soothingly reassuring words. "You're okay, Mrs. Zadeh. Your baby's okay too!" She felt comforted by the words, and at that moment she relaxed feeling that somehow she was safe and everything would be okay as once more she drifted back to sleep.

She didn't know how long she had been there, but finally one afternoon, she managed to open her eyes just a little. She appeared to be in a hospital bed and could hear low voices on the other side of a curtain facing her.

"Becky, you realize that you can't go back to him. Your life is in grave danger."

"I know, Ms. Katy. I don't understand why he keeps hurting me. I've never done anything wrong, and he just picks on the least little thing. But this last time, I really thought he might kill me."

"I hate to tell you this, Becky, but he's not going to change. He's violent. He's been violent his whole life. Matter of fact, he's a danger to the public in general when he starts drinking. You're not to blame for this. You must remember that you don't only have yourself to think about now. You've got to think of the baby and your child's future."

"Ms. Katy, I can't help it. I still love him. I kept hoping that things would be better once we had a baby. I don't think I can manage without him."

"Becky, think about this very carefully. Recently his physical assaults have been increasing. He's also employing other tactics like controlling all the money in your home, emotional abuse, isolation, and threats of harm to the baby. Eventually, you won't be able to act independently without him. He'll box you in, and perhaps next time you won't be able to get out. Your baby will never be safe. This is why there are women's shelters to protect innocent people like you and your unborn child. At the shelter, we can help you. There are a lot of dangerous people out there, some whom we least suspect."

"My head tells me you're right, Ms. Katy. I'll come. I'm just so scared, but I don't really have any other choice. I've got to protect my baby. I think I should move back to Jamaica where my mom can help me, but I know it's not much better there. Men abuse women all the time, and they always get away with it. He might even go there looking for me. If that happens, I think he will kill me."

"The shelter is safe, and he won't find you there. The doctor said that you could leave today. I have a bed for you, actually a room for both you and your daughter. Is that okay? I can help you."

"What if he's watching the hospital?"

"Don't you worry! My husband has a security company, and my dad's a retired immigration officer who now works with him. My dad has promised that he'll be here to help get you safely to the women's shelter. If you really do want to leave the country, my dad has lots of contacts all over the world and might be able to help you with that too. I just don't know if going to Jamaica would be a very good idea. I think that you and your baby might have a better life in Canada, perhaps moving outside of Vancouver. We'll talk about it after the baby's born. You must remember though, Becky, your guy's a terribly dangerous man."

"Yes, Ms. Katy. Everyone warned me about him, but sometimes we have to find out the hard way. We can't help whom we fall in love with, and then it's hard to get out of the situation. I guess I'll be okay, I trust you. I haven't much packing up to do. When will your dad get here?"

As Jas lay listening to the conversation in the bed next to her, she closed her eyes and thought back to the afternoon when Hassan had told her that the Canadian government thought that he was a danger to the public. She also remembered that her own government had warned her that he was a very dangerous man. She recalled how upset she had been when she left the prison thinking about both of those conversations, and that was when she stepped into the path of an oncoming vehicle.

She wondered if both governments were right about her husband. Was Hassan a dangerous man? As quickly as the thought had crossed her mind, she dismissed the idea. Hassan wasn't a violent man. He'd never even raised his voice at her or threatened her in any way.

"Speak of the devil, here's Dad now. You get dressed, and I'll just take him out in the hall to wait for you," the voice of the woman called Ms. Katy interrupted her thoughts.

Jas slowly turned her head and gazed into the bluest pair of eyes that she had ever seen. A handsome older man was standing in the doorway. She felt a spiritual connection to those eyes, as if to instinctively say that this man was compassionate, trustworthy, dependable, and reliable. A person who was not unlike her own father. The blueness of his eyes mesmerized her and reminded her of the gentle sea surrounding her homeland. Instinctively, she knew that the frightened and abused woman in the next bed would be guarded to safety by this man.

The door opened again, and a nurse rushed over to her. "Oh, Mrs. Zadeh, you're awake?"

Jas thought that she caught a flicker of surprise in the man's face as she managed to ask, "My baby?"

"Your baby's just fine, he's just a wee little boy because he arrived a little early, but I'll bring him to see you very soon. You've had a very difficult time. How are you feeling?"

"Him? I have a son?"

"Yes, dear. We've been taking good care of him. He's still in an incubator because he was a little underweight, but you're not to worry, we can bring him in for you to see for yourself shortly. I just want to check all your vitals first and let your doctor know that you've finally come to." Her roommate's visitors smiled at her as they hurriedly exited from the room.

"How long have I been here?"

As the nurse placed the blood pressure cuff on her arm, she said that Jas had been brought there nearly two weeks before.

Then she caught a glimpse of a young woman who hurried out the door; this was probably Becky. Throughout the day, she was poked and prodded by the nurses, doctor, and lab technicians. Finally, she was able to spend coveted, precious time with her son. They allowed him to be wheeled in by her bedside in his incubator, and the doctor had agreed that he could stay there.

At five o'clock, Dana had found her sitting and staring in awe at the tiny baby beside her. Dana recalled the day that she had been at school when a knock had come to the classroom door asking if she could step out to the hallway for a few minutes. The school had received a call from the local hospital that someone whose identification papers said she was a student at the college by the name of Jaslyn Zadeh had been admitted. She had been in a traffic accident and was in a coma.

They had been unable to find any family information on her but had found a little notebook with the name of the Douglas College with Dana's name in it. The police contacted the school trying to find out how to reach Jas's family. After learning that she was a foreign student, they were informed that Dana Jahel was her close friend. To this end Dana had been asked if she could come to the hospital to identify the woman and possibly assist them in contacting her family.

Jas felt so alone, and she was petrified of what her future might hold. When Dana arrived, she couldn't ever remember being so happy to see someone walk through the door. She turned to her friend with a weak smile and said, "Hi, how are you? This is my son. Isn't he beautiful?"

"Don't be silly, Jas," Dana quipped. "Look at how beautiful his mother is. I wouldn't have thought he'd be anything but handsome. My goodness, you've had us so worried! When did you wake up?"

"I've been awake for a few hours now."

"What happened, Jas? Do you remember anything? The hospital said you were in a traffic accident."

"It's coming back to me, and I think it was my fault. I hope no one else was hurt."

"No, apparently not. Noe, his wife, and I have just been concerned about you."

"I wasn't watching where I was going and stepped out when I shouldn't have. I can't remember anything else. I don't even remember having the baby. The doctor said they had to deliver him. How did you find out I was here. Does Hassan know?"

"I think so. Noe called Mr. Connors, his lawyer, and asked him to let Hassan know. The hospital called the school after they found school documents and something with my name. I guess in your purse. I've been taking photos of the baby for you every day for over a week now since the day after I found out you were here. Have you seen the doctor today?"

"Earlier today. I think it was still morning. I'm glad you took the pictures, and I can't wait to see them."

Before Dana could reply, a doctor entered the room and had asked her to step outside for a few minutes so he could examine Jas. Dana said that was fine; she'd just go and make a call and be back shortly.

"I won't be far away, Jas. I'll call Noe and let him know you're awake."

When Dana returned about ten minutes later, the doctor was advising Jas that she could probably go home with the baby by the end of the week.

As he left the room, Jas said, "You know, Dana, I think I'm going to call him Anil after my dad. I don't think Hassan would mind. By the way, the doctor thinks I can go home soon, maybe in a few days. Could you ask Maryam to bring me some things to take him home in?"

"Noe's on his way over. You can ask him yourself. He's extremely pleased to hear you're awake. The school also gave the hospital information, and I think they called your family in Temesekia. If you're up to it, you might give them a call."

"Oh dear, well, after everyone leaves, I'll give my sister-in-law a call. She can explain everything to my brothers. I hope that they aren't planning on coming here."

Jas was thankful when the nurse cut short the visit with Dana and Noe. She had been glad to see them, but she was getting overly tired, and she was anxious to call her sister-in-law. Faith would set her family's minds at ease. As she reached for the phone, she noticed a business card lying on the nightstand beside it. She picked up the card and read that there was both a name and phone number on it. It said "Mrs. Katy Freeman, Social Worker," with the name of an organization. Jas thought that the girl Becky must have left it there by accident, and without thinking, she slipped it into her purse.

44

Jordan Connors had been practicing law for more than twenty years, but he had never seen a situation quite like the one involving Zadeh. A lot of intelligence had been gathered about his client from all over the world. He knew that it was going be an uphill battle to poke holes in much of what they had uncovered. To make matters even worse, he had been informed by the prosecutor off the record that the Americans were carefully watching this case. This was bound to be the most challenging case of his career.

He didn't even know where to begin. His initial hurdle was going to be getting some straight answers from the people whom he knew were associated with Mr. Zadeh. He needed to determine if any of them had knowledge of the organization that his client had been involved in. He wondered if they were also connected to any of the events and whether he personally would be safe in his dealings with them.

His thoughts drifted to the other client that Zadeh's cousin had recently referred to him, Al Zain. Coincidentally, he had been caught using a phony passport trying to leave Canada the day after Zadeh had been arrested. He was curious whether the two incidents were somehow related. Was his haste to leave Canada because of his lost brother, or was it because of Zadeh's arrest? He wouldn't be able to continue representing both men if they were both involved in some sinister plot.

He was also puzzled about the cousin. Was he truly his cousin? He had known Noe for a long time now. He rather liked the chap. He seemed to be a regular kind of guy. He worked, had a nice family, and he had referred quite a few clients to him over the years. It nagged at the back of his mind, though, that he seemed to be connected to them all, even that other guy that they had deported to Kuwait.

He had confronted Zadeh earlier that same afternoon with most of the salient details that the government had been able to amass concerning his activities over the past ten years. He hadn't been able to read anything in Hassan's face. He just sat impassively without any comments or reaction during the entire time Jordan went through the disclosure he had received. Jordan felt frustrated with the difficulty in getting the man to discuss the allegations. The man's cold blank stare had revealed nothing.

He informed Hassan Zadeh that the government asserted that after completing his university degree in Iran, Zadeh had gone to Beirut where he attended the Popular Front for the Liberation of Palestine (PFLP) terrorist training camp. At the camp, he had used the named Mahmoud Bahrami. Zadeh had neither acknowledged or denied this. Connors mentally noted that there didn't appear to be a direct link between his client and the terrorist activities that the PFLP was known to have engaged in at that time.

The government said that Zadeh, while also using the name Bahrami, was present in Paris when several people were killed in the bombing of a synagogue, but the evidence hadn't actually placed the bomb in Zadeh's hands or shown a direct connection to him. Connors grabbed his writing pad and drew a line down the center of it. On the left column, he entered the number 1 and the letters *PFLP*. To the right in the next column, he made a note: "No relevance to organizational activities, speculation, what proof of training activities?"

They also had evidence that he had been in Lebanon. It was alleged that the young man had travelled to Egypt from there and attended the Zagazig University. During this period, he had become involved in a student group called Badr, which distributed Islamic fundamentalist pamphlets, and he authored a weekly periodical. The school records indicated that he was registered in the name Zadeh. While there, he met with two doctors who were leaders in a group called Al-Jihad al-Islami.

He travelled to Pakistan as a member of the International Islamic Relief Organization where he reconnected with at least one of the doctors who had now been convicted of terrorist activities. It was determined that a number of people in the relief organization and the doctor were sympathetic to the Taliban and Al-Jihad's involvement in Afghanistan. The government also had information that Zadeh was a skilled computer expert who had served as a communications assistant between the workers in Pakistan and their leaders in Afghanistan.

Later they uncovered that he had lived for periods of time in Yemen and Azerbaijan using the name Bahrami, but he had no visible means of support. They alleged that he continued to be associated with and was thought to be financially supported by terrorist organizations during that time. His actual activities were unknown.

The Canadian Security Intelligence Service had received documentation of his arrival in Temesekia where he, again, used the name Mahmoud Bahrami. He had married a local teacher within six months of his arrival and remained in the country for a period of three years. He was according to government records still married to that woman as he had never registered the divorce he had undertaken with the Muslim registry as required by law.

Shortly after the failure of his marriage, he left Temesekia for an unknown destination. However, a single fingerprint belonging to him was extracted from a package addressed to the American ambassador in Temesekia. The package had been laced with inhalational anthrax, and the employee who had opened it died. The Temesekian government wanted to question him about the incident and suspected that he had been responsible for the murder.

Subsequent to his departure from Temesekia, the authorities of the country had uncovered evidence of his past involvement in global terrorist activities during the three years he had lived in that country. After the arrest of a former associate of his and a forensic audit of that person's computer, they had uncovered links to several bombings of US embassies in other countries and of political assassinations in several countries using chemical weapons.

When Zadeh finally began talking to Connors, he had insisted that he wasn't the person that the government was accusing him of being. He admitted to some of the minor accusations, like where he went to school and organizations he had been involved with, but was adamant that he had never taken part in any of the attacks that they attributed to him and that he had divorced his former wife.

After Jordan had left the jail, he felt that little had been accomplished by his discussions with Zadeh; however, he also felt that a lot of the information that the government had was based on speculation and innuendo. As far as the so-called former associate was concerned, he may have received instructions from someone, but could they prove that the person giving the orders was his client or had any knowledge of this other man's activities?

He found it hard to believe that this simple man, Zadeh, was not only involved in chemical warfare and sophisticated terrorist activities perpetrated against various governments all over the world but that he was also considered to be possibly the mastermind. The whole thing seemed quite preposterous.

45

In his review of the government's disclosure against Hassan Zadeh, Jordan Connors thought that the single most damaging piece of evidence against his client would be the fingerprint. He thought back now to the badly burned hands of Zadeh when he had first met him. He wondered if Hassan purposely had tried to conceal his fingerprints but dismissed the idea to be too outrageous. However, they obtained the fingerprint they had matched when he applied for permanent resident status.

Suddenly, it dawned on him that the RCMP had plenty of opportunities to check the fingerprint on his Iranian National Identity Card, and nothing had been said about that card. He wondered which fingerprint had matched the one they had found on the package in Temesekia. What a fucking mess, he thought. They might have him in a catch 22 because he had insisted that his real name matched the name on the identity card.

His intercom buzzed, and Jeanine announced the arrival of Mr. Akbari. Connors asked that Noe be shown into his office. He was not looking forward to the discussion that he was about to embark upon, and anxiety was written on his face. However, he was pleasant to Noe as he asked him to be seated and inquired how Mrs. Zadeh and her baby were doing.

After a few informal exchanges, Connors cleared his throat and began, "Before I discuss with you what has transpired concerning your cousin, I need to clarify a few matters with you. First and foremost, I want you to know that Hassan has agreed that I can share the information I will provide to you today."

As Noe nodded, Jordan continued, "Second, I'm going to ask you some very personal questions, and I need you to be frank with me. I have to warn you, though, that anything that you say is not protected information, and I may choose to use it to Hassan's benefit if it becomes necessary. Do you understand? I would not be obliged to keep such information secret. Is that okay?"

"That sounds like a warning to me, but I'll see what you ask me first before deciding if I want to provide you with an answer. You have to understand I have a family to consider, and if that's okay, we can proceed. Does this mean that you won't come with me for this interview I've been asked to attend with the Canadian Security Intelligence Service?" Noe said.

"Well, I'm in a predicament, Noe, as I'm representing Hassan on some very serious matters, I can't represent you both. I'm sorry I feel awful about this as you and I have known each other for a long time. I can refer you to someone else who'll look after you. The law society prevents me looking after you if there's a possible conflict between you and Hassan. Today, I just want to go over some basic background information," the lawyer said, "but I need the truth, and this will be off the record. This is an extremely serious matter, and you have to understand I am only trying to act in Hassan's interests."

"Background information like what?"

"Such as whether or not you are really cousins. If yes, how much you know about his adult life? If not, how long you've known each other and general things like that. It's important that I ask you these questions. I suspect CSIS, the Canadian Security Intelligence Service, will ask you the same questions. Are you all right with that?"

"I think so. There isn't a lot to tell. Hassan is related to my mother's family. In my country, I have many blood relatives. We don't call them cousins, but here in Canada, the immigration people do. I honestly didn't know him very well until he came here. He's a few years older than I am, and my mother didn't see her sister often."

"Why is that?"

"Hassan's mother married a man who practices the Bahá'í religion. My family doesn't. We are devout followers of Islam. My father would not bring shame into our home."

"What do you know about his childhood and his travels?"

"I don't know much about his life, and he was away at the university for a long time before I came to this country. He is actually seven years older than I am. Then one day my father called and asked me if I could meet Hassan at the airport. He was coming to Canada because his family had been killed. When he came, I tried to help him out in the beginning because my father asked me to."

"Are you friends here?"

"Hassan is now faithful to Islam, and we get together to go to the mosque and celebrate special occasions or for dinner with our wives once in a while."

"Do you know which countries he's lived in?"

"I know that he was born in Iran. During his early life, he had lived there before he went away to school. I never knew where he was, just that he was away at school. Recently, he told me that he had lived in Temesekia for a while. It's his wife's home country. I don't know where he attended university."

"Did he ever tell you that he had used any other name?"

"No, why would he? His birth name is Hassan Zadeh. What other names would he use?"

"Well, what name was on the passport he used to come to Canada for instance?"

"I don't know about that. He never told me anything about using any passport."

"Do you know if he's ever been involved in any organizations or Islamic fundamentalist groups?"

"I don't know what you mean by the term *fundamentalist*. Hassan believes in Islam."

"What I'm referring to is extremist groups who advocate violence while promulgating their beliefs."

"Violence? No, we are peaceable people. We follow the teachings of the Qur'an. Islam does not support violence."

"Well, Noe, did you know any of Hassan's friends before he came to Canada?"

"Like I said, he is seven years older than I am. I didn't hang around with him. I was still a boy when he left Iran. No, I didn't know any of his friends. I doubt that he would know my friends either. Why? I don't understand these questions."

"The Canadian government believes that he has been associated with a group of extreme believers of Islam and was once a member of a sect some people refer to as Jihad. They think he has committed acts of terrorism against the United States and other countries and that he is a security threat to Canada and possibly the United States. They don't believe that his real name is Hassan Zadeh."

"This is crazy. Like I said, his real name is Hassan Zadeh, and he's just an ordinary person. I don't think for one minute that he has been involved in these things that you are saying. Why do the Canadian people think this? It must be American propaganda."

"I haven't heard that the Americans have said anything about him yet. I am sorry that I had to ask you these questions, but I have to try and defend Hassan from these charges, and the government have acquired a lot of information. I can't tell you all of it because some of it is classified. Have you ever heard the name Mahmoud Bahrami?"

"Not until recently. Jas asked me about this name. Who is this person? What has Hassan got to do with him?"

"The government believe that this is Hassan's real name. Hassan has admitted to me that he once used this name on a passport to get into Temesekia."

"Really? Well, I don't understand why he would use another name. I certainly have never heard him use it. Why would he use someone else's name to go to Temesekia?"

"He told me his reasons, but I can't share this with you at this time. You'll probably get the same questions put to you by other people when you attend an interview with the investigators from the Canadian Security Intelligence Service. Uh, they're usually just called CSIS. It's best that you stick to what you already know."

"I know nothing about these things."

"Yes, I see. This is good. I don't think you have anything to be concerned about, but I'll give you the name of a good lawyer if you want someone to attend that meeting with you. If you think of anything, I want you to call me. Hassan may need your help. Certainly, he's going to be dependent on both you and his wife," Connors remarked as he scribbled the name and number of a colleague on a notepad and handed it to Noe. Then he rose, indicating that their conversation was over.

"Jas. Does Jas know about all of this?" queried Noe after swallowing hard.

"Hassan is supposed to tell her today. It's not wise for you to discuss this with her, though. Like you, I want her to be spontaneous when she's interviewed by CSIS. Thanks for coming in, Noe, I hope you understand that it would be next to impossible for me to withdraw from Hassan's case now. By the way, the legal aid certificate for Hassan was approved. I'll do the best I can for Hassan, but his wife in all probability will have to get an independent representative too. Good luck to you, son."

46

After Jas had been released from the hospital, she booked an appointment with the prison for a private family visit that would allow her and the baby a weekend with Hassan. She had been looking forward to visiting him because she hadn't seen her husband for almost three months, and he had never seen their son. It had been many months since Hassan's arrest, and she was desperate to feel his arms around her, share the joy of their newborn son, and just have an opportunity to talk privately.

She carefully packed a small suitcase with everything that both she and the baby would need for their visit, following the list provided by the prison of things she wasn't allowed to bring. She was cognizant of the fact that the guards would go through everything before she entered the living quarters, and she was careful to ensure there wouldn't be any problems. Jas called a cab, and as she waited for it to arrive, she wondered how all of this could have happened to her in less than two years.

As the taxi drew up outside, Jas quickly gathered her things, locked the doors, and left for her visit. Over the next two days, the couple rejoiced in the company of their infant son and their time together. The room was confining, but they barely noticed it as they quenched their need to be with one another. For the first day, they were utterly oblivious to their environment and the things looming over their life.

On the final day of their visit, as Anil lay napping, the atmosphere became uneasy, and she sensed a tension in the air as Hassan said he needed to talk about some serious matters. For the next hour, Hassan revealed to her all the charges that the Canadian government had brought before the court. Hassan cautiously disclosed that he was being accused of terrorist activities but pled his innocence. "You have to trust me, Jas, they are wrong."

Terrorist! Jas felt numb. She was dumbfounded that the man she had given her heart to, the father of her child, the polite and soft-spoken man sitting before her could even be suspected of such an outrageous thing. This country's government had to be filled with madmen.

"How could they think such a thing?" she asked as she eventually found her voice.

"You may recall that I told you that I went to Egypt to further my education. While I was there, I joined a student group who produced a weekly newspaper. We cited the many wrongdoings of the Egyptian government who were being influenced by Americans. Many students supported us and agreed that the right path for Egypt was to follow the teachings of Islam. However, some people were connected to the attempted assassination of an Egyptian government official. I was well known to be a member of the organization, so I also came under suspicion."

"Did you know these other people? Were you arrested?"

"Yes, I knew the other students. I wasn't arrested, just interrogated. I had met the students when I was involved in the paper, but I didn't have anything to do with what they did. The government never had anything that actually connected me. They just figured I was guilty by association."

"Surely the Canadian government will demand evidence that suggests that you were involved? From what I've seen, the justice system in this country is reasonably fair."

"I don't know, I think the Americans are causing all the fuss, just because I was there at that time they've convinced Canada that I was involved. The Canadians haven't accused me of direct involvement. It's just the background of innuendo that they've brought into the hearing. However, there is much more that is going on here. I am only telling you this so you will understand what these charges are all about."

"I see. Please go on."

Hassan knew that she didn't really see at all. She was naive and would be horrified at what would come out at the hearings in the days ahead. He needed her to become his ally and not shirk her duty to him as her spouse. She didn't know it but felt that she had the power of his destiny in her hands.

"I actually left Egypt because some of those students were linked to the assassination plot. I wasn't sure what I was going to do. It was an extraordinarily complicated time in my life, and it shook me up very badly."

"Where did you go, back to Iran?"

"No, I went to Pakistan with some friends and a professor to work for a group called the International Organization for Alleviation to aid people who had been victims of a big earthquake. Our group delivered food and blankets, tents for people to stay in, and medicines to treat the injured."

"I remember hearing something about a big earthquake there a long time ago. I think it was about the time my parents died. Surely, that must tell the Canadian government that you are a good man?"

"Someone has convinced the Canadians that the work we performed was not humanitarian. For some reason, probably the Americans, they think I was involved in subversive matters, in Afghanistan, during that period."

"How could they think that? I don't see the connection."

"It doesn't matter. They are wrong. While I was in northern Pakistan, I met a man, an Egyptian doctor. We became good friends, probably because I had studied in Egypt and brought him some current news of his homeland. He had been living in Afghanistan and told us many things that were happening in that country. Jas, I watched him, and I worked with him every day trying to attend to the unimaginable suffering of many people."

"Who was he?"

"I don't think it was his real name, but we called him Dr. Fadl. He had written a book called *The Essential Guide for Preparation* that people in Afghanistan used to train men to fight the Russians, and that is the problem. Some people, again I am sure it is the Americans, suggest that it is a terrorist training manual."

"Did you read this book?"

"Yes, I read the book. It was actually quite brilliant. Most of us did not realize what had been happening in Afghanistan. The Russians were greedy. They wanted control of the trade route through Afghanistan to the Indian Ocean. It was really about the oil and access to the rich minerals of the Afghan lands."

"That's shameful!"

"It was worse than that. It was a revolution between two groups of people with different ideologies. The Russians tried to destroy the culture of the Afghan society. They altered the land and marriage laws, and they attacked Islamic teachings to totally undermine the stability of the country. When the Russians invaded Afghanistan, they tried to force their atheist beliefs on everyone. People like Dr. Fadl stood up and said that they had to be stopped. Then Pakistani military leaders interfered after the collapse of the Communist government and attempted to install Gulbuddin Hekmatyar to run the country against the wishes of the Afghani warlords. The Taliban, who the world claims are terrorists, was the only group that had successfully stood up to these warlords. Later the Americans also attacked the Afghani people, killing many innocent women and children."

"I don't understand what business it was of Russia to begin with, never mind the peoples of Pakistan and America."

"That was just Russia looking to extend their power and control of the markets. There's a lot of history there, and you're right—the bloody Americans and Pakistanis shouldn't have got involved either!"

"Did you ever go to Afghanistan?" Jas innocently asked.

"No, but it's funny that Canada has accused me of actions in Afghanistan even though I was never there. I wanted to go there and help the people, but I was too involved with the work I was doing in Pakistan. When I left Pakistan, I travelled a little until I was able to get a passport in the name of Mahmoud Bahrami, and then I went to Temesekia to start a new life."

"Oh, I forgot," Jas remarked. "When I went home to Temesekia the last time, I was asked by the government if I knew Mahmoud Bahrami. It was a simple question that they just kind of threw out there, and when I said no, they didn't mention it again. They changed the subject and kept insisting that you were still married to your first wife and that you were a dangerous man."

"Jas, I did nothing. I am your husband, and you can choose to believe me or them. Why didn't you tell me that your government asked about Mahmoud Bahrami?" Hassan said with annoyance creeping into his voice.

"I simply forgot about it. It didn't seem significant at the time. I was just so stunned that my government wanted me to leave my marriage and insisted that you weren't divorced."

"Do you remember what else they said? Jas, I have no one else to depend on right now. Things are much worse than you could imagine. You need to remember everything."

"Hassan, I was jet-lagged and overly tired. I was also in quite a bit of a shock at the reception I received, and I found out that the government had investigated my brothers and questioned my best friend and former employer. Some of what happened that day has become an unwanted blur in my memory. Worst of all, they tried to convince me to abort my baby."

"They did what? *La'anatullah*! How could you not have told me this?"

"What would you have done? What could you do? It was so painful to me that I couldn't talk about it. I have never told another soul what they said to me about the baby on that day."

Hassan was so upset about this revelation that he couldn't control his anger, and without thinking, he blurted out, "Well, Jas, that is not the only evil that your sanctimonious government has done. Do you know that I am also accused of trying to kill the United States ambassador in Temesekia by sending him something called anthrax? Of course, that is preposterous! I have never heard of this thing called anthrax until now. I don't even know what it is or where I would get it."

Jas reacted with a slight gasp at Hassan's newest revelation. Just then Anil awoke wailing loudly for a feeding. She quickly looked at her watch and realized that she scarcely would have enough time to feed the baby and pack up their things before her visit would be over. She was at a loss for words in trying to comprehend the entirety of the situation her husband was now facing and was grateful for the distraction her son now offered.

Hassan was totally rattled. He too was thankful for the interruption caused by the baby. He hadn't meant to tell Jas about the anthrax accusation. She was from Temesekia and might have some recollection of the incident from the press. Hassan immediately sought to distract her from what he had just disclosed and began some idle conversation about their son. "Anil has strong lungs. Is he always so loud?"

"The nurse told me that after he had left the incubator, he was the loudest baby in the whole nursery." Jas nervously laughed.

"Who was present when he was born?" Hassan inquired, still trying to make small talk to distract her from the discussion that they had just had.

"I don't know, I was in a coma, and they took the baby by cesarean section. There were just some doctors and nurses as far as I know."

"Was there anyone of our faith?"

"I don't know. It's not the sort of question that you would ask the hospital staff."

Hassan's anger had not subsided altogether when she had revealed the totality of her experience in Temesekia. Now her response concerning the care of his son infuriated him even more. What kind of woman was she? Was their marriage a farce?

"Jas, we talked about this before. It is imperative to the teachings of Islam that the first word that a newborn child hears is Allah. When I was not present you had a responsibility to ensure that he was given the *tawheed* and the *iqama*, the declaration of our faith. Did you not carry these instructions on you at all times?"

"Hassan, the baby wasn't due to be born yet! I had a car accident and couldn't control what happened during his birth or for some time after."

"At the time of a child's birth, parents have an obligation to make the infant aware of Allah in the first moments of life. My question is simple, did you or did you not have instructions in your purse for just such an emergency?"

"No, I didn't. I had been here visiting you and didn't have my usual handbag with me. When I come to the jail, I have to restrict what I carry. I just had my wallet and the house keys."

"Why didn't you just put the instructions inside your wallet? I am extremely concerned that you did not act to protect my son in the event that you were unable to fulfill the requirements of our faith."

"Our son, Hassan—our son. Noe informed me that when he came to the hospital and saw Anil for the first time he ensured that our son was introduced to Allah, and he administered the declaration as well. He came to the hospital the day Anil was born."

"Noe did this? That is good. Did Noe also provide him with a taste of a date?"

"Yes, he said that he transferred all of his best qualities to Anil when he rubbed the date against his mouth as required by Islam."

"Noe is a good man. It gives me some comfort to know that at least Noe acted to protect my son."

"We did everything according to your faith as soon as we could do it."

"Our faith, Jas. Our faith. There is no other faith. Anil must be raised in our faith."

"Yes, yes, of course, I meant our faith."

"Did Noe help you to get a healthy sheep for the sacrifice?" As she nodded, he continued, "Did you remember to cut his hair seven days later and weigh it to determine how much silver to give to the mosque?"

"Hassan, I was still in a coma. All of the circumstances were beyond my control. Noe told me that he took a clipping. We have not had the sacrifice yet, but I will remember."

"Jas, I want you to speak with Maryam and the imam at the mosque and learn how to be a good mother. In this regard, I am very disappointed in you. The sacrifice is so important to his health. You must not put yourself before the interests of my son. This is not the way that Allah instructs us to care for our children. Do you understand?"

The prison guards rapped at the door before Jas could respond. She was deeply distressed by her husband's criticisms but held her thoughts to herself as she packed her belongings. She had never before witnessed her husband's anger, and the fact that it was directed toward her greatly disturbed her.

Hassan quickly changed the subject and asked her to pack his laptop up and send it to Hamid in care of the imam at the mosque just before the two guards entered the quarters. She nodded in agreement and said a quick good-bye to Hassan, promising to be back soon. While Hassan was led back to the cell, he contemplated what else Jas had learned in Temesekia and was perhaps withholding from him.

She had not acted surprised to hear the charges against him, and he now began to wonder how much he could trust her. He was also profoundly troubled about her shortcomings as a mother. He worried that she did not take her motherly duties seriously, and in this respect she was failing Islam. He was deeply disappointed by her. He hoped that she would remove his computer from the apartment quickly as he began to doubt her loyalty and whether he could rely upon her if things got tough.

47

"How are you doing, Dana? It's Noe here," came the solemn sound of Noe's voice.

"Not bad, yourself? What's up? Is Jas okay?" she answered groggily, still half-asleep. Glancing at her alarm clock, she noted that it was not quite six in the morning.

"Jas is fine. Sounds like I woke you up, but I have an urgent problem that you might be able to assist with and wanted to catch you before you went off for the day."

"How's that?" she answered anxiously.

"It's about Hamid. They found out that he had nothing to do with that guy's death, and now they've got a bail hearing coming up about the passport issue."

Fully alert now, Dana gasped. "Oh, I'm so relieved. Is the passport still a problem? I'm glad that they've cleared him on that other thing."

"His lawyer doesn't think the passport issue will be too bad. The immediate problem is that he's got no fixed address. I haven't got room at my place. I remembered that when Jas came to Canada, she said that you arranged a room for her to stay. I wondered if you might be able to help Hamid get a room. They won't release him from jail until he has an address to give to the court. His bail hearing is in three days."

"Oh, that should be pretty easy. Even though, I'm no longer at the school now, I have friends who are on the hospitality committee who can arrange that. I'll see if I can reach someone. I'll just tell them that he's planning on returning to school."

"You're great, Dana! I'll give you my number at the store, and as soon as you find out anything, just give me a call. We'll need a receipt in his name. Umm, there's one other little thing." He sighed.

"Fire away." She laughed.

"I hate to ask you this, but he may need some help getting a surety. I can't get involved with Hamid's case right now. His lawyer said there may be a conflict with Hassan."

"What's a surety? What would I have to do?"

"It's a person who puts up the bail. All you need to do is put up a percentage of the bail money and show them that if he skips out on making the payments, you forfeit the full amount of the bail money that you have the means to pay to the court. Take a paystub from your work and your bank book. I've got the money for you to put up, but I can't get involved because of Hassan. Could you do that?"

"I don't know about that. I don't want someone calling my work. My job has a high-level security clearance, and this could be a problem. Have you spoken with his lawyer about this? There might be some kind of bail program."

"His lawyer asked me to find him a surety. It doesn't have anything to do with your work. They just need to know that you do work. I'll get his lawyer to call you and go over everything with you. If you still don't feel comfortable, you can tell him and ask if there are any other options. I don't know anyone else that could do it. Can you help?"

"Sure," Dana said after a few moments of contemplating the situation, "I'll talk to his lawyer. Tell him to call in the evening. I'll ring you later to let you know if I've been able to find Hamid a room."

"Thanks, Dana. Talk to you later."

Scrambling out of bed, Dana hit the shower still wondering what she had let herself into. By midafternoon, she had found a room and placed a deposit on it in Hamid's name, thankful that she had enough cash that she had been able to facilitate every-thing smoothly. When she later contacted Noe, he agreed to meet on Friday and give her the money to cover her expenses.

Hamid had sat in a jail cell for almost three months before he had been cleared in the death of his cellmate. It had been a pretty grueling experience. He had been ostracized by other prisoners during the entire time. He wasn't sure if they thought he was a murderer, or they didn't like him because he was a Muslim. It didn't actually matter to him, they were all infidels, and fairly soon he would be responsible for the deaths of thousands like them, not just one junkie.

However, he wondered if it had been a set up and whether they had purposely placed him in a cell with a dead guy. Was it possible that someone in the prison knew the man was dead or dying when they had brought him in? He had been questioned for the better part of the day at the police station and hadn't been brought to the prison until quite late in the evening. He'd never spoken to the guy, he was just lying in his bunk when he'd been ushered in, and Hamid had assumed that he was asleep for the night. Perhaps he was already dead.

Hassan thought that the authorities knew that he would make bail easily on the passport charge, but they wanted to hold him longer. He had been questioned extensively about his rela-tionship to both Naz and Hassan. He pretended that he knew nothing of Hassan's arrest and asked them what Hassan had to do with his charges. They had suggested that Hassan had arranged the meeting with Naz. He stuck to his story, realizing that they suspected that he was involved with Hassan in some-thing more sinister.

He'd been pleasantly surprised today when he'd had a visit from a man, Bart Barrett, an attorney. He said that he had been referred by another lawyer named Jordan Connors. He quickly explained that Mr. Connors had been contacted by someone named Dana; however, Mr. Connors couldn't represent him because there might be a conflict with another of his clients. Wouldn't you know it, Dana had come through!

She was a sweet girl and had proven to be a loyal friend. He hadn't wanted to drag her into all this mess, she was the marrying kind, and that he had no intention of ever doing. She was too westernized in his opinion. This Mr. Barrett was optimistic that he'd get bail in a few days and informed him that his friend Dana had also acquired a room for him, so there would be no problem as far as providing the court with an address. When Barrett left, he thought that things could be looking up, but later that afternoon Hamid had a visit from two men who were with something called CSIS, which he later learned was the acronym for the Canadian Security Intelligence Service.

He'd been careful not to leave any connection between himself and any of the other cell members that he and Hassan had been involved with. Generally, he had only worked with Hassan after Sammi had been deported. The school had been a perfect cover for their meetings, and of course they sometimes met in the mosque. Naz was the backup if anything unusual occurred or when they needed documents. Hassan and Naz did all the communications with other members of the cell, both in Canada and the United States. Hamid knew a couple of their first names, but he had actually never met anyone other than Giv.

During the CSIS interview, it had become apparent to Hamid that they were on a fishing expedition. Yes, they had established that Hassan and he were friends, but they were probing to try to establish the depths of that friendship and whether or not they had known each other before coming to Canada. They were surreptitious in their questioning and had even gone so far as to ask him whether he had ever known of someone called Mahmoud Bahrami.

Eventually, the investigators turned their questions to Hamid's activities and friends in Canada. With confidence, he disclosed that he went to school and had met Dana, Hassan, and Hassan's wife as fellow students at the Douglas College. As far as he knew, all of them were simply in pursuit of new lives in Canada. They tried to help one another with their studies and occasionally went out for dinners or to the mosque. Throughout the interview, he wondered what they knew about Bahrami.

Later lying in his cell, he recalled how he had returned from attending university in Saudi Arabia and had only been working for a short period of time when his country had been attacked by the Iraqis. He had managed to escape with some extended family members back to Saudi Arabia fleeing for their lives. When he had eventually returned to Kuwait, all of his immediate family, his workplace, and many of his friends were gone. He decided to go back to Saudi Arabia where he had become involved in the International Organization for Alleviation, which was also known as the IOA.

Several years later the Iraqis threatened Kuwait once again, and Hamid decided that he would explore how to obtain military training to defend his country. Through his involvement in the International Organization for Alleviation, he learned of, and enrolled in, a three-month course in self-defense at a training camp in Lebanon that many Palestinians in the group had recommended. When the Americans invaded Iraq, he returned to Saudi Arabia to work with the relief organization that in turn had led him to relief efforts in Pakistan following a devastating earthquake.

In Pakistan, he had met many people from the Arab world committed to helping others. He had also learned details of the horrific experiences of the Afghani peoples who had suffered from several invasions of their homeland. Although he had never met Mahmoud Bahrami, he had heard about the man from a select few who had worked side by side with him.

He hadn't hesitated to work for Bahrami, when Egyptian members of the organization contacted him upon his return to the Middle East asking him to work on a few projects for Bahrami.

All these activities involved the use of chemicals. Hamid was greatly honored to be recognized by Bahrami, who was becoming legendary within the organization. He recalled a particularly successful project in Lebanon that Bahrami had considered imperative to their cause, and he had been told that Bahrami had been highly impressed with his success.

Hamid had become a hardened militant and no longer was active in the humanitarian efforts of the IOA. He had adapted to the belief that his purpose was to serve Allah and purge the world of infidels, especially Americans. When he was again approached to come to Canada for this American mission, he believed that this was perhaps his most important assignment to date. In this case, the target involved hundreds of thousands of people who lived in various parts of the western United States. He knew that this mission would help bring the Americans to their knees before the entire world.

He had been picked because of his skills as a chemical engineering specialist, and he was instructed that he would be working with one of Bahrami's most trusted associates. Later, Naz had informed him that that man was Hassan Zadeh, a fellow student at the college. He had admitted none of this history to the men from CSIS and shrewdly insisted that he only knew Hassan from the college.

They had questioned him nonstop for many hours and wouldn't even let him get a drink of water or go to the washroom. It was a tactic that they were employing to wear him down, but they hadn't been successful. They had even asked if he knew a man named Nazreh Arz to which he had responded that he had never heard of him. He was pleased with the way he had conducted himself and felt confident that they had suspicions, but nothing tangible that they could put together.

48

Judd sat reviewing the Al Zain file and decided to phone Russ Norman for an informal chat. He had caught Russ as he had been just about to call it a day. Upon hearing that CSIS and the RCMP didn't have enough evidence to prevent Al Zain from making bail, he quickly agreed to wait for Judd at the office. Russ was certain that the man was responsible for an attempt on his life, and he didn't want to have to keep watching his back.

Waiting for Judd's arrival, Russ pulled out Al Zain's file. There wasn't much in it. The Failaka sewage treatment plant had been destroyed by the Iraqi invasion; therefore, he had been unable to verify any of his employment history. For that reason, he hadn't bothered to check Al Zain's education transcript. It showed that he held an honors bachelor of science in chemical engineering. It was from the King Fahd University of Petroleum and Minerals, also known as KFUPM, located in Saudi Arabia and considered one of the top universities in the world.

Judd had seen it all before. Excellent reference from the Douglas College and an interesting interview that didn't amount to anything from another student, Dana Jahel. Russ had asked Judd to get him a photo of the man after the incident with the wine. He sat looking at the picture and was sure he'd never seen him before. He had a long thin face, sported a neatly clipped chevron mustache and a full beard that made him stand out against the majority of young men in the Western world. Russ was sure that his only connection to the man was Zadeh.

To keep Al Zain in detention for an immigration matter, they needed to find evidence that he had materially misrepresented himself when he came to Canada. Once Russ had learned that his previous employer wasn't available to verify his past employment records, it would have been futile to go any further in his present job. It's too costly an investigative process for summer employment contracts. Perhaps, Judd could do it through the Canadian mission in Riyadh. A half an hour later, Judd scrutinized his file. He was grasping for anything that could support an action to continue to hold Al Zain.

"It's a long shot, but perhaps there are still some records of the employees of the Failaka sewage treatment plant. There are still three similar operational facilities in Kuwait. Failaka used to be the fourth. One of the other companies may have obtained any of the salvageable records of Failaka or have hired other former employees."

"There's about a ten-hour difference in the time between here and Kuwait, but I think the consular office in Kuwait City opens in about three hours. I thought you might use your resources to check on his schooling in Saudi Arabia, too," Russ replied.

"I think I'll contact Kuwait and see if they can dig up anything. Did he happen to mention any clubs or associations that he belonged to?"

"Nothing here. He provided two references both connected to the Douglas College. One was from a professor and the other a student who worked on the school's hospitality committee. She's the one who told me that he was a friend of the Iranian. Let's see, yep, she said his friends' names were Hassan and Jas Zadeh; the informant's name was Dana Jahel."

"Jahel? Hmm, that's the only person he's contacted since we arrested him. She hired a lawyer for him. Do you remember if she said anything else of interest?"

"I made some notes. Here, let's see. One interesting thing she mentioned was that both Al Zain and Zadeh had gone to Victoria to see someone. She thought their host was named Nash or something like that. She wasn't sure if that was the name and couldn't supply me with any surname either."

"Wait a minute! I think you just hit a connective chord on the passport charge, anyway. The name's off a little bit, though. Nazreh Arz is the name of the guy we were tailing when we nailed Al Zain. The guy owns a print shop in Victoria, and we think he specializes in providing forged documents. You sure about the name?"

"Perhaps Ms. Jahel got the name wrong. She wasn't sure. What's happened that's got you so fired up?" Russ asked.

"This Arz guy has been under surveillance for a while as a possible people smuggler. Seems he went to the airport carrying a satchel, used the washroom for less than five minutes, exited, and a short time later out came Al Zain carrying the same bag. We think it contained the phony passport that he was caught with."

"I don't think the Jahel woman knew the guy they went to see. It sounds like a weak link. She wasn't sure of the name. Hell, I wasn't sure of the name, and 'Nazreh' doesn't sound like 'Nash' to me."

"Well, we've got some evidence 'Nazreh' shortens his name to 'Naz.' I think it's possible that this Jahel person might have confused the names 'Nash' and 'Naz,'" Judd replied.

"I see what you mean. It could be, or maybe I wrote it down incorrectly. Wait a minute, take a look at Zadeh's file. I think that I recall mention of the word 'Naz' with a phone number, but we thought it was in reference to an Iranian airport."

"I'll do that. Seems like we're getting more questions than answers when it comes to these guys," an obviously frustrated Judd remarked.

"I'd still put my money down that these boys are up to something significant. Al Zain made an application for work at the water treatment plant here. Makes you wonder whether that had anything to do with their plans. Have you run his fingerprints with Interpol anywhere?" Russ said, shaking his head from side to side.

"We're waiting on a response from Temesekia and Pakistan because of his connection to Zadeh. Nothing came back from Kuwait, but I'll try Saudi Arabia too now that I know he attended school there. It has also crossed our minds that he could be another one with multiple identities. We need to get a break on this one. We're hoping something shakes loose *soon*."

"It certainly is a tangled web they weave! Can't they keep him on the passport charges?"

"He's a first offender, and he's got a sob story about a missing family member who's just been found by the allies after being imprisoned by some extremists in Iraq. He says he paid an unknown Chinese fellow that he had heard about around the school to help get him a passport. Supposedly, the guy took his picture right on the school campus and told him to go to the washroom in Victoria on a specific day and at a particular time. He was told that there he'd find a package with a new passport. Claims he doesn't know Arz. The good news is that we've been able to obtain a print off the package that matches Arz."

"That sounds as if it is pretty compelling evidence," Russ remarked.

"We've got enough to hold Arz. We just can't definitively place the two of them together. It's pretty circumstantial, and we've got to consider that it could go either way with a sympathetic judge. You know criminal charges, we've got to prove his guilt beyond a reasonable doubt. I think we can do that for possession, but he'll likely just get a slap on the wrist. I might interview Jahel."

"Sorry I can't be of more help. Did you get anything on this printer fellow connecting him to Zadeh or anyone else?"

"We found some encrypted communications that Arz had with several people in the US and a photographer here in Vancouver but nothing with Zadeh."

"Did you contact the Americans?"

"Yeah, Homeland Security doesn't have much on any of his contacts except that most of them are illegals and working near or with filtration systems and water reservoirs. They've been picking them up and deporting. Both Canada and the US intelligence have people working on trying to break his codes."

"Let me know if and when he's released so I can watch my back," Russ remarked.

"We'll be watching him pretty closely, too. Thanks, Russ. I wish we could find a way to hold the bastard, but it doesn't sound too promising. Considering the tampered wine attempt, I agree we're all going to have to be vigilant. I'll get hold of the overseas missions, see if I can come up with anything else. You know what they say, it isn't over until it's over." He chuckled as he headed out the door.

49

Bart Barrett had waited for the paperwork to be completed and for Hamid to gather his belongings before handing him the envelope with the address and a key for the room that had been arranged by Dana. Hamid was relieved to be released from the prison that had been his home for more than three months and was most grateful to Dana, who had helped to make it possible.

Barrett told him that he would try to get a speedy trial on the passport charge. He thought that by taking a plea and with the two-for-one pretrial custody credit, he might get lucky and receive a sentence of time served with probation. In the meantime, he assured him that there was a process that would allow him to go to see his brother, but he needed to be patient.

He asked Hamid to call his assistant for help in making the proper application for a refugee travel document after they cleared everything up. He warned, though, that if his brother were taken to Kuwait, the travel document wouldn't allow him to go there as he had initially received asylum protection from that country.

"Hamid, stay out of trouble and keep a low profile," he'd remarked as he departed.

It was midafternoon, and Hamid didn't have any idea where he was headed. He was unfamiliar with the name of the street, but the bus driver was helpful and gave him the directions to his new address that the lawyer had provided for him. He was pleased that it turned out it wasn't far from the Douglas College, so he would be in familiar territory.

The first thing he would do would be to take his meager belongings and stash them in the room. The weather had turned cold, and he didn't even own a warm jacket now. He decided to visit the mosque and see if they could help him out. He spent about an hour there chatting with some of the regulars, but as the afternoon sun faded, he was restless about what he would do next. He was eager for news concerning Jas and Hassan and decided to call Dana on her cell to see if she could meet him for dinner.

Dana hesitated a little but reluctantly agreed to meet in the Lebanese restaurant that they had occasionally gone to in the past. When he left the mosque, the thought of the upcoming Arab cuisine gave him a voracious appetite for a decent meal after three months of slop. He looked forward to seeing Dana and was hungry for any information about what was happening with Hassan.

He was also concerned about Naz, but he didn't dare try to contact him. He'd learned from his lawyer that Naz had been under surveillance for some time over forging documents. He was glad to learn that they hadn't been following him and that he'd been able to give them a plausible story of how he acquired the passport. It was unfortunate that they had got Naz's fingerprint off of the passport that Hamid had been caught with. Otherwise, they wouldn't have been able to prove any connection between the two men.

It seemed that much of their operation was going down the drain, and the entire mission would have to be aborted. He didn't know what to do and wished that he could find a way to talk to Hassan. Then he realized that Hassan had already essentially told him it was over. He'd done the only thing he'd been able to do and left the one-word message: "Retreat."

He had been told the code word so many years ago but had never heard it used before during an operation. This was the first failed mission he had ever been involved with, and it sucked! He wondered where it had all broken down after so many years of careful planning. He had never felt so alone.

Moreover, he was a little strapped for money, although he had a few bucks on him, but he supposed until the fiasco with his outstanding criminal charge was over, he'd need to get a job to get back on his feet. He wondered if Noe might lend him some money in the meantime and made a mental note to give him a call later.

50

Shortly after Dana had met up with Hamid, he had found out that Hassan had been imprisoned on something called a security certificate. Jas had been in a car accident and had her baby delivered while in a coma, but mother and son were apparently doing well. Dana was working and moving on with her own life.

"How's Jas taking things?" he inquired, eager for news of the events over the past few months.

"She avoids talking about it. I think Noe knows what's going on, but he doesn't discuss it. They understand more about the security certificate than I do, and I'm not sure that I want to know anymore. I find it better to let some things remain private. There isn't some magical button that you can turn off and on to judge your friends as others see them. We decided not to tell her anything about your circumstances."

"Yes, I suppose you're right. Hopefully, he'll be out soon. Has Hassan seen his son?"

"Yes, Jas has taken him a couple of times when she's been allowed a pass of some sort where she stays with him in housing at the jail for a couple of days. She's had a rough time with the accident and not knowing what's going to happen with Hassan. The government is trying to take away his refugee status."

"I don't know if they can do that. I think it would be pretty difficult, and I don't think they can send him back to Iran to face torture or death. We'll see how it plays out. Dana, I want to thank you for all your help. I honestly didn't know who else to go to. I'll pay you back as soon as I can."

"I didn't do too much, really. Noe arranged for a lawyer and paid the bail bondsman. I just got you a room through the college and told them you were coming back to school. I'm finished there now, and I've got a full-time job. Noe also gave me the funds for your room, which is paid for a month. Now you must tell me, how you got yourself into this mess?" she asked him.

"I received a message from a friend in Dubai who said he had heard that my brother had been found alive but in critical condition. The Iraqis have held him captive for four years."

"I thought you said that your family were all killed in the war with Iraq. Who told you that your brother's alive? Do you believe that the information was reliable?" Dana asked.

"I was told that my family was all killed. As for my brother, I want to believe it. That's why I tried to get there as soon as it was humanly possible. Then, out of the blue, I heard from a friend who grew up with me that he had just learned that my brother was alive. My friend agreed to meet me in Dubai. I had to go. I just panicked."

"What happened that you ended up getting charged with murder?"

"That was so weird and a complete nightmare. I almost think the cops tried to set me up. I didn't get taken to the jail until nighttime, and the other guy in the cell seemed to be asleep in his bunk. I didn't try to wake him. I still don't know whether he was dead or asleep when I got there. They did an autopsy, but the report took a long time before they finally said he had died because of some drugs that he had swallowed."

"You wouldn't believe how surprised I was when the police came to see me and tried to coerce me into getting you to admit that you had supplied him with the drugs. They went to the school to find out my address and showed up one night just as I got home from work. It was terrible. After that, someone from the Intelligence Department of Border Services said that he was investigating you, and he paid me a visit too. He wanted to know who your friends were and if I knew anything else about you. He was particularly interested in your friendship with Hassan."

"Gee, Dana, I'm sorry that they put you through this. How could they possibly think I supplied the drugs? They had searched me before they put me in the cell. What did you tell them about me?"

"Really nothing. What could I tell them? I told them that I knew you from school. In fact, I explained that we all met through the school. At least I think we did."

"What do you mean?"

"I'm not sure where you and Hassan met. I thought you met at school, didn't you?"

"What would make you think otherwise? Of course, I met him at the college. I don't understand why anyone thinks that Hassan and I are anything other than schoolmates. What else did the cops say?"

"They asked if you and Hassan had ever gone to Victoria to meet anyone, and I just said I couldn't remember. What's actually got me upset, however, is that two men showed up at my work stating they were from the Intelligence Department."

"Was it the Canadian Security Intelligence Service? It's called CSIS for short. Do you remember if that was who it was?"

"Yes, I think so. They must have been following me; otherwise, I don't know how they knew where I was working."

"What did they ask you?"

"Just mainly the same sort of questions as the police and the other guy from Border Services had asked. Oh yes, they wanted to know what kind of chemicals we worked with at the college and whether we had access to an outside lab. I got the impression that whatever Hassan is involved in, they think you are too. They asked me if I knew someone named Mahmoud Bahrami."

"Wow! This all sounds like a fishing trip to me. They're probably following me too! I don't know anything sinister about Hassan, though, so they're barking up the wrong tree. They asked me about someone named Bahrami too. I don't know anyone by that name."

"Well, yes, as it happens we apparently both know this Mahmoud Bahrami, only not by that name."

"What? Who told you this? What do you mean?"

Dana observed that Hamid had actually been shocked by this revelation.

"Hassan has admitted that he is this person, Mahmoud Bahrami."

"What? Where did you hear this?" gasped Hamid as he struggled to conceal his dismay.

"Jas told me that he admitted it in the courtroom. He said that he couldn't get a passport to leave Iran because of his religion, so he got a phony passport in this other name."

"Oh, he just used this name to come to Canada?" Hamid asked.

"No, he's apparently used it for many years. He used to live in Temesekia before, and that government knows him by the Bahrami name."

"He is Mahmoud Bahrami? This is amazing. I certainly didn't know that Hassan was this other person."

"Have you ever heard of this Bahrami person before?"

"No." He quickly lied.

"Well, I don't find it strange. After all, you also had a passport under a different name. You've even altered your appearance. I barely recognized you. I wonder what his real name is. Jas told me that other countries know him by this Bahrami identity."

"His cousin Noe calls him Hassan," Hassan pointed out. "He certainly always used the name Hassan with me. I had no idea that he uses other names. I am shocked by this news."

"I've been doing a lot of thinking, Hamid. I'm nervous, and I'm not happy being involved in all of this. I'm afraid! I've got to move on with my life now, and quite frankly, I don't want to be involved in any of this. I've never had dealings with the police before, and I find it kind of scary. The police are asking me a lot of questions, and I'm very worried about how this will affect my job and my future. My work requires that I have a high-security clearance, and I am only on probation at the present time." She continued in a whisper, "Hamid, I hate to say this, but I think that I can't see you anymore."

There she'd done it! She'd finally got the words out. She hoped that he'd understand, but even if he didn't, it wouldn't matter. She had made up her mind that she had to cut all ties with these people. She held her breath for several minutes waiting for his reaction as she let her gaze slide slowly away from direct contact with his eyes.

Hamid knew that she was right, and nothing could be gained by his continued relationship with her. He struggled to find the right words and was silent for what seemed like forever. This was the closest that he had ever let himself become emotionally attached to a woman, but more than that he had considered her to be a reliable friend.

"It's okay, Dana. I do understand. You've done more than enough for me, and for that I will always be grateful. I am sure that this will all get sorted out sooner or later, but you're right not to want to be associated with any of it. You have every reason to protect yourself and your future. I wish that I could repay you for all that you've done. You're probably right—the best thing that I can do is get out of your life."

Dana believed Hamid when he denied knowing that Hassan and this Bahrami person were one and the same, as his eyes had exhibited genuine shock. However, she was just as sure that his demeanor had been a dead giveaway that he knew something about the man's other identities beyond mere recognition of hearing the name muttered once or twice. She suddenly felt the need to get away from him as she glanced around the restaurant and noticed that they were the last two customers, and the owner appeared to be getting ready to close for the night.

"I guess we better head out before we get booted out the door." She laughed nervously, and for the first time, she felt afraid to be with this man.

"Goodness, it is getting quite late. Do you want me to walk you home?"

"No, I moved, and it would be a pretty long walk from here. I'll just grab a cab. I wish you lots of luck. Hamid, and I hope you'll take good care of yourself. I hate final good-byes, so let's just pretend that it isn't really the end of our friendship." She gave him a pat on the arm.

As Hamid had watched her pull away in the cab, he was regretful that things couldn't have worked out differently for them. She was right that their association had run its course. She had the good sense to recognize the need to back away from them all to protect her future.

51

Returning to his room, Hamid's head was reeling with the knowledge that Hassan and Bahrami were one and the same person. It had been a shocking revelation. His worst fears had basically been confirmed; their plans were definitely in serious trouble, if this were true.

His relationship with Hassan had been fairly open, and there were many people who could attest to the close friendship. He felt somewhat disappointed that Hassan had never revealed to him that he was Bahrami. He now felt that his own role within the organization was probably under investigation and might be discovered. He hoped that Naz didn't let on that he knew him.

Hamid's lawyer had informed him that the conviction for the passport charge was the least of his worries. Apparently, the Canadian government could take away his permanent resident status upon his conviction. Hamid knew that if they did that, they also would be looking to find away to take his asylum status. It was also likely that Naz would lose his status in Canada, and their mission would not be able to be fulfilled by anyone in the near future. He began to feel like a hunted animal that had nowhere to hide.

Hamid needed to find out from Hassan if there were any instructions to safeguard the plans for their mission. He could contact Hassan's cousin, but it was likely the government was watching Noe too, he contemplated. However, he needed money, and if anyone was monitoring Noe's phone line, it would be a credible reason for Hamid to contact him without raising any suspicions. Hamid wondered if Noe could get in to see Hassan and privately communicate with him.

Hamid purchased a new smart phone and tried to reach Giv in the United States, but he wasn't answering his cell phone. He then bought an overseas calling card and made an attempt to reach his contact in Saudi Arabia. The Saudi had set him up on this mission in the first place and was the only lifeline that he seemed to have left.

He was exceedingly cautious with overseas transmissions and aware that it was possible that conversations and correspondence could be easily intercepted by the intelligence community who would work diligently to decipher the coded language. He resorted to the simplistic prearranged storyline that he knew his contact would understand.

"Have you had any news on Grandpa's retreat to the nursing home?" Hamid asked as the phone was answered.

"I heard he went there a few months ago, and his situation is not good. Can you come?" After a moment of hesitation, the reply came.

"I was on my way, but I got delayed, a few months ago, when I tried to catch a plane to Iraq to see my brother. I can't leave Canada at the present time. I've got a restriction for travelling."

"Sorry to hear. Grandpa's three brothers have returned. Your uncle and your cousins have been delayed, like you. You are the last to contact us. Grandpa doesn't look good. We need everyone to come soon."

"Are you sure about Uncle? Do you have the directions? I've lost mine."

"Yes, Uncle may not be able to come for some time, and no, you'll need to contact the nursing home."

"I'll try, the nurses are very protective, and it's hard to communicate with the residents. Let you know when I can come, but it won't be for a while. I have a big problem."

Hamid was very concerned as he left his room in search of some food. Things were definitely much grimmer than he had imagined. He had learned that the organization knew the authorities had Hassan, whom they referred to as "Grandfather," and that he was in a prison, which was the term for "nursing home." It appeared that Naz, who was "Uncle," and some of the American operatives, whom Hamid did not know by name, and the "cousins" were all detained as he had been. He had hoped that Naz would have been released by now. Giv, Sammi, and Mohammed, the three "brothers," must have been deported at some point by either Canada or the United States.

This message meant one thing. He was probably the only one free to protect their operation and that he had to find out where Hassan kept the plans. He had to risk enlisting Noe's help. It was their only chance to protect the interests of the organization before the government got hold of the documents that might reveal everything.

Eventually, he decided not to risk calling him and to try and get a "chance" meeting. Every day, he went faithfully to the mosque that Noe attended, hoping he would connect with him there. After four days, he approached another regular he had seen and asked him to contact Noe at his work and request him to come to the mosque. He explained that he hadn't seen him for a long time and wanted to surprise him.

When Noe received the call asking him to come to the mosque for a meeting, he figured that Maryam had signed him up to some committee work and obligingly agreed to come when his relief worker arrived at 4:00 p.m.

Hamid was unsure how much Noe knew about the operation, but he had to trust somebody. Perhaps, he thought, Hassan had kept important papers at Noe's place. It was unlikely that Jas knew anything that would be damaging to any members of the organization. When Noe entered the mosque later that day, he was startled to find Hamid waiting for him.

"Hi, Noe, sorry for the mysterious phone call, but I wasn't sure if your phone has been tapped. I needed to talk to you urgently. Dana told me a little of what's been going on. Have you seen Hassan at all?"

"Only at the courthouse. There's been a couple of hearings."

"Did he leave any papers or a computer at your place?"

"Papers? What kind of papers? As for a computer, it's probably at his home."

"We were working on something. The papers might be blueprints or maps."

"No, he didn't leave anything at my home. He had Jas give me a key to a locker at the bus terminal, though. There was a bit of money in it. Nothing else. There were no papers or maps. I used most of the cash to pay for your room and the bail, though. Your legal aid went through, so your lawyer's fees are covered."

"Can you get into seeing Hassan? I need to find out if he can tell me where these papers are. It's really important."

"They only allow visitors on certain days, so I'll have to see what I can do. I can't promise you anything. Jas usually goes for the visits. I'll meet you back here next week, same time."

"Good. Thanks, Noe. Can you give him a personal message too!"

"Sure, I'll try."

"Tell him that Grandfather's situation does not appear to be good. His three brothers have returned, but his uncle and cousins have been delayed."

"Who are you talking about? His grandfathers have both passed away a long time ago. He doesn't have any brothers, and my father is his only uncle."

"He will understand. It is a mutual friend that we call Grandfather. It's just coded language that has nothing to do with his actual family. I would give the message to Jas, but she does not know that I am back. I didn't want to upset her with my problems."

"No, leave it with me and don't bother Jas right now. She's having a tough time, and I think it wouldn't be wise to put anything else on her. I don't know if I can speak freely in the jail, though. I'll try and see you here next week at the same time."

"I have one other small request. I'm sorry, but I'm really broke and wondered if you could spot me some cash. I'm going to get a job as soon as possible, and I'll pay you back."

"I've only got about a hundred bucks on me. Will that do?" Noe asked as he checked his wallet.

"Yeah, that will help. Thanks."

"No problem, I'll just borrow it from Hassan's stash. He doesn't need it right now, and Jas is financially okay."

"Sounds great. It'll let me eat and get around. See you next week."

52

After meeting with Hamid, Noe contacted Jas and asked if he could accompany her on her next visit to see Hassan. She seemed eager to have the company, and a few days later they met as she dropped the baby off with his wife, and they travelled to the jail together. Although Maryam had mentioned that she was worried about Jas, he was shocked by her worn-down appearance and concerned about her health. Her eyes were saddened and hollow looking, and gone was her shy smile. Most of all, it occurred to him that she had lost the innocence of her youth.

"How are you holding up, Jas?" Noe inquired.

"As well as can be expected under the circumstances. Anil has been a little fussy lately. I think he's started teething."

"You know Maryam would be happy to take him off your hands for a day if you need to catch up on your rest."

"I know. She always tells me the same thing. It's enough that she watches him for the weekly afternoon visits that I'm allowed. I just hate these controlled visits."

"Controlled? What do you mean?"

"There is so much that Hassan and I need to talk about, and the only opportunity we get is at the conjugal visits; otherwise, they listen to every word we say, and we have to talk through a glass partition," Jas disclosed.

"I thought that you get to talk to him every week."

"Yes and no. Hassan told me that those visitation rooms that make you use phones to communicate record all conversations, and someone always monitor whatever we say. He also said that there are small hidden cameras on both sides of the glass separating us, so they can spy on us. Even on the weekend visits, we are not sure of whether there are hidden cameras or microphones in the little cottages we get to use."

"I see, well I'll keep that in mind when I'm talking to him too," Noe replied.

During the bus ride, Noe reflected upon his reason for going to visit Hassan and the possibility that he might implicate himself in something he did not want to be a part of. It was out of the question. He couldn't help Hamid or Hassan if it meant jeopardizing his family.

He had a wife and child, a decent job, and had made a good life in this country. He wouldn't let Hassan's perverted aversion to America and his extremist ideologies that brought shame to the people of his faith alter the happiness he had found. He cautiously resolved that now was the time to stand up for his family and the true beliefs of Islam by distancing himself from the actions of his cousin. He wouldn't mention Hamid's request.

Hassan appeared to be surprised to see him, but Noe assured him that Jas was also in the waiting area for her visit. Noe took only a few minutes as he feigned that he had forgotten to get some information for his father that Iran had requested before releasing Hassan's identity documents.

He never mentioned maps or documents, though, but managed to pass on Hamid's mysterious but seemingly innocent message to him. He asked if Hassan needed anything, and Hassan just responded with a hopeless shrug before abruptly thanking him for coming and asking to see his wife.

A week later, Noe met with Hamid and gave him the lowdown on the highly restricted access rights that he had with Hassan. He told Hamid that his cousin was very tight-lipped about his activities in Canada. He suggested that Hassan probably had stored any documents of importance, like the money, in another place but couldn't speak about these matters.

Noe assured him that he had passed on his message about his grandfather, uncle, and cousins as it had seemed harmless. Then he expressed unease that the government was trying to link each one of them to some disturbing information that they had on Hassan, but no one quite knew what it was. Investigators had been to Noe's home on several occasions and had been relentless in their questions.

He further explained that he been called into CSIS on three separate occasions and grilled over and over again about his relationship with Hassan, Hamid, and other people that he had never heard of. He felt that the government was keeping a close eye on him and advised that they should limit their contact. It didn't take long for Hamid to figure out that Noe, like Dana, appeared to be trying to sever future contact when he suggested that they didn't meet for a while but handed him an additional five hundred dollars that he hoped would help him out.

As the men said their good-byes, Hamid realized that he had no one else to turn to in Canada. He was determined, though, that he couldn't give up yet in the hunt for the plans, despite that the odds were unfavorable. He decided that somehow, it was going to be necessary to get into Hassan's home and search it.

The next day, he began a vigil near Jas's home in an attempt to learn her schedule or perhaps to seize upon an opportunity to break in and search her home. On the third day, it dawned on him that she visited Hassan at the prison, and all he would need to know was the prison visitation schedule.

He recalled that Dana had told him where Hassan was being held, and he returned home to make a phone call. He found out that the next visitation would be in two days. He hoped like hell that he could find and retrieve the evidence before Jas got back and before the cops decided to search her home.

53

Two days later, Jas was flicking through channels on the TV, getting ready for her weekly visit to see Hassan, when she saw a news flash with Hamid's picture on the screen. She turned up the volume as the reporter stated that he had been shot and killed just outside a local mosque early the previous evening. There were no witnesses to the crime, and at present the assailant was unknown. Few details were provided.

As Jas sat in shock, she was filled with sorrow for the man she had considered her friend. She hadn't even realized that he had come back to Canada and wondered how long he had been around and why he had not contacted her. She earnestly tried to find out more, searching local broadcasts on other stations, but no other information was immediately forthcoming. What was happening to the people in her life? Thoughts of terrorism, questions of identity, and now murder were racing through her head. For the first time, fear gripped her, and she longed for the safety of Temesekia.

Russ and Corby had spent the weekend at the cabin and were heading home, when they heard the breaking news on the radio. They had gone up together in Russ's car as Corby's was in the repair shop. They both gasped in unison and glanced at each other, neither of them saying anything for a moment as Russ turned up the volume, and they tried to hear the details.

"Did I hear right?" Corby asked.

"I think so. I'm pretty sure they said Al Zain," Russ replied.

"Jeez! I wonder if Judd knows anything. He might be on shift this weekend. Do you want to head over to see him?"

"Yeah, I'm kind of curious to know how his investigation was going on this guy. He might have rattled a few chains. They were trying to find a way to put Al Zain on immigration hold before he made bail. Unfortunately for him looks like they weren't at all successful."

It took them about another half hour before they pulled into the parking lot and went looking for Judd. He was in his office, but he was entertaining some of the local police, so they went and fetched coffee and doughnuts before joining in on the conversation. Judd made some introductions and confirmed that they were seeking information about Hamid Al Zain.

He suggested that the police might want to talk to Russ as he had been involved in doing some investigative employment checks concerning the deceased man. Judd also advised that much of his own information was privileged as part of an ongoing federal investigation. The police indicated that they had no leads in the case. It was too early to determine if it had been a random act. As far as they knew, Al Zain had kept to himself since being released from prison a few weeks earlier.

The information that they had was that his daily routines were sketchy except that according to the imam at the mosque, he usually came by about the same time every evening, said his prayers, and didn't socialize with anyone. The police noted that he had made it easy for the killer if it was a targeted hit by establishing a clear, routine pattern every evening.

Judd advised the officers that he had been investigating how the deceased had got the fraudulent passport and didn't have any other concrete information to offer them. Russ was aware that Judd was hampered by privacy laws that prevented a federal employee from providing such information to the local cops, and he watched as Judd cautiously answered the questions posed to him. The RCMP, intelligence, and internal investigations, all worked criminal matters under federal jurisdiction, which often couldn't be shared with the local enforcement officers.

Although the murder investigation was a police matter, there were still outstanding federal crimes that the victim had been charged with. However, Russ also knew that occasionally there would be an unofficial exchange of information in the interest of public safety. An hour later, after the local policemen had departed and Judd turned his full attention to Russ and Corby, he asked, "Can you believe this? I was just starting to get some feedback on the guy, and he gets himself killed. The question is, who did it and why?"

54

"You think it was a hit?" Corby asked.

"I think there's a real possibility. We didn't have enough on him, yet. It's all just begun to come together nicely. We've been stacking up evidence to turn over to the prosecution. We were also looking at a possible removal from Canada. I did find out some interesting information about our man. Included is a potential prior connection to Zadeh, before they both arrived in Canada."

"Well, we know Zadeh couldn't have done it or even orchestrated a hit. He's tucked nicely away for now with little chance of communicating with anyone without our knowledge. What kind of connection did you make to him?" Russ remarked.

"It seems that they both worked at one time or another for an organization called the International Organization for Alleviation and were in Pakistan about the same time working with relief efforts after the big earthquake. Nothing absolutely concrete, though, that might prove they knew each other or even that they crossed paths."

"How the hell did you get that?" Corby asked?

"Russ gave me some information that wasn't in his immigration files about his education. I found out about Al Zain's involvement with a local branch in Saudi Arabia through the university he attended. This organization is known to us and other governments, and although it does a lot of charitable work, it has also attracted a radical Islamic group of sympathizers to the whole movement of Jihadist," Judd replied.

"Have you done any background work on the other known parties? The wife, the cousin, or the girlfriend?" Russ commented.

"There's nothing on any of them. Zadeh's cousin didn't come in as a refugee. He married a Canadian citizen. He works, supports his family, corresponds with his father overseas, and attends a mosque near his home like clockwork. We haven't gotten anything connecting him directly to any of the radical things that the others were involved in. We're watching him, though."

"What about the wife?" Corby asked.

"The authorities in Temesekia vouch for the wife. They think she's an innocent party and doesn't understand what she's mixed up in. She's smart, comfortably well-off, and appears to have had the misfortune of meeting Zadeh at the college. She was questioned by Temesekian intelligence about him when she went home for a visit, and the government was satisfied that she didn't know anything about his true identity."

"Didn't that set off alarm bells for her?" Russ asked.

"They tried to warn her to stay clear of the guy, but the investigation was just beginning, and they weren't in a position to divulge anything to her other than the fact that he was already married. She said that she knew that he had been, the operative word being *had*, and chose not to believe them when informed that he wasn't divorced. She was already pregnant at the time."

"I saw her at the hospital when she had the baby. She'd been in a car accident. Even though she was just waking from a coma, it was apparent that she was a beautiful woman. She looked very innocent, and I tend to think she is likely very naive. She may turn out to be a victim in all of this. How about the dead guy's girlfriend?" Russ said.

"Mrs. Zadeh's brothers and the Temesekian government seem to think along the same lines about the wife being love struck and hoodwinked by her unscrupulous husband. The authorities in her country are willing to work with us for her protection. This other girl, Dana Jahel, is the one farthest removed from all of this. We don't think she was actually his girlfriend, just someone he met through the college."

"How do you figure that? Al Zain used her for a reference on his job application. I understand that she's the only one he contacted during the months he was in jail. She even found him a lawyer," Corby remarked, raising his eyebrows.

"The college people say she is an outgoing and friendly person who takes her role in helping new students seriously. Everybody at the college loved her. They also said that her best friend on campus was Zadeh's wife. On the other hand, Al Zain's relationship with Zadeh is another thing. Zadeh and this Al Zain fellow were regularly seen together in various places, sometimes with the two women and sometimes not," Judd replied.

"That doesn't mean that Jahel wasn't sleeping with Al Zain," Corby said.

"From what we've learned about him, she wasn't his type. Seems he was known in the seedier parts of town. He liked women all right, but didn't mess with anyone at the college that we know of. He kept his exploits apart from people of his own faith. He was pretty much a loner and preferred one-night stands or prostitutes."

"That's interesting, I attended a course on identifying terrorists a few years ago, and we were told that more than 60 percent are married, from upper-middle-class families and well-educated professionals usually from the hard sciences such as architecture, medicine, or engineering. He fits a part of the profile, but where does he get his money from?" Russ inquired.

"His family was upper-middle class, and he was a chemical engineer. Quite well educated before taking the courses here at the college. You're right, though, other than student welfare, he had no other visible means of income."

"Doesn't that surprise anyone?" Corby sarcastically asked.

"I think that he was definitely up to something. Hell, he probably could have taught some of those courses with his background. The money is puzzling too, seems he had ready access to funds to be able to purchase a counterfeit passport and fly out of Canada on a whim. The Jahel girl is different, though. She's Lebanese, has been in Canada for a number of years, and is somewhat religious. She and Al Zain were in some of the same courses at the college for the past couple of years but didn't socialize until after the arrival of Mrs. Zadeh," Judd replied.

"Lucky for her," Corby cynically commented.

"She was on a school committee that meets and greets newcomers and was the person who provided Jaslyn Zadeh's reception. When Mrs. Zadeh had the accident, the school provided information that Dana Jahel was her closest friend. She's moved since she graduated and now works full-time. There's been a tail on Al Zain since he got out of Wilkie, and he only met up with the Jahel woman once, at some small diner. We don't think that he's made contact with Zadeh's wife at all. Interestingly, this past week, Al Zain spent a couple of days watching the Zadeh home, but he never approached it."

"I wonder what he was up to. Was he spying on Mrs. Zadeh? Where was the tail when he got shot?" Russ asked

"Still inside the mosque. He'd gone for a whiz. We can only surmise that he wanted something in the Zadeh home but didn't want the wife to know he was there," Judd replied.

"I think we're missing somebody or something," Russ said.

"Yep, I think you've got that right. There has to be someone else, or I'd say we haven't got the whole puzzle yet. It's unfortunate we can't get more out of Al Zain. We even checked his former address where he lived before his short flight, and the landlord told us the room was clean as a whistle when he suddenly vacated it. He had very little inside his current room according to the local police. Just a few papers concerning his passport charges and some items of clothing. One interesting little fact that I just learned from the Kuwaiti visa office on Friday was that he didn't have a brother. He was an only child," Judd acknowledged.

"God, wouldn't that have been powerful enough evidence to prevent his bail?" Corby queried.

"Who knows? The visa office had to dig a little to get that little gem too. We did get some interesting stuff from the warrant we had for the printer Nazreh Arz, though. He didn't get a chance to clean out his place. We grabbed a cell phone and his computer. It gives us a tenuous link between a lot of these characters and some fellows south of the border. The Americans at least have some names to watch out for."

"Sounds like they had a pretty big operation planned. I hope we can round them all up on both sides of the border before something catastrophic happens," Corby commented.

55

Although the news from Hamid had not been good, Hassan was grateful to be able to get somewhat of a clear picture of what the situation was. He felt that his instincts had been right about that Norman fellow. He was sure that much of the evidence that the Canadians had was due to that man's relentless investigations. At least Hamid had taken care of that problem, and the immigration officer wouldn't be around to gloat, he thought.

He found that saddest of all, though, was that the mission would fail. Hamid's message indicated that the Americans had deported or detained most of the chief operatives in the United States. The deportations were probably based on illegal status, but he was curious why the others had been arrested. He hoped that Jas had sent his laptop to the imam and Hamid had recovered it.

Disappointingly, Hassan concluded that the operation wouldn't be able to proceed at this time. Thinking about his most trusted operatives, Hassan realized that Sammi, Tarik, and Khurram had left the country; Naz, Hamid, and himself had been arrested; and Bashir and Shahid were dead. All that he had left of this entire fiasco was Noe, Jas, and his son. He felt that Noe's usefulness had been stretched to its limits. He debated on whether he could trust his wife, but he still had things that needed to be taken cared of; it was just a matter of who he could trust to get it done.

There was no point in him staying in Canada any longer, and he wondered how he could best broker a deal to leave the country without admitting to the crimes he was accused of. Tomorrow, he would check out the law in the prison library and figure out a plan. Noe had said Connors was good. Now would be the time to prove it and get him out of the country without turning him over to Temesekia or the United States for prosecution. He rolled over and went into a fitful sleep.

Meanwhile, the men who had gathered in Judd's office continued their discussions about the man in Victoria. They agreed that he was posing as an ordinary joe, but he had a more ominous role within a suspected terrorist organization. Perhaps he was the person who cleans up the loose ends, and they'd need to keep him in custody for as long as they could.

"I don't think that it was a random act that got Al Zain killed. I think he had become a loose end. Do you think the printer wanted him out of the way and found a way to get rid of him?" Russ asked.

"Yeah, what about the printer? He had to have been worried that this guy might testify against him," Corby tossed out.

"Nope," Judd remarked, "he couldn't have done it. He's still in the clink. Everything we got from his cell phone and his computer suggests that most of his contacts were in the United States, and they've all been rounded up down there. They did get one connection in Vancouver, a photographer, but he's on criminal hold, too. He did photos for all kinds of the documents manufactured by the guy in Victoria, and we recovered a lot of the prints and negatives there. The photographer wasn't as careful at destroying things and apparently hadn't realized that the printer had been nabbed."

"Have they linked any of these guys to Zadeh?"

"Not yet, they're working on it. However, they found the letter that Al Zain received from the water treatment plant at Arz's shop, and they found a lot of evidence in the photographer's studio that have been very eye-opening to the investigations," Judd remarked.

Russ was astounded when he learned that the photos had included numerous shots of the plaza where Kendrick's offices were located and close-ups of many of the Watchdogz employees. They'd also found negatives that proved to be photos for a number of people whom they'd had dealings with over the course of the past two years. These included Al Zain, the baggage handler, and his Hong Kong friend that Russ had encountered.

He wondered if any of the photos had matched the suicide bombers. Judd explained that they were still trying to put names to all the faces, and they had been able to get enough to show that there was some prior relationship between the deceased Hamid Al Zain and both the photographer and the printer.

"That Zadeh is one shrewd dude, though. We know he knew Al Zain through school and possibly met in Pakistan. We've got nothing else. As for Nazreh Arz, I reviewed the intake file from the airport and found the slip of paper that you confiscated with the writing of the word 'Naz' on it and what appears to be a phone number."

Russ and Corby glanced at each other as they recalled their conversation about how Azizi had said it was a reference to the Dasht-e Naz Airport in Iran. They were even more shocked when Judd revealed that they had the tape of the interview translated by another interpreter and found that Azizi had only made his own assumption about the connection to the airport, thus misinforming the officers at the time of the interview. Zadeh had simply replied that the name was common, such as in the Dasht-e Naz Airport.

The men concluded that it appeared that they had rounded up most of the people who were involved in whatever their plans had been. However, they were still left with the mystery of who had killed Al Zain and what was their ultimate mission.

"Do you think Arz could have contracted someone about to be released from the prison for the job?" Corby asked.

"I think I'm inclined to agree with Russ," Judd said. "There's got to be someone we're missing—a sleeper."

56

Jas carefully packed the suitcase with necessities for her monthly conjugal visit with Hassan. She had faithfully taken Anil to stay with his father at least once a month, when they would improvise a normal family environment in the "cottage" that was within the confines of the prison walls. This month's visit would be different, however, as Anil was on medication for an ear infection, and she wasn't allowed to take any drugs into the prison.

Maryam had consented to mind Anil overnight. Other than the few hours she went for her weekly visits, it would also be the first time she had been separated from her son for any length of time since they had left the hospital. It was also the first time she would have Hassan's undivided attention in many months where there was no one listening in on their conversation and without the interruption of the baby.

She was apprehensive about this visit as Jordan Connors had called to advise that Hassan had lost his refugee status. He had also warned her that the Canadian government probably would not renew her own minister's permit that had allowed her to stay in Canada while the hearings had been taking place. She was no longer eligible for a student visa.

The most disturbing news was that they would be deporting him to what they considered being a "safe third country." She'd inquired whether or not they could go to Temesekia. He said that the authorities had received information that connected Hassan to a murder in Temesekia, and he might face the death penalty there if they could prove their case.

The previous evening she had confided in Dana that she had discussed the possibility of appealing the decision; however, Mr. Connors had said that it was out of the question. They didn't have any grounds such as an error of law or an error of fact that might get them to a higher court.

Although Hassan emphatically denied having done any wrong, the government prosecutor did not need to prove this in the criminal standard of beyond a reasonable doubt. They only had to show that there were serious reasons to believe that he had committed acts of terrorism. Jas had confessed her own fears when she had learned about the unsolved murder of Hamid and that she no longer felt safe in Canada. Anil was almost seven months old now, and this continued uncertainty in their lives had to be resolved. She thought back on parts of the conversation that she had divulged to Dana about the harsh reality that she was facing.

"Have you thought about going back to Temesekia, Jas?" Dana had asked.

"Continually. Now I've learned, though, that Hassan cannot go there. I don't know what to do. Mr. Connors said that Hassan will be sent to another country. I can go if I want, but I don't think that will be in the best interests of Anil."

"Jas, I don't understand what has exactly happened. Nothing makes sense. You tell me he's wanted for murder, and Noe and Hamid told me that they were holding him on some kind of a security issue. I honestly don't understand what that means."

Jas softly began to cry as she told Dana, "They think that Hassan is a terrorist threat, maybe even an actual terrorist. They've accused him of doing terrible things, not just this one murder. The government says that he is responsible for the deaths of many, many people. They didn't let me sit in the court, part of the time. Hassan said that they didn't even show Mr. Connors all of the evidence that they are using against him."

"Can they do that? I didn't think Canada had secret trials."

"Mr. Connors said that they can in circumstances like this. The judge sees the evidence, but I don't know how Hassan is supposed to defend himself."

"It doesn't seem fair, but it must be very serious. Do you think you should go with him?"

"Mr. Connors said that it's something to do with a 'danger opinion' and special rules. You know, it was my government that first warned me that Hassan was a dangerous man. They didn't tell me that he was a murderer or a terrorist, though. They told me that he was a bigamist because he was still married. Hassan told me that it wasn't true, and I believed him. When Hassan was first arrested, I genuinely thought that this was all about the marriage business. I know nothing about these other things. I don't know what to do."

"Oh, Jas, I don't know what to say. Perhaps, you should talk to your brothers. What options does Hassan have now?"

"Canada wants to find another country that's willing to take him. Somewhere that we would always be outcasts just because of these proceedings. I'm so worried about Anil's future, our future."

"Jas, you have to think about Anil. You understand that this isn't just about you and Hassan. You've got to think about what's best for Anil. You know these men that have come across our lives really frighten me."

"What do you mean? What men?"

"Both Hamid and Hassan. I didn't want to worry you after Hassan was arrested, and then you had the accident, but some scary things happened with Hamid, too! He was in jail before he was murdered. Perhaps Hassan isn't innocent."

"What do you mean? Why was he in jail? What kind of things do you know about?" Jas asked.

"Hamid suddenly said that he received a message that they had found his brother was alive and had been held as a prisoner of war. It was the same day that Hassan went missing. Heck, I didn't even know he had a brother. I never heard him talk about him. I thought it was a strange coincidence."

"It's possible that Hamid was telling the truth. He told me too that he was going to see his brother. Nobody told me that he had returned to Canada. Then I saw on the news that he had been murdered," Jas shivered as she recalled the bulletin on the evening news.

"Well, Jas, the truth is he never left Canada. He was arrested and charged with possession of a forged passport. They even suspected him of murder."

"A forged passport? He didn't leave? Where was his? Why did they think he murdered someone?"

"I don't know, but he was trying to leave the country on a passport in someone else's name and another student who used to attend the college worked for the airline and recognized him, even though he had shaved off his beard and tried to disguise his appearance on the very day that we found out Hassan had been arrested. As for the murder, I don't know all the details, but his cellmate at the jail was found dead."

"Oh my God! Who was the man? You say Hassan had disguised himself? I don't know what I'm mixed up in. I've been very scared since Hamid's death."

"That wasn't the worst of it. He was in prison for several months because of the man in his cell that died the first night he went to jail. Hamid was initially accused of murdering him. I know all of this because he contacted me to get him a lawyer and arrange his bail."

"Oh, this is terrible," exclaimed Jas.

"Yes, I'm thinking that death seems to follow both of these men around. Do you think Hamid and Hassan were previously involved in something? I mean, I only met Hamid at the college because we took some of the same courses. I'd never actually socialized with Hamid before the day you arrived in Canada. If you stay with Hassan, what life will Anil have? Moreover, can you trust him?"

As Jas recalled the conversation, she was determined that today, she was going to try and get answers to those very questions. She felt lucky that Anil was better, and she could leave him with Maryam to give her the opportunity to go to see Hassan. The doctor had assured her that there was no danger to his cousin, and Jas was confident that the two infants would be company for each other.

She packed another small overnight bag for Anil and wrote out some instructions for Maryam regarding his medication and then placed it in the carrier of his carriage for the short walk to the SkyTrain that would take her to Noe's. Once the baby was settled in, Jas returned to her apartment, retrieved her overnight case, and called a taxi to take her to the prison.

57

Jas made decent time getting to the institution, and she expected that she would see Hassan just after lunch, following the extensive search that she would have to undergo. It was a bright and sunny day when she'd left home, but by the time she reached the prison, it was raining cats and dogs. The weather was so unpredictable in Vancouver!

As she entered the cramped living quarters, Jas felt slightly queasy and awkward. On her last visit, they had talked a lot about the death of Hamid and the memories that they shared about him. It was the first time that Jas could remember seeing her husband so visibly shaken. They had become close friends, almost like brothers, and Hassan had taken his death hard.

On this day, she knew that they would have to make some important decisions about their future, and she sensed that her life would never be the same. She tried to steady herself by keeping occupied. She had brought a change of clothes and some sleepwear that she put into the upper drawer of the small chest, put her basic toiletries in the washroom, and went to the kitchen to wash down the counters and tabletop, waiting until Hassan was brought into the unit.

"Where's Anil?" Hassan asked as he entered the premises.

"Maryam's looking after him overnight. He's had an ear infection, and they wouldn't let me bring him because of the medication," she answered.

"Perhaps you shouldn't have come. If he's sick, he needs his mother."

"No, he's really much better. It's just that he needs to finish the medication. Besides, he likes to visit Maryam. I'm only staying tonight. I promised Maryam I'd be back early tomorrow. I didn't have any way of letting you know that I wouldn't be coming, and I didn't want you to worry about us. Besides, there are things we need to discuss."

"What kind of things? Have you been talking to Connors?"

"Yes, Mr. Connors has told me that Canada has taken away your immigration status here. He also told me that I might not get an extension on my permission to stay in Canada, too!"

"Right now, I'm thinking I'm hungry to hold my wife. We'll talk about these things later. Let's just have some time together. It's been too long since we've been apart. How is Anil doing other than the ear infection? Has he got any teeth yet?" Hassan ably deflected the conversation.

"That was going to be a surprise." Jas laughed. "He got one on the bottom, and I can see the top of the one beside it just breaking his gums. He was so cranky, drooling all over the place and wouldn't eat. When he developed a fever and diarrhea, I didn't even realize he was sick."

"How could you not know he was ill?" Hassan exclaimed with disapproval.

"I thought it was just another tooth. You know Maryam's smart, she didn't think the fever had anything to do with his teething, she said it was too high. She's the one that told me that I should take him to the doctor. Maryam told me that her doctor told her she should check out a fever in an infant and not just assume it's because of a baby cutting teeth."

"Maryam's a good mother. It's good that she's helping you. You have so much to learn," he murmured as he caressed her cheek.

"Yes, she told me that she grew up with younger siblings and learned a lot from her mother. My mother was such a good mother too, but I was the youngest and never got a chance to learn the little things that mothers pass down to their daughters," Jas sadly conveyed her biggest regret with a tear in her eye.

Sensing his wife's melancholy, Hassan reached for her and gently held her for several minutes. As his arms encompassed her, Jas regained her composure. She was hungry with her need for him, and she had missed his tenderness and caring. Her senses spun out of control as her heart beat rapidly in anticipation of his lovemaking. He had been growing distant from her recently and was continually critical of everything she did. But today, he seemed to have some of the same needs, and the afternoon was theirs.

Nothing else mattered during those few short hours as they replenished the depths of their love. It was as if the rest of the world ceased to exist, and nothing or no person could separate or harm them. After taking a shower, Jas went to make them an evening meal from the food that had been ordered through the prison program.

"Has there been any news about Hamid's murder?" he asked.

"Nothing. Noe has even asked Jordan Connors because there has been nothing reported recently. No one knows anything. Noe said that Mr. Connors thought it was a random racist attack. There just isn't any other explanation!"

"What happened to his personal belongings?"

"I don't know. Dana said that he had cleaned out most of his belongings or taken them with him when he went away to try and find his brother. I don't know what they would do with his things. Why?"

"I was just curious. I didn't even know he had a brother."

"I don't think that he knew that his brother was alive. But you're right, I never heard him mention a brother before. Dana found him a room when he came back, and she said all he had was a small satchel, so I don't think he had very much that anyone would worry about."

"That's good then," Hassan answered, sounding slightly relieved. "Did he find his brother?"

"No, he was apparently arrested for travelling on a false passport. I'm not really sure what all happened. Maybe Noe knows.

I didn't hear from him when he got back. I was a little surprised when I saw his picture on the news. He left so suddenly, and Noe said he'd only been back about a week or so." Jas was careful not to reveal anything about the suspicions that Hamid had murdered his cellmate.

"How are you managing for money?"

"Noe gave me some. He said that your uncle got hold of some money from your father's assets and sent it for your defense."

"Did he give any more to Jordan Connors?"

"He said he did because legal aid doesn't cover everything. I was really worried because things have become so complicated, but Mr. Connors told me that everything was taken care of."

"Come on, let me help you with the dishes and cleaning up this mess before I have my wicked ways with you again."

"That sounds like an interesting proposition. You're on," whispered Jas.

The evening had pretty much replicated the afternoon until the couple fell into a peaceful sleep. In the early morning, Jas realized that she had been distracted by Hassan's boyish charm and passion. After breakfast, Jas was fiercely determined to pursue the discussion that had been put off the afternoon before.

"Hassan, we need to discuss your options after you're released from here," Jas opened the conversation shortly after breakfast.

"The options are simple, Jas. They'll keep me here indefinitely, or they'll find another country that will take me."

"Here? Do you mean in Canada or in jail here in Canada? What other country? Will they send you to Iran?"

"No, there is no possibility of that. They can't send me to Iran. They know I'd probably be tortured and killed. I'm not sure where they'll deport me to. They've mentioned Sudan, Algeria, and Yemen. If I stay in Canada, there's a distinct possibility I'll be kept in prison."

They spent a couple of hours talking about the potential countries that might accept Hassan. However, it always came back to the three that he had told her earlier in the discussion. Hassan seemed to favor Algeria and raved about the capital city of Algiers.

"I don't want to go to any of those countries. I don't speak their language, and they wouldn't be good places for Anil. What about England or France?"

"Jas, I don't have a choice here. If Canada thinks I'm a terrorist, England and France wouldn't take me either. We'll be together as a family wherever they send me. That's all that is relevant. As for language, most of the people speak Arabic, and you'll need to learn the language to teach Anil."

"No, Hassan, I think you're wrong. If you're innocent of these charges, then you should fight them. Are you a terrorist? Did you commit these crimes? You have to consider Anil's future. There's nothing in Algeria for him. What about my family?"

"What do you mean if I'm innocent of the charges? First, you show me what a lousy mother you are, and now you show me how disloyal you are. I can look after my son and give him everything that is important for his future. Forget about your family. From now on, we are your only family. You are my wife, and your duty is to obey my wishes," he scolded.

"Hassan, I don't obey anyone." Jas was appalled at his comments. "I am not a lousy mother nor have I been disloyal to you. To me marriage is a partnership. I have loved you, and I have always believed in you. You can't ask this of me. I will not sever my relations with my family, and I will not let my son go to one of these countries," Jas declared just as a knock came to the door, indicating that the visitation period was over.

As Jas walked toward the door, she was astounded at the last private words that she heard from Hassan as he threatened, "Listen, you little bitch, he's my son. Over and over again you've proven to be an unfit mother. It is Anil that I am only thinking about. You don't know what love is, lady. It's not just the lustful ways of the Western women. I don't care what you want to do, but mark my words—my son will join me. I have lots of friends on the outside, and if you choose to defy me, I promise you that when you least expect it, you'll never see my son again."

Neither Jas or Hassan looked at each other as he was led away and taken back to his cell. Fear engulfed Jas as she gathered her suitcase and headed to the prison exit for her belongings to be examined. She called a taxi to take her across town to fetch her son. With her pulse racing and her heart pounding, Jas began to shake uncontrollably as she thought about her visit with Hassan.

She was alarmed by the words she had heard him utter at her. This was a side of him that she had never seen. She realized that he had become increasingly critical of her parenting, but she thought he was just frustrated by his situation. There appeared to be a part of him that she didn't know. She trembled with terror from the sheer brutality of his words. Could there be some truth to the accusations against him? What did she really know about this man who was her husband? Was he capable of things like kidnapping and murder? What was she going to do?

58

A visibly shaken Jas hurried home and packed a large suitcase. She filled it mainly with things for her son, her software disks, and a few personal things. Taking a quick look around the apartment, she fetched a cab and went to pick up Anil.

Jas had known that Maryam would invite her to stay for dinner, but she had carefully crafted an excuse that she was going away with a girl from school for a few days. She didn't want to face anyone with the fear that was bursting in her. The waiting taxi provided her with a quick opportunity to leave. She hoped that this would buy her some time before Hassan could put into action his threat.

At first she didn't know where to go; she only knew that she didn't want to return home. She instructed the cab driver to take her to the hospital where she knew that lots of people would be around. Hopefully, it would provide her safety while she thought about what to do. Driving toward the medical center, she recalled the woman who had visited the girl in the bed next to her when she had the accident. Digging through her purse, she found the card for Ms. Katy Freeman.

About twenty minutes later, thankful that Anil was settled comfortably in his stroller, Jas approached a pay phone.

"Ms. Freeman, my name is Jaslyn Zadeh, and I desperately need your help. Can I see you?" Jas whispered into the phone as she connected to the party she was calling and hoping that no one overheard her in the hospital reception area.

"How can I help you, Ms. Zadeh?" Katy replied, slightly taken aback,.

"Myself and my child are in danger, and I need a place to stay for a few days. I need it right away."

"Where are you? Is anyone with you?"

"I am at the main entrance to the hospital, near the inquiry desk. No one is with me, but someone may be watching me," Jas explained.

"Are you hurt? Who do you think is watching you?"

"My husband said that he has people watching me."

"Do you live with your husband? Why would he have someone watch you?" Katy could sense the fear in the woman's voice and thought that it could be attributed to a psychotic episode. Not that she would refuse to assist her, but how she chose to respond depended on whether the woman was in a real or imaginary danger.

"My husband is in jail. He's mixed up with some very evil people, and he wants to take our son away. He says that these people will take my baby. Please help me," Jas pleaded.

"All right, you stay right where you are until I get there. I should be there in about twenty minutes. Will you be okay? How will I recognize you?"

"Yes, I'll be okay. If you come into the waiting area, I'll know you. I saw you once here at the hospital when you visited my roommate." Jas replaced the receiver and wondered how much information she would have to tell Ms. Freeman.

She was afraid that the shelter wouldn't take her and Anil if they knew her husband was a suspected terrorist. Perhaps, the people there would feel that her presence placed everyone else in danger. Jas made the decision that the next day she would contact the Temesekian consulate and obtain a travel document for Anil and take him to her homeland. Hopefully, they would leave Canada within a few days.

It was late afternoon, and Katy decided to let the young, obviously frightened mother settle into the shelter without pushing her to reveal her problems at this time. She assured Jas that the facilities were safe, and she gave her a quick tour of the main desk, the sitting room, kitchen, and dining room before showing her to a small, sparsely furnished private room with a crib and en suite bath where she could stay for the duration of her visit.

The following day, Katy was tied up with prescheduled appointments and didn't have an opportunity to meet with Jas for more than a few minutes to check up on her and schedule an appointment for the next afternoon. Jas made use of her time to contact the Temesekian consulate and made inquiries about obtaining the travel document for her son. To her utter disbelief she was informed that her request would be denied.

Although Anil was born in Canada and throughout most of the world he would be recognized as a Canadian citizen, Temesekia was not one of those countries. The archaic laws of her country did not recognize dual citizenship and for all intents and purposes considered her son to have the nationality of his father. Temesekia would only allow her son entry into the country as a temporary visitor with his father's permission.

Even if Hassan authorized his initial visit, Jas was advised that Anil would have no status in her country. Anil would only be permitted to attend school as a foreign student, and he would need to obtain a tourist's medical coverage at continuing financial costs. She knew that this meant that even as an adult, his job choices would be restricted, and he'd always have to have a work permit. The most appalling thing of all, though, was that Hassan could demand his return to him at any time.

Her life was one huge mess, and she didn't know where to turn. Coupled with her fear, she was overwhelmed with shame. By the time she finally sat down to discuss her dilemma with Ms. Freeman, Jas had recalled the conversation she had overheard in the hospital and thought that maybe she could hire the social worker's father to help her. She recalled that he was a private investigator who had previously worked with the Immigration Department.

"I can't tell you everything, partly because I don't understand it all myself, and it is very serious. My son and I are in grave danger, and I need a place to stay until I can figure out how to leave the country with him. I think your father might be able to help me, and I'd like to hire him?"

"My father? Do you know my father?"

"I saw you at the hospital once with him. Part of my problems are with immigration and the laws of my country. I heard you say he used to work in immigration matters. He may be able to help me. The girl in my room, I think you called her Becky, she must have left your business card on the nightstand. I found it, and that's how I knew how to contact you."

At this revelation, Katy thought back to the time she had gone to the hospital to get Becky and the woman who had been lying in a coma in her room had suddenly awoken. She didn't know the extent of her problems, but one thing was sure, though—the woman was afraid.

"I don't know if my father is available, but I'll try and get a hold of him. I won't promise you anything, but I'll speak with him and let you know tomorrow, Mrs. Zadeh."

59

Russ was dumbfounded as Katy conveyed Jas's request. A vague picture of Mrs. Zadeh flashed through his mind. He recalled the glimpse he had of her when she was in the hospital. Russ felt chills along his spine at the mention of the woman's name in the same breath as his daughter, though. He wondered what had triggered her to contact the shelter.

"I don't know what the hell this is about, but if this woman thinks that she's in danger, I suspect that she might be right. I know exactly who she is, and I remember seeing her when we went to pick up Becky in the hospital."

Russ quickly advised his daughter that her client's husband was being held for deportation as a convicted terrorist and that he personally had a long history with the man. He explained that Corby had interviewed him when he'd arrived in Canada. He told her that he had escorted the man to the detention center the night he'd arrived in Canada. When her father conveyed that the man's best friend had recently been murdered, Katy gasped.

Russ was curious about what had fired Mrs. Zadeh up but hesitated about meeting her. He pointed out that he had left the government more than a year before, so he didn't necessarily have a conflicting interest; however, ethically he might not be her best choice. He promised to discuss it with Kendrick and get back to her.

Kendrick was apprehensive for both Russ and Katy as he recalled the incident involving the tampered wine that was still not fully resolved. He wondered if Mrs. Zadeh might be involved in setting a trap of some sort, and somehow the people involved in that incident had also learned that Katy was Russ's daughter. Was Mrs. Zadeh as naive as everyone seemed to think, or perhaps she was planning something a little sinister herself?

Eventually, Russ and Kendrick contacted Judd and apprised him of the situation. All the men agreed that Mrs. Zadeh might have finally accepted that she was in danger and to be truly in need of help. This was one of those instances when they all knew that you could be damned if you did or damned if you didn't respond. To minimize the risks to others, the men came up with a plan.

Russ contacted his daughter advising that Judd would pick Mrs. Zadeh up at the shelter in the morning and bring her to a secure meeting place. She was to bring no personal belongings except necessities for her baby. He suggested that Judd would circle the block a couple of times to make sure that no one was watching the premises.

Katy had protested that the woman was terribly frightened and that he could meet Mrs. Zadeh in her office. Katy's opposition to their meeting under the terms Russ described was so intense that Russ eventually was forced to confide his fears to her. After learning that the mysterious woman at her shelter was affiliated with the perpetrators of the tainted wine, Katy grudgingly accepted the arrangements the men had come up with.

Jas was just finishing her breakfast when Katy found her the next morning. Katy explained the meeting arrangements and sensed Jas's perplexity. Jas was initially resistant and stated that she felt safe at the shelter and was highly nervous about leaving the premises. Finally, Katy confided to her that her father's line of work necessitated taking precautions to ensure not only the confidentiality and safety of his clients but also those people around, like the other women and children in the shelter.

"Mrs. Zadeh, obviously you need help about a serious matter. You have to trust someone. I would like to help you, and I'm trying very hard to work with you on this without knowing all of your problems. I have young women who arrive here under circumstances much the same as you; however, I have to admit that your request to meet with my father is rather unique."

"Okay, Mrs. Freeman. You're absolutely right. I do have to trust someone, and that is why I must meet with your father. I don't know of anyone else who might be able to help me in my situation."

"Do you want to talk to me? I'm here to help you. I might not be able to personally resolve your problem, but I have access to a wide network of people who probably can."

As if Katy hadn't even spoken, Jas began to gather her things and asked when the driver would arrive. While Jas returned to her room to prepare for the meeting, Katy reflected on the information she did have. Instinctively, she felt almost certain that Mrs. Zadeh and her son were in peril. She prayed that she wasn't putting her father in harm's way, too!

60

On the drive over to meet the woman, Russ wondered what the hell was going on. As far as he knew Zadeh was still in holding. He had to admit that he was curious if this somehow might be connected to the unsolved murder of her husband's friend.

When Judd arrived at the shelter, Jas was waiting with her son and Russ's daughter. Katy was adamant that she would accompany the woman to the meeting. Signs of strain were evident on Mrs. Zadeh's face. Judd was concerned about her obvious distress. What was the purpose of her request to meet with Russ? Was she planning a cold-blooded attempt to murder him, or was she truthfully a victim and seeking his help?

A half hour later, the mysterious woman and her son, Katy, Judd, and Russ gathered in the office. He noted that the woman was trembling and seemed determined but afraid. Katy had the foresight to bring some bottles of water, which she placed on the table and invited everyone to help themselves. As they settled in, Russ thought that he would take the lead to open the conversation.

"Mrs. Zadeh, I understand that you have sought assistance at the shelter, and I must stress that my daughter and perhaps the police are better equipped to help you sort out any problems you might have."

"Mr. Freeman, I think you might be able to help me. I have a legal problem."

"Mr. Norman. Freeman is my daughter's married name. My name is Russ Norman. What kind of legal problem do you have, Mrs. Zadeh? I'm not a lawyer. My daughter can probably help you find some good legal advice if that's what you need."

"I'm sorry, Mr. Norman, my situation is very unusual. I know that the police and the people at the shelter have probably never encountered anything like it. I think you may be able to help because I overheard Mrs. Freeman tell someone at the hospital that you have a lot of knowledge about immigration matters and contacts outside of Canada. Please listen to my story first, and then you can decide if you can or cannot help."

Jas shyly related how and why she had come to Canada, her meeting with Dana and Hamid and ultimately Hassan. She emphasized that there had been an instant attraction between them. Hassan was an expert at computer programming and had taken an interest in her business ideas, and he subsequently became involved in helping her develop her software programs. Over time, they had simply fallen in love, decided to get married, and were looking forward to settling in Canada. They had both been excited by the news that she was expecting a baby, and they had thought they both had a promising future.

Jas suddenly hesitated as if struggling to find the right words. Katy, Russ, and Judd waited for her to continue, giving her the time she needed to gather her thoughts. Haltingly, she described her visit home, the accusations of the government security people in Temesekia, and her confrontation with her husband concerning his first marriage upon her return to Canada. She mentioned that when she told her husband what had happened she forgot one detail: The government had queried her about whether she knew someone by the name of Mahmoud Bahrami, and she had no idea who this person was or the significance of this name.

She briefly talked about his friend Hamid and the shocking news of his murder. Finally Jas relayed the events surrounding her husband's arrest and detention, the charges, and the ultimatum that her husband had given her. She stated that she recently had learned that this "Bahrami" was a name her husband had used, and in fact, he had admitted it in court. The government of Temesekia apparently had some evidence that linked him to what they termed was a "terrorist attack" that resulted in the death of a worker at the US Embassy in her country and an attempt on the life of the American ambassador.

Russ thought that she was articulate as well as beautiful but appeared to be oblivious to her own attributes. More importantly, he felt she was genuine. It was evident that she valued integrity and honesty. She had probably led a remarkably sheltered life and would have been like putty in the hands of her shrewd husband. She was taking her time, telling her story the way that was comfortable for her. The group patiently listened and waited for her to get to the problem that was now causing her fear, but Russ and Judd knew that much of her story was the truth.

After explaining his last threatening words to her, Jas concluded that Hassan was probably not as innocent of the charges as he had pretended to be, and she now believed both her and her son were at great risk. She was more afraid than she had ever been in her life. She had decided to cut all ties with everyone that she and her husband had known in Canada and wanted to return home; however, she couldn't and was caught in a legal conundrum that wouldn't allow her to take her son with her. She had been checking on returning to her country before she had spoken to him on that final day. She now pleaded that she needed Mr. Norman's help to find a way to resolve the technicalities that prevented her from returning to the safety of Temesekia.

Jas looked down at her son with his big trusting eyes and his broad smile; it pulled at her heartstrings. She instinctively knew that she was doing the right thing. Would anything else ever matter to her again? It was his safety, his well-being, and his future that would be her guide. She couldn't imagine life without him now, and her faith, not some distortion of religion, would protect them both.

"Mrs. Zadeh—," Russ began.

"Jas, please call me Jas. In fact, my maiden name is Jaslyn Koh."

"Okay, Jas, I was going to say that your husband may have believed that he was divorced. Some followers of the Muslim faith don't realize that when they go through the *talaq* ceremony of repudiating the marriage, the divorce must still be registered and ultimately granted by the courts. This provides a legal record of the divorce that all countries can rely upon. He may have gone through the verbal ceremony, repeating his decree—"I divorce you"—three times, but he never had the divorce granted by the court," Russ informatively offered her as some consolation for her loyalty to the man.

"Oh, I see. Yes, he might not have realized this. As for me, I don't understand some of the technical aspects about the Muslim religion at all. I converted to his religion after we were married. However, that is not my biggest problem right now. I must care for my son," Jas responded. Gripping the side of her chair, Jas pleadingly looked at both Katy and Russ, stating that she now believed that her husband did have the means to carry out his threat.

Jas began to cry and said that she had caught a glimpse of the most distorted look of pure evil in Hassan's eyes and face such that it made her shudder in remembrance of it. He had told her that she meant nothing to him as if she were disposable. His best friend had been shot and killed on the streets, and she didn't understand why. Her government had warned her that her husband was a very dangerous man, and right now, she believed them.

"Jas, he can't harm you when he's locked up," Katy commented.

"Yes, I believe he can. Someone murdered his friend Hamid. I also know that they had friends that I never met. When I went to Temesekia the last time, Dana told me that they had gone away to visit someone in Victoria. Hassan said that they only went sightseeing. He and Hamid went off together all the time, but I have no idea whom they met or where they went. In the court, not all of the evidence shown to the judge was disclosed. I am sure that there is more, but I don't know what it is."

"How do you think we can help you, Mrs.—I mean—Jas," Russ asked.

"I need protection until I can go home to Temesekia, and there is a significant problem preventing me from going there. My country will only grant visitor status to my son, and I need his father's permission to take him to Temesekia. In my country, a child has the citizenship of his father. He will never have a normal life. He would need permits to go to school or work for the rest of his life, and I will always have to buy expensive medical insurance and pay foreign tuition fees. I hope that perhaps the government of Canada can assist me in talking to my government about how I can overcome this. Hassan would never give his consent. He wants to take my son from me. I can pay your company for your time. I have my own money, and my brothers will help if I need them."

"Okay, Jas. I'll look into things and talk this over with my boss. I'll get back to you in a few days. Katy will be our go-between but don't leave the shelter unless you have Katy check with me first. Your instincts may be right, so we'll be cautious until we can see what we can do," Russ answered and prepared to leave.

61

Russ headed back to his office after agreeing with Judd to meet up later that afternoon. Judd was a lot more familiar with the intricacies of the case, and he had indicated that he had talked to the authorities in Temesekia. It was one consulate that Russ had never dealt with, and he hoped that Judd could help make contact with the Temesekian government.

Later that day, Judd suggested that perhaps the RCMP should accompany Mrs. Zadeh when she went to pick up her belongings as there was no telling what they might find among her husband's personal effects that might cast some light on what this man was planning in Canada. He surmised that Al Zain was after something in her home before he died. Russ agreed and said he would like to accompany her to the flat as well.

During the next several days, Dana anxiously tried to contact Jas. She checked with the college and continued to call on the phone several times during the day and evening, all to no avail. By the weekend, her despair was so great that she reluctantly contacted Hassan's cousin, Noe. He also went to the flat several times and even spoke to the imam at the mosque. Dana and Noe finally realized that Maryam was the last person to see Jas. However, Maryam said that she had appeared to be fine when she picked up Anil after her visit with Hassan. With growing apprehension, Noe decided he would pay his cousin a casual visit to see if he might know where she had gone.

Noe was caught in a conundrum. He didn't want to alert Hassan that Jas was missing until he had a better understanding of whether she had simply learned truths about the man she had married and gone into hiding. He decided that he would let Hassan talk for a bit and see if he divulged anything.

It didn't take long before Hassan confided in his cousin that he was going to be deported to another country, likely Yemen or Algeria, and Jas had refused to come with his son. Noe had heard of the exploits of his cousin in the name of his alter ego, and he understood without further words that Hassan had likely threatened to take Anil from Jas. He was pretty confident in making the assumption she was on the run. She must have finally reached the realization that she was living in a fearfully dangerous world. He made small talk for the duration of his visit without divulging that Jas was missing and promised to keep in touch, when he received the signal from the guard that his time was up.

He sympathized with Jas because he too had lived in fear of this man. Noe had played along with everything that had been asked of him by Hassan because he had known for a long time that he had power over the life and death of those he came in contact with. Noe knew that Hassan had many associates who would willingly follow his commands.

Noe had been apprehensive about the safety of his own family from the moment he had learned that Hassan was coming to Canada. He had even dared to hope that when his cousin had married Jas, things would be different. Now all that he could do was pray that she and Anil would be safe. For these reasons, he had not revealed to Hassan that she was gone.

As he waited at the little Lebanese restaurant for Dana to arrive, Noe wondered how much he should reveal to the unsuspecting young woman who was truly concerned for her friend Jas. He thought she was owed at least part of the truth. He couldn't give her all the answers, but he was optimistic that he might give her some peace of mind.

"Hi, Noe, did you find Jas or where she might be?"

"Whoa, Dana! Let's wait until we've ordered our food to talk. I have some critical matters to discuss with you. I don't even know where to begin."

"Oh my, you sound very mysterious. I hope you have good news. I was thinking of calling the hospitals and maybe even the police."

When the food arrived, Dana said, "Okay, spill it. Tell me what's going on, please."

"Dana, this is not going to be easy, and I only know some of the details. I'm asking you to keep our conversation confidential. There could be some trouble brewing. Do I have your word?"

"Yes, yes, of course."

"People's lives may depend on you not repeating anything I am about to tell you."

"You're scaring me, Noe."

"I don't mean to, but I'm dead serious. I think that Jas is safe and is trying to hide. She may have even left the country."

"Why? I don't understand. Why would she do that without telling me? I'm her friend."

"She is scared. Hassan has been found guilty of some very serious things. He is probably going to be deported to Algeria or Yemen, and he wants her and Anil to go with him. Apparently, she refused to go, and they had an argument. I am not positive, but I can almost be sure that he threatened to have Anil kidnapped so that he could go with him."

"Without Jas? He couldn't do that, could he? The Canadian government wouldn't let him take the baby without Jas, would they? Why would he say that?"

"Legally, I am sure he can't leave with Anil. That wouldn't stop him, though. He has other ways. He knows many people who would be willing to kidnap the baby and get him away from Jas. Believe me, I know."

"What do you mean?" Dana gasped.

"Dana, I know that Hassan has lived in many countries before and that he knows many dangerous people. He is what one might call a master of terrorism. He planned a lot of terrible things that others carried out. He controls evil people who are very loyal to him and his beliefs. I know that the Canadian government is right: He is a big threat. He will stop at nothing. I, too, have been afraid for myself and my family since he came to Canada."

"What kind of terrible things? Have you told anyone?"

"These things I cannot speak about. I have no firsthand knowledge and only heard rumors from others. I am not his confidant. He is very misguided since he lost his family, and I believe he is mixed up in this jihad. There is some truth to what happened to his family, but he was away at school at the time, and it was because of their loyalty to the shah. Hassan blames the Americans for the deaths of his family and wants revenge. He became involved in a radical group with similar hatred."

"What does this mean? He is in Canada. This is another country that has given him opportunities. He has a wife and son. Why would he believe in jihad? Have you talked to Jas about this?"

"I've talked to no one. I don't know anything that I can prove. I also have family and Maryam's family in Iran. None of our family has been safe, unless we do exactly what he says. I do know that both he and Hamid were involved with people here in Canada and others in the United States who were planning a major attack there of some sort. Those two men were two peas in a pod. It is rumored that both of them did many terrible things, although I don't think Hamid knew that Hassan was the actual leader."

"Hamid was involved in all of this? This is scary."

"Yes. There were others too. Hamid wanted me to give Hassan a message, and I think that he wanted him to know that some of his people have been deported and others are also in jail in the United States or Canada. I don't know if there are more people involved. Hamid was murdered by someone, but I don't know who or why. You must try and forget all of this, though. I don't believe that you are a threat to anyone. In fact, I think Hamid liked you and tried to protect you a little."

"Poor Jas. I don't think she knew any of this. She really loved Hassan, and she liked Hamid, too. When is Hassan expecting to leave?"

"I called Jordan Connors, and he said that it would be very soon, probably at the end of the month. He'll keep me informed."

"You'll let me know, please. Surely, they're not just going to let him go and live somewhere else? Don't you wonder if anyone will really ever be safe from him?"

"I don't know, Dana. I hope that when Hassan has left, we'll be safe here in Canada. Live your dreams, get married, and forget all of this. That is best. I have to go now. Maryam is expecting me to be home early. We are both afraid, too, but I'll let you know when he's going."

"Good-bye, Noe. I hope you and Maryam will be safe too! You are a good man. I know Jas would be pleased to know that you're not involved in all of this. I hope you are right and that she's fled from these evil people. Take special care! You don't mind if I call you later in the month and see if you've heard anything more about Hassan's removal from Canada? I really won't feel safe until I know that he's gone."

62

It took a lot of wheeling and dealing, but Judd was finally able to secure an agreement from the Temesekian government that they were willing to negotiate an accommodation for Jaslyn Koh and her son. It was going to be touch and go, though. The authorities had agreed that Anil could be granted citizenship, by special decree, but it was conditional. Jas had to divorce her husband, and both she and the baby must return to Temesekia before the child's first birthday.

The divorce courts were busy, and Anil was already eight months old. Russ and Katy arranged to acquire the services of a reputable family law attorney, Ray Neville, who agreed to take the case. He advised that he might be able to pull a few strings with the British Columbia divorce registry to expedite the divorce without either party appearing before the court, due to the unusual circumstances in the case.

Russ also managed to arrange with Jas that two RCMP officers, Judd, and himself would accompany her to the flat she and Zadeh had rented to pick up her belongings about a week later. The men assumed that it might take the better part of the day and made the decision to set out early. Russ agreed to bring his old pickup truck so that they could cart the items that Jas wanted to keep.

The RCMP was going to bring a van to transport Hassan's belongings and packing cartons for anything they might want to seize. They had all hoped that someone at the shelter would look after the baby, but Jas would have none of that. She wouldn't let the little guy out of her sight, and everyone gave up trying to convince her otherwise. Who could blame her?

Fortunately, the flat was on the ground floor of a small house and consisted of just two bedrooms, living room, kitchen, and bathroom. They decided that they would start with the living room. Jas didn't want to keep anything from it except for a photograph album. She had simplified matters by deciding to leave the bulkier furniture sitting in the house for the next tenant or give it to charity. Russ suggested that the shelter might know of someone in need of furniture and a TV, at which Jas nodded her head in agreement.

The RCMP officers tossed all the cushions and even checked underneath every piece of furniture in the room. The four men got down on their hands and knees to examine all of the floorboards. They were looking to see if any were loose and serving as a possible hiding place of whatever. There was nothing!

Next, Jas led them into the kitchen where she decided that she didn't need or want anything. Again, she watched the men systematically check every nook and cranny in all the cupboards and drawers, even looking inside bowls, cups, and pots for any hidden items that might be of some value to their investigation. They scrutinized every kitchen tile, the refrigerator, and the stove as they looked for hiding places that might contain further evidence against her husband.

Glimpsing at the kitchen clock, Judd commented that they were making significant progress, only two rooms and the bathroom to go, and they had been there for less than an hour. However, each of the men was cognizant that the real work was probably ahead of them as they grabbed some packing cartons and headed to the master bedroom, punching the boxes into formation, ready for use.

There was a large mirrored dresser, two chests of drawers, two nightstands, a bed, and a closet to go through. A crib and baby change table sat next to the window; Jas told them that she had acquired these after Hassan was arrested. Pointing to the large dresser she indicated that it was hers, and its matching chest of drawers belonged to her husband.

"What about the other chest of drawers?" one of the officers asked.

"It was the baby's, and I took everything to the shelter from it."

Russ stepped forward and offered to help Jas pack her personal things from the large dresser, while the other men each grabbed one of the drawers from the chest and placed it on a portion of the bed to sort through its contents. They began tossing Hassan's neatly folded clothes into the empty boxes, checking pockets as they went. They found nothing unusual and were getting slightly discouraged. Then one of the officers picked up his empty drawer to lean it against the wall, and Judd noticed a package taped to its underside. Matter of fact, it was soon discovered that several of the drawers had similar packages underneath. Jas looked startled as each of the hidden packages were revealed.

As they opened each package, it became apparent that they had hit the mother lode! It appeared that they had discovered some of the key research materials for the terrorist's latest project, and it was mostly written in English. There was substantial information about the entire California, Nevada, Washington, Oregon, Idaho, Utah, and Arizona water supply and distribution systems, all obtained from Internet sources. It looked like they had uncovered their targets.

There were photocopies of maps, charts, photographs, even personnel records for employees for each of the reservoirs and aqueducts throughout those particular American states and the cities that were serviced by those facilities. Several sheets contained listings for over nine hundred testing facilities and a notation of their monthly testing schedules.

Russ was silently delighted that he had been a party to at least temporarily throwing a monkey wrench into this operation. His gut feeling was that judging from Al Zain's Canadian job application, he would have played a prominent role in this undertaking as a person familiar with chemicals. The information was thorough but far from perfect, and it appeared that they had been still in the planning stages of a major attack on multiple United States water reservoirs.

Some of the maps had color-coded marks on them with numbers, perhaps indicating a perceived soft target. However, there was no indication of how many people were involved in the operation or who the players were. At least they had a pretty clear idea of what the terrorists were up to, and the Americans would be put on full alert.

Judd went over and pulled out the last drawer of the chest and shook out its contents onto the bed so they could see under it, but it was clean. They grabbed the few belongings that they had emptied out of the drawer and shook out the items and pulled out the pockets before boxing them up, too. One of the officers walked over to the large dresser and pulled it away from the wall to look behind it and the mirror.

"What's this? I think there's a false backing behind the mirror," he'd announced.

"Anybody got a pocket knife?" the other officer inquired.

"I have a long nail file if that will help," Jas said.

"I think so. Let's try it," Judd said.

"Well, I'll be damned. There's nothing there but a lot of cash. It did look promising, though. I imagine this belongs to you and your son now, Jas." Russ grinned.

"Not so fast. I'm sorry, but we'll have to take it as evidence, at least for now. You might be able to get it back at some later date. I can't promise you, but I hope you understand it may be classified as proceeds of crime if we find out it's from an illegal source. I'll give you a receipt for it," the RCMP officer said as he began counting it out.

"You have to do what you must. I didn't even know that the money was there, so it doesn't matter to me one way or the other," Jas informed him. She was truly perplexed at the staggering sum of money they had uncovered. She had been draining her trust fund to help Hassan while he had hidden almost half of a million dollars right in their home.

After they had finished counting the money, they gave Jas a receipt. Then the men quickly checked out the rest of the room, including Jas's dresser, the pockets of the clothes in the cupboard, under the mattress and bed, the walls and floorboards, in fact, every inch of the room, before they separated and folded everything that still needed to be packed in the boxes that were lined up to go with Jas or those holding Hassan's things that the RCMP would take. Finally, they were satisfied that there weren't any other discoveries to be made in the room.

Anil was becoming rather restless, and Jas knew he was long overdue for a nap. She warmed a bottle for him, and within ten minutes, the little tyke was fast asleep. Suddenly a knock came to the front door of the flat. Everyone stopped dead in their tracks. Russ placed a finger vertically over his mouth and motioned to Jas to remain where she was.

"I'll get it," he whispered as the other men protectively huddled around Jas.

Russ stepped into the hallway, peered through a peephole, and then opened the front door.

"Can I help you, ma'am?" Russ's voice boomed.

"Oh, I'm looking for my friend that lives here. Her name is Mrs. Zadeh. Is she home?" A woman's voice was carried into the house.

"Sorry, I can't help you. I'm afraid that the people who lived here recently moved out."

"Oh, are you the landlord or the new tenant? Would you happen to know the forwarding address?"

"Afraid I can't help you there, ma'am. I'm just looking at the property for a contractor who's going to do some remodeling. Like I said, sorry I can't help you."

"Yes, I'm sorry too. Well, thanks anyway."

Russ watched the young woman cross the road and move down the street. It had taken him all of about two seconds to figure out that she was probably Dana Jahel, which Jas confirmed moments later. Jas confided that she felt guilty about not letting Dana know that she was safe and what was happening; however, she just didn't know whom to trust anymore.

"You're absolutely right, Jas! You have to put those people behind you. However, I think we'd better finish up here as soon as we can before anyone else shows up."

"We're going to take the computer with us and just dump all the contents from the desk in the boxes here. Is there anything in here that you want, Mrs. Zadeh?" one of the officers asked.

"My computer software templates and business plans are all on that computer. Can I just open my files and send them by e-mail to one of my brothers in Temesekia?"

"That's no problem, and you can take a quick scan through all this paperwork and books for anything else you think you might need," he replied.

About an hour later, everything had been packed and carted out to one of the two vehicles. Jas jotted down the name and phone number of the landlord on a piece of paper and asked Russ to contact him to advise that they had a family emergency and had to move unexpectedly. Jas didn't have a problem forfeiting the month's rental deposit they had made, and she said that she surmised that it would give the landlord ample opportunity to find new tenants. Climbing into the car, she handed Russ her house keys and took one last look as they pulled away.

No one had seen Dana, who had hidden herself from view and watched as the vehicles were loaded. They hadn't fooled her for one minute. She had spotted Jas's purse sitting on the kitchen counter just before the man closed the door. He had been blocking her view during most of the conversation but moved just enough so that she had a bird's-eye view of the kitchen.

She had an uncanny feeling that whoever he was, he'd watched her departure. She had circled the block and then bought a newspaper before returning to find an inconspicuous place to watch the small bungalow. She had read the paper twice, without really reading it, from cover to cover. She had only booked half a day from work and was about to leave when she observed a couple of men bringing out boxes and loading them into two separate vehicles.

She wondered who all the men were until she saw Jas and Anil come out under the apparent protection of the four men. She figured it must be the police. Watching them carry the computer to the van, she surmised that they had separated her things and were taking Hassan's belongings elsewhere. Dana smiled with satisfaction knowing that Jas and Anil were safe.

63

During the next several months, Russ learned that Hassan had appealed the decision to vacate his refugee status, which delayed the process of removing him from Canada. Jas remained apprehensive, while Ray Neville continued with his efforts to obtain her divorce within the time constraints that the Temesekian authorities had set. The documents found in the Zadeh flat had been shared with the Americans, and they had placed all of the targeted facilities under high security. It felt like everyone's lives had been placed in limbo waiting for something to break.

Katy was the first to get the news that Ray Neville had the divorce certificate, which set off a mad scramble to get Jas and Anil on a flight and notify her government. Just four days shy of Anil's first birthday, Russ, Corby, and Katy had escorted Jas to the airport to board the plane back to Temesekia. Her government had made a last-minute request by diplomatic note for the Canadian government to provide her with an escort to accompany her to Hong Kong where she would be met by two Temesekian government representatives and one of her brothers to ensure her safety home.

In Canada, the Department of Foreign Affairs had contacted the minister of public safety to see if the local Canada Border Services office, who often did prisoner escorts to foreign countries, could do the trip. The director had called a meeting with his senior managers and requested a volunteer for the job. Russ had laughed when Corby had told him that he was taking her. It seemed kind of fitting that Corby, who had played a key role in keeping everyone alerted to the danger of Hassan

Zadeh, would be the person to lead the man's latest innocent victims to safety.

Jas shyly thanked everyone for their help and said she would remain forever indebted to them but would likely never see any of them again unless they came to her homeland. She confided that she had experienced enough adventure to last her a lifetime. Katy squeezed her business card into Jas's hand and appealed to her to let her know how she was doing when she and Anil were resettled. Russ suggested that if anything cropped up, especially with regard to the release of the money, he would contact her through Katy. Jas was relieved when she finally got on board and the plane took to the skies.

A couple of weeks later, Russ, Corby, Judd, and Kendrick got together for a few beers and a game of poker at Russ's home. It was a pleasant evening, and all of the guests were quite intrigued when Judd informed that the federal court had denied Zadeh leave to appeal his deportation. In the interim, Canada had been trying to negotiate with several countries who might be willing to take him.

Judd remarked that Yemen had agreed that Zadeh would be permitted residence there after the Al-Islah tribal confederacy agreed to sponsor him. He was going to be flown to Seattle, and the Americans were going to provide him with an escort to Sanaa, Yemen, with some of their own removal cases. It was expected to happen very soon.

"Shit, I wouldn't want to be in Zadeh's shoes. Yemen's got one of the highest rates of capital punishment in the world. He better stay out of trouble if he goes there," Russ commented.

"Can't say I feel any sympathy for the guy. However, al-Qaida has training bases there too, so I'm sure that he'll be tempted to continue his life of terrorism and get right back into the thick of things. I'll just be glad to see him gone," Judd replied.

"I hope Jas will be safe from him in Temesekia. If he gets hooked up with more terrorists, I'm sure it won't take him long to figure out that she's gone home," Corby said.

"I think she'll be safer there than anywhere else," Judd replied. "She seemed to be a really decent girl that just met up with the wrong man. It's ironic that she came to you, Russ, looking for help."

Russ agreed and then told Judd and Corby that all of the furnishings and miscellaneous items left by Jas at the house were given to a young, abused woman, Becky, who once shared a hospital room with Jas. Russ recalled that he had gone to the hospital to pick up Becky with his daughter and had been flabbergasted to discover that the other occupant of the room was Mrs. Zadeh. He recounted that first instance that he had heard her name and came face-to-face with the woman.

He had later learned that Jas had overheard Katy and Becky talking about the shelter, found one of Katy's business cards left on the nightstand, and later contacted Katy for help. He commented that his daughter, Katy, was immensely pleased about passing the well-kept furnishings and household items to the other woman who had left the shelter only a few days before Mrs. Zadeh's arrival. Each girl had helped each other from that brief encounter.

"Did you get anything off of the Zadeh computer?" Russ inquired.

"Oh yeah! It took them a bit longer, and they lost some of it. He'd booby-trapped most of his personal folders with a firewall. Instant destruction if anyone tried to break into several of his codes. They had to bring in someone to get past his sophisticated programming, and it took some doing. He was a computer expert. One of the most disturbing sites that we found was that these two were exploring the use of some other biological and chemical toys as well and were targeting a substantial number of medium-sized cities throughout the American West. We got a list of them and passed it on to the people in the American Central Intelligence Agency."

"Humph! How the hell would they get their hands on biological supplies?" demanded Kendrick.

"Some of these chemicals are provided for other purposes and can be found in common usage in specified industries. It's all about knowing where to look. For instance, entomologists use potassium cyanide to kill insects and still preserve their bodies intact. Al Zain probably had lots of access to such toxic materials and knew how they could be used both beneficially and harmfully. There was information on the computer about ricin too, which comes from the castor oil plant. It can be homegrown, and a minute dosage is all that one needs to kill someone," Judd informed them.

"Sounds as if these guys were fairly knowledgeable about some scary things," remarked Kendrick.

"That's the new face of worldwide terrorism. They have educated, mobile, young recruits," Corby piped in.

"Enough of the shop talk! Hopefully, it's all over now. Who's for pizza?" shouted Russ as he reached for the phone.

64

On a Wednesday afternoon, about ten days later, Judd was packing up for the day when he received a call from Corby advising that Zadeh was being shipped out that evening. Hanging up the phone, he felt that this case had been a bittersweet victory. He wondered what happened to these men when they deported them. Would he live to endanger others until some other less tolerant country would put a stop to him?

As he walked to his car, Judd thought about the horrendous costs to Canadian taxpayers that had been involved in getting the man removed. The legal costs alone had been well over a hundred thousand dollars. There had been significant costs to the Immigration and Refugee Board for the numerous hearings from the time he had first entered the country. Canada Border Services had also incurred substantial investments in research and manpower, the federal court had heard appeals, and then the Canadian public had picked up his tab for his legal team every step of the way.

The costs of holding a prisoner in maximum security was more than two hundred dollars per day, and before that Zadeh had been given free schooling and lived on social assistance for a couple of years. Yet a reading of his file had indicated that he was somewhat of a computer technology genius who could have made a significant contribution to modern society. Why had he turned to terrorism? What would become of him? Would Jas and her child be safe?

Russ was at home preparing the barbecue for the arrival of Kendrick and Katy, when he also received a call from Corby advising that Zadeh's removal was imminent. Russ informed him that he had followed the criminal trial against the printer and the photographer, and they had both been found guilty of various charges, including fraud and conspiracy to commit fraud involving their business in forging Canadian and other foreign passports. Although Russ was pleased that both Canada and the United States had been successful in getting rid of these particular terrorists, he still worried whether the young mother and son would ever be free of living in fear from her former husband. For that matter, he also wondered, how many more operatives they'd missed in the roundup?

Judd had just finished his dinner when his cell rang. He listened to the conversation coming from it for several minutes and asked the caller to keep him posted. He placed a call to Russ and advised him to turn on the television for a few minutes. As Russ flicked on the television, a special news report was blaring across the air as a satellite picture showed a plane exploding in midair over the Pacific Ocean. The announcer stated that the plane had been en route from Seattle, Washington, to Yemen. The cause of the explosion was unknown, and all one hundred and sixty-three passengers and flight crew had been instantly killed.

"You won't believe this," Judd quipped. "That's the flight they put Zadeh on. I'd say that Jaslyn Zadeh's problems are now definitely over."

"The sad part is that almost everywhere that man has gone a lot of other innocent people have died. It looks as though the bastard took a lot of people with him, even in death," Russ sadly commented, "but who the hell blew up the plane? For that matter, it's still a mystery who murdered Al Zain."

"I guess we'll never know, but hopefully it has put an end to the threats to Zadeh's wife and son," Judd replied.

There wasn't much more on the news that night, but in the weeks to come, the men knew there would be lots of speculation about the cause of the explosion, the search for the black box, and attempts to identify the people who had perished. It appeared that the terrorist had been killed by another terrorist! Both men knew that somewhere there still had to be a sleeper. They had an uneasy feeling that there were still operatives at large and were at a loss on where to begin to look for them.

65

The imam at the mosque had been busy with a whirlwind of activity in the growing Muslim population in British Columbia over the past few months. There had been a major clothing drive to help war-torn brothers and their families overseas, a family potluck, organization of sporting activities, and tutoring for the youth membership in addition to the regularly scheduled teachings of Islam and daily prayer.

He had been saddened to learn of the corruption that had almost threatened the stability of his community involving Hassan Zadeh and his friend Hamid Al Zain, who had been murdered only steps from the front door of the mosque. Thinking about the men, he suddenly recalled that he still hadn't been able to return the parcel that he received from Jaslyn Zadeh that he had simply forgotten to pass on to the deceased Mr. Al Zain before he died.

Mrs. Zadeh hadn't been back to the mosque in many months, and the imam wondered if she hesitated to rejoin the community because of the shame she felt about the alleged terrorist activities of her husband. Fetching the parcel, he noted the return address on the outside of it and decided to return it to her with a brief note inviting her to return to the fold of the community. He recalled that her young son would be more than a year old by now and hoped that he would personally be able to play an instrumental role in guiding him in the years to come.

New tenants had moved into the flat where the Zadehs had once lived, and when the parcel from the mosque arrived for Mrs. Zadeh, they had hung on to it for some time. The landlord, Mr.

Murray, came around only periodically, and so they had waited on his next visit before turning it over to him in the hopes he knew the person whom it was for and could forward it to her.

Murray was a pleasant man who had genuinely liked Mrs. Zadeh and had been sorry to lose her as a tenant. She kept the apartment immaculate, paid her rent in a timely manner, and instead of just vacating the flat, she had a very nice gentleman contact him and let him know that she had an emergency that required her to leave. The man had given him his business card in case there were repairs that the Zadehs might be financially responsible for after their departure. As he looked through his wallet, he was pleased that he still had the information to contact him.

Russ was quite surprised when he received a call from the landlord but even more shocked when he noted that it was a parcel that Jas had sent to the late Mr. Al Zain in the care of the imam at the local mosque that the parties had frequented. Initially, he wondered if the property should be turned over to the RCMP or returned to Jaslyn Zadeh.

An uneasy feeling swept over him, and he wondered if the "naive" Mrs. Zadeh had perhaps outfoxed them all. After observing that the package had been sent to the mosque months before, he decided to open it. As far as he was concerned, she had given him the authority to look after emptying the contents of the apartment and to settle all matters with Mr. Murray, her landlord. It might not be anything significant. Perhaps just some things that Al Zain had left at her place, and she didn't know what else to do with it.

When he opened the parcel, he initially found a note from the imam to Jas; it was taped to another inner wrapped parcel, which contained a box with a note taped to its exterior and addressed to Hamid. The imam simply stated that he was returning the package to her and invited her to reconnect with the mosque. In eager anticipation, Russ turned his attention to the second piece of correspondence addressed to Al Zain.

It was a short note in which Jas had conveyed that she was enclosing Hassan's laptop at his instruction. She informed Al Zain that Hassan had said that it contained some documents that he had been working on. Russ wondered why she had failed to mention this at the time they seized the desktop computer. Russ knew that critical and relevant evidence might be found on the computer.

Through his years working at the border, he knew that proper collection and examination of its contents would be critical to preserving those contents and avoid spoliation. Although Kendrick employed good computer technicians, Russ realized that this time, he should enlist the assistance of a skilled computer forensics professional. The best resource that he could access in the business would naturally be with the RCMP. With this in mind he called Judd and told him of his latest discovery.

Both Russ and Judd were anxious to find out what was on the computer; however, the men agreed that they would need the help of an encryption expert to find the password and possibly to open any individual files. Judd phoned Doug, one of the RCMP officers who had been previously involved with the case. Doug warned them that the RCMP generally use a program called "dictionary" to randomly test multiple password combinations until they could find the right one. There was no guarantee, however, that they could crack the code.

The following day, Doug introduced the men to Kian, their technological expert. Kian had been recruited from a university-sponsored Hackathon held at UBC just a year earlier. He was considered to be one of the brightest technological young men in Canada with a keen interest in using his knowledge and talents for issues related to public safety. The government had finally wizened itself up to the fact that private industry was snatching up a lot of the top university computer science grads that were badly needed to keep ahead of the criminals and terrorists.

Kian advised the men that if the password could be decoded, it would probably take some time, anywhere from hours to weeks. He also explained that computer-savvy guys were generally using multiple levels of encryption on individual files, and that some had advanced to a system called steganography, which could hide data from third parties. This method would involve hiding messages in images or within what might appear to be some other innocent-looking cover text.

He was very professional and thorough in preparing for the task at hand and requested as much background information about the case as the men could provide. He told them that he hoped to not only open the files and find out what was on them but to also perform a number of related checks on the laptop by checking what web sites the user had visited, what files had been downloaded, when data had been accessed, whether records had been deleted, and hopefully who had authored the files in question.

Kian had just returned from a comprehensive antiterrorism training program run by the US government and could also access some highly sophisticated equipment for breaking encryption codes through them if need be. Doug gave Russ a receipt for the computer, which he promised to return if it contained nothing of interest to the overall investigation and some of the loose ends that had not been closed off; otherwise, he would contact Judd.

Several weeks later, Judd called to advise Russ that the findings had been stunning. They had discovered aerial shots of a ship, a map, and blueprints of the entire ship that had been imprinted with the name USS *Whitton*. It was a US naval vessel that had been destroyed in the Gulf of Aden in what was believed to have been a terrorist attack a couple of years earlier.

The ship had been at port for refueling and was docking for the night while on assignment trying to protect commercial ships in the waterways from the Somali piracy that frequented the area. It had been hit by a series of missiles and literally blown out of the water in a matter of minutes. There were no survivors. American intelligence had never been sure whether extremists from Somalia or Yemen were responsible. It was the reason why foreign countries now sent at least two escort ships to patrol the area, which was a critical shipping route.

Another file contained instructions to operatives in North America regarding a plan of attack on American reservoirs in the western part of the United States, which appeared to be authored by someone called Bahrami. They were still working on identifying the recipients of the directives and had shared the information with the United States.

A third file contained abundant information about the civil war that had occurred in Lebanon also a few years earlier. Included in this file was a list of persons, an itinerary, and even a menu with respect to a particular event. Judd recalled the assassination of the head of one faction in that country's civil war. If his memory was correct, he thought that it had happened on that day and at that event held in Beirut. He said that it had been reported that the drinking water had been laced with potassium cyanide. He asked if the name Hamid Al Zain was anywhere on the file and found an e-mail addressed to him, again authored by Bahrami.

"Zadeh was doing this stuff way back then," Russ said. "That's interesting. It's an established fact that he was in Temesekia at that time."

"He may have been elsewhere, but it's clear that he was commanding the operation and that he knew Al Zain," Judd replied.

"Somehow, I'm not surprised," Russ commented. "When I screened Al Zain's employment application, I was amazed at his academic credentials, and I couldn't understand why he was undergoing a college course here in Canada that should have been below the level of experience that he had already attained. I didn't know that he had ever been in Lebanon, though," Russ responded.

"We can place him in Beirut for only a few months, but during that time he attended a PFLP training camp. Zadeh using the Bahrami name had been in the same camp before he arrived but left about a week before the assassination. I wish we had that information on Al Zain when we were holding him on the passport charges. Then again, maybe not, the son of a bitch would probably still be alive and another costly case for the Canadian taxpayers to fund."

"Christ, I wonder why the hell he kept all this information," Russ said.

"It's almost as if he kept it just like a psychopath who collects trophies. Russ, there's so much information on the computer, including names of operatives, details of past terrorist kidnappings, hijackings, and bombings; and he even had a list of kill targets. By the way, just as we suspected, you were the latest name that was added."

"That bastard! Can't say I'm sorry that somebody took him out. I'm still curious who, though. More importantly, I can't figure out why Jas didn't tell us about the computer."

"Why don't you write her and ask if her late husband had another computer? That some information has turned up with another IP address. See if she comes clean."

"That sounds about all I can do. Yep, I think I'll pass on the news of her husband's death and slip it into the letter. I hate to think that she played us."

66

"Where's the blue hat, Anil," Sherlyn coached her little godson while she was reading him a story. Jas laughed and clapped her hands together as she watched him point correctly at the picture.

"Good boy, Anil. You'll have him reading in no time, Sherlyn."

"I'm telling you, Jas, you can see the difference at school in children whose parents have spent time reading to them. There's a good selection of books out there designed with first words to teach toddlers. As you can see, Anil may not be able to say the words, but he understands what they are, and he can identify them by pointing."

"Between you and my brothers, I'm going to have a little genius before he enters school."

Anil stretched out his chubby, little arms to his mother, and Jas informed her guest that it looked as though she had exhausted him. He was ready for his nap time. Before leaving the room to put him in his bed, she handed Sherlyn a letter that she had received a few days earlier from Canada suggesting that she might like to occupy herself with reading it till she got back. Glancing at the signature, Sherlyn recognized the name and remembered that Katy Freeman was the social worker who had helped Jas to return home.

It wasn't a long letter, and it began with a few simple pleasantries expressing her good wishes for both Jas and Anil. She extended greetings from her father and informed her that many of her possessions had been given to a girl named Becky, whom Jas might have recalled from the hospital. Then she went on to say that her father thought that she might like to know that Hassan had died in an airline mishap and that she and her son never had to fear him again.

Sherlyn gasped as she read that he had been on a plane travelling to Yemen when it had exploded in the sky, killing everyone on board. Mrs. Freeman hadn't been able to provide any other details of what had occurred but suggested that Jas might want to read about it on the Internet if she had access. She explained that her dad and his friends were not sure if they'd ever know what happened aboard that plane, but he hoped that she would find lasting peace.

She had ended by saying that her father was wondering if either she or Hassan had owned a second computer because some correspondence had been found with information sent to him that hadn't appeared on the computer the RCMP had seized from their home. She suggested that it could be either a laptop or desktop computer.

"What do you think of that?" Jas inquired, reentering the room.

"Wow and wow again! Do you believe it? It's shocking."

"Yes, I checked out the stories about it on the Internet. It may be inappropriate for me to say this, but I'm relieved. A part of me is sad. Sherlyn, I loved and trusted this man. He was the father of my son. In the end, however, my eyes were totally opened that he was not the person whom I thought he was. I never have imagined that such an evil person lived on this earth. He was so captivating, and my friend Dana was also fooled by both him and his friend Hamid. I liked Hamid, too, for that matter! They were both extraordinarily talented men. It was such a waste of human intelligence."

"Maybe now you can market your software. There's nothing to stop you anymore. He was the only one who had ever seen it, wasn't he?"

"Yes, he helped me so much with developing it. It's almost like he put his mark on it. He encouraged me and perfected it. He was a brilliant man. He could have had the world by the tail. He really did help with the software. When he was first imprisoned, he encouraged me to complete it saying that it would protect Anil's future."

"Maybe, it was his way of trying to ensure that Anil would be taken care of, Jas. Try to remember some good things about him. I don't think you would have fallen for someone who was all bad. I don't know what happens in a person's life that makes them do horrible things. I look at children almost every day, and they are all so innocent, but somehow we end up with good guys and bad guys."

"He told me such horrific things about his boyhood in Iran. He claimed that all of his family were tortured and killed by that government. I don't know what to believe. I don't know whether he was ever truthful to me. I think he was bitter and that he was easily influenced by others that he met in his travels throughout the world. I've wondered about his first wife, too. Did she know the things he did? How did that marriage end?"

"Jas, don't! You mustn't think about trying to find out. You need to close the door on that chapter of your life. Think of this letter as a brand-new start and try to forget."

"I don't think I will ever forget what happened. One day, I will have to figure out how much I need to tell Anil. I don't know what I'll say."

"When your parents died, Jas, it traumatized you, too. Time is a healer. You don't ever forget those you have loved, but you do need to move on. When the time comes, somehow you'll find the right words to share with your son. Peter, Colin, and Faith will be there with you. So will I, for that matter. You have to return to your beliefs and trust in God."

"I was terribly misguided. I wanted adventure. International experiences. What I received was international intrigue and adventure that led me into a living nightmare. My experience with Hassan doesn't even belong in the same stored memories of my parents. He took my innocence and led me into his world of terror."

"He also gave you the best little boy in all of Temesekia. Don't ever lose sight of that!"

"Yes, I think I'll write Mrs. Freeman back and thank her for the update. She deserves to know that I'm doing okay too. I'll talk to Peter and Colin about the software. See what they think. I need to start making some money. I also realized that there was another computer. Hassan said that Hamid needed it, and I sent it to him care of the imam at the mosque. I had forgotten all about it until now."

"That a girl! I need to scoot too and prepare my lesson plans for the week, or I'll be looking for a new job, too." Sherlyn laughed.

"You jest. They wouldn't let you go. I'll bet you're the best teacher on the island. I'm counting on you for when Anil walks through the school doors." Sherlyn jumped up and gave Jas a sisterly hug before she helped her clear and wash the teacups.

She thought Jas didn't know it yet, but she was starting on the road to recovery. It had been so distressing for all of those who loved her to see her when she had first returned home. Today had been the first time since her return to Temesekia that Sherlyn had witnessed her friend endure a conversation concerning her experience without bursting into tears.

It was a healthy sign. She had first met Jas when she was at rock bottom, at a time when providence had taken her parents. At that time, it had taken Jas nearly five years to learn to live again. She was a stronger woman today, and that little boy would keep her together. Eventually, she'd find someone who would love her and accept her and her child, but indeed it would take time. As Jas scurried to the sounds of her waking son, Sherlyn called out her good-byes and slipped out the door.

67

Russ was ecstatic with the news that Katy and Kendrick shared with him one Saturday afternoon. He was going to be a grandfather! The small family had gathered together at his daughter's home for a backyard cookout when Katy had made the revelation. With that earth-shattering announcement, Russ immediately began to ponder the new moniker that he would have. He didn't particularly like the sound of *grandpa, gramps, granddad,* or *granddaddy.*

"Pops!"

"Come again," said Katy.

"Just thinking out loud. I'm trying to imagine what the little one will call me. I'm thinking *pops* or maybe *papa.*"

"Oh, Dad, you're so vain," chuckled Katy.

Breaking out with a snicker, Kendrick added, "Perhaps, *old man* would be good."

"Enough of you two! When's the big day? Do you know if it's a girl or boy?" Russ laughed.

"I haven't verified it with my crystal ball, but I'm thinking around the end of August, Dad. So don't be planning any fishing trips then." Katy teased. "And no, we don't know if it will be a boy or girl. We want a surprise. You know we'll be satisfied with whatever the dear Lord has in store for us."

The warm afternoon slowly turned into a cool evening, and though they had enjoyed the barbecue feast, the first of the spring season, they headed indoors. The men went into the small room, off the master bedroom, to discuss plans for outfitting it for the new arrival, while Katy cleaned up. Russ offered to paint the walls or put up wallpaper, whatever they decided. Heading back into the living room, he offered to ask Corby to help with any renovations that they might want to do to baby proof their home.

Rejoining the men, Katy said, "Speaking of Corby, that reminds me that I received a letter yesterday that was addressed to you care of me."

"A letter for me? From Corby? Don't tell me he ran off and got hitched?" Russ asked.

"No. Not from Corby, silly. When you mentioned his name, it reminded me of Jas. I think that the letter is from her. It came from Temesekia."

"That's nice. I wonder how she's making out. The last time you heard from her, she appeared to be getting on her feet, and I was rather relieved when she revealed the facts concerning the laptop computer. She took the news pretty well that Zadeh was no longer with us."

Katy went and fetched the letter, handing it to her father; she eagerly awaited to hear how the mother and son were doing too. It was quite bulky, unlike her usual communications. Russ slit open the envelope, and what appeared to be a second letter fell out. Or at least it was a photocopy of another letter. He noted that it was signed, "Your faithful friend, Dana."

How on earth had Dana found her, Russ silently thought. Then he settled down to read the cover letter first as Katy and Kendrick looked on in anticipation. He carefully read it twice, before he went on to read the second letter with fascination. Turning to Katy and Kendrick, he said that the letter was indeed from Jas.

Jas stated that she had recently received the "attached" letter from the Douglas College. It had taken some time to reach her because the school had sent it to her last Canadian address. Apparently, they received a letter that was marked Confidential with a request for forwarding to her. When the post office returned it to them, they sent the unopened letter to Jas care of her brother's home in Temesekia. Her brothers were still cautiously protecting her, and they had apparently held on to it for a while, dreading what might be inside.

Jas wrote that she was sorry that she had forgotten about Hassan's laptop computer as it seemed so long ago that he had asked her to give it to Hamid. As Hamid had temporarily left Canada, Hassan had instructed her to send it to their local mosque care of the imam. She assumed that Hamid had the laptop, which supposedly just contained some of Hamid's school research. He had used Hassan's laptop as he didn't own one of his own.

Jas went on to say that the letter that was attached might help provide a lot of missing answers in matters that had concerned her and was enclosing a copy of Dana's letter for him. She had suggested that he was free to share it with anyone that he thought might find it useful in providing closure to everything that had taken place.

"I'll read you the second letter, from Dana," Russ quietly said.

Dear Jas,

I hope this letter finds you and Anil safely. I was so worried about you, but I observed some people helping you to go away from all the dangers you were surrounded with. I figured that it was the police, and you were both safe for the time being. When you are reading this, Hassan will be dead. For that matter, so will I. You and your son will never need to fear him again. I learned from Noe that the Canadian government was going to send him to Yemen on a specific date and flight from Seattle, Washington. I know that you cannot be safe from him as long as he lives. I came to love you like a sister, and I knew that you were another innocent victim in all of his evil activities.

You probably won't understand some of this, but I thought that I would try and explain most of it to you. I know that the people he knew would change his appearance, give him a new identity, and he'd have hunted you down. In the beginning, I didn't know who Hamid or

Hassan were. I only knew that a person named Mahmoud Bahrami was responsible for the death of my brother in Lebanon several years ago.

My brother had returned to assist one of the leaders in the civil war and was highly involved with one of the political parties. The leader, some of his friends, including my brother were, all victims of a treacherous plot to kill them by mass poisoning at a gathering. I later learned that the man who orchestrated those murders was none other than Mahmoud Bahrami, whom you know as Hassan. I received some information from some of my friends in Lebanon that they had heard Bahrami was in a Canadian jail. I also learned that some people believed that it was a Kuwaiti chemist who actually performed the actual murders in Lebanon at Bahrami's request.

When Hamid tried to flee Canada at the time of Hassan's arrest, I realized that he was involved in Hassan's sinister plans. He confided to me that he had once been in Beirut, and I knew of his expertise in chemicals. Although he didn't know that Bahrami and Hassan were one and the same person, I learned that he definitely knew who Bahrami was. It didn't take much for me to conclude that he was the person who actually murdered my brother at the direction of Bahrami.

I came by to see you one afternoon soon after he was released from prison and saw him watching your home. I thought he planned to search it for evidence or plans as Noe told me Hamid had asked him if Hassan had left some maps with him. I also became very worried that Hassan might try to harm you when you told me that you didn't want to go to another country with him. After seeing Hamid by your home, I thought he might be going to harm you at Hassan's instruction.

I carefully chose the most opportune time and place, and I killed Hamid to stop him from hurting you and others. There isn't a government anywhere in the world that can piece all the things together that those two men have been responsible for. For the past several years, I had hunted these men, and I was shocked to hear the police tell you that Bahrami and Hassan was the same person. However, I knew then that both of these men would have to die.

When you disappeared, I met with Noe because I was frantic about your safety. I learned that Hassan had terrorized both Noe's and Maryam's relatives in Iran for years. Hassan was so evil that he also made his own relatives his victims, living in constant fear of him and the people he knew. Shortly after, Hamid died, Noe confided in me some of the traumas that he and his family had suffered from Hassan. Noe also figured out that you were in hiding but kept it from Hassan and prayed for your safety.

Later, Noe found out from his lawyer that Hassan was going to be sent to Yemen on a flight via Seattle, and when it was scheduled to happen. He agreed with me that he thought that his family, you, and Anil would always be in danger from Hassan, no matter where he went. Hassan held incredible power in his organization and could plot and manipulate people to commit appalling acts against others. Noe said that he had even had someone hideously burn his own hands to try and fool the Canadian government before he came to Canada.

I regret that many more innocent people will die when I blow up the plane he will be travelling on, but I can assure you that it is much more likely thousands more will live because of my actions. I don't know if Noe and his family will ever be safe from Hassan's associates, but I hope you and Anil will.

Blessings. Jas, have a good life.

Your faithful friend, Dana

Clearing his throat, Russ looked up and spoke, "Well, I'll be damned. I think everyone is accounted for now. Looks like we've got a confession of sorts. Dana was the sleeper!"